TATTOOED TEARDROPS

TATTOOED TEARDROPS

TAMARA'S TEARDROPS #1

P.D. WORKMAN

ISBN: 9781989080023 (IS Hardcover)

ISBN: 9781989080016 (IS Paperback)

ISBN: 9781989080009 (KDP Paperback)

ISBN: 9780993768767 (Kindle)

ISBN: 9780993768774 (ePub)

pdworkman

ALSO BY P.D. WORKMAN

Tamara's Teardrops:

Tattooed Teardrops

Two Teardrops

Tortured Teardrops

Vanishing Teardrops

Medical Kidnap Files:

Mito

EDS

Proxy

Toxo

Pain

Between the Cracks:

Ruby

June and Justin

Michelle

Chloe

Ronnie

June, Into the Light

Breaking the Pattern:

Deviation

Diversion

By-Pass

Stand Alone YA novels

Stand Alone

Don't Forget Steven

Those Who Believe

Cynthia has a Secret

Questing for a Dream

Once Brothers

Intersexion

Making Her Mark

Endless Change

Gem, Himself, Alone

AND MORE AT PDWORKMAN.COM

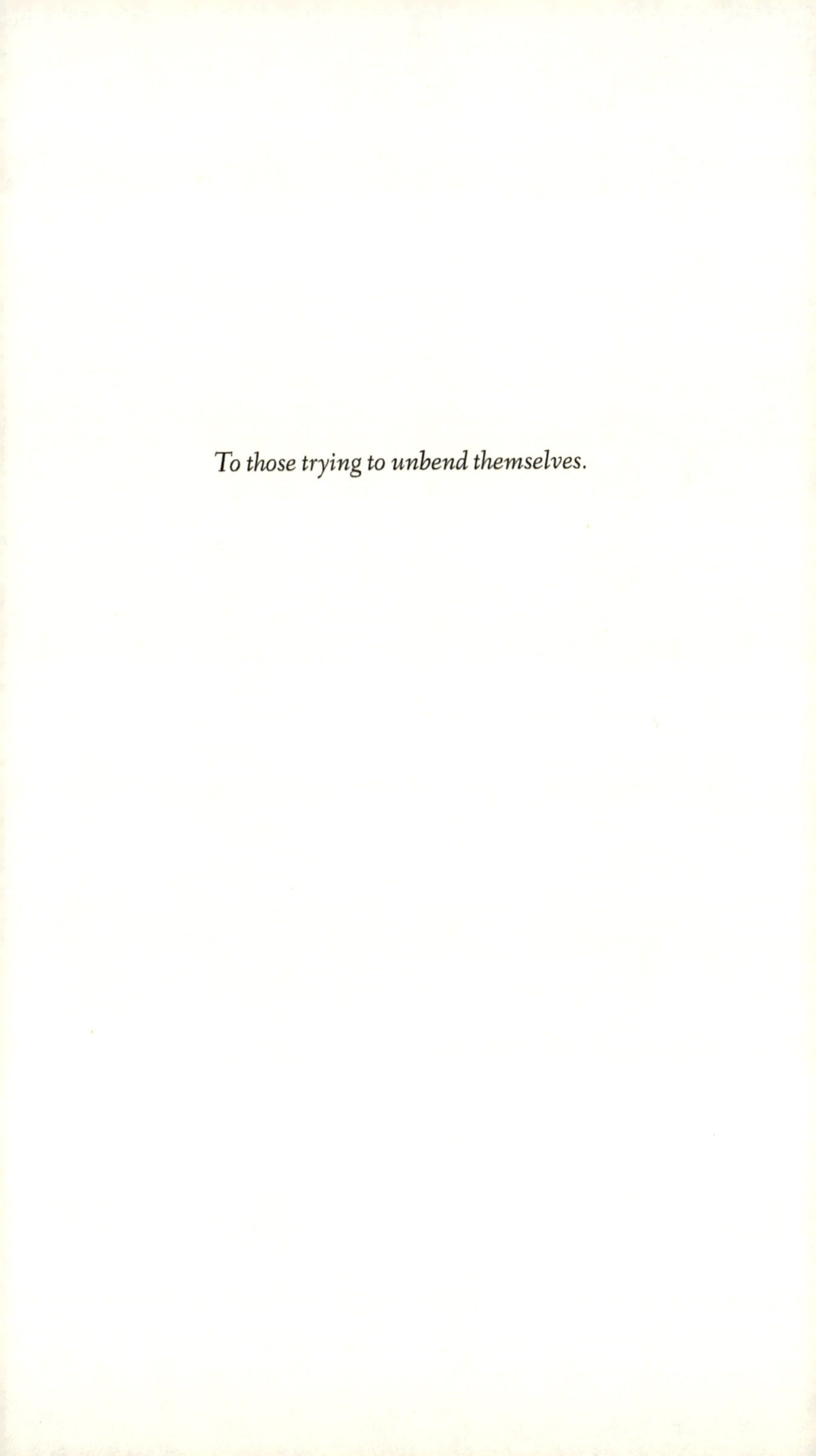

To those trying to unbend themselves.

ONE

(i)

TAMARA FRENCH HAS BEEN *a model inmate throughout her incarceration.*

Great reference. You could go far on that one. Tamara sat on an uncomfortable bench in the brightly-lit lobby waiting for her ride. It was strange being on the other side of the guard booth. She stared at the too-white sneakers that stuck out below her dark pant cuffs, wondering what kind of life she had to look forward to with that ringing endorsement. She jiggled her legs up and down, trying to resist picking her nails. Eventually, a tall, middle-aged woman with a bun came in and stood before her. Tamara stared at her boxy black shoes for a moment before reluctantly looking up at her.

"Tamara?" the woman said.

"Yeah."

"Ready to get out of here?"

"I guess."

"I expected a bit more enthusiasm," the social worker said with a hint of a smile in the corners of her lipsticked mouth.

"I'm sorta nervous," Tamara said.

"I guess that's understandable. Come on, let's go."

Tamara sat there for another moment, then finally stood and followed the woman out of the juvenile facility. She got in the car and buckled up, holding her bag tightly on her lap.

The social worker introduced herself, but Tamara paid no attention, completely forgetting her name the next minute. The woman attempted small talk a few times, but Tamara turned on the radio and stared out the window, freezing the social worker out. Eventually the woman got the message, and stopped trying to engage her.

(ii)

They pulled up in front of a brick house that was at least a hundred years old and needed some work. There had been an attempt made at landscaping, with some flowers and bushes bunched around the concrete steps leading up to the porch and the front door. There was peeling paint on the fence and mailbox post.

"Here we are," the social worker announced. "Let's go in."

Tamara unbuckled and got out slowly. The social worker took her in, knocking on the front door and entering without waiting for an answer.

"Hello, Marion, come on in," a woman's voice called from up above. "I'll be right down."

Tamara stood beside the social worker, waiting. She held her paper bag awkwardly at her side, wishing that she didn't have anything to hold onto. She made a show of examining the front hall and living room of the house, but in all honesty, she didn't care what it looked like. It wasn't prison. Her concern was not with the house, but what the foster parents were going to be like. The front room was fairly neat and presentable. No children's toys scattered about. A load of laundry neatly folded in the basket sitting on the couch. The TV shut behind the doors of an entertainment center so it would not be the central focus of the room. The furnishings were nice, not thrift store or destroyed. There were footsteps on the stairs, and Tamara looked up for her first glimpse of her foster mother.

Mrs. Henson had a pleasant, round face. Blond hair that had been lightly styled in an attempt to hide that it was starting to thin. She didn't look more than forty. She was overweight, but not grossly. She just looked soft and comfortable. She was wearing a sweater and pants, and inconsequential gold jewelry. She didn't look anything like Mrs. Baker, but that was no guarantee.

"Hello!" her voice rang out cheerfully.

"Gerry, this is Tamara," Marion introduced as Mrs. Henson reached the bottom of the stairs. "Tamara, Mrs. Henson."

"Hey," Tamara muttered, without meeting her eyes. "Where do you want me?"

"Your bedroom is at the top of the stairs. First door on the right," Mrs. Henson offered. Tamara made the trek up the stairs. There was a dark wooden bannister, ornately carved. Not too scarred for being in a foster home. Tamara turned at the top of the stairs and opened the door to her right.

There was a bed and a crib, and Tamara stood there, her heart speeding up, wondering if she'd been sent to the wrong room. Surely they wouldn't have given her a room with a crib in it? She could almost see Julie's still form lying on the high mattress... Mrs. Henson was there a moment later, having said a quick good-bye to Marion. She breathed a little heavily after her trip back up the stairs.

"Go on in," Mrs. Henson encouraged. "We sometimes take teen moms, to help teach them how to take care of their babies. We don't have any right now, so you get this room. That way you don't have to share."

Tamara walked into the room. The walls were a light green,

freshly painted, with a white board wainscoting all the way around it. There was a pull-down blind with gauzy green curtains around the window. Tamara tossed her bag onto the bed, where it sat looking pitiful and inadequate.

"The others will be getting home soon," Mrs. Henson offered. "I'll introduce you then."

"Yes, ma'am."

"I'm happy to have you join us, Tamara. I was very impressed with your file."

Sure. It was certain to be the last place she went that anyone was impressed with her prison record. She'd wowed them all at her parole hearing. There had been tears, and not all of them hers. So many of the inmates protested their innocence and refused to take responsibility or express remorse at their parole hearings. Tamara had been working on her performance for three years, and it was good. The board's vote was unanimous. Now she was free. But to what kind of life?

Mrs. Henson stirred, making Tamara jump, startled. They both looked at each other, not knowing what to say. Mrs. Henson smiled and nodded.

"Make yourself at home," she encouraged, motioning around the room.

Tamara nodded. Mrs. Henson backed off, and left her alone. Tamara stretched out on the freshly-made bed to wait. If there was one thing she was used to doing, it was waiting.

(iii)

There were no bells that rang to mark the passage of time and the transition from one activity to another. Instead, disconcertingly, it flowed along with small shifts and gradual transitions. Tamara heard the front door open and close several times, with voices reaching her ears even through the closed bedroom door. Mrs. Henson did most of the talking and others answered her questions or made comments during the pauses. Tamara couldn't tell what any of them were saying, just the tone of voice. They all seemed to be casual and relaxed.

There was a knock on Tamara's bedroom door, and before she could get up to answer it, Mrs. Henson poked her head in.

"We're going to get dinner going," she said. "Why don't you come down and help? Then you can meet everyone."

Tamara studied her for a moment, assessing her options. Was it a choice? Was there a consequence for not complying? She was so unused to making her own decisions that she wasn't sure what to do when faced with one.

"Come on," Mrs. Henson encouraged, motioning for Tamara to come.

Tamara got up slowly and followed her foster mother down the stairs and to the kitchen. She was suddenly confronted with a whole pack of new people to meet. All bigger and older than her. Tamara made an effort to unclench her fists and not look confrontational. This wasn't juvie. She didn't have to prove herself physically here.

It hadn't occurred to Tamara when she had met Mrs. Henson that the foster children would not all be white like her. But of course, she already knew the statistics. There were more non-white children in foster care, and very few non-white parents. So they couldn't pair black children with black parents. Tamara was intimidated by all of the dark faces looking back at her. She wasn't prejudiced, but juvie had taught her to be acutely aware of race relations, and how her white-faced, blond-haired presence could be aggravating to others. They would immediately judge her as stuck-up, privileged, and ignorant.

Tamara was fifteen, and not tall. There were only four other children, Tamara realized, not the mob that she had originally perceived them as. They were all bigger than her. Most of them taller than Mrs. Henson. Studying their faces, Tamara figured that they were seventeen or eighteen. One boy seemed even too old to be eighteen.

"Everyone," Mrs. Henson said, "this is Tamara, our new foster child. I know you'll all make her feel comfortable and help her get settled in."

They all nodded, smiled, and waved. Tamara nodded back.

"Hey."

Her voice was hoarse, the greeting barely audible. Tamara wasn't sure any of them had heard her. She nodded again and didn't repeat the greeting.

"Okay, are you ready?" Mrs. Henson asked with a wide smile. "This is Nita," a Hispanic girl with long hair and perfectly plucked eyebrows, "Deshawn," the darkest face, a girl with corn-rows and a brilliant white smile, "Jason," black skin, close cropped black hair, probably eighteen, "and Harry." Harry seemed a particularly non-ethnic name for a boy who appeared to be some mixture of black, Hispanic, and native. He smiled nicely for her, but his resting face was serious, contemplative. He was the one that Tamara was sure must be older than eighteen. He should have already aged out of the system.

Tamara nodded again and swallowed. Now what? Was she supposed to repeat them back? Greet each one separately? Shake hands? Tamara just stood there, lost, then looked at Mrs. Henson for direction.

"Okay, let's get started on dinner," Mrs. Henson suggested. "Nita, why don't you show Tamara where the dishes are, and she can help you set the table..." She went on, but Tamara didn't hear the rest of the instructions she gave to the remaining kids. She had her instructions. Go with Nita and set the table. She made her way across the room to Nita, and Nita smiled at her.

"Welcome," she said in a low voice that was almost a whisper. "I hope you like it here."

Tamara nodded. "Yeah. Thanks."

"Well, come on. The dishes are in this cupboard here, and the glasses, and the cutlery." Nita indicated each location.

"How many...?" Tamara asked. She cleared her throat. "Is there a Mr. Henson? Or anyone else?"

"Yeah, Jesse will be home for dinner. That's Mr. Henson. So seven altogether."

Tamara counted out the plates and trucked them over to the table, where she put them down carefully. Her hands shook slightly as she set them down, and it was an effort not to let them clatter. There was a baby's high chair, pushed against the wall. Tamara looked away from it and continued with her work, breathing shallowly. Setting the table only took a couple of minutes, and then Mrs. Henson gave them various other small tasks until everything started coming together for the dinner. She looked at her watch.

"Thanks guys. Take a break for about twenty minutes. Then everything should be done cooking, Jesse will be home, and we'll eat."

The kids dispersed. Tamara headed back up to her bedroom. Deshawn stopped ahead of Tamara, blocking her way into her bedroom.

"Do you need anything?" she asked Tamara.

Tamara shook her head.

"Sometimes... people don't come here with very much," Deshawn said. "Missus buys up extra toothbrushes and all, and we all share clothes..." She glanced over Tamara's figure. "My pants won't do you much good, but if you want a shirt, some accessories..."

Tamara stood there and contemplated the idea. For three years, she had worn nothing but an orange prison jumpsuit. Social Services had provided her with two very basic changes of clothing for her release. T-shirt, pants, socks, underthings. One pair of white tennis shoes. It was more fashion than Tamara had access to in all her time in juvie, but she was aware that it was sorely inadequate for a teenager on the outside.

Deshawn made an encouraging motion.

"Come on. Let's see if there's anything you want to borrow," she said.

Tamara followed her to one of the other bedrooms.

"Nita and I share the room," Deshawn commented. Nita was not there; maybe she had gone to watch TV or something. The room was painted sky blue. There was a utilitarian set of bunk beds, a couple of dressers cluttered with scarves, jewelry, and books, and a closet that was jammed full. The knobs on either side of the open closet door had been pressed into use to hold more hangers full of clothes. "It's mostly thrift store," Deshawn said, "but you can find some pretty good stuff if you look hard enough. Sorry, it's sort of a mess. Come on. See what you like."

Tamara went to the closet and looked over the hangers full of brightly-colored clothing. It didn't appear that either Deshawn or Nita went for anything understated.

"If you want t-shirts, they're in the dresser," Deshawn pointed, "and just grab whatever you see that you like. Just bring it back or throw it in the laundry when you're done with it."

Tamara saw herself in the mirror mounted on the back of the closet door. There hadn't been any full-length mirrors at juvie. And the only mirrors that had been there were polished metal or plastic, and you could never really see your reflection very well. Tamara had grown up a lot in juvie. She wasn't the soft, shy little farm girl she had been when she went to the Bakers. They had changed her. And juvie had changed her. The years had not been particularly kind ones. But she had developed a figure now, and was going to have to learn how to dress it up, instead of simply shrouding it in a jumpsuit. She had tattoos and piercings that she hadn't had before her incarceration. Her hair was dull and lank, like everybody else's in juvie. Tamara wound one lock around her finger, staring at the stranger reflected in the mirror.

"Why don't we do something with your hair?" Deshawn suggested. "There's not much time, but if we blow-dry, we could be done before supper."

Tamara raked her fingers through her limp blonde hair, disgusted with it.

"Yeah. Could we?"

"Mmm-hmm," Deshawn agreed with emphasis. "We'll shampoo it in the bathroom, and use leave-in conditioner..." she led the way out into the hallway, still chattering away to herself what they would do. Tamara just followed.

Tamara knelt by the tub while Deshawn used the hand-held shower attachment to quickly wet her hair down. The warm water felt so good on Tamara's scalp, she wished she could get in for a full shower, and just luxuriate in it for hours. Three years of quick, cold showers. But Deshawn turned off the water way too soon, and applied a fruity shampoo with strong, capable fingers; working it in and then rinsing it back out. She handed Tamara a towel and while Tamara rubbed her hair, Deshawn rifled through the myriad toiletries lining the back of the counter, the medicine cabinet, and a couple of deep wicker baskets under the sink.

(iv)

"Girls! Dinner!" the impatient call came again from downstairs.

Deshawn poked her head out the door.

"Just one more minute," she called back. "We'll be right down!"

She returned her attention to Tamara.

"Okay, just sit still for one more minute, girl," she instructed.

Tamara sat frozen, while Deshawn wound sections of her hair around the fat curling iron, holding it and then releasing. There was no way that she was going to be done the whole thing in another minute. But Deshawn worked quickly, sure of herself.

"That will do it for now," she announced.

She laid the curling iron down on the counter and unplugged it from the wall. Standing Tamara up, Deshawn shuffled her over and turned her to face the mirror.

"Ta-da!"

Tamara looked with astonishment at the face in the mirror. She was amazed at what a big difference a hairstyle could make. She still didn't have on any make-up, hadn't changed her clothes or accessories, all she had done was let Deshawn clean and style her hair. Her image in the mirror was no longer so harsh and plain.

"You're gorgeous," Deshawn gushed. "You've got really good color and proportions. We can have a lot of fun glamming you up. For now, this will do."

Standing behind Tamara, Deshawn used her fingers to wind and readjust a couple of curls. She lowered her head so that it was on the same level as Tamara's, and gave her a smile.

"What do you think?"

"It's... it's really pretty. Thanks," Tamara said. She cleared her throat, realizing that she was whispering. She had learned in juvie to use a strong, confident voice, not to be soft or timid. The Henson's home was so different in atmosphere, she felt like she was in a library or something. That she needed to be quiet to avoid upsetting the peace of the place.

"Come on, we've got to get down to dinner, or Missus will not be happy!"

Tamara followed Deshawn back downstairs and to the dining room table that she and Nita had set. It was now covered with serving dishes, and everyone was seated, waiting for them. All eyes turned to Tamara as she looked at the three empty chairs, trying to decide which one she should take.

"Tamara, doesn't that look lovely," Mrs. Henson complimented. "Here, sit down. These boys will eat everything before we even get a bite, if they have to wait much longer."

She gestured toward the empty chair nearest to her, and Tamara went over and sat down. Deshawn took what appeared to be her usual seat, beside Nita, which left one empty chair at the table of eight. Tamara looked for the first time at Mr. Henson. Slim, on the tall side. Handsome boyish face. Short-cropped curly red hair. He smiled at Tamara.

"Welcome, Tamara. I'm Jesse."

Tamara nodded, looking down at her empty plate. Her stomach tightened and it was suddenly hard to breathe. The only men that she had been around for three years had been guards, doctors, and administrators. The last man she had lived with before that... her foster father, Mr. Baker... that had been a bad scene. A very bad scene. Tamara swallowed. She tried to slow her breathing, but it just made her breath louder in her own ears. She was sure everyone would be hear how loudly and quickly she was breathing.

"Dig in," Mrs. Henson said, and Harry and Jason acted like two Rottweilers just told to attack, diving into the serving dishes immediately. Conversation started up around the table, and rather than trying to follow any of it, Tamara just let it wash over her like white noise. She served up small portions of each of the dishes that passed her, and dutifully passed them on.

"So tell us about your last home, Tamara," Nita said. "Where did you come here from?"

Tamara looked at Mrs. Henson. The woman just smiled and gave her a small nod, and didn't jump in to help her out. If Tamara didn't want to answer questions, she was going to have to be assertive and speak up. The conversations around the table quieted as the others paused to listen for her answer. Tamara swallowed a very dry mouthful of potatoes. They stuck right in the middle of her chest.

"I wasn't at a home," she said finally, careful to keep her

voice up, not to duck her head down. She was not vulnerable and had nothing to be ashamed of. She was strong and knew how to take care of herself. She had just as much right to be here as any of them. "I was in juvie."

There was an initial silence, and then conversations started back up again without further comment on Tamara's answer.

"Sorry," Nita said. "I didn't know."

"It's okay," Tamara said, shaking her head. "It's not a secret. That's where I was."

Nita nodded.

"Most of us have been in trouble at one time or another."

Tamara glanced around at their faces. None of them looked particularly troubled. They seemed happy and relaxed. At peace with themselves. Maybe they had been in trouble before, and maybe they hadn't. You couldn't always tell by looking at someone.

"Harry's probably spent the most time in juvie," Deshawn contributed, nodding to her brother. "How much time, Harry?"

"All together?" Harry questioned, laughing. "I don't know. Longest stint was two years. But I had plenty of shorter stays before that."

Tamara studied him more closely. He met her eyes and nodded.

"Harry's twenty," Mrs. Henson said without being asked. "So he's not officially a foster child anymore. But we told him he could stay on here while he does some more schooling and gets on his feet."

Tamara nodded, looking back down at her plate.

"That's really nice of you."

"It's to our benefit too. Harry contributes a lot to the family, and since he's working part-time, he's also paying a bit of rent to help keep us afloat. So it works both ways."

Tamara bit into some sort of casserole.

"I guess you'll learn about everyone's backgrounds gradually," Mrs. Henson said. "We try to be open with each other. Everybody's been through some pretty tough stuff. We don't judge. We just try to help."

"That's cool," Tamara said, pushing her dinner around on her plate. She wasn't hungry.

She watched everyone else chow down, and conversations flowed back away from her again. Tamara watched for the appropriate time to leave the table. There was no end-of-dinner bell anymore. She had to relearn all the social graces. How to judge the end of a conversation. When one could politely leave the dinner table. How long she could look at someone before they decided she was being too aggressive. It was like living in a foreign country. A dangerous foreign country.

"Not very hungry?" Mrs. Henson observed, as dinner conversation started to peter out.

Tamara looked down at her plate, still nearly full.

"No. I'm sorry... it's good... I just feel kind of... my stomach hurts."

"It's all right. It takes time to adjust. You can scrape it into the garbage. Nita can show you where. Everyone rinses their own plates and puts them in the dishwasher."

"Sure," Tamara agreed. She stood up, grabbing her plate, and Nita got up and led the way back into the kitchen, where they took care of their dishes. Tamara looked back at the dining table. "Do you want help with clean-up?" she asked Mrs. Henson. "Or would I be in the way?"

"Of course you can help. Usually, I'd probably tell you to go do your homework while I cleared, but you don't have any today, so why don't you and I clean up together?"

Tamara nodded, and she and Mrs. Henson bussed the serving dishes back to the kitchen, found lids for things, and put them into the fridge. Mrs. Henson turned the dishwasher on and wiped down the dining room table.

"You can watch some TV or take some 'down' time. In bed at nine, and lights out at ten."

"Okay," Tamara agreed.

She wandered around the house a bit, but wasn't comfortable sitting down with anybody else, and so she made her way back to her bedroom. As she approached, the door to the other girls' bedroom opened. Nita peeked out.

"Hey," she said. "You need anything? Do you have pajamas?"

Tamara shook her head.

"No," she admitted. "If I could borrow a t-shirt or something..."

"You bet. Come in."

Nita opened the door the rest of the way for her, and Tamara went in. Tamara looked down at Nita's feet, nails freshly painted and toes spread apart while they dried. Nita giggled and hobbled on her heels over to the dresser.

"You want to do yours?" she asked. She pulled out a handful of shirts and tossed them at Tamara.

"No. Thanks," Tamara said, fumbling with the shirts to see what her options were. "I'm going to hit the sack."

She found herself strangely unable to choose one of the shirts. There were three of them. They were all cute. Any one of them would work. All she had to do was decide which of the three she liked best. Nita was watching her, head cocked slightly.

"The blue one is a really good color for you," she suggested.

Not the blue one. Tamara looked at the other two. She didn't know which she wanted, but she had to decide before Nita made another suggestion. She had to make her own choice. Tamara tossed the blue one back to Nita, and with a knot in her stomach, tossed Nita the pink one too. Tamara looked down at the purple and blue patterned shirt in her hands.

"This one is good," she said.

She felt a little sick. Worried that she had made the wrong

choice. How silly was that, to be worried that she had picked the wrong t-shirt to wear in the privacy of her own bedroom? But she was. She had an overwhelming feeling of dread.

"Have a good sleep," Nita said with a smile.

"Thanks."

Tamara went back to her room. She changed into the t-shirt, long enough to reach her mid-thighs. She lay down on the bed and stared at the ceiling. There would be no bell ringing to tell her when to go to sleep. Would her body know when it was time, without the bell? Would she be able to adjust to a new schedule? Not feeling the least bit tired, Tamara lay staring at the ceiling, twitching her foot and waiting for sleep.

TWO

(i)

TAMARA AWOKE. SHE WAS confused at first, disoriented by the sight of a bedroom around her instead of her familiar cell. Turning her head to look at the clock beside the bed, Tamara saw that it was five forty-five on the dot. The usual time for the reveille bell. Groaning, she rolled over and slid out of bed.

She didn't know what time the others usually arose, but she imagined there would probably be a bottleneck waiting for the shower. Moving as quietly as possible, Tamara tiptoed across the room and opened her door. She listened for any sounds of movement. There was a light on down the stairs, but it wasn't bright. It could just be a streetlight through a window, or a nightlight. The shower was not running, so Tamara darted into the bathroom, shut the door, and turned on the light. She started the shower running and stripped down. For the first time in three years, she stepped into a warm shower. The tantalizing sample of the night before when Deshawn had helped her wash her hair didn't even come close to the luxury of a hot, whole-body shower. Tamara took a deep breath. She could get used to this.

More out of habit than anything, Tamara very quickly soaped up and rinsed off. She forced herself to shut off the water again immediately. Even though she would have loved to have stayed in the shower for an hour, until the hot water ran out and people started banging on the door to tell her to get out, she knew she had to be considerate and leave some hot water for the others. With a family of seven, you couldn't be selfish and use it all yourself. Shivering, Tamara grabbed the closest towel and dried herself off. She realized with dismay that she hadn't brought in any clothes to change into. She only had the makeshift nightshirt she had just taken off. Tamara swallowed and steeled herself. She wrapped the worn towel around her body. It didn't cover much, and wasn't long enough to tuck it back into itself. So holding the towel with one hand, Tamara tucked her shirt under her elbow, and used the other hand to open the door.

Her room was conveniently right across the hall from the bathroom, so she only had to take three steps, and she was safe in her own room again. She heard the click of another door down the hall, and a minute later, the bathroom door closed and the water turned back on. Had whoever was in the shower now seen her in her dash from the bathroom? She hadn't dared to look for anyone. Tamara pulled on her sad little Social-Services-provided outfit and looked for a comb. She found one in the top drawer of the dresser, along with a few other necessities. As she carelessly pulled the comb through her hair to get it in order before it finished drying, Tamara's eyes sought out her reflection in the mirror over the dresser. Did she want a prison hairdo for the first day of school, or something nice, like Deshawn had done for her last night? But the curling iron was in the currently-occupied bathroom.

Trying to breathe calmly through her anxiety, Tamara

crossed the hall to the bathroom door. The shower was still running. She knocked on the door and opened it up a couple of inches.

"Can I just get the curling iron?" she asked.

She didn't look toward the shower or the foggy mirror. She just kept her eyes down, waiting for a response.

"Sure, go ahead," a male voice answered. The voice was deep, probably Harry, but Tamara wasn't sure.

She opened the door far enough to rifle through the contents of the vanity and the baskets underneath, and found the curling iron, a brush, and some hairspray. Tamara retreated from the warm, misty bathroom and hurried back to her own room.

(ii)

Breakfast at juvie was served promptly at six and was over at six thirty, so by the time Tamara was finished styling her hair, she was starving. She went down to the kitchen to see what she could find to eat. Mr. Henson—Jesse—was eating a bowl of cereal on the kitchen island, reading through a newspaper. Tamara stopped short. He must have heard her footsteps on the stairs, though, because he looked up at her and smiled.

"Come on in, don't be shy," he invited.

Tamara approached cautiously, not getting too close. She knew foster dads. She'd dealt with a foster dad. But she'd learned how to protect herself in juvie. How to be careful and not leave herself open.

"You're an early riser," Jesse observed, dropping his eyes back down to his newspaper and taking another bite of cereal.

Tamara watched him for any change in attitude, any extra watchfulness. He glanced up again, then back down at his paper.

"There's juice in the fridge. Cereal and bread in the cupboard," he pointed. "Coffee's fresh."

"Thanks," Tamara said.

She kept an eye on him while she opened a couple of cupboards to locate the mugs, and poured herself a cup of coffee. Tamara inhaled the soothing aroma while she waited for it to cool down a bit. Perhaps Jesse could feel her gaze, because he looked up at her expectantly, eyebrows up. Tamara looked away.

"Sorry," she said. "I'm a bit dopey. Still getting the engine started."

He chuckled.

"Did you sleep well?"

"Well... okay, I guess. The bed is really comfy and every-thing. It's just..."

"Somewhere new," Jesse finished for her, nodding. "That's perfectly understandable. It will take a while before it feels natural. Like home."

"Yeah."

Tamara wondered if she would ever feel like this was home. She had been warned that parole wouldn't be easy. She knew inmates who had been back within a week of being released. Some had intended to follow the rules, and slipped. Some had never intended to follow any rules. She remembered when Mitchell had come back. Tamara had thought that she would make it. Mitchell was tough, one of the few who had managed to survive juvie without getting in with one of the gangs. She was strong-willed, and made it known that once she got out, she wasn't going to be back. She would do whatever it took to stay on the right side of the law and make a life for herself. A straight, honest life.

On her return, Mitchell's dark eyes were underscored by shadows. She looked almost haunted.

"I just couldn't do it," she told Tamara, as they both stood at the sinks in the restroom. "I felt so... exposed. I didn't belong out there."

She had held up a convenience store at knife point. With no mask. In full view of the security cameras. Not because she needed money, but because she wanted to go back. Back where she belonged.

Tamara sipped her coffee. She considered what else she might want for breakfast. Her stomach was still growling. She wasn't going to be able to make it to lunch on a cup of coffee. She was used to a full breakfast at juvie.

With another careful look at Jesse, she went over to the cupboard that he had pointed out, and got herself Cheerios and a slice of bread, which she threw into the bright red toaster on the counter. She prepared the cereal and started to eat, leaning against the counter and waiting for the toast to pop.

"You can eat at the table," Jesse said. "You don't have to eat standing up just because I am."

Tamara didn't move. He didn't pursue it. She and Jesse continued to eat in silence. Mrs. Henson joined them as Tamara moved on to her toast, searching the fridge for some jam.

"You're up early," Mrs. Henson observed. "Couldn't sleep?"

Tamara nodded. She moved to the dining table as Mrs. Henson entered the kitchen, feeling crowded, anxious at both foster parents being in such close proximity. Mrs. Henson gave her a smile and got herself a cup of coffee. Tamara took a few quick bites of her toast and then laid the remainder down.

"Sorry, I took too much," she said. She dumped the toast in the garbage and slotted the plate away in the dishwasher. Then she retreated to her room.

As Tamara got upstairs, Deshawn was knocking on the bathroom door.

"Come on, Jason! Time's up! There's a line-up out here."

She smiled widely at Tamara as she waited for a response.

"Hey, girl," she greeted. "Go on in." She gestured toward her own bedroom. "Help yourself to whatever you need. Nita's awake, she's just playing possum."

Tamara hesitated.

"Go ahead," Deshawn pressed. "You going to go to school without putting your face on?"

Tamara had no experience with makeup, but she knew most of the other girls at school would probably be wearing it, and she didn't want to look any more different than she had to. So she nodded and went into the bedroom, tapping lightly on the door before she went in.

Nita didn't play possum, but propped herself up on her elbow, yawning.

"Mornin' sunshine."

"Hey. Deshawn said..."

"Yeah, of course. Help yourself to whatever you see. Except that orange scarf over there," Nita nodded at it. "That one's calling to me this morning."

"I'm kind of sick of wearing orange," Tamara said.

Nita snorted. "You don't say," she said with a giggle.

Tamara looked over the clutter of accessories on top of the dresser. She tried on a couple of necklaces before settling on one with a large, brassy sun-and-moon medal on it. She put in chunky earrings. She looked at the makeup and didn't know what to do with any of it.

"You want some help?" Nita offered.

Tamara hesitated, not wanting to owe Nita anything. She felt vulnerable letting anyone help her. Nita sat up and swung her feet over the side of the bed. She stretched and stood up.

"Why don't you sit?" she suggested, motioning to the chair in front of the small mirror and pile of makeup.

Tamara sat down. Nita started pawing through the makeup, sorting out what she wanted to use. Without further discussion, she started by applying some moisturizing cream. Then she brushed on some blush.

"Is everyone always so nice and perfect around here?" Tamara asked, watching Nita's actions in the mirror.

Nita laughed.

"We're far from perfect. We still have our fights and rough spots. But..." She paused while she moved onto selecting a shade of eye shadow. "We've all been there. Moving into a new home. Starting over again. Trying to figure out your place. First day of school. It works better if you're nice to newcomers rather than getting all territorial. A lot less grief."

"Oh."

As if to underscore her words about not being perfect, Deshawn pounded on the bathroom door, yelling at Jason again to quit being inconsiderate and get his bony butt out of the bathroom. Tamara and Nita laughed.

"And luckily, Deshawn and I both love having sisters to share with. Neither of us grew up with much family."

Tamara was going to nod, but thought better of moving while Nita worked on her.

"Me neither," she agreed.

"Yeah? Well, there you go. Now you've got two sisters who are going to love dressing you up and showing you how to do your makeup."

Tamara studied Nita's face in the mirror. Nita was beautiful. The lines of her face were almost perfect. Her smile was bright and even and could have been an advertisement for a dentist. There was the tiniest shift to the lines of her nose that made Tamara wonder if it had been broken at some point. Without thinking, Tamara touched the bump in her own nose. Nita stopped for a moment and pushed Tamara's hand away.

"Don't you worry about that," she said. "It's not obvious unless you're looking for it."

Tamara put her hand back down again. Nita handed her a tube of lipstick.

"I think you can do this part," she said.

Tamara screwed the lipstick out, and applied it to her lips. She looked at her face, at the overall effect of the makeup. It still looked like her. There was nothing too obvious or stark about the makeup. But her face was softened, more feminine. Framed by the silky blond waves, she could almost be pretty.

Nita was over at the closet, pushing clothes around. She was wearing a long Minnie Mouse nightshirt that reached her calves. She pulled out a couple of button-up shirts.

"Now how about one of these layered over your t-shirt?" she suggested. "I think that would be really cute."

Tamara took one of the shirts from her and pulled it on, then shook her head and took it back off.

"Not really my style," she said.

Nita shrugged.

"You want anything else? Don't be shy, just try on whatever you like."

Tamara joined Nita at the closet, and looked through the offerings. She pulled out a black jacket with silver hardware, and tried it on. Nita looked her over and nodded.

"You like it?" she asked.

"I think so."

"It's yours."

Tamara smoothed it with both hands and nodded, smiling shyly. "Thanks."

(iii)

Neither of the other two girls went to the school that Tamara would be attending, so she was on her own. Mrs. Henson offered to make the proper introductions at the school, but Tamara shook her head.

"Just drop me off," she said. "I can find the office and they'll give me what I need."

She didn't need to look like a little girl who couldn't manage to go to school on her own. She was strong. Mrs. Henson agreed. She drove slowly, pointing out landmarks that would help Tamara to find her way around the neighborhood in the future.

Tamara stared out the window, not commenting, her stomach in a tight, sick knot. She was not looking forward to school. Of course she'd gone to all of her classes in juvie—not like she had been given a choice—but public school was not something she was looking forward to.

She checked in at the office, was given a locker, schedule, map, textbooks, and a number of covert looks. She was told who her guidance counselor was and invited to set up an appointment with him any time.

Tamara went to her morning classes, and at lunch went looking for the students' illicit smoking hangout. She had a few cigarettes left over from juvie, but getting her hands on more might be difficult. It didn't take long to find a small knot of students wreathed in smoke. Tamara nodded briefly and cupped her hand around a cigarette to light it. She drew the smoke into her lungs, the tension in her stomach subsiding slightly.

"Sucks being new," one girl offered.

Tamara nodded.

"Especially halfway through the year," she agreed.

"I'm Sybil." She had dyed black hair, a post through her lip and a piercing in her nose. Her makeup was stark, but not goth.

Some of the others offered their names.

"Hi. Tamara."

"You're staying with the Hensons?"

"Yeah." Tamara shifted her feet. "You know 'em?"

"They go through a lot of kids there. Some of them go to school. Some don't."

"Uh-huh."

Since Tamara was not yet sixteen, she didn't have a choice about school attendance yet. It was mandatory. Especially if she wanted to stay out of juvie. One of the boys, slim and pale and wearing a black leather jacket, looked her over curiously.

"So being with the Hensons, does that mean you've been in trouble?" he inquired.

Sybil rolled her eyes.

"Smooth, Jason," she objected. But that didn't stop her from listening with obvious interest for the answer.

Tamara blew out smoke in a thin, white stream. It was a question bound to be on everyone's mind.

"Yeah, I've been in trouble."

"What kind of trouble?"

"I just got out of juvie. Three years. Made parole." Word would get out one way or another. It might as well come from her and at least be accurate to start with. The more she tried to hide her past, the more the rumors would fly.

Jason whistled through his teeth.

"Wow. What for?"

"Murder," Tamara said flatly. No emotion in her voice or expression. Nothing that would show weakness or vulnerability.

"You're pulling my leg. Seriously?" he demanded.

Tamara shrugged. He could interpret the gesture as he liked.

"Who'd you kill?"

"None of your business."

"Some guy who asked too many questions," Sybil teased, and cracked up.

Tamara grinned at Sybil. Jason opened his mouth to ask another question.

"Shut up, Jason," Sybil snapped.

He closed his mouth and rolled his eyes. They continued to smoke. After a few minutes, Jason stepped on his cigarette butt and left. Sybil looked at Tamara.

"You want to walk?"

"Sure."

They walked in silence for a while. Tamara tried to make her cigarette last, not knowing how hard it would be for her to get another pack. In juvie, it was surprisingly easy. Here, she was going to have to get someone who was old enough to buy them for her, once she could get her hands on some money.

"News travels fast," Tamara observed.

"The grapevine is humming away," Sybil agreed. "Some of Henson's kids have made things... interesting around here, so when word gets out that they got someone new—well, the news travels."

"Great."

"Sorry. It'll die down again. Unless you're planning on making a splash."

"I'm not looking for attention."

Sybil nodded. They continued to walk and make small talk.

"So what was it like?" Sybil asked, and at Tamara's questioning look, elaborated. "In juvie."

"Not somewhere you'd like to be."

Sybil waited for more information, but Tamara shook her head and didn't enlighten her.

(iv)

The teacher walked up to Tamara while she was doing her classwork, and put a slip of yellow paper on her desk. Tamara looked down at it, and looked up at the teacher questioningly.

"You're wanted down at the office. That's your hall pass."

Tamara looked at it for a minute, and then closed her books and stacked them up. She picked up the yellow paper and headed out of the room and down the stairs. She got turned around a couple of times, but eventually found her way to the administrative office where she had started her day. She presented her yellow slip to the gray-haired woman at the reception desk.

"Yes. Tamara," the woman said, looking at the paper as if there was something wrong with it. "You are in conference room B."

Tamara looked around, and the receptionist pointed to a closed door behind her.

"Right there. Go on in."

Tamara wasn't sure what was going on. Was she in trouble for something already? Maybe someone had reported her for smoking. Or maybe it was something they always did at the end of the day when a student transferred mid-term. Checking up to make sure that everything had gone all right. That they had found all of their classes, hadn't had any trouble...

She put her hand on the doorknob. The receptionist had said to go right in, but she didn't feel right about it. Tamara knocked lightly on the door, and opened it, poking her head in. It was a small meeting room, four chairs around a small table. A tall black man sat in one with his long legs stretched out in front of him. He was dressed in a suit. His head was bald, maybe shaved. He smiled, but didn't show any teeth. The smile didn't reach his eyes. His face immediately fell back into a tired, grim look.

"Tamara," he greeted. "Come on in. Shut the door and have a seat."

Tamara obeyed, trying to analyze him. Not the principal. Maybe a counselor, if he'd been a cop in a previous life. He had the air of one of the guards in juvie. Not one of the day-to-day guards, but one of the supervisors or something. Higher up the food chain. More reserved, not as quick to pull out his baton or taser. Tamara sat down in the chair across from the man and waited.

"My name is Chad Collins," he introduced himself. "I'll be your parole officer."

"Oh." Tamara blew out her breath. Now it made sense. She wasn't in trouble. Not yet. This was her new shadow. The man who would be watching for her to fail. "Hi."

"I've read your file, and I think that you can make this transition successfully, if you put your mind to it."

Tamara nodded.

"It will be hard," he went on, "but you can choose to be a different person than you were before you went to juvie. Or while you were at juvie. It's a pivotal time for you. This is your chance to turn things around."

He rubbed his chin, looking down at the slim file in front of him.

"Okay," Tamara said.

"You don't want to be sent back for something stupid. It's important that you understand the terms of your parole."

Tamara nodded again.

"So what..." she started. She cleared her throat and tried to strengthen her wavering voice. "What are the rules?"

He pulled a single sheet out of the file and placed it in front of Tamara.

"Okay, let's go over it." Pointing to the top line, he started out. "I will tell you when and where our meetings are, and you'll be there. On time. Every time. You're living with the Hensons, and you're not allowed to move anywhere else without my say so. You have a nine o'clock curfew. No matter what, you're home by nine o'clock every night. Right?"

"Yes, sir," Tamara agreed.

"No weapons, no alcohol, no drugs. Not on your person, not in your room, not anywhere near you. You don't associate with anyone carrying weapons, alcohol, or drugs. You'll submit to random drug testing. Whenever I say. On the spot. You are not allowed to be around anyone who has been convicted of a felony."

"What if..."

"No one. No 'what ifs'. It doesn't matter if you knew them in juvie, before juvie, or met them since. No criminal associations."

"Okay." Tamara nodded.

"You're not allowed to be around young children. No one under six. And you'll attend mandatory counseling at least weekly."

"Yes, sir," Tamara said. "What kind of counseling?"

"Something to help to ease the transition, give you the skills that you need to stay clean outside of juvie. Anger and stress management. Addictions counseling, if you need it. Anything that I or your therapist decide that you need."

Tamara nodded and swallowed.

"Okay."

"Do you have any questions?"

"No, sir."

"What are you going to do if you think of questions? If you're not sure about something?"

She continued to stare at the paper in front of her.

"I guess I call you," she said.

"That's right." He pointed to his contact details at the bottom of the page. "Do you have a cell phone yet?"

"No."

"When you get one, you put me on your number one speed dial. I'm the person you call if you have any questions."

"Yes, sir."

"What if you slip up and break a rule, what do you do?" he demanded.

Tamara picked at the skin around her nails, hiding them under the table.

"Fix it," she suggested. "Don't do it again."

"The first thing you do is call me. You report yourself. 'Mr. Collins, someone offered me a beer and I was stupid enough to drink it.' 'Mr. Collins, I was ten minutes late for curfew.' 'Mr. Collins, a friend from juvie called me up, but I hung up on her.' Any violation, no matter how big or small. You call me. Got it?"

"Yes, sir."

"Things will be much worse if I hear it from someone else, or it shows up in a drug test or something. Tell me, and you might not get sent back to juvie."

"Okay."

Tamara had an overwhelming desire to bite her nails, and it was only with a huge exercise of will that she was able to keep her hands in her lap, hidden, away from her face, still picking at the cuticles.

"What if you have some other kind of problem?" he questioned.

Tamara looked up at his face, the slight flare of his nostrils and curl of his lip.

"Call you?" she suggested.

He nodded.

"Now you're getting it," he agreed.

Tamara mirrored his nod. Neither one of them said anything for a while, and Tamara eventually looked back up at Collins again, wondering what else she was in for.

"How was your first day?" he asked.

Tamara relaxed a little in her seat, letting out a pent-up breath.

"Okay. Not bad. The Hensons all seem really nice."

"They're a good family," Collins agreed. "They've dealt with a lot of tough cases. Everything is pretty calm there now, and I'm hoping that you won't make things too difficult for them. Give them a bit of a rest."

"I don't plan on getting in any trouble."

"Good. But it can be harder than you would think. These things are rarely planned. But temptations show up, catch you at a weak moment. You feel loyal to a friend or family member and think nobody will know, nobody will get hurt."

"I don't do drugs," Tamara said. "Or drink. I never even had a cigarette before juvie."

He studied her, eyes narrowed slightly. Tamara felt the need to defend herself further. She might not care what the kids at school or the Hensons thought, but she thought her parole officer ought to know what kind of a person she was.

"I'm not a troublemaker," she said. "You look at my juvie file. Or my school records before... before it happened. I never got in any kind of trouble. Ever."

Collins rubbed his chin, his dark eyes boring into her.

"You have admitted to the murders more than once. In court and to the parole board."

"Yes."

"What does *that* say about you?"

Tamara stared back down at the paper again. She picked at her cuticles under the table.

"It was a bad situation," she said. "I was trapped, and hurt, and the hormones... made me so foggy and emotional. I didn't know what to do. I know it doesn't make sense when you say it like that, but I was so... confused."

There was silence from Collins at first.

"This time," he said finally, "you have someone to talk to. You're not alone."

Tamara looked at him again. His voice was low, almost gentle.

"Call me," he said, tapping the piece of paper with the eraser end of his pencil. "For any reason."

"Okay. Thanks."

Tamara nodded. She felt very teary and emotional all of a sudden, and she didn't like it. She couldn't let her guard down. Couldn't make herself vulnerable. Collins' lips pressed together in a thin line for a moment, then the look vanished. Collins unfolded himself from the chair, towering over her. Tamara scrambled to get to her feet. He offered his hand, and Tamara shook it, feeling a bit awkward.

"Call me tomorrow before curfew," he instructed.

Tamara nodded.

He was still holding her hand, and looked down at it. Tamara saw that her fingers were bleeding around the nails, and pulled her hand out of his grasp, hiding it behind her back.

"I'm not the enemy, Tamara," Collins said. He sighed. "I'll get you in to see the therapist as soon as possible. Transition and stress management. You'll go."

"Yes, sir."

"Talk to you tomorrow, then."

Tamara nodded, and he left the room. The door swung shut behind him, clicking softly into place. Tamara put her hands over her face and tried to calm and compose herself. She was tough. She could manage it. She'd show Chad Collins that she wasn't like any of his other parolees. He didn't know her. She could make it.

THREE

(i)

TAMARA WATCHED CAREFULLY OUT the bus window for her stop, looking for the red brick building that Mrs. Henson had pointed out to her on the way to school. She kept thinking that she had gone too far, nothing seemed familiar and she had been on the bus for forty-five minutes. Anxiety built up in her stomach, and her breathing sped up. She felt like she couldn't get enough air. Finally, she started to recognize some of the street names, and saw the bank. She pulled the cord and got off. Looking up and down the street, disoriented, she eventually identified which way was home. A couple of blocks to walk, and she was looking at the Hensons' old bungalow. Sighing, Tamara went up the steps and in the front door.

Mrs. Henson came out of the kitchen, wiping her hands on a dishcloth.

"Oh good, you made it," she said, the wrinkles on her forehead smoothing out. "I was beginning to worry that you got lost."

"The bus takes a long time," Tamara snapped. The words

were out of her mouth before she had a chance to moderate them. She regretted her tone, and shrugged a little in a 'what can you do?' gesture.

"You must have missed the first bus. Did classes run late, or did you have to talk to a teacher...?"

"I got pulled out to meet with Mr. Collins, my parole officer. It's not my fault."

Mrs. Henson nodded.

"He stopped by this afternoon to talk to me too."

"Why?" Tamara demanded, irritated.

"Because I need to know your parole terms and conditions as well. And who to get in contact with if there are any problems."

Tamara scowled and shook her head. So everyone was going to be spying on her and reporting to her PO. She had just gone from one kind of prison to another. They might act like she was free now, but freedom was a relative thing.

There was a buzz from downstairs, and Mrs. Henson looked at her watch.

"That will be the laundry. Could you please go down and swap the clothes to the dryer?"

So, the beginning of the endless list of chores had begun. Just like at the Bakers. Tamara pressed her lips tightly shut. Complaining would only make it worse, bring the punishments down all the faster. She put her school books down on the coffee table and followed the noise of the washer down into the dark, cold basement. The stairs were rough plank steps. The laundry room was lit by a single white bulb. The appliances—several washers and dryers—looked like they had seen their prime back in the seventies. At least there would be no complex programming required. The washer quieted as she approached it, as if it were an animal that heard her coming. Tamara opened the lid. The first few handfuls of clothes were okay, a bit wet, but when she got down to the bottom, she found that several inches of water hadn't drained from the tub. Tamara went back to the bottom of the stairs and yelled up.

"Missus! Missus!"

Mrs. Henson appeared at the top of the stairs. The light was behind her and Tamara couldn't see the expression on her face.

"What is it, Tamara?" she asked.

"The washer didn't empty all the water out. Do you want me to squeeze them out, or run it again, or what?"

"It didn't empty?"

"No."

Mrs. Henson swore under her breath.

"You'd think with three washers we'd be able to keep *one* of them running," she complained. "Just do your best to squeeze them out before putting them in the dryer, and I'll get Jesse to look at it again."

Tamara went back to the washer again.

The water was cold, and by the time she finished wringing out all of the clothes, her hands were cold, sore, and rough. That did not improve her mood any. She slammed the door of the dryer and turned the timer all the way up. She stomped up the stairs and slammed the door at the top.

"Take it easy," Mrs. Henson soothed.

Tamara picked up her school books.

"Before you go up to your room, would you set the table, please?"

Tamara whirled around to look at her.

"Are you kidding me?" she demanded, her voice rising in pitch. "I just spent ten minutes wringing out your bloody clothes! Someone else can set the table!"

She stomped up the stairs and slammed her bedroom door without looking back.

(ii)

Tamara hadn't had a chance to cool down and relax before there was a knock at her door, and Deshawn popped her head in.

"Hey, girl. Dinner's on."

She withdrew again and was gone. Tamara obediently got up from her bed where she was pouting and headed downstairs, wondering even while she walked why she was bothering. It wouldn't hurt her skip dinner, and she really didn't want to be around the perfect happy family right now. But she was used to obeying the activity bells at juvie, and her body reacted to the invitation almost before her brain processed it. At juvie, if she decided to skip dinner, it would mean a follow-up by one of the guards to get her on her way, and if she still refused to go to the cafeteria or to eat when she got there, she would be on her way to the infirmary for a chat with Dr. Eastport and an exam. It was better just to go and appear to be compliant.

Tamara flounced down into her chair, scowling at anyone who dared to smile at her. There were a few glances exchanged around the table, those infinitesimal messages shared with a slightly raised eyebrow, wink, or nod. They waited for a couple more minutes for Jason to make it to the table, and once his butt touched the chair, Mrs. Henson nodded.

"Go ahead," she invited.

Tamara took each dish that was passed to her, but didn't make any effort to reach the ones that stayed in the middle of the table. She wasn't really hungry, and didn't feel like trying to choke down the food.

"How was school?" Deshawn asked. "First day, and all."

"Fine," Tamara muttered.

"Meet anyone? Make any friends?" Nita prodded for details.

"A couple. Not a lot of people are interested."

"It can take people a while to warm up," Nita agreed cheerily.

Tamara rolled her eyes.

"Who did you meet? Maybe we know someone in their family," Deshawn said.

Tamara chewed on her food for a while, avoiding answering and hoping that other conversations would distract her foster sisters from pursuing the line of questioning. Anxiety gnawed at her stomach. She already had Collins on her case. And Mrs. Henson watching her, reporting back to him. She didn't need the girls prying into her private life as well. They could mind their own business. She chewed the corner of a nail.

"Who did you meet?" Deshawn took up the question again, raising her eyebrows and staring at Tamara.

"Girl named Sybil," Tamara muttered.

"Sybil? That's not a very common name," Deshawn and Nita looked at each other, considering. Tamara could see them evaluating Sybil, what kind of a friend she would be. Sybil was obviously one of the school rejects; rebellious and outspoken, a disruptor. Not preppy and together, like Deshawn and Nita. Not a cheerleader.

"There's nothing wrong with her," Tamara growled.

"No one said anything against her," Nita pointed out.

But Tamara could see it in their eyes. They had already judged Sybil, decided that Tamara couldn't be allowed to hang out with her.

"I can't have who I want for friends?" she demanded. "My choices of friends have to be vetted through you, now? You're not my real family; what right do you have to decide who I can be friends with?"

"Tamara, cool it," Jesse said. "No one has criticized your friends."

Tamara's gaze flashed over to him, and as always, the knot in her stomach grew tighter at the sight of him, at the thought of another foster father trying to control her, forcing her. She felt like throwing up.

"Leave me alone!" she told him.

"Tamara. Take it easy," Mrs. Henson said, from Tamara's other side.

Tamara stood up, anxious at being pincered between them. She was on guard, warily looking from one to the other, watching for the coordinated attack.

"You have every right to choose your friends," Jesse soothed. His voice sounded mellow and reasonable, and it made nervous goosebumps break out on Tamara's arms and back. Her breath caught in her throat. Mr. Baker had a tone like that too, when he wanted something from her. "As long as they're not felons or trying to get you to break your parole."

"Is that what you think?" Tamara demanded. "You just want me to go right back to juvie. You don't want me here!"

"If we didn't want you here, you wouldn't be here," Mrs. Henson said.

Tamara shoved her chair back into the table with a bang. She wasn't going to be sitting back down. She wasn't going to be eating.

"So why don't you just call the stupid social worker, then?" she shouted. "And tell her to come and pick me up. Because I'm not staying here!"

Tamara ran back up to her room, shut the door, and flopped face down on the bed, hot tears of rage and fear trying to burn their way out of her eyes. Her throat was tight and hot. She swallowed, shaking all over, and hugged the pillow tightly against herself.

(iii)

In the morning, she kept waiting for the consequences. Mrs. Baker would never have let her get away with talking back like that. Even if Tamara had to wait a day or two, there was always a consequence. And always severe. Tamara was sick with anticipation.

She was hungry. It was way past time for the breakfast bell, but Tamara couldn't make herself leave her room. She'd have to go downstairs, and see Jesse, and then Mrs. Henson. They would have a list of chores, and her punishment for misbehaving. Her skin crawled in nervous anticipation of having to face them.

There was a tap on the door, and Nita poked her head in.

"You up? I didn't hear you in the bathroom."

Tamara covered her face with her hands, her heart pounding. She shook her head and tried to breathe evenly, a sob catching in her throat.

"Tamara?"

Nita shut the door behind her and walked across the room to the bed, where Tamara sat waiting for the world to collapse around her.

"Tamara, it's okay. What's wrong?"

"I can't go down," Tamara whispered. "They're gonna *kill* me!"

"What?"

Nita touched Tamara's hands, getting her to lower them. Nita looked into her face.

"Mister and Missus?" she asked incredulously. "You think they're gonna be mad at you?"

Tamara nodded, struggling to find her voice, to put it into words.

"What for?" Nita said.

Tamara looked at the smooth, glowing skin of Nita's face.

"Because... I got mad and mouthed off last night. At supper."

Tamara swallowed, and looked anxiously at Nita's eyes. They crinkled up at the corners when Nita laughed.

"*That?* That was nothing, Tamara." She reached out to touch a lock of Tamara's hair that draped next to her face. "Mr. and Mrs. Henson have been foster parents for years. To lots of teenagers. You think they'd last if they took all of the hormones and angst seriously?"

Tamara frowned.

"What?"

"Some of the melodrama and meltdowns this house has seen!" Nita exclaimed. "Baby, you've got nothing on them. A little bitchiness after your first day at a brand new school? I doubt if they've even thought about it this morning. You didn't even break anything."

Tamara studied Nita, her breathing easing gradually. Nita nodded.

"It's true," she insisted. She sat down on the edge of Tamara's bed. "Look, even if you came into foster care after living with your own family your whole life, and it was all roses, and you just went into foster care because they died and you didn't have anywhere else to go... it's still different, scary being somewhere new. Different rules. Things don't work the way you expect. You'd still have a few blow-ups, trying to get settled in." Nita traced the lines of stitching on the quilt. "And when you come here from *juvie*... well..."

Tamara looked out the window, embarrassed. Nita went on.

"It was a few years ago that Harry got out of juvie last, but I remember what it was like. He seems all mellow and easygoing now, right?"

"Uh-huh."

"Well, when he got out of juvie..." Nita shook her head and whistled. "Bruce-Banner-Incredible-Hulk! You looked at the guy the wrong way and he'd go off. And not just shouting. Throwing around furniture, trying to go after Jesse, running away... but Mister and Missus stayed cool about it. They've seen it all. And they're not going to let a little bitchiness or a teenage tantrum get in the way of the job. Okay?"

Tamara nodded.

"Okay."

"Now we'd better get you ready for school. You don't want to be late."

(iv)

In gym later on that day, Tamara fell back, panting, and headed for the bench, letting another student sub in for her.

"Hey, Tamara, right?" Mr. Wilson, the phys ed teacher was looking at her.

"Yeah."

"You're not bad," he complimented. "Are you interested in joining the volleyball team?"

Tamara shrugged awkwardly.

"I dunno. I haven't played for a long time. We didn't play volleyball... at my last school."

"Well, from what I've seen today, you've got what it takes. If this is you after not practicing for a long time, things will only improve from here."

Tamara glanced around at the other girls. The game had paused between serves while everyone listened in on the conversation. New girl getting singled out for being better than everybody else was not good. Not when you wanted to make friends or fly under the radar.

"I don't know," she said, looking down.

"After school today, be here."

She continued to stare down at the floor. Mr. Wilson left her alone and continued to circulate around the gym.

(v)

Tamara was tempted to just forget about the volleyball team tryout. She had enough to worry about without adding sports to the mix. And she wasn't in good shape or practiced up.

On the other hand, playing on the volleyball team could solve some of her problems, too. She would get to know some of the other girls, maybe make friends with a couple of them. She would have something physical to do to get her mind off of other difficulties, something to burn off the excess energy. She would be a part of something, instead of just hanging around the fringes of the school, trying to break in somehow.

When the dismissal bell rang, her feet took her back to the gym instead of out to the bus stop. Tamara should probably tell Mrs. Henson what she was doing, but she didn't figure she would take too long. She would still catch the later bus and be home in time for supper.

The other girls were already changing into their practice clothes when Tamara walked into the room. They quieted and looked at her with various expressions of confusion or challenge. Tamara didn't say anything, just went to her gym locker and started changing.

"What are you doing here?" questioned a tall, straight-haired blond changing close by.

"Mr. Wilson asked me to come," Tamara said.

The girl considered this for a few moments.

"You can't join the team mid-year. We already started."

Tamara shrugged.

"I just transferred in. I dunno. Mr. Wilson said to come, so I came."

"He probably wants her to take Holiday's spot," a petite redhead said.

"Maybe," the first girl admitted. "It's not like Holly's coming back."

"What happened?" Tamara asked. "Did she get hurt? Or transfer somewhere else?"

"Got herself *pregnant*," the blond said, arching her eyebrows. "Talk about stupid."

"Oh. And she's not getting an abortion?"

"Her family doesn't believe in it. Some religious thing. So she's gone for the rest of the year. Even if she wants to come back to school after she has the wretched thing, it won't be until late next year. By the time she can play, she'll be in high school instead of here."

"Sucks," Tamara nodded.

The blond pulled on her shoes and tied them up, then looked at Tamara for a minute with her hands on her hips. Then she appeared to have made a choice, and stuck her hand out toward Tamara.

"I'm Emily," she said.

"Tamara."

She took Emily's hand and gave it a brief shake before withdrawing again.

"I hope you're good. Because this team really needs a kick in the rear. We're pathetic this year."

"I'm not in shape," she warned. "Haven't been practicing. So don't expect much."

"Great. Oh well, at least we get *someone* to replace Holly. Better than leaving a hole in the team. You get a couple of people out with injuries, and you start hurting for replacements. Just having someone to jump in when we start to get tired is better than nothing."

Tamara nodded.

"Okay. Come on. I'll introduce you to the coach."

(vi)

"Coach McClure," Emily called, as they entered the noisy gym.

A group of boys were setting up the volleyball nets, others were standing around talking, or shooting hoops at the opposite end of the gym. The man that Emily was calling turned around.

He had a lot of gray hair and a kind-looking face. He had a prominent nose and silver wire frame glasses. The wrinkles around his face were cheerful, pointing up. He raised his eyebrows questioningly.

"Emily?"

"Coach, this is Tamara. I guess Mr. Wilson told her she should come out for practice tonight."

He nodded.

"Okay. Good to meet you, Tamara. You're interested in joining the team?"

Tamara's face got warm. She tried to look confident, to keep her gaze focused on his face instead of dropping it to her feet.

"I dunno. Maybe. He thought I should try."

"How much volleyball have you played in the past?"

Tamara shook her head.

"Not much. And I'm out of practice."

"She's good," a voice boomed out, coming from behind Emily and Tamara. Tamara looked and saw that it was Mr. Wilson. "Her 'out of practice' is better than some of the girls already on the team. She's a shoo-in if she wants it."

"Well, let's take a look," Coach McClure agreed.

When the boys finished setting up the nets, they were all shooed out of the gym, and the volleyball team gathered in a group around the Coach. They worked on several different drills, and then moved on to a short practice game. Tamara was awkward and clumsy, knowing that everyone was watching her and evaluating her skills. It wasn't easy to perform when you knew the focus was all on you.

She nearly collided with one of the other girls, forgetting to call the ball, and they ended up both missing it.

"Chill," the curly-haired brunette told her. "Stop trying to show off and just have a little fun."

Tamara settled back into her place, thinking about it. If she was going to be miserable trying to make everyone think she was better than she was, there was no point in joining the team. If she wanted to have fun, then she had to just shut off the competitiveness, and try to enjoy herself. If she was going to join the team, it would have to be because it was enjoyable.

So she tried to relax. Bump the ball to other teammates, let other people run for it. Every now and then she managed to nail a brilliant spike, or to save the ball when it looked like a bust, and that made her smile. When a teammate complimented her, she smiled and blushed, feeling warm from her face right down to her toes.

When practice was done, McClure blew his whistle, and everyone sat down in a semi-circle around him. He reminded them of the drills that they had started with, and assigned them more work before the next practice. Looking around at the group of pink-faced, sweaty girls, he pointed at Tamara.

"It's yours if you want it, Tamara," he said. "So are you interested, or not? It's a commitment, and I don't want you to start if you can't follow through. What's it going to be?"

Tamara glanced around at the other girls. None of them seemed particularly angry or jealous about her being recruited. There didn't appear to be any resentment over it. Emily nodded encouragingly at her.

"Okay." Tamara nodded. "I'll join."

She was nervous about it. What if she ended up getting bounced back to juvie, and letting the team down? She was committed to coming out to practices and games, but she couldn't promise to be there when it came down to the wire. She wondered if she should talk to McClure after the practice. Explain the situation, so he wasn't surprised if something happened.

"Good," McClure approved. There was a murmur from the assembled girls. "We'll get you a uniform. The practice schedule is online. One of the girls can e-mail it to you, or set it up on your phone. Lotta, stay after. Team dismissed."

They all jumped up and headed for the locker room. Tamara lingered for a moment to explain to Coach McClure about her parole, but he motioned for her to join the others in getting changed. Lotta, the girl he'd asked to stay behind looked at

Tamara nervously, waiting for her to leave. She was a small girl for a volleyball player, as Tamara was herself, but she had plenty of energy that seemed to make up for it, showing up when she was needed, and keeping the team pumped up. She was a brunette, wavy hair pulled back into an untidy ponytail. Slim. She had a sort of tentative air with the coach, as if she was afraid of doing the wrong thing. Tamara sighed and headed down to the locker room. The showers were already all running and occupied. Tamara stripped down and wrapped a towel around herself, waiting for one to come free.

"Not bad today," one of the other girls told her. "Keep it up, and maybe we'll win a couple of games."

Tamara forced a smile that she hoped looked interested.

"You don't have a good record?" she asked.

"No. We really need some more power. Things were already bad, but when we lost Holiday," she shook her head. "Everything just went down the drain. Even Coach seems like he's not quite 'on'. Distracted or something. I don't know."

One of the girls exited the shower, and Tamara jumped in. She cast a glance around quickly. Showers were a dangerous place at juvie. Tamara didn't like to be there any longer than she had to be. She quickly rinsed off the sweat. She let the warm water run through her hair for a moment, closed her eyes ever so briefly...

There was a crash across the locker room. Someone shutting their door a little too hard. It just about made Tamara jump out of her skin. Her eyes flew open, and she looked quickly around the showers for any dangers. You couldn't see much of the locker room from the showers, so she couldn't see what was going on. Tamara stepped out of the shower to let someone else get in, toweled off briefly, and wrapped the towel back around her.

Lotta was getting back to the locker room as Tamara went to her locker. Tamara glanced at her curiously, wondering what she'd been kept back for. Lotta dropped her eyes when she caught Tamara's gaze. She looked upset, teary-eyed. Lotta headed toward the showers, not talking to anyone. Tamara raised her eyebrows at Emily, dressing next to her.

"What's up with her?" Tamara asked. "She mess up or something?"

Emily's face was a mask.

"None of my business," she said.

"Okay..."

"I got enough of my own stuff to work on," Emily said. "I just keep my head down."

Tamara finished getting dressed in silence.

FOUR

(i)

MRS. HENSON TRIED TO stop Tamara as she went up the stairs.

"Tamara. You're late again. Is everything all right?"

"Fine," Tamara said. She didn't stop. She went straight to her bedroom and put down her books. By the time Mrs. Henson made it up the stairs and to Tamara's door, she had the books spread out and was in a pose that indicated she was deep in thought and didn't want to be interrupted. Mrs. Henson tapped on the door and came in.

"Tamara."

"What?"

Mrs. Henson sat down on the edge of the bed.

"Did you miss the early bus?"

Tamara looked up. She tried to keep her face expressionless.

"I was trying out for volleyball."

Mrs. Henson's eyebrows went up, surprised.

"Really? How did that go?"

"I'm on the team."

"Congratulations!" she said with a broad smile, and reached as if to give Tamara a hug. Tamara pulled back, but she couldn't help smiling in response.

"Yeah."

"That's excellent. It will be a lot of fun, and a good way to make friends. I didn't know you were interested in volleyball."

Tamara nodded.

"You should tell Mr. Collins about it," Mrs. Henson said.

Tamara frowned, her excitement over sharing the news evaporating.

"Why?" she demanded.

"You know, parole officers don't get to hear a lot of good news. You want to share the positive stuff with him, so he can see how you are progressing. You need to call him tonight anyway, right?"

Tamara traced a circle on the bedspread.

"Yeah. I'm going to... I just don't think he'll care about me making the team."

"Trust me. He'll care. Share it with him."

Neither of them said anything for a minute. Mrs. Henson reached out to touch her hand. Tamara pulled back.

"Tamara, you need to keep me informed when your plans change. Just a call after school to tell me that you're staying to try out, so you'll be late getting home. Then I don't have to worry."

"I don't have a phone," Tamara said. "Are you going to give me a cell?"

"The school has pay phones out front, phones in the office that students can use if they don't have any change, and most of your friends probably have phones that you can borrow. I'm not buying you a phone, but you have access to plenty of phones. Okay?"

Tamara rolled her eyes, sighing in exasperation.

"The schedule for the practices is online," she said. "They

didn't have a hard copies to give out. And I don't have a computer either," she looked pointedly around the room, bare of any electronics.

"We'll look it up, and I'll print it off for you. It would be a good idea to have a copy on the fridge too, so that we can double-check whenever we need to."

Tamara nodded. She knew it was too much to hope that a foster family would give her a phone or computer. That just didn't happen. It was obvious that the Hensons were not well-off. They probably needed every penny that they made through fostering for things like upkeep of the house. And the washing machine. If Tamara wanted to be able to have things like phones and computers, she'd have to get an after-school job. Which she couldn't really do if she was on the volleyball team and had to go to a lot of practices and games.

The doorbell rang, and Mrs. Henson glanced at her watch.

"I'll get the door if you'll run down and check on the chicken. Make sure it's not burning."

Tamara followed her down the stairs, and separated from her to go into the kitchen. The chicken in the oven looked just fine. Tamara poked at it with a fork to see whether it was dry or pink inside, but it looked perfectly done. She turned the oven temperature down to keep it warm.

She could hear Mrs. Henson talking with someone at the door, both of their voices sounding concerned. She peeked around the kitchen doorway at them, but couldn't get a good view of the visitor, just a back view of Mrs. Henson. They spoke for another minute, and then Mrs. Henson shut the door and came back to the kitchen. At Tamara's questioning look, she shook her head, rolling her eyes slightly.

"That was Mrs. Phipps from two doors down. One of her cats seems to have gone missing."

Tamara shrugged her shoulders.

"An outside cat?"

"Yes. She has a few that run the neighborhood, I chase them out of the garden every now and then, for all the good that does."

Tamara nodded. "Cats are a nuisance," she agreed.

Mrs. Henson nodded, and checked on the chicken. She moved to turn it down, and saw that Tamara already had. She closed the oven and leaned back on it, facing Tamara.

"They are," she said. "People should keep them inside. At least in the city. It's not like you need them to keep down the mouse population in the barn or something. Anyway. Mrs. Phipps is missing her black and white male cat. If you happen to see him, he apparently answers to the name of 'Toodles'."

Tamara snickered.

"She's quite concerned," Mrs. Henson sighed. "She hasn't seen him at all the last two days, and that's very unusual."

Tamara went to the cupboard and started getting out the plates to set the table, heading off any instructions that Mrs. Henson could give her.

"Anything could happen to a cat you let roam outside," she said, getting the plates down and then heading over to the dining table. "I knew a girl in juvie..." She trailed off, deciding that maybe she didn't want to reveal anything about Glock. It wasn't exactly the kind of thing you discussed over dinner.

Mrs. Henson looked at Tamara when she didn't finish.

"A girl in juvie who what?" she asked. "Lost a cat?"

Tamara shook her head, and looked for another subject to segue to.

"Nothing. Do you think I could get a volleyball to do practice drills?"

"There's probably one kicking around already. Check the shed out back for a ball and a pump. We've had them in the past."

"Okay."

Tamara went back to get cutlery to lay out beside the plates. Mrs. Henson watched her, frowning slightly.

(*ii*)

The clock on the wall didn't seem to be advancing at all. Every time Tamara looked at it, expecting ten or fifteen minutes to be marked off by the progress of the hands, they seemed to be in exactly the same place as they had been last time she looked at it. The last class of the day seemed like it would never end.

She didn't have any volleyball practice after school, so she had a break to do what she wanted. And what she wanted was to meet with Sybil after school and walk over to her house. It was the first invitation that Tamara had received since getting out of juvie. She felt like a kindergartner on her first play date. She had a friend. A friend who deemed her important enough to invite Tamara over to her house. It wasn't like they were going to do anything exciting or earth-shattering. Tamara just had a warm feeling, a sense of well-being. She had a friend. She was going to her friend's house. All was well in the world.

"All done your work, Miss French?" the teacher questioned.

Tamara looked down at her notebook, where she had barely done more than write down the first problem. She grimaced.

"No, sir."

"You'd better get to it, then. No point in wasting class time and having to do more work at home," he pointed out.

Tamara nodded and tried to focus on the problem, surreptitiously looking back up at the clock again. She couldn't believe how slowly the clock hands were moving. Tamara let her breath out slowly in a long, thin stream, like she was blowing out cigarette smoke. It wasn't loud enough for the students sitting closest to her to be disturbed, but it helped to soothe Tamara. Helped to calm the butterflies in her stomach. *She got to go to a friend's house today.*

She packed everything up quietly, her eyes on the second hand circling the clock face. The teacher raised his eyebrow at her, but Tamara ignored the look, counting down the seconds until the bell finally rang. When the dismissal bell shrilled, Tamara shot out of her seat. She was the first one out the door, and sprinted down the hall toward her locker until the flood of students exiting their various classes clogged the halls, and she had to slow down to avoid running anyone over. She growled impatiently. Not loudly enough for anyone to hear. When she finally reached her locker, Tamara shoved her books haphazardly into the denim backpack that Nita had lent to her, and shutting her locker door, headed for Sybil's locker to meet up with her.

"Tamara!"

Tamara searched the sea of students in the hallway, and saw Sybil heading toward her, raising a hand above everyone's heads to wave at her. Tamara grinned at her. Sybil pointed to a side hallway, and they both worked their way toward the quieter hall instead of directly down the middle of the main hall toward each other. Breaking free of the crowd, they both laughed.

"It's crazy out there!" Sybil said. "It's like rush-hour traffic."

"Worse," Tamara countered. "At least in rush-hour no one runs into you."

"If you're lucky." Sybil laughed.

"Yeah. Can we get out this way?"

Sybil nodded.

"Follow me."

It wasn't the most efficient way out of the school, but it was probably a lot faster than trying to cut their way through the knot of students in the hallway. Tamara tried not to act too excited about going to Sybil's house, even though her stomach and heart were bouncing all over the place excitedly. She didn't want Sybil to think that she was some kind of emotionally-needy loser, or that she had invested too much in the friendship. They each lit up cigarettes almost the moment they walked out the doors and were outside, even though they weren't supposed to smoke within three hundred meters of the school.

"Finally," Sybil said, taking a big inhale, and then blowing the smoke out away from Tamara.

Tamara took a pull on her own cigarette and held the smoke in her lungs for a few seconds, feeling the nicotine rush spread from her middle to warm and relax her entire body. She let it out again slowly.

"Did you pick up smoking in juvie or before that?" Sybil asked.

"In juvie," Tamara said. "Helps to fit in."

Sybil grunted in agreement.

"What about you?" Tamara asked. "What made you take up something so stupid?"

Sybil laughed.

"My mom smokes. I don't know. It was just natural for me to pick it up too. Pick up one of her cigarettes from the ash tray one day, take a drag to see what it's like. By the time she figured out what I was doing, I was hooked. She was not happy about that, I'll tell you."

"What's she going to say, if she smokes? She can't exactly say 'I smoke, but you can't.'"

"Well, she did, actually. But I didn't take it seriously. People can tell you how bad it is, but when you're a kid, you don't understand. And once you're hooked, and you figure out how bad it is for you... then it's too late."

"We could quit," Tamara said.

"Yeah. Could. My mom has a few times. But it never sticks."

"She shouldn't have smoked in the house, around you."

"Suppose not."

They continued to walk, smoking.

"You live close by?" Tamara asked after a few minutes.

"Yeah. Not much further now. Where do the Henson's live? All the way over on the east side, somewhere, right?"

Tamara nodded.

"About an hour on the bus."

"Yech. What a pain. I hate taking the bus."

"It's better than not being able to go anywhere."

Sybil looked at her sideways and chuckled.

When they reached Sybil's house, they stood outside, finishing off their cigarettes.

"I don't like to smoke around the others," Sybil explained.

"They don't smoke too?"

She laughed.

"Not yet. Mom doesn't smoke in the house anymore and I'm not supposed to either."

Tamara looked the house over as she finished her cigarette. It was a nice-looking house, a bungalow, brick facade, white-framed windows. Not as big or old as the Henson's house. They had a flat green lawn, not much landscaping. Tamara and Sybil stood there smoking in silence for a couple more minutes. They both ground out their butts, and Tamara noticed several others on the sidewalk and in the gap between the sidewalk and grass.

Sybil led the way up the sidewalk to the house. She used her key in the lock without trying the door first. As they stepped in the front door, Tamara heard squeals and running feet.

"Syb's home!" one little voice shouted as others giggled and they apparently tripped over each other, by the noise.

Sybil took a look around the disaster area in the front room.

"I'd better not catch whoever's been eating crackers in here!" she shouted. "You're gonna get it!"

More squeals.

Sybil dropped her backpack and started picking up the couch cushions that had been pressed into use as a play fort and shoving them back into place without regard as to where they belonged or what direction the zippers were facing. Tamara gave her a hand. Sybil kicked a collection of stuffed animals, dolls, and action figures into a pile at the side and picked up what cracker pieces she could. Tamara followed Sybil as she went into the kitchen and threw out the bits. There was movement down the hallway, and Tamara turned to see a couple of elfin faces peeping out of one of the doorways. They giggled and retreated. Tamara laughed.

Sybil opened the fridge and pulled out a jug of milk. "Everyone do their chores?"

There was a patter of feet, and Tamara looked around as a little blond girl of four or five came into the kitchen, one finger in her mouth.

"I did my chores," she announced.

Sybil poured some milk into a plastic animal cup and handed it to her. "There you go, then, Boo."

The little girl's eyes turned to Tamara, and looking into her clear blue eyes, with a heady rush, Tamara was suddenly back at the Bakers, a sick, terrified feeling in her stomach. Corrine. Blue eyes, blond hair. That little heart-shaped face. Tamara's hands clenched into fists. Nausea ripped through her, turning her legs to jelly.

"Hey, are you okay?" Sybil asked.

Tamara couldn't answer.

"Sit down. You're white as a sheet," Sybil said, pulling a kitchen chair out and guiding Tamara toward it. "Are you sick? Do you feel faint?"

Tamara held onto the chair, steadying herself.

"I gotta go."

"What? You just got here." Sybil's brows drew down. "What's wrong? Do you want me to call someone to pick you up?"

"No. No, I just have to get out of here."

Sybil stood there looking at her, eyes wide.

"I'm not supposed to be around kids," Tamara said, trying to make her voice sound calmer and more reasonable. "My parole terms."

Sybil swore. "Seriously? Why not?"

Tamara didn't try to answer the question.

"I'll just tell them to stay out of our way, how about that? You don't have to be in the same room."

"I don't know…" Tamara looked down at the little girl, swallowing.

"Go play with the others, Boo," Sybil told her, shooing her away. "Me and my friend need some space, okay?"

The little girl took another sip of her milk and handed it back to Sybil. Sybil put it in the fridge and returned the jug of milk as well. Then the little pixie scampered away. Tamara breathed a sigh of relief.

"Sorry," she said. "I didn't know you had little kids."

"Is it okay? You can stay here, if they stay out of our way?"

"Yeah, I think so," Tamara said. Her own answer nagged at her. She should call Collins to make sure. If she had any questions, she was supposed to ask him. But Tamara was worried that Collins would tell her no, she couldn't stay, and she didn't want to go home. If she didn't call him, she could still honestly say that she wasn't around children. She'd made sure that they were out of the way. Collins hadn't said she couldn't be in the same house. He hadn't said she had to be a certain distance away. So it was up to Tamara to decide what 'around' them meant.

"Good," Sybil said, satisfied. She opened her mouth with an inquiring expression, and then shut it again. Tamara saw the doubt chase across her face before Sybil managed to blank her face. She had decided that she didn't want to know, just like Tamara didn't want to check with Collins. Sybil smiled. "Good. Then we can get down to business. Come on."

Sybil led the way to her own bedroom. It was a small room, and couldn't hold much more than the bed and dresser that were in it. The walls were light pink, but little of the paint was visible, as the walls were papered with posters of musicians, actors, and some scary-looking men that Tamara thought were wrestlers.

"Cool," she said.

Sybil sat down on the bed, then lay back.

"Make yourself at home," she invited, and Tamara flopped down beside her.

(iii)

Tamara's eyes were closed while they talked. She felt Sybil shift her weight on the bed beside her, and then felt her lean in close. Tamara opened her eyes and saw that Sybil's face was about two inches from hers. She blinked.

Sybil chuckled.

"I want a good look at your tat," she explained.

Tamara held still while Sybil examined it.

"So you got that in juvie, right?" Sybil said, sitting back.

"Yeah."

"That's *so* cool. Did lots of the inmates get tattooed?"

Tamara nodded. "Most of them had at least one."

"Two tears means... two deaths, right?" Sybil asked tentatively.

"Yeah. There can be other meanings, but..." Tamara trailed off.

Sybil didn't ask for more details about who had died. Who she had killed. Tamara had noticed that while Sybil admired her and was interested in Tamara's prison experience, she was careful not to ask for too many details on what Tamara had actually been convicted of.

"Do you have any other tats?" Sybil asked.

Tamara held her hand out, showing Sybil the inside of her wrist. Sybil studied the arrangement of five dots.

"What does that one mean?" she asked.

"It just means you've done time," Tamara said with a shrug.

"So what's it like? Does it hurt, getting a prison tattoo like that?"

"Not bad. Not like piercing."

Sybil raised her brows.

"Piercing isn't bad," she countered. She had several piercings of her own.

"Not when you get it done with the right equipment at a professional place, maybe," Tamara said. "Bit different when you're using a safety pin or sharpened bed spring."

Sybil winced.

"You gotta be kidding. Yeouch. What did you get pierced?"

Tamara hesitated. She lifted up her shirt and showed Sybil her naval ring. Sybil examined it closely, touching the ring gently to take a look at the hole.

"Looks like it healed up okay," she observed.

"Yeah. Didn't have much trouble with that one." At Sybil's questioning look, Tamara rolled her eyes ceiling-ward, feeling her face and ears getting warm. "Piercing in juvie is against the rules. Without proper equipment, it isn't hygienic. And they don't want you using your jewelry as a weapon. You can only get pierced where the guards won't notice it and take your jewelry away. So you pierce places even more likely to get infected."

"So you've got...?" Sybil motioned, her cheeks getting pink.

"Don't know if I'll keep them. But for now... yeah."

"And you didn't get any infections?"

"Nothing *really* bad." Tamara thought back to this rite of passage and gave a little shudder. No one had thought that she would actually go through with it. They wouldn't take her seriously. So she had done the first piercing all by herself. Surprised a lot of people. Tamara decided to move Sybil's focus away from herself. If Sybil wanted to hear about tats and piercings, Tamara would entertain her with stories of tats and piercings.

"One girl managed to get her tongue done, and the guards didn't find out about it for almost a year. She wouldn't talk to anyone while there were guards around, because they might see it and take it out. They thought she was mute!"

Sybil laughed. "You're joking. I'd never be able to do it. I'd yawn, or be playing with it, or they'd see it while I was eating or something. She would have had to be so careful!"

"Yeah. They always find out sooner or later. Someone informs on you, or the guards find it in a body search, or something. They take whatever jewelry they find, but they can't stop you from putting something else through the hole again later to keep it from closing up. Some of the girls were really good at making jewelry."

"Too cool," Sybil breathed, her eyes shining.

"Don't plan on spreading it around," Tamara warned. "I'm not showing everyone."

Sybil giggled at the thought.

"But you must have shown someone at juvie," she pointed out. "Otherwise, why get it done? And the person who did it for you saw."

"No privacy in juvie," Tamara agreed. "Everyone sees everything."

(iv)

The doorbell rang during Sunday dinner as Tamara poked at her slightly dry roast, trying to decide whether she was hungry enough to eat anything more. A bit of gravy, and the roast would be fine. But she wasn't really sure she was hungry.

Mrs. Henson put down her knife and fork with an exasperated sigh.

"If that's *another* neighbor looking for their lost cat or dog, I'm going to scream. Mrs. B. Thinks someone is going around opening back gates to let them free."

She got up and went to the door. It was a male voice, and Mrs. Henson was back to the table again almost immediately. Not long enough to have a detailed discussion about what he could do about his lost pet. Behind her was Chad Collins. Tamara put her fork down with a loud clink.

"What?" she demanded. "I didn't do anything!"

She looked around the table at the rest of the family. Did one of them report her for some minor infraction? Say that she had done something that she hadn't? One word could get her sent back to juvie, whether it was true or not.

"Sunday dinner is a rather odd time for a visit," Jesse agreed, looking at Collins questioningly.

"I need to see you," Collins said to Tamara.

She gripped the edge of the table.

"What? Why? What's this about?"

Collins stared at her steadily.

"Come on, Tamara. Any time, any place, I can request a meeting, and you need to be there. Well, the time is now and the place is here."

Tamara didn't get up from the table. She felt like she was frozen in place. It didn't make any sense that Collins would want to see her now. She was supposed to be meeting with him on Tuesday. Why would he show up unannounced on Sunday?

Collins sighed and held up a clear plastic cup with a screw-on lid.

"Tamara. I need a sample. Now."

There were giggles around the table. Tamara stood up, her face hot. She worked her way around the dining room table over to Collins.

"Really not appropriate during dinner," Jesse joked to Nita, sitting beside him. Nita let out a high giggle. They all continued to eat. Furious at being mocked, Tamara was glad to get out of the room. She snatched the cup from Collins and stomped up the stairs to the bathroom. At first she was too angry to provide a sample, and just sat there, steaming mad. Collins waited and did not take up pounding on the door telling her to hurry up. Eventually Tamara unclenched her body enough to do what was required. She screwed the lid onto the cup and opened the bathroom door. Collins took it from her with gloved fingers, and sealed it into a bag marked with her name. He scribbled his initials across the seal. Tamara watched him strip off his gloves and drop them into the wastepaper basket.

"Good. Since I'm already here, I'd like to spend a few minutes with you. Your room?"

He gestured toward Tamara's bedroom. It took her by surprise that he knew which room was hers, but on reflection, Tamara realized that he had visited the house before while she was out, and that the Hensons had acknowledged having Troublemakers before. Collins had probably been in the house on previous occasions, if he had dealt with any of their previous foster placements.

Tamara opened her door and led the way into the room. She sat down on the end of the bed. Collins walked around the room, eyes analyzing everything. He opened and closed a few drawers on the dresser, pushed clothes around in the closet, and eventually turned around to look at Tamara.

"Everything seems to be fine," he said. That helped Tamara to relax a little, knowing this was not going to be a confrontation over some imagined infraction. She blew out her breath. Maybe it was all just routine. Nobody had reported her. It was just a random visit. "Do you have anything to report to me?"

Tamara shook her head. "No."

"Nothing I should know about?"

"Uh-uh."

He waited for a couple of minutes, letting the silence draw out uncomfortably.

"Anything you have any questions about?" he persisted.

Tamara's mind flashed back to being at Sybil's house with the little sisters around. But she had already decided that was okay. She didn't need to ask him about it. So she stayed stubbornly silent, just shaking her head.

"How's the volleyball going?" he asked, gazing down at her.

Tamara was surprised by the question. She raised her shoulders in a shrug.

"Fine... I've been getting playing time, not just sitting on the bench. The team isn't great. But we won the last game."

"I saw that. Good job. I think you being on the team is a great idea. I'm glad it's working out."

Tamara nodded.

Collins looked at her, waiting to see if she had anything else to say.

"And how about your counseling? How is that going?"

Tamara sighed and rolled her eyes. "I dunno. I'm sure Dr. Frank has probably given you his report. He's got a better idea of what's going on in my head and whether I'm doing okay or not than I do. I go to my appointments. Dunno what else I can tell you."

"Is it helping you?"

"Helping me what? Fit in? Volleyball is good for that. Make the transition from juvie?" Tamara shook her head. "I still feel like I'm just out on a day pass and I'm going to have to go back tomorrow. My body still wakes up with the bells, even though they don't ring here. It's weird."

Collins nodded.

"Don't worry. It can take time to adjust to being free. Just because it is what you have wanted for three years, your body and brain still need time to cope with the change."

Tamara raised her hands. "Sure," she agreed.

"Okay. We're meeting on Tuesday anyway, so there's no need to prolong this. Just keep abiding by your terms, and you'll be fine. Call me if you have any concerns. Okay?"

Tamara nodded. Collins looked down at her like he wondered if she would get up and shake his hand. She did not. He left the room, and Tamara listened to his steps recede down the stairs. She just sat there, breathing, trying to calm the tightly wound spring in her belly that made her feel like she was going to either explode or throw up every time she had to talk to Collins. Or think about having to report to him. He was the one who was waiting to throw her back in jail. The one watching and waiting for her to screw up.

(v)

There was a knock on the closed bedroom door, which made Tamara just about jump out of her skin. She gasped for breath and held her hand over her chest.

"Sheesh... What is it?" Tamara yelled.

The door opened, and it was Jesse. Tamara pulled her feet up onto the bed, putting her knees in front of her chest, forming a shield between them. Her heart, still pumping hard from the knock on the door that had startled her, did not slow down now that she saw who it was.

"There's pie," Jesse said, smiling. "I assume you would like some."

Pie. Tamara considered it. Her stomach was tense and nauseated. And Coach McClure had warned her that she should lose a few pounds in order to improve her performance on the volleyball court. She grimaced and shook her head.

"Tell Missus I'm not feeling good."

He stood there for another minute, studying her as if trying to figure out if she was telling the truth, or if he could persuade her to come down and have dessert with the family. Then he nodded.

"Okay. I'll eat your slice." He grinned.

Tamara rolled her eyes. "Go ahead."

Jesse retreated. It couldn't have been more than ten minutes before Deshawn was there, poking her head in the door.

"Everything good, Tam?" she asked.

Tamara frowned. "Tam?" she repeated. "Don't call me that."

"Oh. Okay. Just checking... I know it's embarrassing to be pulled away from the dinner table to pee in a cup—"

"Really? How many times have you had that happen?"

"Well, I haven't, exactly, but I get it—"

"You don't get it," Tamara snapped, "or you wouldn't be in here bugging me about it! Why can't everyone just leave me alone for once?"

She heard Nita behind Deshawn. "Hey, is she all right?"

Deshawn turned, trying to head Nita off, but it was too late.

"Leave me alone!" Tamara yelled. "Both of you just get out and leave me alone!"

She jumped up to shut the door, and the two girls retreated.

"We're gone. Sorry. Just wanted to make sure you were okay."

Tamara slammed the door shut. She flounced back to her bed and threw herself facedown. Unbelievable.

Of course, it wasn't very long before Mrs. Henson had to stick her nose into it too. She opened the door quietly without knocking, came in, and shut it behind her.

"Tamara," she said, "I know you're upset. But the girls are just concerned about you. They're not teasing or making fun of you. They truly do just care about whether you are okay."

"Leave me alone," Tamara insisted, not raising her face from the pillow she was hugging to herself.

"Tamara..."

She put her hand on Tamara's back. Tamara flipped over, slapping Mrs. Henson's hand away. She jumped to her feet, holding her fists high in front of her chin and dancing back.

"Don't touch me! Don't you *ever* touch me!" she yelled. The force of her yell ripped her throat raw. Her hands were clenched in tight fists. Her heart was pounding so hard and fast it felt like it would burst from her chest.

"Tamara," Mrs. Henson tried to calm her.

"Get out of here!"

Mrs. Henson hesitated, looking for a way to take control of the situation. But Tamara wasn't about to allow anyone else to get the upper hand. She wasn't going to let herself get caught in a situation like at the Bakers. Not again. No one was going to touch her. She wouldn't let anyone hurt her. Mrs. Henson took a hesitant step toward her, reaching out a hand. Tamara shifted her stance, readying herself. Mrs. Henson backed up.

"It's okay," she said, her voice calm. "No one is going to hurt you, Tamara. I can see that you're scared."

"Then get away from me," Tamara dropped her voice to a low, threatening growl. Glock had tried to teach her how to use her voice. Screeching wasn't going to convince anyone that she was in control. She had to use all of her resources. The right voice, the right threat, could change everything.

"We'll talk later," Mrs. Henson suggested.

She backed out the door and pulled it shut, leaving Tamara by herself.

FIVE

(i)

"I GOT SOMETHING FOR you," Sybil said quietly to Tamara at school the next day.

Tamara didn't say anything at first. She pulled out her cigarettes and her lighter and got a hit of nicotine. Sybil waited, her eyes bright, bouncing a little on her heels. She was hyped up about something.

"Well?" she prompted impatiently.

Tamara breathed the smoke out.

"Okay," she said, rolling her shoulders. "What is it?"

Sybil pulled out a flip phone and held it out to Tamara in the middle of her palm.

"What?" Tamara said.

"Look. I had an old one laying around. So I had it activated on my account, on a shared plan. All calls and texts between phones on the same account are free. And the minutes are shared. I know you're not going to run me over. You can just use it when you need it, and you and I can talk or text any time, without it costing anything."

Tamara took the phone from Sybil. "Really?"

Sybil nodded, smiling. Her eyes danced. "Am I good or what?"

Tamara flipped it open and watched the keys and the LCD screen light up.

"Show me how to use it."

Sybil laughed. "Just like any phone, honey. Dial and press talk. That's all there is to it. My number is programmed as speed dial one."

A voice echoed in Tamara's head, making her pause.

"I'm supposed to make my PO speed dial one."

Sybil stared at her. "You're telling me it's one of your parole terms that you have to put him on speed dial one?"

Tamara shrugged. "Yeah."

"That's the weirdest thing I've ever heard."

"Can we change it?"

"Yeah, sure," Sybil took the phone out of Tamara's hand and reprogrammed it, smiling. "Okay, what's his number?"

Tamara recited it slowly.

"There you go." Sybil handed it back. "He's one, and I'm two."

Tamara grinned.

"This is great! Thanks." She looked down at it, feeling warm. "I can't believe that I have my own phone."

(ii)

The warm-up for practice was brutal. Gasping for breath, Tamara slowed to a walk. She held a stitch in her side, trying to slow her breathing and get enough oxygen to continue on.

"Tamara. No walking," Coach McClure shouted from the other side of the gym.

Tamara didn't start running again immediately. She walked a few more steps, taking deep breaths, and then started a slow jog.

By the time she rounded the gym so that she was running past him, she was struggling again, gasping.

"Tamara."

She looked at him, and he motioned for her to come over. Tamara gladly broke away from her laps and walked over to him, where she stopped and put her hands on her knees, dragging in the air. McClure watched her.

"You want to know why you're in such bad shape?" he asked, raising an eyebrow.

Because she'd sat on her butt in juvie for three years? Tamara knew very well why she was in such rotten shape. She had not been one of the inmates who had a strict calisthenics routine and worked on burpies and bodyweight exercises in order to stay in condition. She didn't eat much, so she didn't gain weight, but she certainly hadn't made an effort to stay in shape. She had developed some muscles by fighting, but not any cardio benefits. Tamara just glared at McClure, daring him to tell her.

"You smoke," McClure pointed out. "That's why you're having such a hard time breathing. Give it up, and you'll have a much easier time."

Tamara hadn't thought about that.

"What makes you think I smoke?" she challenged, between gulps. "Maybe I've got asthma."

"You think I don't know the difference? You don't wheeze, you don't have an inhaler. And anyone who has stood within three feet of you can tell that you smoke."

Tamara's face got hot. She glanced toward the rest of the team self-consciously.

"You stink," McClure said, smiling to soften the words. "You reek of smoke. I don't have to catch you with a cigarette in your hand to know. Give it up. I can help you with a program to quit, if you want. You don't want to limit yourself, do you?"

Tamara clenched her jaw. Give up smoking. It was the only thing that had helped her to fit in. And despite Glock's assurances that she wouldn't get enough chances to smoke in juvie to get addicted, she knew very well how she felt if she had to go a day without a nicotine hit. Quitting wouldn't be easy. She didn't need that on her plate right now too.

McClure waited for her answer, and when Tamara didn't say anything, he sighed. "Go finish your laps, then."

Tamara started out again, circling the gym, now even further behind everyone else for having had to stop and talk to McClure. As much as she tried to catch back up, she just couldn't manage it, making her more angry and frustrated. Eventually the rest of the team was sitting in a circle, and McClure was chivvying her along.

"Come on, Tamara. Pick up the pace. Push through it. Everyone is waiting on you!"

Anger at the humiliation made her take longer, faster strides, but not without consequence to her lungs. She finished her last lap, and mowed down McClure, crashing into him. He was heavier than Tamara was, but she had momentum and knocked him out of place.

"What the...? What do you think you're doing? You want to get suspended from the team?" McClure yelled, his face turning a deep red.

Tamara bent over, chest heaving, black spots before her eyes. She ignored Coach McClure, trying to keep from passing out. She finally got her breath back and straightened up. McClure silently pointed at the seated team, and Tamara walked over to sit down with them.

"Quit being such a prima donna," Bernadette sneered, too quiet for the coach to hear. "You're not the only one on the team."

Tamara immediately kicked her over, then threw herself on top of the bigger girl. Bernadette barely even defended herself, putting her arms in front of her face rather than hitting back. Tamara's rage overflowed and she pounded Bernadette for all she was worth. Multiple hands hauled her back. McClure and several team members held her in place.

Bernadette's nose was bloodied, but it didn't look like it was broken. She was crying like a baby. Disgusted at her show of weakness, Tamara tried to kick at her, but McClure jerked her back.

"You dis' me, you'd better be ready to fight," Tamara snarled at Bernadette.

The girl just sobbed.

"Go to the office," McClure ordered Tamara. He motioned to Emily. "Go along and make sure she gets there."

"I know the way," Tamara said sullenly. "I'll go myself."

"Yeah, because you've been such a great example of self-control," McClure's tone was heavy with irony.

Tamara shook off the hands that were restraining her and headed for the door. Emily trailed behind her, not getting too close. Tamara could hear McClure speaking comforting words to Bernadette and the others behind her. She hit the door angrily and strode down the corridor toward the office. She turned to Emily, needing to vent her fury.

"She deserved it!" Tamara insisted. "No one gets away with talking to me like that!"

Emily cringed back, but when it became apparent that Tamara wasn't going to go after her too, she stood tall and walked beside Tamara.

"This isn't juvie, you know," Emily said.

Tamara scowled at her, fists clenching. "What's that supposed to mean?"

"It was just talk. We don't beat each other up. We're a team."

"Oh, and she was being a team player?" Tamara challenged.

"Let Coach handle it. He would have."

"McClure was already on my case."

"Trying to get you in shape," Emily said. "So that you can keep up with the team. That's his job!"

Tamara walked on in silence, reviewing it in her mind. She had reacted like she'd been conditioned to in juvie. But like Emily said, this was not juvie. Bernadette hadn't attacked her and probably didn't even know how to fight. Tamara didn't have to protect her reputation in order to survive. There were no gangs waiting for a sign of weakness. No one watching for that instant of vulnerability to take advantage of. They were just normal girls. Girls who wanted to play volleyball.

But Tamara couldn't tell her pounding, racing heart that. She couldn't convince her primitive brain. There was no way to short-circuit three years of conditioning. Tamara swore under her breath and looked at Emily in dismay.

"I screwed up... am I off the team? Did I mess everything up?"

"You did a pretty good job of it, yeah."

By the time they made it to the office, Tamara's anger was fading, replaced by anxiety over what she had done. She was shaking. Tamara and Emily walked in the office door, Tamara dragging her feet by now, staring down at the carpet. The secretary looked surprised to see them.

"What's going on, girls?"

Tamara stared down at her feet, feeling her face going red. Sweat trickled down her temples.

"Tamara got in a fight," Emily eventually filled in, when it became obvious that Tamara was not going to answer for herself. "Coach sent her down."

The secretary shook her head.

"I think Mr. Van Rhyn is still in. Wait a moment."

She turned away as she dialed an extension on her phone and spoke quietly. Then she turned back around as she hung it up.

"He'll be right out."

One of the inner office doors opened, and Tamara faced the vice-principal. Tall, hair long and slightly shaggy, a brown suit that made him look like he was playing dress-up. But at the moment, Tamara wasn't amused. She was terrified. Now what? She felt suddenly light-headed, and distant from the situation. Like she was watching herself on a screen. Mr. Van Rhyn looked her over.

"Ms. French. Come in."

Tamara staggered after him, her knees weak, feeling lost in space. He motioned to the visitor chair in front of his desk, and Tamara sat down. Van Rhyn sat on the edge of his desk, looking down at her.

"You want to tell me what happened?"

Tamara pressed a hand to her forehead.

"Coach was getting after me. One of the other girls, Bernadette... she started calling me names..."

Tamara put her face in both hands, elbows on knees.

"And...?" the vice-principal prodded.

"And... I lost it..."

He waited.

"I hit her," Tamara admitted.

"You hit her."

She nodded.

"You know we can't condone violence of any kind," Van Rhyn said.

Tamara nodded again, suppressing a sob.

"Wait here," he told her.

He walked out of the office, shutting the door behind him, leaving Tamara there alone. Tamara took the opportunity to wipe away the tears that were leaking from the corners of her eyes. She tried to calm herself down. She didn't know what would happen. Would she be expelled? Have to start again at yet another school? She would be off of the team for sure. Mrs. and Mr. Henson would not be happy.

The sounds were muffled by the door but Tamara could hear Coach McClure's and Bernadette's voices in conversation with

Mr. Van Rhyn. Tamara imagined that their descriptions of what had happened would be far more dramatic than hers. There seemed to be a lot of coming and going before Van Rhyn returned to his office. This time he sat down in his chair at the other side of the desk. Without a word to Tamara, he busied himself with writing. Tamara waited, time stretching out like a long, taut cord. Tamara rubbed her arms, cold sitting in the air-conditioned office after a hard workout. She had goosebumps. As she rubbed her arms, she noticed that she'd split the skin over her knuckles. She flexed them.

Mr. Van Rhyn tore off a sheet, and handed it across the desk to Tamara. Tamara took the form that he had filled out, and looked down at it.

"You need to get that signed by one of your foster parents before you can come back," he told her.

Tamara nodded, and waited for the rest.

"Am I suspended?" she asked, trying to decipher the form.

"You are suspended until you get that signed."

"If I bring it back tomorrow...?"

"Then you can come back tomorrow. Our zero-tolerance policy requires that there is some sort of suspension. Sometimes that might be an in-school suspension, or a signature-required suspension. I think... you need some more time to settle in. Acclimatize."

Tamara raised her eyes to him in disbelief.

"Really?"

"We know where you're coming from. I think you need some more time."

Tamara nodded.

"It won't happen again," she promised. "I swear. It won't."

"You can do it," Van Rhyn told her, holding her gaze. "Come and talk to someone if you are getting too stressed. Walk away if you are upset about something. I know you're working with a therapist. I believe you can do it."

Tamara breathed. "Thanks."

(iii)

Tamara walked from the bus more slowly than usual. Her stomach was one hot lump of lead. She hesitated at the front door, knowing there was going to be trouble now. She could delay walking in the door, but that wasn't going to help anything. Swallowing hard, Tamara turned the doorknob and walked in.

Mrs. Henson came down the stairs before she could get up to her bedroom.

"Tamara? You're home early. I thought you had a practice today."

Breathing in a slow, controlled rhythm, Tamara handed her the suspension sheet without a word. Mrs. Henson's eyes flicked over it. Tamara waited.

"What happened?" Mrs. Henson asked, her voice calm and even.

Tamara licked her dry lips and swallowed. "I messed up," she said, trying to keep her voice from shaking. "A girl was bugging me... and I hit her..."

"Hit her?"

Tamara shifted, looking up the stairs toward her room. She wanted to just go hide in her room and not have to talk to anyone, not have to explain what she had done. Just bury her face in her cool pillow and not have to deal with it.

"I... kicked her down... and I hit her... in the nose, in the face... they pulled me off."

Tamara's voice cracked. She cleared her throat and stood there, waiting for the explosion. Mrs. Henson walked into the kitchen, jerking her head for Tamara to follow her. Tamara did. Mrs. Henson took a pen out of the jar beside the phone.

"What are you going to do to keep this from happening again?" she questioned.

Tamara cleared her throat again, and ran her fingers back through her hair.

"Walk away. Go talk to someone. Call Dr. Frank."

Mrs. Henson nodded.

"Has Dr. Frank given you some work to do? Relaxation exercises? Meditations? Journal questions?"

"Yeah... I should probably spend some more time... working on it."

"Yeah, you should," Mrs. Henson agreed.

She signed the form and handed it back to Tamara.

"Call Mr. Collins."

Tamara's heart sank.

"No..."

"Yes." Mrs. Henson nodded to the phone. "Do it now before it gets any harder."

She walked away. Tamara stood there, staring at the phone. She hadn't even thought about having to call Collins about the fight. Breathing hard, Tamara picked up the receiver and dialed. Collins picked it up after a couple of rings.

"Yeah?"

"It's Tamara."

"What's up, Tamara?"

Tamara took a deep breath, and explained it all as quickly as she could. Then she waited. Collins sighed.

"Can you think of any reason I shouldn't send you back to juvie?" he questioned.

Tamara gasped.

"What?"

"You think this is a minor violation?" he demanded. "That I shouldn't act on it?"

"I didn't—I didn't violate any terms," Tamara protested.

"Committing assault doesn't violate your parole terms?"

"I didn't... commit assault! I just... I just lost my temper... hit someone."

"Hitting is assault, genius. And assault is a crime. Which makes it a breach of your parole."

"But..."

Tamara listened to the silence on the other end of the line and tried to figure out what she could say to him to persuade him not to send her back to juvie.

"The vice principal... he said I just need more time to settle in."

"Did he. How long is your suspension?"

"I can go back tomorrow. Missus already signed my sheet off. She said I just had to talk to you."

"Well, there are still going to have to be some consequences here."

"Okay..."

"I want you to write an apology to this girl. I want to see a copy."

"Okay."

"And you apologize to your team, and to the coach."

"Yes, sir."

"Discuss it with Dr. Frank."

"Yeah."

"You call me before and after your next practice, if you're allowed to stay on the team."

"Okay."

More silence.

"All right," Collins said finally. "We'll see how that goes."

Tamara blew out her breath, the muscles in her stomach shaking.

"Okay. Thanks. Okay."

"Go work on your apologies."

SIX

(i)

NIGHT WAS STARTING TO fall, the sky beginning to cloud over and get dark. Tamara reproached herself for forgetting yet again to search the shed for an old volleyball and pump while it was still daytime. She never seemed to remember until she had finished dinner and her homework and it was too dark to find it. There was still enough light to see shapes. If the ball wasn't too well-hidden, she might be able to find it before the sun dipped down over the horizon and it got too dark to search.

She found a soccer ball first. It was white, it was the right shape and size, but it wasn't going to do her much good. Tamara pushed old furniture and camping gear around, growling to herself impatiently. How hard was it to find a ball? She found other sports equipment, including hockey pads and skates. Who had played hockey? Jesse? One of the boys? Some foster kid that had moved on years ago? Tamara pushed back a crinkly blue tarp and found a barbecue.

"Seriously?" she muttered. "All I want is a volleyball!"

Almost as soon as she said the word, she saw it. In the corner by the foot of the barbecue, wedged between a bin and the side of the shed. Tamara pounced on it triumphantly, pulling it out. It was flat, but otherwise seemed to be in reasonable condition. If she could just find the air pump, she'd be set. But the sky was darkening rapidly, and she could now barely see the inside of the shed. She hurried back into the house.

"Do you have a flashlight?" she asked Mrs. Henson. "And do you know where the air pump would be, in the shed?"

"Hmm." Mrs. Henson went to the back closet and found a flashlight for Tamara. She flipped it on. It worked. Not super bright, but it worked. "I'm not sure where the pump would be. I think on the left-hand side. It might have even be beside the shed; there is some equipment leaning up against the shed, and it might be in there." She sighed. "I really need to get Jesse to clean that stuff up."

"Yeah."

Tamara hurried back out to the shed. The wind was picking up. The neighbor's screen door was swinging loose and kept banging shut and then flying back open again. There was still some light in the sky, but the inside of the shed was now pitch black until Tamara shone her light inside it. She searched along the left hand wall, hoping to find the pump leaning against it. No such luck. The flashlight threw weird, misshapen shadows around the shed. The screen door banged again, making Tamara jump. She thought she heard footsteps, and turned around, shining the light behind her. There was no one there. Maybe someone had been walking down the back lane. Tamara flicked the light down it, but couldn't see anyone. And she wasn't about to go looking for trouble.

With an exasperated sigh, Tamara shone the light in the pile of junk next to the shed. Old doors and windows, lumber, and equipment. Some of it looked like there had been an attempt to make a neat and orderly stack, but other stuff had just been thrown haphazardly on top or shoved into the spaces at the bottom. Tamara ran the flashlight methodically over the jumble, starting at the top and moving back and forth, left to right, and right to left, and back left to right again. There was the snap of someone stepping on a branch behind her, and Tamara whirled around, trying to find them with her light. But there was no one there. It must have just been the tree moving in the wind.

Tamara looked back at the pile of rubble. It probably wasn't worth looking for the pump any more tonight. She would just have to wait another day, and hope that she remembered to look for it earlier tomorrow. She played the flashlight along the bottom of the pile. She'd lost her place in the more methodical search. Then she spotted what looked like the foot of an air pump. Tamara dove in and grabbed it, trying to wrench it out. It moved, but seemed to be caught on something. Tamara saw the end of the hose, and grabbed it as well, pulling both the body and the hose, wiggling them back and forth to try to get it unwedged. There was the sound of running feet, and she looked up with her heart pounding. It must have been further down the lane, and the wind was just disorienting her, making noises sound like they were closer than they really were. Tamara continued to pull on the pump. It was coming out, but obviously dragging something else with it. With another yank, Tamara pulled it free. She shone the flashlight down to see what else she had pulled out. It was a black, shapeless lump, a piece of a child's teddy bear or something.

When Tamara shone the light on it, she could make out the four legs and fur, but then realized it wasn't a toy. It was an animal. There was dried black blood, red flesh, maggots, no head.

Struggling to hold back the nausea, Tamara ran back into the house, tripping over the uneven bricks of the walkway. The door slammed behind her, and Mrs. Henson looked up to reprimand her.

"Tamara? What's wrong, you're white as a ghost!"

Tamara held onto the wall. She dove into the tiny back bathroom and threw up. Mrs. Henson hovered somewhere behind her.

"Are you sick? Tamara?"

"Out there..." Tamara coughed and gagged. "There's a dead animal. Something dead. By the shed."

"A dead animal?" Mrs. Henson repeated. "What is it? A squirrel or something?"

Tamara shook her head. She couldn't blink her eyes. Couldn't close them.

"No. Bigger. A cat... or dog."

"What?" Mrs. Henson went over to the stairs and called up. "Jesse? Can you come down? Please?"

He must have heard the worry in her tone, and came down the hall and the stairs quickly.

"What's wrong?" he asked, his eyes going to Tamara. "Is she okay?"

"She said there's a dead animal. By the shed."

"Okaaay..." he drew the word out, frowning.

"Would you go see? Take care of it?" Mrs. Henson said, taking the flashlight from Tamara's numb hands and handing it to her husband.

"Sure," he agreed.

He stopped in the kitchen for a garbage bag. Tamara saw him take another look at her before going outside, shaking his head. He must think she was being weak, a stupid girl going into hysterics. But when he came back a few minutes later, his bag was empty, and he was pale. His complexion was almost green.

"I think we should call the police," he murmured to Mrs. Henson.

"The police? Why?"

"It's one of the missing cats."

"Yes...?"

"It's a real mess, Gerry. Someone... mutilated it."

Mrs. Henson's eyes widened. She looked at Tamara, still standing near the toilet, hunched over, not sure she was done being sick.

"Oh, no."

He nodded.

"I'll give them a call. You keep an eye on Tamara, make sure she's okay."

Mrs. Henson agreed.

Jesse looked in at Tamara. "I'm sorry you saw that, Tamara. It's pretty bad. Are you going to be all right?"

Tamara nodded wordlessly.

"She's so pale, she looks like she's going to faint," Jesse said to Mrs. Henson.

"So do you," she said.

Jesse shook his head and went into the kitchen to make the phone call.

(ii)

When the police arrived, Tamara was wrapped in a blanket, on the couch with Mrs. Henson. The policemen went out back with their big lights and cameras and equipment and took whatever pictures and evidence they needed. One came back into the house to make further inquiries.

He sat on an easy chair, his jacket still zipped up, and pulled out a notepad. His name badge read 'Bright.'

"So you're the one that discovered the cat?" he said, focused in on Tamara.

He was young, the lamplight shining on him making him look positively boyish. Maybe that's why he was the one who had been sent in to deal with Tamara. To put her at ease.

Tamara nodded her head.

"What were you out there for?"

"Looking for the volleyball and pump."

"Where were they?"

"I found the volleyball in the shed. Missus told me," Tamara nodded to Mrs. Henson, "that she thought the pump might be beside the shed. So that's where I looked."

"And when you found the pump, and pulled it out, it snagged the body of the cat."

Tamara closed her eyes and held her hand over her mouth, her stomach still writhing. She nodded.

"Yeah."

"You couldn't see it before that?"

"No. It was dark, and jammed way in there."

"Who has been in the backyard lately?" Bright questioned, switching his gaze to Mrs. Henson.

"None of us have spent any time back there lately. There's no lock on the gates, anyone can get in."

"Have you noticed anyone suspicious? Anyone prowling around the house? Hanging around the neighborhood? Anything?"

"No," Mrs. Henson shook her head. "I haven't noticed anyone. But... we have noticed the neighbors complaining about missing animals lately."

His pen hovered over his notepad for a moment as he thought it through.

"More than one?"

Mrs. Henson nodded. "I think... there have been three or four."

Bright wrote something very deliberately in his notepad. He tapped the end of his pen on the paper thoughtfully.

"If you'll excuse me for a moment... I need to talk to the others."

He got up and went back outside. Mrs. Henson reached over and gave Tamara a brief back rub.

"How are you doing, Tamara?"

Tamara groaned. "Okay."

"Good. You should probably get off to bed soon. I don't know how long the police will be here."

"I don't know if I can sleep. Every time I close my eyes..."

Mrs. Henson rubbed her back some more.

"I'm so sorry you had to see that," she said.

Tamara nodded. So much for the tough girl from juvie. Reduced to throwing up and practically having a nervous breakdown over a dead cat. What Glock would say if she could see Tamara now...

Bright returned after a few minutes. He sat down and looked Tamara over.

"You look tired. I should let you go off to bed. I don't need to bother you with any more questions."

Tamara looked at him. "I'm okay."

He met Mrs. Henson's eyes, and she seemed to understand some non-verbal signal.

"Go on up to your room, Tamara. I need to talk to the officer alone."

Tamara got up slowly, gathering the blanket around her. She looked from one to the other, wondering what was going on.

"I'll come up and see how you're doing in a bit, okay?" Mrs. Henson said. "Make sure that you're settled in."

Tamara obediently went up the stairs and to her room, shutting the door firmly behind her. She lay down on the bed, snuggling in the blanket, and thought back over that last look. Bright wanted to talk to Mrs. Henson alone. Without Tamara there. So it must either be something he knew would upset Tamara more, or something about her. There were a number of things that might have upset her more. Maybe they'd found the head. Or another pet. Or something that indicated who had done this. But why else wouldn't he want Tamara in the room? Maybe he wanted to ask Mrs. Henson about her.

Tamara supposed that he knew she was a foster child. It hadn't been discussed in front of her, but the Hensons had probably made it known to the police who had come to the scene. If they knew she was a foster child, they might know that she had just come from juvie. Would that make her a suspect in the torture and slaughter of the cat? Tamara could imagine the conversation between Mrs. Henson and Officer Bright.

"How much do you know about the girl's history?"

"She had a very good record at juvenile detention. No problems there."

"And before that?"

"She didn't have a record before that, so we don't know very much."

"Killing animals is a common sign of a serial killer..."

"She was in juvie for murder..."

Tamara flashed back to her cellmate at juvie. During a nighttime chat with Glock, Tamara had asked her about what she was in for. At first, Glock didn't answer. Tamara didn't think she was going to. But then Glock spoke.

"This time... some stupid animal cruelty charges. Can you believe that they can actually throw you in the clink for animal cruelty?"

Tamara rolled onto her side, so that her face was closer to the edge of the bed.

"Really?" she said. "I didn't know that."

"Yeah, me neither. Maybe pay a fine or something if you got found out. But not juvie."

Tamara thought about it for a minute.

"Well... what did you do?" she said softly.

Glock chuckled to herself.

"Are you sure you really want to ask me that?" she asked. "You really want to know how bad you have to be to get thrown in here over some stupid stray cats?"

Tamara thought about it, and felt a little queasy. Glock was right. She probably really didn't want to know.

"It's all about profiling," Glock exploded. "You know, they

used to just say: 'it's only animals,' or 'they'll grow out of it,' or whatever. But ever since profilers started saying that serial killers start out by mutilating animals, suddenly anyone who kicks a puppy is a potential killer. Stupid. People can't think for themselves."

"Well... that doesn't mean you're a serial killer," Tamara agreed, trying to be tactful and agreeable.

"Hell, they're probably right," Glock said, with a little laugh. "I mean, what kind of person vivisects animals for entertainment?"

Tamara wished she could erase the memory. Could go back to not remembering it. That's what Bright was going to be talking to Mrs. Henson about. Profiling Tamara. Trying to press Tamara into the mold. See if they could make it fit. The neighbors were probably already thinking it. Tamara got out of juvie and went to live with the Hensons, and pets started disappearing. Now they knew the animals—at least one of them—had been tortured and killed. Obviously, it was Tamara. She was the only variable. The only suspect.

Tamara hugged her arms to her stomach. She wasn't going to throw up again. There was nothing left in her stomach. But she still felt sick.

(iii)

At her next counseling session, Dr. Frank smiled reassuringly at Tamara, leaning back in his seat.

"Sooooo..." He drew the word out long and looked expectant.

Tamara leaned back in her chair, trying to relax her tense muscles.

"So, what?" she demanded.

"It sounds like you've had a pretty rough time the last couple of days."

She nodded, rubbing her fingers along the arm of the chair that she sat in.

"Yeah, it's been kind of..." She trailed off, looking for a word to describe how unsettled she was feeling. She was foggy and had a dull headache from not being able to sleep. She was terrified that Collins was going to decide that she was behind the pet killings, and send her back to juvie. She had already admitted to messing up once, in the fight at school. If he decided that she was also torturing and killing animals, he wouldn't hesitate to send her back.

"Kind of what?" Dr. Frank prodded. "How are you feeling, Tamara?"

"Scared, I guess."

"Scared of what?"

"Of going back to juvie," Tamara said. She looked down at the doctor's carpet. An indeterminate color designed to never show the dirt. Instead it looked institutional. Always dirty. "I don't want to go back."

"Why do you think you're going to go back to juvie?"

"If you tell Mr. Collins that I didn't do anything... he'll believe you, right?"

"That you didn't do what?"

"I didn't kill that cat," Tamara said, her voice rising. "I wouldn't do that. I didn't do anything to any animals. You know that. You know I wouldn't do that."

He considered her for a few minutes before answering.

"It doesn't fit what I know about you," he agreed.

Tamara didn't like the sound of that. Not an outright 'no'. He was hedging.

"You think I did it?"

"No, I don't think you did it."

He didn't *think* she did it? He was supposed to know. He was supposed to be able to tell Collins that she definitely was not the culprit. That they should be looking for someone else, not sending her back to juvie for something she didn't do.

"I admit I got in a fight at school," Tamara told him. "But I didn't hurt the cat. I wouldn't do something like that."

He looked at her, his hands pressed together, palm against palm. He was obviously not convinced. And now he was probably wondering if she was protesting too much. If it was a sign that she was, in fact, guilty. Torturing and killing animals wasn't anything like getting into a fight at school. The fight had been a flare of temper, a conditioned response from three years in juvie. That wasn't the same as torturing and killing innocent animals. But then, she hadn't gone to juvie for getting into a fight. That hadn't been a flare of temper either.

"I feel bad for what I did before," Tamara told him. "That was... just a bad situation... I'm not that kind of person who hurts animals. A... a torturer, or a serial killer."

"You feel bad for what?" Dr. Frank questioned, studying her with watery blue eyes.

"You know. What I did before. The murders."

She hated to talk about it. It always made her uncomfortable. It was like it had happened to another person, not to her. She wasn't the same person that she had been back then. Before juvie. With the Bakers. With all of the abuse, the fogginess from the hormone shifts, she hadn't been in her right mind.

"You have said before that you feel bad, that you're sorry," Frank said.

"Yeah. And I am."

She forced tears to her eyes, held them wide open until they started to sting and water. She blinked rapidly to make them fall down her cheeks. She *was* sorry. He could see she was sorry. Dr. Frank rubbed his chin, and jotted down a note on her file. Tamara shifted uneasily.

"How did you feel at the time?" Dr. Frank asked.

"At the time... when I did it...?"

He nodded, waiting. Tamara cleared her throat. This was not going the way she wanted. He wasn't helping her to transition to life on the outside. He wasn't helping her with stress management. He wasn't supposed to be asking her about her crimes. That was all in the past. She scratched at a scab on her arm, thinking.

"I felt... confused. Trapped. Things were so messed up. I don't know."

The pink area under the scab started to bleed. Tamara pressed her thumb over it, waiting for it to stop. There was a ragged edge on her thumbnail, and Tamara tried to smooth it out with her teeth. Nita would get after her for chewing her nails.

"How are you feeling now?" Frank asked.

Tamara saw the trap and avoided it.

"It's not the same now. I feel okay. Just... scared that I'm going to get blamed for something I didn't do."

"I see."

"I didn't hurt those animals."

"*Those* animals?" Frank repeated. "I thought there was only one."

"They only found one," Tamara explained, her heart pounding faster. "I think. Unless they found something else later, after I did. I only found one. But there were other missing animals. I just assumed..."

She cleared her throat and didn't know what else to say.

"Why do you think they were hurt too?"

"I just did." Tamara shrugged. "I thought it was all connected."

"Animals disappear from time to time. Why did you think they were connected?"

Tamara shifted in her seat.

"Mrs. Henson thought they were. She's the one that said it."

"I see." Frank nodded, watching her too closely.

(iv)

Tamara felt like she was in a fog. She had gone back to school because she knew that was what she was supposed to do. But maybe she should have faked sick and stayed in bed. She couldn't focus on any of her lessons. People kept trying to talk to her, and she just brushed them off, shaking her head. People asking her about the fight with Bernadette, mostly. Trying to find out all the details. The news had spread. Everyone wanted the inside scoop.

But the fight didn't matter. Tamara couldn't see why everyone thought it was so important. It was the trouble with the animals that filled her thoughts. She couldn't shake it. Something was going to happen. Something bad. Tamara kept looking at the clock, wondering if Dr. Frank had reported back to Collins yet. Reported that he thought Tamara might have been responsible for the disappearances and killing of the neighbors' pets. Tamara knew that he would. And then Collins would send her back to juvie. Would he come to the school to pick her up? In front of everyone? Would he wait until she got home? Maybe she shouldn't even go home. Maybe she shouldn't just sit around waiting for them to send her back. She could just leave right now, run for it. It seemed like the only way that she was going to stay out of juvie now.

"Tamara? Tamara!"

Startled, Tamara focused in on Sybil. They had sneaked out of social studies to grab a quick smoke, but Tamara didn't have a clue how long they had been out there or what Sybil had been talking to her about.

"Um, sorry, what did you say?"

Sybil raised an eyebrow. "Are you on something today?" she demanded. "You're totally zoned out!"

"No," Tamara pulled on her cigarette, hoping it would stimulate her brain to start working again. "It's just... stuff happening. I'm sort of... distracted."

"No kidding. Is it because of the team, you mean? You taking out little Miss Smarty Pants?"

"No. Well, partly. Other stuff too."

Sybil nodded. "So are you done with the team, now? They're pretty lame."

"No, I still want to play." Tamara sighed, and started to pace down the sidewalk and back. "I still want to be on the team, so that means I have to apologize. I had to write out an apology for Bernadette."

"Seriously? McClure is making you do that? Or the school?"

"My PO. So I gotta, you know."

"That's just stupid. Why don't you just dump the team?"

"I don't even know yet if they'll let me keep playing. But I want to."

"He shouldn't make you do that."

"Yeah. Whatever. I shouldn't have attacked her for being a butt head. She probably can't help it, right?"

Sybil snorted. "Yeah. Pretty much born that way, little Miss Sissy Pants."

That seemed to satisfy Sybil as far as the fight went. She smoked in silence for a few more minutes.

"So what else?" she asked. "What else is it that's bothering you?"

Tamara wondered whether she should share it. Sybil was her only real friend. If Tamara told her in confidence, she'd probably keep it to herself. It would feel good to be able to talk to someone else about it. Someone who wasn't an adult, judging her every move and thought. Tamara blew out a long stream of smoke, and scratched the back of her head.

"Okay. Here's the thing..."

She gave Sybil all of the details of the disappearing pets, and

Tamara's gruesome discovery. Sybil's eyes were wide, her lips parted as she listened raptly.

"Whoa. That's some serious stuff. That's like... serial killer stuff..."

Tamara's stomach gurgled. Everybody knew that. Sybil looked at Tamara thoughtfully, evaluating.

"And you didn't do it, did you?" she said, and it was more of a statement than a question.

Tamara shook her head.

"Do you think that you're in danger? You, or someone in your family or something? What if this guy comes after you next?"

Tamara looked at Sybil's concerned expression, surprised. Sybil was the first one to show any concern for her safety. The only one to make the assumption that Tamara wasn't the culprit, and to follow it through to its natural conclusion. If Tamara wasn't the cat killer, then someone else was. Someone who could be a danger to all of them, including Tamara.

"I... don't know..." she stuttered. "I didn't really think..."

She remembered the noises in the yard and the lane before she discovered the body. Footsteps. Twigs snapping. A feeling that someone was there, watching her. She had written it all off as the wind and the falling darkness. But what if there had been someone there, in the yard or close by, someone who was a killer and who knew she would find the corpse? Tamara shuddered.

"Man," Sybil grabbed her around the shoulders and gave her a sideways hug. "I'd be super freaked out. No wonder you can't focus on anything."

(v)

It was not a practice day, so Tamara went home on the early bus. She stared out the window, not seeing anything. The ride passed slowly. Tamara just wanted to get home, lock herself in her room, and not have to talk to anyone else or think about anything. Just crawl under a blanket and go to sleep. When she walked up the sidewalk, Tamara again had the uneasy feeling of being watched. The street was quiet. There was no one about that she could see. No dogs barked. Everyone must be keeping their pets inside, while the police tried to sort out the trouble. Tamara didn't go right up to the front door, but took the pathway that led to the back yard. She looked around. She'd been avoiding the back yard, but everything seemed normal. The police had taken all of the evidence with them; there were no grisly remains left behind. The shed had been closed and locked back up. She didn't see any sign of the ball pump.

A twig snapped behind her, but this time Tamara didn't move. Didn't turn to see who it was. A breeze ruffled her hair, but it was nothing like the wind the night she found the dead cat.

"Looking for something, Princess?" came a low, rough inquiry from behind her.

Tamara knew that voice without turning. She'd heard it hundreds of times before.

It was Glock.

SEVEN

(i)

SO IT'S YOU," TAMARA said.

"Yeah," Glock said, "it's me."

"You've got people thinking it's me killing those cats," Tamara said, her voice hard. "You're gonna get me sent back down."

"You?" Glock sounded genuinely surprised. "Why would they think it had anything to do with you?"

"I get here and animals start disappearing. I'm the one who found the cat," Tamara said, motioning toward the shed where it had been. "What are they supposed to think?"

"Well, you weren't supposed to find it," Glock said. Tamara listened to her footsteps drawing closer, until Glock was standing directly behind her. She still didn't turn to look. "It was supposed to stay hidden."

"How did you even know where I was?"

"I have my sources. Gotta keep track of my girl."

Tamara felt Glock's big hands close over her shoulders. Glock turned her around so they were face to face. Tamara looked her over. Glock's face was as familiar to Tamara as her own. Maybe more than her own, after three years of not having a real mirror. Tamara had seen Glock's face every day, until Glock had been released. She was a big girl; taller and broader than Tamara, and muscular like a boy. Her black hair hung lank around her face. Her eyes were dark hollows, slightly bloodshot. Tamara supposed that Glock's features were Hispanic, but only vaguely so. Glock was in a mellow mood, relaxed, smiling slightly at Tamara. A real smile from Glock was rare.

"You're looking good," Tamara said, backing up slightly.

"Not as good as you," Glock teased, touching the blond curls that rested on Tamara's cheek. "You really do look like a princess now."

Glock was so close, Tamara could smell her. The familiar spice of her sweat and breath that was as unique to Glock as her fingerprints. The scent Tamara had breathed every day they shared a cell. Tamara glanced toward the house. Anyone could look out and see the two of them standing there together. And if Collins found out that she had been in contact with Glock, he would violate her parole.

"You have to get out of here," Tamara said. "I can't be seen with you, or they'll put me back in juvie."

Glock rolled her eyes.

"No one is going to see us back here. You're not usually home yet. Most of them are out."

Tamara forced herself to breathe slowly, trying to keep calm. Glock had been there the whole time. Watching her come and go and noting her schedule. Capturing and killing the animals. Maybe torturing them right there in the back yard while Tamara ate and slept.

"You can't stay here," Tamara insisted. "Everyone is watching now. You gave yourself away. You have to go."

Glock shrugged.

"Let's go for a walk," she suggested, gesturing toward the alley.

Tamara hesitated. She couldn't stay there talking to Glock in the back yard. Mrs. Henson and Jesse would know as soon as they saw Glock that she was a felon. But if Tamara went for a walk, other people might see her with Glock too. More people, more risk.

Glock didn't wait for Tamara to waffle through and make a decision. She had always been the decision-maker. She grabbed Tamara's arm and pulled her toward the alley. Her grip was hard, just like Tamara remembered. Tamara knew better than to protest or pull back. Not unless she wanted to *really* get hurt. She stumbled along beside Glock, and after a few strides, Glock let her go, and they walked side-by-side down the alley.

"So... why are you here?" Tamara asked.

"To see you. What else?"

"But... you've been here since I got out, and you haven't talked to me until now."

Glock nodded.

"I figured I could leave you alone, just watch you... but once you figured out I was here..."

"How did you know... that I knew...? I mean, I kind of did, but..."

"I knew when you saw the cat, it wouldn't take long for you to put it together."

Tamara nodded. She looked at her feet as she crunched through the gravel down the alley. Glock gave her a shove that made her stumble sideways. Tamara clenched her fists, squaring off.

"Hey, what the...?" she started.

"You already forgotten everything I taught you?" Glock demanded, laughing. "You don't look at your feet while you walk. You keep your eyes up. Watch for danger."

Tamara started walking again, keeping her head up this time.

She felt more confident. Not just because her head was up, her body language stronger, but because Glock was there. Glock had been her protector and her teacher. Glock always knew what to do, what Tamara should do. Having her back was something that finally felt right. She had been so adrift since leaving juvie. The loss of routine, of everything that had grown familiar to her, had left her feeling vulnerable and alone. With Glock there, Tamara finally felt normal again.

(ii)

Tamara spent all of the next day at school dreading it. She knew that the next volleyball practice was after school, and she couldn't focus on any of her classes. She took several smoke breaks or just wandered the halls, trying to calm the pounding of her heart and the worm writhing around in her stomach. Her nails were chewed to the quick, and the cuticles raw and bleeding. She wished she could just time warp to the practice and get it over with.

The final bell rang, and Tamara put her books into her locker and went down to the change room. She called Collins to report in on her way down. Tamara dragged her feet and was one of the last ones there. Everyone quieted as she entered, their eyes following her to her gym locker, then they averted their eyes as she started to undress. The only one who ignored her presence was Bernadette, who had received Tamara's handwritten apology earlier in the day. Tamara pulled her gym clothes on jerkily, without looking at anyone, and walked back up to the gym. She was one of the first ones in the gym. Coach McClure was assigning drills. He looked at Tamara as he spoke to Emily and raised his eyebrows. Emily turned around and saw Tamara. She nodded at whatever McClure was telling her, and broke away to do her drills. Tamara approached the coach, swallowing hard.

"Tamara."

"Coach... I'm sorry for my behavior last practice. I shouldn't have run into you. And hurt Bernadette." She took a deep breath. "I was disrespectful and I acted like a little kid. Not like a team player. I'll do better, if you'll still let me be on the team."

She pressed her lips together to keep any excuses from running out, and waited for his response. McClure nodded.

"I appreciate the apology. It's not easy to admit when you've made a mistake."

"I've given Bernadette a written apology already," Tamara offered. "And... if I could get a minute to apologize to the team, too..."

"If I give you a chance, and something like this happens again..."

"I know. I won't let you down."

He considered.

"Go drill with Emily," he said. "I'll put it to the team for a vote after your apology."

Tamara went to join Emily, the worm still writhing in her stomach. She just wanted it to be over. She had assumed that McClure would tell her yes, and the apology to the team would be routine. But now everything hinged on how it went over. Put it to the team. What if all of them thought, like Bernadette, that she was being a diva? If they hated her, they would vote her off, no matter how good the apology was or how sincere it sounded.

Emily walked Tamara through the drill without asking her about what McClure had said. After everyone was changed and had been doing drills for a few minutes, the coach called for them to assemble. They all sat around him as usual. He looked at Tamara and nodded.

Tamara stood up, and went to the front of the group. She rubbed her sweating hands on her shorts.

"I wanted to apologize," she said. "For having a bad attitude, and being disrespectful to Coach, and hitting Bernadette. I haven't been a team player. If you'll give me a second chance, I'll do better. I'm sorry."

She looked at McClure and didn't know whether to sit back down or wait where she was. McClure faced the team.

"I'll put it to a vote," he said. "Do we give Tamara a second chance on the team, or is she done?"

The girls murmured to each other, too low for Tamara to hear what they were saying. She shifted anxiously.

She had thought that they would all vote individually, with the majority winning, but they came to a consensus. It was Bernadette who spoke for the team.

"We'll give her a second chance."

Tamara breathed out. She met Bernadette's eyes.

"Thank you," she said, relieved.

Coach McClure motioned to her.

"Go sit down, then, and let's move on."

(iii)

For a few days, everything seemed to settle down and go back to a normal routine, and Tamara avoided any trouble. She kept the news of Glock's return to herself, knowing that the instant she told Collins, he'd have her back in juvie.

"Why don't we go to your house today?" Tamara suggested to Sybil when they bumped into each other in the hall, not wanting to go home.

Sybil nodded.

"Sure. No practice today?"

"No."

"Great. I'll just get my books."

Tamara went to her locker to dump the books that she didn't need. She didn't want to take any homework, but she knew she'd better if she was going to keep up with her classes. Collins wouldn't be happy if her marks suddenly went down, with no explanation. He might think it was because of volley-ball and tell her that she had to quit the team. She took what she had to, and waited for Sybil to make it back through the jostling crowd.

They were walking toward Sybil's house, smoking. Tamara was starting to relax, let the stress of the day go. Things were difficult lately. Lots of pressure. But she thought she was over the worst of it now. Collins had been right in his prediction that it would be hard. But now, Tamara thought, she was over the hump.

She was lost in her own musings and wasn't really listening to Sybil as they walked. But as they made their way down the street, Tamara's eyes caught on a figure smoking under a big tree half a block down. She slowed down.

"Tamara? You okay?"

"Yeah... just..."

She was sure she was only seeing what she was because she had just been thinking about Glock. There was no way Glock was going to be all the way over here, near the school. She would be near the Henson's house, waiting for Tamara to come home. Which was why Tamara was not going home yet.

"You know her?" Sybil asked, following Tamara's gaze.

"No."

But Glock peeled herself away from the tree and started to walk toward them. It was Glock, without a doubt. Tamara couldn't wish her away.

"Hey, sweetie," she greeted. "Aren't you going to introduce us?"

Tamara swallowed, looking at her two friends. "Hey," she said. "Glock, this is Sybil. Syb... Glock."

The two girls looked at each other. Sybil smiled up at Glock, her eyes wide and excited. Glock's eyes were narrow.

"Hi," Sybil said. "Are you a friend of Tamara's... from juvenile?"

Glock nodded. She put her arm around Tamara's shoulders, giving her a rough hug.

"Yeah," she agreed. "Frenchie and me were cellies for a long time."

Sybil giggled. "Cellies?" she repeated.

"Cell mates," Tamara explained.

"Oh yeah, sure. That's cool. Did you just get out?"

Glock shook her head. "No, I got out more than a year ago."

Sybil smiled. "Well, it's nice to meet you... Glock."

Glock snorted. She looked at Tamara. "So, we going to your girlfriend's house?" Glock nodded at Sybil.

Tamara opened her mouth, but didn't know what to say. We? Girlfriend? The question was so loaded, she didn't know where to start.

"Sure," Sybil answered. "Why don't you come along too? You guys can get... caught up. I'm sure Tamara will be happy to talk to someone she knows from before, for once."

Glock's eyes slid over to Tamara.

"Huh. Yeah. I'm sure she'll be happy to talk to her old cellie," she agreed.

So Sybil led the small group down the street. Glock already seemed to know where they were going. Tamara sucked in a large lungful of smoke, hoping it would soothe the growing knot in her belly. Glock knew where Sybil lived. Knew that Tamara was going to go there after school, when Tamara herself had barely decided. Just how closely had Glock been shadowing Tamara since she got out?

Sybil managed to chatter on, holding Glock's attention. Which was good, because Tamara had no idea what to say to her. They had never had anything in common. Just the forced uniformity of juvie. Same routine, same classes, same cell, same clothing, same food... Everything they ate and did was the same, and it covered up the fact that their personalities were completely different. Glock had taught Tamara how to fit in there, how to not draw attention to herself, how to protect herself. Glock and juvie had forced Tamara to be just another offender, like everyone else. Now they were out, and Tamara had no idea how to talk to Glock.

When Sybil unlocked the door to her house, they found the little girls playing in the living room with dolls and toys, the TV blaring away in the background, unnoticed. Sybil turned the TV off immediately.

"You guys know you're not supposed to be watching TV after school," she told them. "Now scoot. Any of you got homework?"

There were three of them, all blond, including the little one that Tamara had seen last time she had visited. None of them seemed big enough to have any homework, and none of them admitted that they did. Tamara couldn't help staring at the littlest one. Maybe four years old. Not old enough for kindergarten, but maybe she had some kind of ECS class. Who picked her up from it? One of the other little girls?

"Okay. I told you to scoot. Go play in your room, quit messing up the family room. Me and my friends want some space."

"Si-i-ib," one of the two older girls whined, "we were already playing here..."

"And watching TV. You want me to tell Mom that?"

"We already brought everything out..."

"Then take everything back. Go on. Grab your stuff and go."

With a bit of whining and malingering, the three little girls gathered their toys together and went back to their bedroom. It took a couple of trips back and forth to get everything picked up. Tamara tore her eyes away from the little girls to look at Glock, and found her former cellie studying her thoughtfully. Tamara felt her face flush.

"Okay, then?" Sybil asked. "Now they're out of the way?"

Tamara swallowed and nodded. "Yeah, okay," she agreed.

"Cute kids," Glock commented, her eyes still on Tamara.

"They're okay," Sybil agreed with a shrug. "Sometimes it's nice to be able to tell someone else what to do," she said with a laugh, "after having to listen to adults all day."

Glock chuckled at this. Tamara did not. Glock sank into the couch and put her feet up on the coffee table. "You got anything to drink?"

"Well, no. Just soft drinks or Kool-Aid," Sybil said with an apologetic shrug.

"Your dad doesn't drink beer?" Glock persisted.

"Step-dad. No, he doesn't drink anything, and Mom doesn't think it's good to have alcohol around the little kids. Bad influence, and all. Actually, she probably wants to keep it away from me, but she doesn't say that." Sybil laughed.

Glock sighed. "Soft drink, then, huh babe?"

"Okay." Sybil went to the kitchen to get the refreshments.

Glock's gaze shifted to Tamara. "Does she think she's tough, or something?" She rolled her eyes.

Tamara thought about it. "She's just... I dunno... a groupie. She kind of... pretends to be tough... but..." Tamara made a motion that indicated their surroundings, "she's got a home and a family and all."

Glock nodded. "A wannabe," she agreed. "She's kind of cute, though, huh?"

Tamara grunted.

"And the little kids?" Glock said, raising her eyebrows. "You *like* the little girls?"

Tamara shook her head vehemently.

"No. The little one... reminds me of someone. I don't want to be around her. And I'm not supposed to, on my parole terms."

"Or around me," Glock said with a smirk.

Sybil returned to the room with three glasses, passing Glock and Tamara each one.

"So what was it like being Tamara's cell mate?" Sybil asked conspiratorially, nodding to Tamara.

"Oh, I could tell you some stories," Glock said.

"Yeah? What was it like?" Sybil sat down.

"Frenchie here was pretty green," Glock said. "Never been in any trouble before. Didn't know the first thing about fighting. All sweet and pert and fragile."

Sybil laughed.

"But you changed that, eh?"

Glock looked at Tamara, giving her an affectionate cuff. "Well, we toughened her up a little," she agreed. "There was the time I busted her nose..."

Sybil laughed, a high-pitched giggle. "Why did you do that?"

"It was an accident. She sort of walked into my fist."

Sybil looked at Tamara for confirmation. Tamara rolled her eyes.

"Yeah. An accident," she agreed.

Glock flexed her arms, and Sybil was distracted by her tattoos.

"Hey, can I see your tats?" she said, getting up and coming closer.

Glock was happy to show them off. She showed her various inks to Sybil, telling her something about each one. The last one was a blue-white-red striped flag prominent on Glock's right bicep, with a crown in the middle of it.

"What's that flag?" Sybil asked.

"French," Glock said. "With a princess crown. Colors are harder to cook up in juvie." She looked at Tamara. "Did you show her yours?"

Sybil nodded, but Tamara shook her head.

"No, not that one," she admitted.

Sybil and Glock both looked at her, waiting. Tamara pulled down the collar of her shirt to reveal the black tattoo at the top of her left breast in the shape of a handgun.

"Cool," Sybil admired it. But she obviously didn't get the significance.

(iv)

Tamara looked at the time on her phone.

"I'd better be getting home," she said. "They'll start wondering where I am."

"Just call them and tell them you're staying here for supper," Sybil protested. "That'll give you another hour or two. Why wouldn't they want you to make friends?"

Tamara considered.

"I dunno... stuff that's been going on lately..."

She didn't look at Glock.

"Come on, Tamara. We're just getting warmed up," Sybil coaxed.

Glock elbowed her sharply. "Make the call," she ordered.

Decisions were easy when Glock was around. Scowling, Tamara rubbed her bruised ribs with one hand, and dialed Mrs. Henson's cell number with the other.

"Hi, it's Tamara..."

"Tamara, where are you? I was expecting you home soon."

"I know... I've just been visiting with a friend. She invited me for supper, is it okay if I stay over a bit longer? We're doing our homework together."

"I don't like you being out too late on a school night. By the time you eat and do your homework and catch the bus back here, it's going to be getting dark."

Tamara waited, holding her breath. She had an idea that Mrs. Henson didn't like to be coaxed. If Tamara started begging and making promises, Mrs. Henson would just out-argue her.

Mrs. Henson sighed on the other end of the phone.

"We'll give it a try this once," she agreed. "I don't want to discourage you from making friends. But if there are any issues, you know what the answer will be next time."

"Yes, ma'am. Thank you!"

She pressed the 'end' button before Mrs. Henson could offer any other advice or requests.

"Nice addition with the homework thing," Sybil approved. "That's probably what got her."

Tamara slid the phone back away, her heart pounding, and let out her breath. "I've got a while, but if I stay too late, she won't say yes next time."

Sybil nodded. "And I'd better get some grub going. The kids will be getting hungry too. You guys okay with mac' and cheese?"

Tamara nodded. Glock patted her belly.

"How many boxes are you making?" she demanded.

"We've got this bulk thing. I'll make lots," Sybil promised, grinning.

She got up and disappeared into the kitchen. As soon as she started banging around pots and pans, the door down the hall opened, and the littlest girl came out again, seeking Sybil out.

"Syb, what are you making? I'm hungry."

"I know you are, Boo. Have a banana."

"Don't want a banana," the girl whined.

"Then wait for supper."

"Why is dinner so late? Why are those girls here?"

"They're my friends, and we've been visiting. They're going to have dinner too."

Tamara saw the little face peeping out the kitchen doorway at them. That little elfin face, clear blue eyes... Tamara started to sweat. She saw Corinne's face. Corinne's little, naked body. Lying still after all the fight drained out of her. Still as death. And the baby laying in the crib, like a child's doll. Tamara lurched to her feet. She stumbled away from them, down the hallway, looking for the bathroom. She knew which room was

Sybil's. Which was the little girls'. The bathroom had to be on the other side. Tamara threw open the door, stepped in, and slammed the door shut behind her. She hovered over the toilet, not sure whether she was going to be sick, or faint, or if the shakiness would just subside. She knew she was hyperventilating, and tried to stop, tried to force herself to slow down and breathe in and out calmly and normally. She looked away from the bathtub, turned her back and sat on the edge of it, shaking all over. She breathed, and breathed, and breathed.

As the ocean-like roaring in her brain quieted and the shakes subsided, Tamara could hear Glock's voice at the other end of the house, repeating several times: "No, just leave her alone," more loudly each time. Tamara got to her feet and splashed cold water on her face. Patting it dry again, she opened the door and returned to the living room. Glock was standing at the end of the hall and took a couple of steps toward Tamara. She grabbed Tamara's arm and guided her back to the couch. Her expression was amused.

Sybil hovered between the stove and the kitchen doorway, obviously concerned about Tamara and wanting to help, but nervous of Glock and still working on dinner.

"Is she okay?" Sybil asked.

Glock walked over toward the kitchen, her back to Tamara, voice lowered now. "Sure, she's fine."

"I don't understand what's the matter. I know she said she's not supposed to be around kids, but I don't get..." Sybil trailed off.

"Well, you *know* she killed the little kids at the last foster family she lived with," Glock said baldly.

There was a crash from the kitchen.

"What?" Sybil demanded, her voice high.

Glock leaned on the doorframe and chuckled, low and slow. "Or maybe she didn't tell you," she laughed.

"No, she didn't tell me," Sybil said in a loud whisper.

"Yeah. She's always been a bit shy about it. It's the one thing she'd never really talk about. I know she confessed to the court, and the probate board. But they don't make juvenile records public so you can read them."

"But how could she? Why...?"

"I know some of the stuff that was going on," Glock confided, "but..."

"I'm still here!" Tamara said, getting back to her feet and confronting Glock. "Don't talk about me like I'm not here!"

Glock grinned down at her. "Oh, now you're getting feisty, hey?" she questioned. "After practically swooning over a little kid?"

"Well, I'm not swooning now. So don't spread my business around!"

Glock just laughed.

Sybil came over, trying to put her arm around Tamara. "Are you okay?"

Tamara pushed her away.

"I'm fine." Tamara's face burned with embarrassment. She couldn't believe that Glock had outed her. And that Sybil was still being sympathetic about it instead of worrying about her baby sisters. Glock watched Tamara and Sybil eagerly, like it was a scene from her favorite television program.

"I'm sorry," Sybil said. "Maybe we shouldn't have come here. I thought it would be okay if I just told them to play in their room."

Tamara shook her head. "Whatever. Don't worry about it." She tried to brush the whole thing aside. "Just let it go."

Sybil stepped back, looking at Tamara's face. "Okay." She turned toward the stove. "You ready for some dinner?"

"I'm not that hungry," Tamara said.

"I'll eat hers," Glock offered. "Always did in juvie."

"A little bit?" Sybil coaxed Tamara.

"Okay, just a few bites."

Sybil pulled a stack of bowls out of the cupboard. "I'll dish the kids' first, and take it in to them. They can eat in the bedroom today. They'll think it's a big treat."

Tamara looked at Glock as Sybil took bowls to the children. "Where are you staying?" she asked.

"I got a place. Not sleeping in your back yard or something."

Tamara had actually wondered. Glock grabbed a bowl and helped herself to a large portion of the remaining macaroni.

"You could come stay with me," Glock suggested.

"No. I'm good with the Hensons. I just... wondered."

Glock sat down at the little kitchen table and started to shovel pasta into her mouth. "You don't have to stay there," she pointed out. "You can decide for yourself where you want to live."

"That would break my parole terms."

"Yeah, so?"

"I don't want to do that. I don't want to get sent back to juvie."

"They can't send you back to juvie if they don't know where you are. Get a clue, Princess."

"I couldn't..."

"It's easy."

Tamara shook her head. "I want to do it the right way. Start over, a new life."

Glock shook her head.

"If you want to start a new life, then start a new life. New name, new place, where nobody knows your past. That's how you start a new life. You're still living the same life. Everyone knows who you are, what you did. Everyone watching for you to make a mistake. How is that starting fresh? You got this whole thing hanging over your head all the time."

Tamara frowned.

"No... if I can make it through the parole, then they seal my juvenile record, and no one has to know about it. I can finish school, and get a job..."

Glock scratched her ear, looking at Tamara with an expression of disbelief. "You always were gullible," she said.

Sybil returned to the kitchen. She looked at Glock eating her big bowl of pasta, and then at Tamara.

"You didn't have to wait for me. Just dish up. How much you want?"

"I'm not hungry."

Sybil put a few large spoons full of macaroni into a bowl, and handed it to Tamara along with a fork.

"Eat something," she encouraged.

Tamara poked at the mac' and cheese, uninterested. Sybil dished up a bowl for herself and sat at the table with Glock. She patted the chair next to her.

"Come sit."

Tamara sat down beside Sybil, looking across the table at Glock. "I gotta go home, soon."

"Not yet."

"Soon."

"When's your curfew?" Glock demanded. "Not until nine o'clock, right?"

Tamara stared at her. "How do you know that?"

"I know everything, baby girl."

Tamara looked at Glock's face, and back down at her bowl.

"Does everybody get a nine o'clock curfew, or did you hack my file or something?"

The corners of Glock's mouth curled up in a satisfied-looking smile. "I'm more a brute force kind of girl than a hacker," she pointed out.

Sybil's mouth dropped open and her eyes widened. "You broke into the parole records?"

Glock's eyes were on Tamara. "I didn't say that," she teased.

"You're gonna get me in big trouble," Tamara said.

"How would me getting a look at your file cause you any trouble?"

"They'll think it was me, or they'll figure out that I'm associating with you, or something..."

"You worry too much. You think Collins has got time to worry about one file? He's got a hundred parolees. Nobody knows who looked at which files, or if it was just a random break-in. How's that gonna get back to you?"

Tamara pushed her bowl away, unable to eat a bite. "I gotta go."

(v)

It had been a long, hard, practice. Tamara dragged herself, with the other limping and shuffling girls, to the locker room to shower and change. The team was fairly quiet, exhausted after the grueling workout. They murmured a word or two to one another and groaned over their sore bodies.

"Better be worth it," Emily muttered. "You think we can beat Central?"

Tamara shook her head, quickly wrapping a towel around herself.

"I dunno. Haven't seen them play. But I know their record..."

"Yeah," Emily agreed. "Exactly."

"Coach says we're ready," one of the other girls interposed. "Don't be negative, or you'll jinx it!"

Emily grumbled and went on getting changed. Tamara went over to the showers and removed her towel to quickly shower and rinse off the sweat. Her uniform had been soaked by the end of the practice. She lathered up quickly, anxious to get done and get out. The locker room showers reminded her too much of the ones at juvie.

"French!"

The soap squirted out of Tamara's hand and went spinning across the floor. She whirled around, fists up to protect herself.

"Whoa, whoa. Holy crap, are you jumpy!" Bernadette observed, holding her hands up, palms out, in a surrendering gesture. "Sorry. I'm not looking to get my nose broken or something. Sheesh."

Tamara stayed on guard, not lowering her hands. Her heart was racing wildly, brain measuring escape routes, her stomach one big knot of anxiety.

"I was just gonna ask if I could use your soap," Bernadette said, smiling slyly and raising her eyebrows. "I left mine in my locker and didn't want to go back and get it. I can use someone else's..."

Tamara didn't jump in with an offer that of course Bernadette could use hers. It still sounded like a set-up. She'd bend over to get her soap, and someone would jump her. Or maybe it would happen when she reached out to hand the bar of soap to Bernadette. It wasn't like they were friends. They had already fought once. Tamara would be stupid to open herself up to attack like that.

Bernadette looked at her for a moment longer, then shook her head and went on to the next shower to ask someone else.

"Head case," she muttered, under her breath so that Tamara would be the only one who heard it.

Tamara didn't move. She looked around, analyzing all of the risks. There didn't seem to be any immediate danger. Tamara used her foot to retrieve the soap from the corner and pull it back toward her. Then after another quick look around, she bent her knees and retrieved it. She didn't use it, but quickly rinsed off under the water, which was starting to get cold now, and grabbed her towel to wrap back around her.

"Are you okay?" Emily asked, as Tamara hurriedly toweled off and pulled on her clothes. "Something wrong?"

"No. Fine."

Emily raised her eyebrows.

"Okay..."

Tamara did up her pants and pulled on a shirt, relieved to be covered back up again. Less vulnerable to attack. She shoved her sweaty clothes and wet towel into her gym bag and fled.

When she got out to the main school doors, she saw Sybil waiting there. Sybil laughed.

"Hey, I just texted you," she said. "I didn't know whether you were out of practice yet."

"Oh." Tamara felt for her phone, but it wasn't in her pocket. She frowned. It wasn't in either of her pants pockets. She put down her bag and checked through the front and side pockets, with a sinking feeling. "I didn't lose it..."

"You leave it in the gym?" Sybil suggested.

"No, we're not allowed... I put it on the bench in the locker room!" Tamara swore. "I gotta go back and find if. If no one else picked it up."

Sybil cocked her head, raising her eyebrows.

"I guess you'd better," she agreed, making no move to come with Tamara.

"I'll be right back," Tamara sighed.

She walked all the way back to the locker room, passing most of the team as they left.

"Did you see my phone?" Tamara asked Emily.

Emily shook her head. "No. Everyone's gone. Do you want me to go with you?"

"No. It's not locked yet, right? I'll be fine."

In fact, she'd be a lot more comfortable in the locker room if there was no one else around. Provided that she found her phone. Sybil was not going to be happy if Tamara had lost it. Tamara picked up the pace and hurried back to the locker room.

She could still hear a shower running, so not everyone was gone yet. Tamara looked at the bench where she had laid down her phone, but it wasn't there. She looked under the bench, and then all over the floor of the locker room. Relieved, she spotted it under the edge of the nearest row of lockers. Tamara scooped it up and immediately opened it up to make sure that it wasn't wet or cracked. She started to text Sybil back to let her know that she had found it and was on her way back.

But then she heard the sobbing. Or it finally forced its way into her consciousness. There were two voices, very soft, barely audible over the sound of the shower. One seemed to be crying. Tamara started toward the showers, then hesitated. She didn't owe anything to anyone on the team. It wasn't her job to look after anyone, soothe their bruised egos after a tough practice. If they couldn't handle it, maybe they shouldn't be on the team.

But she couldn't ignore the heartbreaking sobs. So she crept toward the showers. Tamara realized that it was Lotta, who the coach had kept behind again today. Was he giving her a hard time? Tamara didn't think Lotta had been playing that badly. Maybe he had some special coaching to give her. The shower shut off, and with the background noise eliminated, Tamara realized that the second voice was male. She stopped where she was, frozen. She could just barely see them from her perspective. Lotta stepping out of the shower into the towel that Coach McClure held up for her. He wrapped it around her, enfolding her in an embrace, pulling her to him. Lotta sobbed.

Tamara turned and ran.

EIGHT

(i)

WHAT'S WRONG?" SYBIL QUESTIONED once they were outside. "What happened that you're so upset about?"

Tamara shook her head. Her heart was racing and she felt like she was going to be sick. She chewed her nail, and Sybil produced a cigarette as a substitute. Tamara lit it up with shaking fingers and sucked in the smoke, wishing it would hit her like it did the first time she had tried smoking in juvie. Just hammer her with the first taste of nicotine and make her forget everything else.

She looked around anxiously. Had he seen her? Did he know that she had seen him? Had he followed her out, to track her down and demand her silence? Tamara saw a tall figure walking toward them, but knew instantly that it was Glock, not the coach. She knew that figure, that stride. Sybil turned to see what Tamara was looking at. She smiled at the sight of Glock, rather than groaning or complaining about Glock imposing herself on them again, as Tamara thought she might.

Glock recognized the instant that she looked at Tamara that something was wrong. She pulled Tamara roughly to her, and gave her a squeeze and a clumsy kiss on the top of the head.

"What happened?" she asked Sybil.

Tamara wriggled to free herself from the embrace, still holding her lit cigarette.

Sybil was shaking her head. "I don't know. She hasn't said. Something must have just happened. She was okay a few minutes ago."

Glock looked closely at Tamara's face, and took a quick scan of their surroundings, looking for trouble. "Well, if something happened here, then let's put some distance between. Come on."

They started walking, following Glock's lead.

"Should we go to my place?" Sybil suggested.

Glock narrowed her eyes at Sybil and shook her head. "No, we don't need the fuss over little kids too. Why don't you go home and look after them, and I'll see to Frenchie?"

Sybil shook her head, smiling.

"No, I don't think so. The little ones will be fine for a while. They'll be happy I'm not making them do homework. Where to, then?"

Glock jerked her head.

"We'll go to the mall. Blend in with the crowd."

No one argued, and they continued to follow Glock's lead.

"So," Glock said to Tamara, "let's have it. Someone say something to hurt Miss Prissy's feelings?"

Tamara shook her head.

"It's not me. It's... another girl... Lotta."

"Lotta what?" Glock quipped.

Tamara took another steadying drag on her cigarette.

"Lotta's on the team, right?" Sybil said.

Tamara nodded.

"So what happened?" Sybil prompted.

"Why would we care?" Glock countered. "I'm sure Lotta can take care of herself. She don't need us getting in her business."

Tamara gulped, and told them as quickly and clearly as she could what she had seen.

Sybil gaped. "You gotta tell someone," she insisted. "Call the police, or the principal, or something."

Glock shook her head. "Girl's old enough to look after herself. You know what to do if some guy tries messing with you again, right?" she said to Tamara. "Kick him where it counts, make sure he ain't ever even gonna think of trying that again."

"I can't just ignore it," Tamara protested. "She was crying."

"What difference does that make? It's none of your business. Just leave it alone."

"Really?" Tamara frowned as she walked, drawing on the cigarette. "I don't think that's right."

"You keep saying how you want to stay straight, be a normal person," Glock said. "So why do you want to get mixed up in something like that for? You know it will come back to bite you. No one will believe you. And he'll say that you're lying, just trying to get back at him for being too tough on you in front of the team. You think I don't know how this kind of thing turns out? You start digging in the mud, you're going to get it all over your own hands and face. Nobody's going to believe a juvie like you."

Tamara walked in silence for a while.

"Maybe I was wrong," she said finally. "Maybe he was just there to help her, because she was upset about something. Maybe it was innocent."

"You wouldn't want to accuse him if he was just being helpful," Sybil admitted. "You could ruin someone's reputation forever. What do you think? Was he just comforting her because she was upset, or...?"

Glock laughed. "Yeah. Because he's supposed to be in the girls' locker room, right?"

Tamara and Sybil looked at each other. Tamara kicked a rock across the road angrily.

"I don't want to get in trouble," she said. "I don't want to make waves or get sent back to juvie just because I'm trying to do the right thing. Why do *I* have to report him? Why doesn't someone else do it?"

"Because you're the one who saw," Sybil said. "No one else was there."

"I don't know what I saw," Tamara maintained. "It was probably nothing. I overreacted. I was already nervous about the showers, and I just saw what I was expecting."

"Sure," Glock agreed. "It's just your imagination."

They had arrived at the mall doors. Glock motioned in the direction of the food fair.

"Let's get something to eat," she suggested.

Sybil looked at Tamara. "You'd better call your mom, right? They'll be expecting you after practice."

Tamara realized that she was right. "You guys find something to eat," she suggested. "I'll find us a table and call Mrs. Henson."

(ii)

"Where are you, Tamara?" Mrs. Henson questioned after answering the phone. "I'm expecting you to be home for supper today."

"I'm just going over to Syb's. She asked me to help her with some homework," Tamara lied.

"I'd like you to come straight home."

"She really needs help," Tamara said, "or she's going to fail English. I want to help her."

"Tamara—"

"I'll be home by curfew. Just like last time, right? I got home in time before."

"You have chores to be done. And I've just been on the phone with Mr. Collins. He has some concerns."

Tamara gritted her teeth. She just couldn't take any more bad news right now. What did Collins have to be worried about? She'd been following all of her parole terms.

"About what?" she demanded.

"Some of your teachers have reported that you've been having problems in class. Not able to keep focused, not turning your homework in on time..."

"Well, that's why I'm going to Sybil's," Tamara said with exasperation. "So I can work on my schoolwork."

"You said you were working on hers."

"We'll do both. Together."

"I have to admit that I've had some concerns too."

Tamara kicked at the pedestal of the table she had picked out.

"Mrs. H, I thought you wanted me to have friends!"

"Of course I want you to have friends. This has nothing to do with friends. Our job is to help you to succeed, and that's what I want to do. Help you to work things out."

"Yeah?"

"I know you've been upset since you found that cat. You've been having trouble sleeping, you haven't wanted to be home, and now your teachers are reporting these problems. Have you talked to Dr. Frank about it?"

"Yes."

Mrs. Henson was silent, waiting for more.

"I didn't hurt that cat," Tamara insisted. "Why does everything think that was me?"

"I don't think it was you," Mrs. Henson protested immediately, and Tamara was relieved by the sincerity in her voice. "I saw how upset you were, Tamara. I just mean that Dr. Frank could help you through that stress. Help you to find ways to relax, get past it."

Dr. Frank obviously hadn't passed on to Mrs. Henson that he thought she was the one who had done it. Maybe he hadn't said anything to Mr. Collins either. He said that what they talked about was confidential between them, but Tamara had her suspicions about just how far that confidentiality went. She was pretty sure that he still had to report back to Mr. Collins if he thought Tamara was a danger to others. And if he thought she was the one killing the animals, then he would think that she was the one who was a dangerous psychopath, too.

Tamara looked around the food fair for Glock. She and Sybil were talking, gesturing at the various food concessions to decide what to get. Tamara worried that the two of them were getting too close to each other. Sybil didn't know what Glock was really like. She'd only seen the bigger girl in a good mood, so far. She didn't know how dangerous she could be. And Tamara hadn't confided to her that it was Glock who had killed the cats. She couldn't bring herself to say it out loud.

"Tamara. Tamara!"

Tamara focused in on the phone she was holding to her ear. "Sorry," she said. "You cut out for a minute there. What did you say?"

"I think my battery is getting low. I'd like you to come home, Tamara. Why don't you arrange to spend some time with Sybil tomorrow, during the day? And catch the bus so you can get home."

"We're already getting dinner," Tamara said. "So don't wait for me. I'll come as soon as we are finished, if I can come over tomorrow."

"Okay," Mrs. Henson said. "Good. I'll see you in an hour or so?"

"Bit longer," Tamara said. "Depends how long I have to wait for the bus."

(iii)

Sybil and Glock got to the table and put down their loaded trays of food. Tamara looked over them, raising her eyebrows.

"Don't you think you went a bit overboard?" She laughed.

"Most of it's for her," Sybil laughed, elbowing Glock.

Glock reacted instantly to the physical contact, sweeping her arm out and shoving Sybil violently away. Sybil stumbled backwards into other chairs and tables with a crash. Tamara rushed over to help Sybil up, apologizing to the people they had disturbed. She gave Sybil a hand and pulled her to her feet.

"You okay?"

Sybil's lip was quivering.

"What was that about?" she demanded.

"You can't touch Glock," Tamara whispered, trying to quiet her. "She doesn't like it."

"*You* touch her," Sybil protested. "She's always grabbing you and hugging you and everything."

"That's because..." Tamara trailed off. "That's just different," she said lamely. "That's her touching me."

Sybil scowled. She wiped her mouth with the back of her hand, and went purposefully back to their table and sat down across from Glock. She didn't look at Glock or apologize for nudging her.

"Awww," Glock mocked, looking at Sybil, "is the little baby gonna cry?"

Tamara sat down on the side, between them. She tried to give Sybil a warning look, to silently communicate with her how to react to Glock.

"I'm not crying," Sybil said. "You just caught me off guard."

Glock took a big bite out of her burger, and chewed it, studying Sybil. She glanced at Tamara, her pupils dilated; big, black holes.

Tamara knew that look. "Don't," she warned.

Sybil looked at Tamara, frowning. "What?" she asked.

"Don't, please," Tamara repeated to Glock. "Just leave her."

Glock gave her a smile, but her eyes didn't change.

"Don't what?" Sybil persisted.

"Frenchie thinks I'm going to hurt you," Glock said, taking another bite of her burger.

Sybil rolled her eyes. "I'm fine," she told Tamara. "I'm not making any trouble. We can get along."

Still holding onto her burger with one hand, Glock reached out casually and caught Sybil's hand, holding it between two fingers. Sybil gave her a puzzled half-smile. Tamara watched helplessly as Glock extended Sybil's wrist to the limit of its range of motion, and then with a grim smile, pushed it further.

"Oh!" Sybil said. "Ow, don't!"

Glock kept bending it. Sybil stood, following the pressure, trying to relieve the pain.

"Stop," Tamara said, using her most persuasive voice. "Glock, come on..."

Tears were starting in Sybil's eyes. Her uncertain smile had disappeared, and she stared at Glock in horror, trying franticly to free her hand.

"Ow, aaah, please," Sybil shrieked. "Stop, stop!"

Heads were turning as her voice cut across the buzz of conversation. Tamara's eyes were squeezed into a wince, waiting for the snap of the bone. Glock released Sybil's hand. Sybil collapsed back into her chair, hugging the hurt wrist to her body. There was no question that she was crying this time. Tears streamed down her face. She sat there sobbing and moaning slightly, cradling the injured limb. Glock hadn't even put down the burger in her other hand. She took another bite, and watched Sybil, her eyes enormous, drinking it all in.

Tamara deliberately picked up a few of Glock's fries and ate them without looking at her.

Glock brushed Tamara's cheek with the back of two fingers. "You gonna pout now, baby girl?"

"I asked you to leave her alone."

"I didn't break it," Glock pointed out. "I let her go."

"You didn't have to hurt her."

Glock chuckled, the laughter bubbling up from her. "Well, I kind of did," she said. "She was asking for it." She looked across the table at Sybil. "Look at those big fat tears."

Sybil wiped at her face with one hand. She didn't say anything, but Tamara could see that she was reevaluating her opinion of Glock. Realizing that Glock was more than just a novelty. That she wasn't just interesting to know, a prop to boost Sybil's bad-girl reputation. Sybil's and Tamara's eyes met, and then Sybil looked away, sniffling and swiping more tears away.

(iv)

The next day, Tamara knocked on Sybil's door. There were squeals from within the house from the little girls, and a few minutes later, a woman opened the door. Tamara hadn't met her before. But she could see the resemblance to Sybil's fine features.

"You must be Tamara," she greeted with a smile. "Come on in. Sybil will be ready in a minute."

Tamara stepped in the door and waited in the entryway. Sybil's mom motioned to the couch.

"You can come in. Make yourself at home."

Tamara shook her head.

"It's okay."

Tamara waited uncomfortably. She stared down at her shoes, not wanting to run into the little children again. In a couple of minutes, Sybil came out of the hallway.

"Hey, Tamara," she greeted with a cheerful smile.

"Hey. You ready?"

Sybil nodded and grabbed her backpack. She winced and changed hands to pick it up.

"Okay, I'm going now, Mom," she called out.

Her mother came out of the kitchen, drying her hands on a towel.

"I'll see you tomorrow, then, sweetie. Have a good time."

She gave Sybil a peck on the cheek. Then Tamara and Sybil headed out. Outside the door, Tamara picked up her backpack from where she'd dropped it beside the steps.

"Have you been to Glock's before?" Sybil asked, as they started on their way.

Tamara shook her head. "No. I guess it will be okay... I didn't want to sleep over at your house, though, with the kids."

Sybil nodded. "It's gonna be great," she said, a bit too enthusiastically. "Just the three of us girls, hanging out, having a party? It will be so much fun."

Tamara nodded. She tried to convince herself that it was a good idea. They could just hang out without any parental involvement, and she could forget all about school, and Coach McClure, and the tortured cats, and her parole. She could pretend she was a normal girl. They walked in silence for a while.

"It'll be okay, right?" Sybil said. "I mean... with Glock...?"

Tamara bit her lip and sighed. They both knew that staying over at Glock's probably wasn't the best idea. But Glock had insisted. Tamara knew she had to do what Glock said, or take the consequences.

"Yeah, sure. I mean... I hope so."

"When you were in juvie... did she...?" Sybil trailed off.

"Hurt people?" Tamara finished baldly. "Yeah, whenever the mood struck."

"At least there were guards there."

Tamara grunted. "It still takes time for guards to get there and do anything about it."

"Oh. Yeah, I guess. Did she—" Sybil started, and then decided she couldn't finish the question.

Tamara shook her head warningly at Sybil. She didn't want

to answer any more questions about juvie, and especially about Glock. Sybil didn't pursue it, pasting on a smile and acting like she had no concerns.

They caught the bus back toward the Hensons' house. Tamara looked up the address that Glock had given to her on her phone so they knew what bus stop to get out at. They walked along the street looking at building numbers, and found the dilapidated apartment block with the right house number. At the front entrance, Tamara pressed the button on the notice board to buzz Glock's apartment. There was no response. Tamara pressed it again. Sybil pushed the inside door.

"It's open," she said.

"Oh. Yeah."

They went in. The building smelled like garlic, cigarettes, and rotting oranges. Tamara hoped that she'd get used to it quickly. They looked at the numbers on the doors, and Tamara knocked loudly on Glock's. She could hear Glock's heavy footsteps, and then the door opened. Glock grinned.

"Hey."

She stepped back and motioned for them to enter. Tamara led the way and Sybil followed. They stepped through the kitchenette; a single sink and short counter equipped with a hot plate and a plug-in beer cooler. The living area was an all-purpose room. A fold-out couch still pulled out in a bed. A big flat-screen television was playing some music video. There was a door that Tamara assumed was the bathroom, and a rod anchored to the wall with a couple of shirts hanging from it.

"*Mi casa*," Glock said, spreading an arm to indicate it.

"Nice," Tamara said, and sat down on the bed. At least one of them was going to be sleeping on the floor tonight.

Sybil didn't sit down right away. She stood there, looking around, like she figured there was more to see somewhere.

"You want a drink?" Glock suggested, motioning to the cooler.

Sybil opened it up to take a look, and pulled out two bottles of beer, holding one out toward Tamara.

"No," Tamara said. "Not for me."

Sybil put the second one back.

"I didn't buy any kiddie drinks," Glock told Tamara.

"Fine. I'll drink water."

Sybil tipped up her bottle. "Good stuff," she approved.

"So you're staying?" Glock verified. "All weekend? Overnight?"

"Yeah," Tamara said. "I told Mrs. Henson that I was staying with Sybil, and Sybil said she was staying with me. So... we're both safe."

"And your curfew?"

"I told Mrs. H that Collins said it was all right, as long as I checked in with him at nine."

Glock snickered. "She should know better. She's had parolees before. You're lucky she didn't check."

Tamara hadn't thought about that. She shrugged. Maybe Tamara had been confident enough in getting a 'yes' answer, that Mrs. Henson had not been suspicious.

"Well, just throw your stuff wherever, and let's go out."

"Go where?" Sybil asked. "We just got here."

"And you think I want to spend all my time in this dump?" Glock demanded, putting out her hands to indicate their surroundings. "Nah. This is just somewhere to crash when you're too smashed to party anymore. We're going out."

Tamara and Sybil both left their bags on the floor, and Glock led the way out of the apartment.

(v)

Tamara got up in the morning for school, but her stomach was writhing and crampy and she couldn't stay out of the bathroom. Everyone wanted the upstairs bathroom to shower and get ready for school and work, so Tamara went to the tiny main floor bathroom and waited for her stomach to settle down.

But whenever she thought about going to school, about having to deal with the Lotta situation, it would cramp up again, and she'd be back in the bathroom. As the time for breakfast past and the arrival of the bus approached, Mrs. Henson tried to have a conversation with her, while she sat at the table with her arms folded across her stomach.

"What's going on, Tamara?"

"I just don't feel good. I don't think I can go today."

"Did you do something over the weekend that might have bothered it?"

"No."

"Are you hung over? Have you been drinking?"

"No," Tamara protested. "No alcohol, no drugs. I wouldn't do that."

"What did you guys do?"

"Listened to music. Danced. Watched some TV. Talked. You know; painted our nails." Tamara shrugged. "Girl stuff."

Sure, the music and the dancing had been at a club, but Tamara had not had anything to drink. The worst she did was smoke cigarettes between destinations, and that wasn't against her parole terms. It had been a fun weekend, and Tamara had been able to forget about the trouble at school for a while. But it had all come back Monday morning, and she felt worse than ever.

"Is there something on your mind? Something you want to talk about?" Mrs. Henson questioned, studying Tamara's face.

Tamara turned away, not wanting her to read anything there.

"No. It's just my stomach. Must be a bug or something."

"Okay... why don't you head back to bed? Get some rest."

Tamara nodded and got up for one more trip to the bathroom before hiding in her room.

(*vi*)

Tamara was surprised by a visitor in the afternoon after school let out. Sybil missed her at school and stopped by to see how she was doing. Rather than getting up, Tamara made space for Sybil to lie down beside her on the bed, and they stared up at the white ceiling.

"I'm just sick over what to do," Tamara confided. "This whole thing about Coach McClure and Lotta. I just don't know..."

"Well, maybe you don't need to do anything," Sybil said. "Maybe it's not really any of your business."

Tamara turned and stared at her. That was Glock's opinion, not Sybil's. Sybil turned slightly pink.

"Well," she said defensively, "you're not sure, right?"

"I don't know... I could have misinterpreted... I kind of expected the worst... but why would he be down there, in the showers with her?"

"She was upset... he wanted to make she was okay... there wasn't anyone else around to check on her..."

Tamara thought about Coach McClure's face, so kind and cheerful, and his usually soft-spoken way. He had let her on the team mid-year, and then had allowed her to stay on even when she had defied him and gotten into a fight. She'd seen him after games, giving players congratulatory hugs, or hugs of consolation. Sure he'd yelled at her, but only when she deserved it. He seemed like a really good guy, and she'd never gotten a bad vibe off of him. He'd never said or done anything inappropriate to her. Of course, she'd only known him a few weeks, but she was shocked at the thought that he could be in some kind of relationship with Lotta.

"Maybe," she said doubtfully.

"If he was that kind of guy," Sybil said. "Then wouldn't the team have figured it out? I mean... he just started with Lotta?

He's never had anything to do with any of the other girls? What's he been like with you? No come-ons?"

"Fine. No troubles," Tamara admitted.

"Well, then... maybe it *was* just innocent."

"Maybe," Tamara echoed hopefully.

"Do any of the other girls seem funny around him? Or jealous of Lotta or something?" Sybil suggested.

The only one she had asked about Lotta was Emily, and Tamara remembered Emily's cold 'not my business' when Lotta looked like she was upset. Similar to the way that she had referred to Holiday's trouble. No one on the team had seemed particularly concerned about Lotta's tears.

Tamara stared at the baby crib across the room. *Holiday.* Sybil could see that something had struck Tamara, and raised her brows questioningly.

"What?"

"The girl on the team that I replaced."

"Yeah...?"

"Holiday."

"Holly?" Sybil asked. "Yeah, I know who she is. Whatever happened to her? Did she transfer?"

Tamara shook her head.

"Emily said she 'got herself pregnant' and couldn't get an abortion."

Sybil's jaw dropped. She propped herself on her elbow, looking at Tamara.

"And we both know she didn't get herself pregnant. You kinda need a boy for that part," Sybil said.

"Did Holly have a boyfriend?" Tamara waited for Sybil's reassurance that indeed she had, and that they were obviously intimate.

But Sybil shook her head.

"No. Not that I ever saw. She was on the team, but not real popular. Kind of shy."

"It was him," Tamara said, certain. "Coach got her pregnant, and she had to quit school. And the team knows it. They know that he's taken up with Lotta now. But why wouldn't anybody say anything?"

Sybil shook her head.

"Maybe they did, and were just told to stay out of it. And nothing happened. Sometimes that's what happens. You read it in the newspaper: There were complaints, but the administration just ignored them..."

"Then what am *I* going to do? If I report it, and no one does anything..."

"You have to try," Sybil said.

"Will you help me?"

"Well... I wasn't there. You're the one who saw..."

Tamara could see that Sybil didn't want to be dragged into this either. She knew not to get her hands dirty.

Glock had warned Tamara that if she got involved, she would end up getting in trouble. She could end up getting sent back to juvie, if they didn't believe her and thought she was just being a troublemaker. Glock knew how it worked.

NINE

(i)

TAMARA GOT OFF THE bus and walked toward school, her feet feeling like lead weights. She knew she had to report Coach McClure. She had to do what she could, even with the rest of the team turning a blind eye. Lotta didn't want a relationship with him, she had been crying both times. Holly hadn't wanted to end up pregnant, out of school, and off the team. Had he interfered with anyone else who was on the team? Sybil was right, whenever these stories ran in the news the perp had always been messing around long before he was caught, ruining the lives of countless children. She was sure that McClure was no different. Everyone looked at his kind, gentle face, and didn't believe that he could be a predator.

What exactly was the proper protocol for reporting a sex offender at the school? She supposed she could have called the police. Maybe that would have been better. She went instead to the school office, deciding that she could talk to the principal. Or to Mr. Van Rhyn. Van Rhyn had been kind to her when she had gotten into the fight with Bernadette. If no one else was there, she could try her guidance counselor.

The secretary looked at Tamara questioningly when she came up to the counter.

"Yes, dear?"

"Um, I'm Tamara French. Can I see... Mr. Van Rhyn? Is he here?"

"He's taking care of something else right now, but if you'll have a seat, he should be able to see you in a few minutes. All right?"

Tamara nodded and went to sit down. Her heart was pounding wildly. She thought she had been through all the stomach cramps she could manage the day before, but they were back again, her guts in knots over the whole business. She hoped that Mr. Van Rhyn wouldn't take very long to finish up whatever other business he had. The sooner she could get this off her chest, the better.

Time crawled by. The opening bell went, and she knew she wasn't going to make it to her first class on time now. But helping Lotta was more important than getting to class. McClure had to be stopped.

The receptionist put her phone down, and looked across the office at Tamara with a frown.

"Did you say your name was Tamara?" she questioned.

"Yeah."

"You need to go up to your locker."

"What?" Tamara frowned. "I wanted to talk to Mr. Van Rhyn."

"He'll meet you by your locker. Please go straight there."

Tamara stood there for a moment, flummoxed. The second bell rang, and she started on her way back to her locker.

(ii)

When she got to her locker, Mr. Van Rhyn was indeed there. So was Mr. Collins. And a couple of uniformed policemen. Tamara caught her breath and stopped where she was. Had someone reported her? For what? She stood there with her feet rooted to the floor. If her parole was violated, then she should run. She should get out of there before they could take her back to juvie. It was her only chance.

"Tamara," Collins said. "Come here, please."

Tamara's feet followed his instruction. Tamara stood looking at him mutely.

"This is your locker?" he questioned, pointing to it.

"Yeah."

"Anything you want to tell me?"

"No."

"Open it, please."

Tamara looked around at the other people. What was going on? Why was everyone there?

"What?"

Collins held up a folded piece of paper.

"This is a warrant to search your locker. In case the school refused to allow me access. But they haven't. Mr. Van Rhyn is here on behalf of the school. The police are here to perform the search. Now open it, please."

Tamara approached her locker, and twirled the combination lock with shaking fingers. It wouldn't open. She tried again, and it still wouldn't open.

"What's the combination?" Collins questioned, shouldering her out of the way.

"Thirty-two, twenty-four, three."

He spun the dial this way and that, and jerked it open. Taking the lock off, he swung the door open.

"Does everything look like you left it?" he asked. "Anything out of place?"

Tamara's head whirled. Why would anything be out of

place? She looked over the rather disordered contents of the locker. How was it possible to make such a mess in the few short weeks she had been there?

"I... don't know... yeah, it looks normal."

"Have you given anyone your combination, or access to your locker?"

"No. I don't understand..."

Collins stepped back, and motioned for the police officers to search the locker. Tamara swallowed. She chewed on her thumbnail, looking at Collins.

"What's going on?"

"We'll talk after."

Tamara looked at Mr. Van Rhyn.

"I was coming to see you today... there's something I need to tell you..."

"Does it have anything to do with your locker?" he asked, his voice quiet.

"No."

"Then it will have to wait."

She stood there watching the officers methodically removing and searching each item in her locker. No one looked at her. The other students were all in their first period classes.

"There it is," one of the cops said, and held a bag up for Mr. Collins and everyone else to see. None of them had any doubt what the dried leaves inside were. Tamara's mouth dropped open.

"What?" she spluttered. "Who put that in there? That's not mine!"

But they weren't listening to her. One of the cops already had his hand on her arm. "Tamara French, you are under arrest for possession of marijuana..."

Tamara shook her head. "It's not mine," she insisted.

She didn't fight the two cops. The one speaking to her gently guided her to the wall, where Tamara automatically placed her hands and assumed the appropriate position. She closed her eyes while he patted her down. He pulled her hands back away from the wall and behind her, and the cuffs closed over her wrists.

"It's not mine," Tamara repeated, tears starting from her eyes. "I know you won't believe me, but it's true. Someone planted it there. I haven't taken any drugs. I don't do drugs. Ever. It's not mine."

"Are you holding it for someone else?" Collins questioned.

"No. No, I haven't even seen it before. Someone planted it in my locker. You gotta believe me."

"I'm sorry, Tamara. I can't."

Tamara felt like her heart was being squeezed. She gasped at the pain. "Don't send me back. I didn't do anything," she insisted. "I swear, it's not mine!"

"I'll see you at the police station," Collins said to the officers.

They nodded, and led Tamara away.

(iii)

Tamara sat in the chilly interrogation room, her elbows on the table and face in her hands. She wasn't crying. Not anymore. But she was overwhelmed by the developments and didn't know what to do. There was no way that Collins would believe that the drugs weren't hers, but she had to try to convince him. But where had they come from? Tamara's first thought was Glock. Her ex-cellie seemed to know everything, to be everywhere, it only made sense that she was the one who had decided to store her drugs in Tamara's locker. Maybe she wanted to blackmail Tamara, force her into some action by holding the drugs in her locker over her head. But someone else had seen the drugs. Someone else knew or suspected about them and reported her. There was no reason for Glock to report her, was there?

Tamara was pretty sure that Sybil didn't have anything to do with the pot. She might do pot, and certainly had been comfortable with it over the weekend, but she wouldn't have any reason to put it in Tamara's locker.

The door opened, causing a whoosh of air that made Tamara's arms prickle into goosebumps and her ears pop uncomfortably. Collins came in. He stood there, towering over Tamara, his expression one of disappointment and disapproval.

"Tamara."

"It's not mine, I swear," Tamara said, the tears again welling up and spilling over her cheeks.

He sat down in the other chair.

"Denial is not going to get you anywhere, except straight back to juvie. Tell me what's been going on. I thought you were doing well."

"I was. I am. You have to trust me, I'm not doing drugs. Test my urine. My hair. I haven't had any drugs. I swear it."

"Then why were they in your locker?"

"I didn't put them there. Someone planted them. Why would I have drugs when I know they would get me sent back to juvie? I don't want to go back!"

"Because you are under a great deal of stress. And drugs are one way to deal with a lot of stress. You want to mellow out, feel better. But it's not the way."

"I wouldn't do that. I am stressed. I know. You don't know the half of it. But I wouldn't take drugs. I didn't drink, and I didn't take drugs, and I didn't hold them for anyone else. Mr. Collins... you have to believe me."

"I don't have a lot of reason to believe you right now."

"I've been good! I haven't broken the rules. Why won't you trust me?"

"I hear," he said slowly, his eyes hard, "that you spent the weekend with a friend."

Tamara swallowed. She tugged at a lock of hair that hung beside her face, pulling it so hard that it brought fresh tears to her eyes. How had he heard that? Mrs. Henson must have talked to him about it after all.

"I didn't break any rules," she maintained. "Sleeping over with a girl from school, that's not breaking any rules. I didn't do anything I wasn't supposed to. We just talked. Just girl stuff. Nothing illegal."

"You didn't break any rules?" Collins questioned. "I know you don't believe that. You told Mrs. Henson that you had checked with me, because of your curfew."

Tamara's stomach was shaking, shuddering like a leaf in the wind.

"That's just... I wasn't *out*. I was in at nine. I didn't break curfew."

"Curfew says that you are at the Hensons' house at nine o'clock. Not at a friend's."

Tamara shifted, squirming in her seat.

"That's just a technicality," she said. "I thought it was okay, if I was in. That's not enough to violate my parole, is it?"

"You knew it was a breach, or you wouldn't have lied to Mrs. Henson about talking to me."

Tamara nodded, staring down at the scratched, scarred table.

"I... yeah. I thought it would be okay... but I didn't want to ask, in case you said no..."

"And I would have," Collins agreed. "There's a reason for the rules."

"I'm sorry."

He folded his arms across his chest.

"You're sorry. Well then, I guess that makes everything okay."

"No. I know. I'm..." Tamara lifted her hands in a gesture of helplessness. "I won't do it again."

"No, you won't," he agreed. "Tamara, breaking curfew is not the issue here."

"I told you the drugs aren't mine. I don't do pot."

"What did you mean when you said I don't know half of it?"

Tamara balked. "What?"

Collins shifted, crossing one ankle across his knee.

"When I said that you were stressed, you said I didn't know the half of it. What did you mean?"

Tamara picked at the skin around her nails.

"I dunno."

"You're supposed to be letting me know everything that's going on. What is stressing you out that I don't know about?"

"Nothing you don't know about," Tamara said. "Just... you don't get how stressful it is. Especially... about the cats."

He considered this.

"Why don't you tell me about that?"

Tamara looked down at her hands.

"It's just... I know everyone thinks it was me. And it wasn't. I felt... sick... I'd never do that."

He nodded.

"Did you talk to Dr. Frank about it?"

"Yeah. But he doesn't believe me. He thinks I did it."

"Does he?"

Tamara nodded. "I think so."

"So you felt... rebellious...? You wanted to numb your feelings? Escape?"

Tamara looked at him, the pain in her chest reasserting itself. She breathed heavily.

"It's not my pot," she insisted. "Not because I was stressed or anything. It wasn't mine." She wiped at tears. "I don't want to go back to juvie!" she said angrily.

"Tamara... everyone makes mistakes. Parole is not a smooth path. It's not easy. People make mistakes. But you remember what I told you at the beginning. You have to be honest. Tell me when you make a mistake. Don't lie and cover it up. Don't keep trying to convince me that you're perfect. You need to talk to me."

Tamara resisted the urge to explain again that it hadn't been her pot. He was telling her what to do, and it wasn't to keep denying. If she wanted to make it better, to impress him, she had to confess. She held his gaze, willing herself to say the words.

"Okay," she said, breathing out. "I... I made a mistake, Mr. Collins."

He nodded encouragingly.

"I... was feeling stressed... like you said."

"Uh-huh."

"I thought it would help to mellow me out. I'd be able to relax."

"People often use drugs to self-medicate."

"I didn't actually take it, though," Tamara said. "I just..."

She saw his disapproving expression and stopped. Just one more thing that he wouldn't believe.

"Okay," she admitted. "I did."

"At the party on the weekend?" he suggested.

Tamara wiped her tears, taking a deep breath. She nodded. "Yeah."

"You should have called me."

"I know," Tamara said. "But please... please don't send me back."

He sighed, studying her.

"I think you have promise, Tamara. I really think that you could do it. But you need to be willing to follow the rules. To be open with me about your problems."

Tamara nodded. "Does that mean...?"

"You're going to need to wait here for a while," he told her.

(iv)

It was a long time before Collins came back. Tamara had begun to think that he had lied to her and that they were waiting for the juvie bus to come and take her away. She folded her arms and put her head down in them on the table. She should be used to waiting. She'd waited for three years to get out. She could wait a few hours to find out if she was going to be released.

Finally, the door opened and it felt as if all of the air was being suctioned out of the room. Collins came back in.

"Okay," he said, "sorry for taking so long. You wouldn't believe how complicated these things can get."

"Can I go home?"

"Here's the thing. You've violated parole, and you've also broken the law. You've been charged with simple possession. Your first drug offense, you would normally be released ROR after being processed. But since you have also breached parole, that complicates things."

Tamara held her stomach.

"No," she protested, her heart squeezed, knowing what was coming.

"You're not going back to juvie."

She took a deep breath.

"What, then?"

"You're going to have to be held over here for a day or two, until you've appeared before the judge. I'll give my recommendation that you be returned to parole, and then you can go back to the Hensons."

"What if the judge doesn't listen to you?"

"The judge always listens to the parole officer."

"What if he doesn't?" Tamara repeated, her voice rising.

"Tamara. Take it easy. He will."

Tamara rubbed her eyes with her fists. So this was it. Back behind bars again. It had been a nice idea. A nice dream. But now it was back to reality. It was all over.

"Okay," she said, holding out her wrists to Collins. "Let's go, then."

(v)

It was all routine. Handcuffs, strip search, and change into the jail uniform. They made her remove all of the jewelry from her piercings. Took pictures of her face and her tattoos. It was almost a relief to be back in custody. She didn't have to make any more decisions. Didn't have to worry about messing up. Didn't have to figure out how to get along with the normal people on the outside, with the foster family. Everything was familiar and comforting.

After being booked, a guard escorted her to the police station cell block. Tamara was used to the closed-wall cells at juvie. The open-bar cells where she could see all of the other inmates were new to her, but she decided she preferred being able to see what was going on. The guard opened up a cell that was currently unoccupied, and Tamara went in. He shut the door behind her, and Tamara turned back around and put her wrists through the access hole so that he could unlock and remove them. She went over to the bunk and sat down, leaning back against the cinder block wall.

"What a greenie," one of the other inmates sneered. "Look at the pretty little blond."

"Shut-up, Webster," another woman snapped. "You're blind. She ain't green, are you, blondie?"

Tamara looked over at the women in the next cell, considering each one of them. She turned her head back and closed her eyes.

"No, I ain't green."

"Not with those tats and that walk, you aren't," the woman agreed. "Anyone who ain't blind can tell that. What'd they get you for?"

"Drugs and parole violation."

"You going back?"

"Probably."

The woman continued to chatter on, but Tamara paid no further attention. She kept her eyes closed, thinking about going back to juvie. She was surprised that after working so hard to stay out of juvie, she now felt no anxiety about being sent back. It was a done deal. Nothing she could do about it anymore. And juvie was something familiar. She knew what to do there. She didn't have to worry any more about looking normal. Staying out of trouble. Reporting Coach McClure. All that was over and done now.

But something niggled at the back of her mind. How had the pot gotten into her locker? Her first thought had been Glock, but reviewing that idea now, Tamara was pretty sure that it hadn't been. If Glock wanted her to be arrested, all she had to do was be seen in Tamara's company. No need to break into the school to look up her locker combination and then plant the pot in her locker and report her. All Glock had to do was to show up at the house or the school and ask for her. Anyone looking at her could tell that she was a felon, someone Tamara couldn't have anything to do with. Or she could have gotten them all arrested over the weekend, starting a fight or taking them to a nightclub that would report them instead of looking the other way. She could do any number of things. No need to interfere at the school.

Sybil was the next most likely suspect. She was close to Tamara. She used weed and must have had access to it somewhere. She could possibly have watched over Tamara's shoulder as she had unlocked her locker, figured out her combination. But Tamara couldn't think of any motive that Sybil would have. She liked hanging out with Tamara. It boosted her bad-girl reputation. She liked having someone to talk to about prison tattoos and what went on in juvie. She even liked hanging with Glock, though she was much more careful since the incident at the food fair. And if she wanted to violate Tamara, all Sybil had to do was to report that she had little kids at home. Tamara had admitted to being there. Had permission to be there. Sybil planting drugs in Tamara's locker didn't make any sense.

There were other kids at school... Bernadette or any of the

other girls on the volleyball team who might be resentful or jealous of her. Jason or another boy that had showed obvious interest in her whom she had turned down, not wanting to get entangled in any kind of relationship while she was sorting her life out. But none of them would have access to her combination. Only the office had a record of her locker combination. And why would any of the teachers or administration want to get rid of her? Because they didn't want any JD's in the school? There were plenty of other kids who had been in trouble at one time or another. Tamara certainly wasn't the only one. There was no reason for any of the staff at the school to dislike or resent her.

Except for Coach McClure.

If McClure had seen her in the locker room on Friday, or thought that she had been there or that she suspected what was going on, he'd have plenty of reason to set her up. He had every reason in the world to want her to go back to juvie. To discredit her. McClure wanted her out of the way. Tamara was too dangerous to him.

(vi)

"French."

Tamara was sitting with her eyes closed, shutting everything out, just letting her consciousness drift while she waited for time to pass. It was an important skill to learn, when you had a lot of time to serve.

"French!"

She started to become aware of someone calling her name, but still wasn't fully conscious.

"French!"

The loud and annoying noise of a baton being dragged across the bars of her cell forced Tamara to return to the real world. She opened her eyes and looked at the impatient guard scowling at her.

"What?"

"You have a visitor," he snapped, and stepped back out of the way so that Tamara could see Mrs. Henson. Tamara looked at her for a moment without moving.

"What do you want?" she questioned, arms still folded across her chest, back to the wall, wishing that the guard hadn't bothered to wake her up for this. There was nothing Mrs. Henson could do now.

"Hi, Tamara. Mr. Collins told me about what happened, and I came to see how you are doing. Are you all right?"

"I'm fine. Looks like I'm headed back to juvie, so you won't have to worry about me anymore. You can get another mom with a baby."

Mrs. Henson cocked her head.

"I'm not looking to get a mom with a baby right now. You're still our foster child. And Mr. Collins said that he expected the judge to return you to parole. You're not going back to juvie."

Tamara shook her head slightly.

"Don't count on it."

"Why?"

"I know how it works. The judge is gonna take one look at me, and at the charges, and say I'm not ready. I'm a danger to the public."

"You're sounding really down... I know how disappointed you must be about being arrested. But it's not over, Tamara. It's one mistake. Other kids make mistakes too. Other adults. The judge knows that. He'll take Mr. Collins' recommendation."

Tamara shrugged. What was the point in arguing and speculating? In a few days, they would all know.

"I guess I should have talked to Mr. Collins when you asked me about sleeping over with Sybil," Mrs. Henson said. "I thought it sounded fishy, but you said that you had talked to him."

Tamara closed her eyes. "I lied."

"Yeah. I gather. So... maybe Sybil's not as good a friend as you had hoped. Not if she's encouraging you to lie, and to smoke pot."

"That was all me. No one else. Sybil's not a bad girl. She just likes people to think she is."

Mrs. Henson chuckled. "Oh, I've seen that kind before. But you should maybe be focusing on other people. Who are a bit safer and will help you to keep in line."

"Uh-huh."

Since she wasn't going back, she didn't have to worry about Mrs. Henson's recommendations of friends anymore.

"Maybe spend some time with some of the girls on the volleyball team?" Mrs. Henson suggested. "Get to know them."

Tamara opened her eyes and scowled at Mrs. Henson.

"They don't care about anyone but themselves," she growled.

Mrs. Henson raised her brows in surprise.

"Oh? You seemed okay with them before."

"I thought... I thought they were different then."

Mrs. Henson frowned.

"Do you want to talk about it?" she asked. "What happened?"

Tamara shook her head.

"I wanted to this morning. Now, I don't care anymore."

"Was it something to do with the locker search? Was that initiated by one of the girls on the team, or something?"

"Or something," Tamara said.

"If you think that someone on the team has a grudge against you, you should talk to Mr. Collins about it."

"Doesn't matter anymore. Mr. Collins wouldn't believe me anyway."

"We're here to help, Tamara. The family, Mr. Collins, Dr. Frank. Even your schoolteachers and principal. We all want you to succeed, and we want to help you out."

"Too late now."

Mrs. Henson gave a long sigh.

"We'll talk about it when you get home, then."

(vii)

"You're on the bus too," the guard told Tamara. "Get up. Let's get moving."

Tamara got to her feet and walked to the front of her cell. The guard shackled her wrists. He opened the cell door and added a waist chain and leg shackles, and chained it all together.

"All right, let's go."

He held her elbow and escorted her to the waiting transport vehicle. She got a seat near the front, where he secured her to an anchor. Tamara thought about the movies where prisoners escaped from prison buses. She never figured out how it could really be possible. Maybe some little county bus somewhere, where they had one guard with a shotgun on a retired school bus, or something like that. Certainly it wouldn't be easy to escape from any prison transport she'd ever been on. Tamara took a wary look around at the other prisoners, some of them the women who had been in the cell block that she had been jailed on, and some of them men, dirty and scruffy looking. No one said anything or made any sign. They were all properly secured. Nothing she needed to worry about. Tamara just sat and waited, letting her mind wander.

At the courthouse, she was taken to a holding room, but almost instantly Mr. Collins was there, and she was taken to a small conference room and sat across from him. Collins stretched out his long legs, studying Tamara.

"How are you doing?" he questioned.

Tamara shrugged.

"Tamara. How are you?" he persisted, not accepting her non-answer.

"Fine."

"I really want to know. It's not just a 'hello'. It can't have been easy for you, these last couple of days."

"Sitting in a cell is easy. It's being out that's hard."

"Mrs. Henson is worried about you."

"Well, after today she won't have to worry."

"You're bound and determined that you're going back to juvie, aren't you?"

Tamara nodded.

"The judge will release you to parole," Collins said.

"We'll see," Tamara said with a shrug.

"Is there something else going on here?" his eyes drilled into hers. Tamara looked away.

"Like what?"

"Hmm. Sounds like there is. What else is going on here?"

Tamara shifted her hands around, trying to move them without jangling the chains. She could really use a cigarette. She had a killer headache after two days of nicotine withdrawal.

"Mrs. Henson said you were upset about something to do with the volleyball team," Collins said.

Tamara nodded.

"What's going on there?"

Tamara looked at him, then away.

"Has there been more trouble because of the fight?"

"No."

"Something else?"

Tamara bit her lip. She glanced around the conference room. "Can you smoke in here?"

Collins shook his head. "You can't smoke inside any city building. By-laws. So what's bothering you with the team? You're not getting along with them?"

Tamara sighed. "I get along okay... but they don't care what happens to each other. They're not... not a real team."

"You have problems with their team spirit?" Collins asked disbelievingly, eyebrows up.

"No."

"I can't just keep guessing here, Tamara. Is the problem with the other girls or the coach?"

Tamara breathed through her mouth. Her chest was hurting. This was the conversation. She had decided that she wasn't going to tell, and now here she was.

"The coach," she said shakily. "He... he's... messing with the players."

Collins' eyes narrowed. "You mean he's damaging their sports careers?" he suggested. "You don't think he's a good enough coach?"

Tamara pressed her lips together and swallowed. She breathed out slowly. She was not being clear enough, not really wanting to say the words.

"No. He's... molesting them."

Her mouth was suddenly so dry she could hardly form the words. Collins stared at her, brows drawn down so that he looked angry.

"That's a very serious accusation, Tamara."

"The girl I replaced on the team, she got pregnant. She didn't even have a boyfriend."

"It's quite a jump from there to accusing the coach."

"I saw him in the showers with Lotta. In the showers—he's not even supposed to be there. He was touching her. She was crying."

Collins scratched the back of his head. "When did this happen?"

"Last Friday, after practice."

"Why didn't you tell anyone?"

"I was trying to figure out what to do... I wasn't sure... and I was so sick, worrying about it... Tuesday when I finally went to school... I went to the office to tell Mr. Van Rhyn."

"Why didn't you call me?"

"I just... didn't know what to do."

"I told you to call me if you had any problems or concerns. About anything. Don't you think this qualifies?"

Tamara stared down at the table, nodding.

"How do you think it looks coming to me now, after you've been arrested?" he questioned. "Now it just looks like you're being vindictive."

"Was it Coach who said to search my locker?"

"You know I can't tell you that."

"How would he know there was weed in my locker?"

"I guess another student might have told him. A student who didn't know what to do, and went to a mentor for advice," he said with heavy irony.

"Yeah. I should've talked to you," Tamara admitted. "But you think juvie taught me to trust people? I'm still trying to work it out."

Collins sighed and rubbed his temples.

"And how am I supposed to trust you?" he countered. "You don't talk to me, you sneak off for the weekend, and get caught with marijuana? I don't know what else you might have done that I haven't found out about. But you expect me to believe that the volleyball coach is a child molester, and that you don't have an ulterior motive to say so."

Tamara shrugged.

"Whatever. You asked. Won't affect me, I'll be in juvie."

(*viii*)

Tamara remembered the last time she had been in court. She spent most of the trial with her head lying in her folded arms on the table, shutting everything out. She had no family or friends. Her court-appointed lawyer hadn't spent a lot of time talking to her. They hadn't connected. Eventually, he had convinced her that the best thing to do would be to confess. He wrote the confession. Tamara read it to the court in a small, shaky voice. And then the judge had sentenced her.

And here she was again. She had confessed to Collins, and he read her confession into the court record. There was no lawyer at her table, just Collins. It took all of Tamara's focus to sit up and look like she was paying attention rather than dissociating like she had before. She just wanted to close her eyes and shut it all out. It was a short hearing, but even so, she still caught her mind wandering, eyes closed, far away from reality. She tried to look at the judge, an elderly woman, to look like a repentant sinner, a kid who could still make it. But she didn't believe it herself, so she wasn't sure how convincing she was.

"All right, Mr. Collins," the judge said. "Your recommendation is to return her to parole? You think you can help her?"

"Yes, your Honor. She has promise. I think with some more work, we can turn things around, make her a contributing member of society."

Tamara looked at the judge, focusing on the bridge of her nose. This was the moment of truth. Her last few seconds of freedom.

"So be it," the judge said, banging her gavel. "Remanded to her parole officer. To appear before this court in... four weeks, on the charge of simple possession."

Everyone stood up and started talking. Tamara looked up at Collins in disbelief. He smiled thinly and nodded.

"What did I tell you?"

Tamara didn't answer. Didn't move. The guard who had escorted her in caught her elbow and stood her up. Tamara didn't move as he unlocked the shackles and pulled them off.

"You got something to change into?" he asked.

Tamara shook her head. Mr. Collins cleared his throat.

"Mrs. Henson will have something. I asked her to bring them with her."

"Missus...?" Tamara looked around, and saw that Mrs. Henson was, in fact, in the spectator seating, watching her.

The guard nodded. "Go ahead and get it from her," he told Collins. "I'll get the girl changed. She'll still need to be formally signed out of the jail, but she can leave here with you."

Collins went to the rail and Mrs. Henson passed the clothing over to him. He handed them to Tamara, and the guard led her out of the courtroom to a small anteroom, where she removed the jail clothes and put on the street clothes Mrs. Henson had brought. She smoothed the shirt lightly, not quite believing that she was, again, free.

TEN

(i)

MRS. HENSON SMILED AT Tamara as she started the car.

"I hope the clothes are okay," she said. "The girls pulled together your ensemble. I had no idea how you would feel about it."

Tamara looked down at her street clothes. Her own pants. A pink button-up shirt layered over top of a white t-shirt with an eyelet pattern. A few items of clunky jewelry.

"It's okay," she said, shrugging. "It's kinda preppy for me, but what do I care? It's not juvie orange."

"Be sure to tell them thanks. They wanted to do something for you, but I didn't want to bring them to court in case it might upset you."

Tamara nodded.

"Yeah, okay."

"Can we talk now about some strategies to help you succeed? Now that you know you get a second chance?"

"Go ahead."

"No, Tamara. This is a discussion, between two people. Not a lecture."

Tamara swallowed. She thought about it.

"You don't think I should see Sybil."

"I don't think you should be spending much time over there. Maybe she could come over to our house. That would be okay. She could come for supper, and you guys could do your homework here."

"She has to—" Tamara cut herself off before revealing that Sybil had little sisters to take care of. Her face got hot. That would be a really stupid thing to reveal. "Yeah. Maybe. I'll ask."

"And maybe there are some other friends that you could do things with too. There's no reason you need to just have one friend that you spend all of your time with. You can have lots of friends."

Tamara ran her finger up and down the seams of her pants.

"I'm not that good at making friends," she said. "And once people know I've been in juvie... the ones you'd like don't want to be friends with me."

"I'm sure we can figure something out. If you're not getting along with the girls on the volleyball team, maybe there's another club or something that you could join, get to know people that way."

Tamara rolled her eyes and sighed.

"Okay," said Mrs. Henson, realizing she wasn't going to get very far along this line. "No more sleepovers for you. Check with me about going anywhere else before you leave school, not once you're already somewhere else." Tamara nodded. "How about the drugs? What can I do to help you avoid that temptation?"

"I dunno."

"Does Sybil have drugs in her house?"

"No!"

"Where did you guys go to get it, then?"

Tamara tried to invent an answer that would be acceptable.

Somewhere they might have gone that she could promise not to go again. A way not to get Sybil any deeper into this than she already was. Her head pounded and she closed her eyes, rubbing her temples.

"Umm... it was just spur of the moment. This guy at the convenience store. We just went to get drinks. Soft drinks. He asked... We thought... no biggie... just help to take the edge off..."

"So, that's not a good idea. You stay away from there. Just snack on what is already at home. Was this a guy from school?"

"No. Just a random guy..."

"You guys shouldn't be stopping to talk to some random guy on the street. He could be dangerous. You don't know what that pot might be laced with, or if he might follow you home or have somebody working with him. That's dangerous."

Tamara nodded.

"Yeah, I guess it was stupid," she agreed, opening her eyes again.

"What can we do to help reduce the stress a little? You're already seeing Dr. Frank. Does he have any suggestions?"

Tamara picked at her nails.

"I don't really... like Dr. Frank."

"Oh... well that doesn't help, does it? Is there something in particular...?"

"He..." Tamara breathed out heavily. "Nothing. Never mind."

"I'd like to hear. If we're going to find you another therapist, we're going to need to know what to look for. What won't work."

She chewed her thumbnail.

"He thinks I killed the cats."

"No, he doesn't. If he thought you had, he'd have to report it to Mr. Collins, recommend that you be remanded."

"He doesn't think I *didn't* do it," Tamara countered.

Mrs. Henson made a sucking noise with her lips, thinking about that.

"He's not sure, you mean."

"I guess, yeah."

"Okay. Let me talk to the team about it and see if we can find someone else for you. Do you want a female therapist? Someone younger? A certain kind of professional? Anything particular?"

"No... just someone who doesn't think I'm psychotic."

Mrs. Henson snickered.

"Yeah, okay. I'll work on that."

(ii)

Almost the instant Tamara got home, her phone buzzed in her pocket, making her jump. She glanced at Mrs. Henson to make sure that she hadn't seen.

Tamara went up to her room and closed the door before pulling out the phone and flipping it open. She was lucky it still had battery power left. They had powered it down at the police station before putting it away. She looked at the message on the screen, from a number she didn't know.

Go outside for a smoke.

She knew who it would be. She texted back.

They'll be watching me.

The reply came back a moment later.

Tell them you're going for a walk.

Tamara took off her pink shirt and pulled a blue-jean jacket out of her closet. She'd borrowed it from her foster sisters earlier and hadn't yet returned it. Neither of them was really into the distressed look and they hadn't asked for it back. She went back downstairs, and heard Mrs. Henson cursing over the washing machine in the basement. Even better.

"Missus, I'm going out for a walk."

"Umm... okay Tamara. That sounds good. Get some fresh air. Try to be back in an hour or so, okay?"

"Okay."

She went out the back door, and looked quickly around the back yard. She couldn't see Glock. She went out to the back lane. Glock was leaning against a power pole, smoking.

"There's our Princess," she said.

"Hey." Tamara motioned to Glock's cigarette eagerly. "Gimme."

Glock grinned and held it out to her. Tamara's heart raced as she took it and put it to her mouth. She took a deep lung-full of smoke and held it. Her headache gradually receded. Her body relaxed. She breathed out slowly, closing her eyes.

"Better?" Glock asked.

"Mmm-hmm."

"Let's walk, then."

Tamara opened her eyes and looked at Glock. Glock stared at her, one eyebrow lifted. Tamara wanted to argue, but her stomach clenched into a tight knot. All she had to do was open her mouth and say one word of disagreement, and Glock would do whatever it took to convince her. After all of their time in juvie, it didn't take much to convince her anymore. That one look was enough. Tamara fell in beside her, and they walked down the lane.

"Told'ya in juvie you shouldn't take up smoking," Glock teased. "Terrible habit."

Tamara shook her head.

"Yeah, right," she said. Of course it had been Glock who insisted that she take those first few cigarettes and got her hooked.

They walked in silence for some time. Tamara looked around anxiously, worried that they would be seen. But she knew better than to argue with Glock about it.

"Happy to be home?" Glock asked.

"Happy to be out," Tamara said. "Don't know about home."

"You're not havin' fun playing house with the Hensons anymore?"

Tamara shook her head.

"It's just... so hard. Trying to fit in and act normal after juvie..." She shook her head. "Being back in jail was easier."

Glock nodded.

"First they make you into an outcast, then they try to straighten you out. Doesn't make much sense, does it?"

"They keep saying I can do it, but they don't make it easy," Tamara admitted.

Glock ran a lock of Tamara's hair between two of her fingers. It was once again limp and lank.

"How long before you figure out that it's just talk? No one expects you to make it. They know what they've made you. It's just to soothe their consciences."

Tamara scowled.

"You don't believe me?" Glock demanded. "How many JD's do you know that have reformed? How many living that 'normal life' you keep talking about?"

"I only know the ones that came back to juvie," Tamara pointed out. "And I'm not allowed to have contact with anyone from juvie out here."

"Uh-huh," Glock agreed. "Convenient, eh?"

"People make it," Tamara insisted.

"Do they?"

"Sure they do. I could do it."

"That's what you've learned so far?" Glock snorted. "You never were a quick study."

She held out her hand for her cigarette, and Tamara returned it to her.

"They gave me a second chance," Tamara argued. "They could have just sent me back to juvie this time."

"They want you to think that it's up to you," Glock said. "That you can choose whether to succeed or fail. But it's got nothing to do with what you choose. They're just waiting for you to make a big enough mistake that they don't have to feel guilty about sending you back."

Tamara shook her head.

"Well, I'm not going to make one."

Glock chuckled.

"Yeah, baby. You just keep telling yourself that. They know what they made you. They just have to wait now."

"I can choose," Tamara insisted. "I can be straight."

"You think you're still the same person you were before juvie? Before going to that foster home?"

Tamara knew the answer without thinking about it. But she didn't answer immediately.

"No. I'm stronger now," she said, chin lifted.

"Yeah, you're stronger," Glock agreed, "but you're bent the wrong direction. You're not straight, Princess. And you can't unbend yourself."

"I can."

"You think if you don't make any mistakes, you won't go back to juvie?"

Tamara nodded.

"Like you weren't set up this time?" Glock prodded.

Tamara narrowed her eyes at Glock. "What do you know about that?" she demanded.

"I know you wouldn't even get close to the weed we had last weekend."

Tamara stared at Glock, trying to determine if Glock was telling the truth, or if she had been involved in planting the pot and tipping Collins to search her locker.

"I don't need to set you up," Glock said. "The game's already rigged against you. It's going to happen sooner or later, without me doing anything."

Tamara pulled her gaze from Glock and looked ahead as they walked. "I think it was the coach," she said.

Glock nodded. "He know you saw him?"

"I think so."

"Then he's not gonna stop there."

Tamara nodded, biting her lip.

"How long before you see that the only way out is to leave?" Glock questioned. "Get out of the game and just make a run for it. It doesn't make any sense to keep trying to play it by their rules. They'll just send you back."

Tamara shook her head. "I have to try."

(iii)

Tamara glanced at the time on her phone as she returned to the house. She had been over an hour, but just by a bit. She didn't think that Mrs. Henson would be that strict about her being exactly an hour. Taking a calming breath, she opened the door and braved the lion's den.

Mrs. Henson was in the kitchen, starting to prepare supper.

"Hi. Did you have a nice walk?" she asked.

"Yeah. Nice to... be able to stretch my legs."

"Good. It's a beautiful day out there today."

Tamara nodded.

"You need help with dinner?" she asked after watching Mrs. Henson for a few minutes.

"Shouldn't you be doing homework?"

"I'll have to get it tomorrow. I don't know what I've got to do to get caught up."

"Monday," Mrs. Henson amended.

"What?"

"Tomorrow is Saturday. You'll have to wait until Monday."

"Oh. Yeah, I guess."

"You don't have any unfinished assignments from last week? Studying?"

"If tomorrow's Saturday, I'll do it then."

"Well, I've never been one to turn down the offer of assistance. Can you chop some veggies for the salad?"

"Sure."

Mrs. Henson got her started at the cutting board, supplying her with a mound of vegetables to start cutting, and went back to give her pot a stir. The doorbell rang. Sighing, Mrs. Henson wiped her hands on a towel and went to get it. Tamara breathed slowly and evenly. It wasn't likely to be Mr. Collins; she'd just seen him, and she hadn't had time to get in any more trouble since then. He had plenty of other parolees to keep track of. No one else would come to see Tamara.

She heard an irate man's voice rising.

"He was chained, and the gates were latched. There's no way he could have gotten out of the yard without someone intentionally releasing him! I've called, and called, and there's no sign of him. He always comes when he's called!"

Tamara listened closely.

"Tamara couldn't have had anything to do with it," Mrs. Henson said. "She hasn't been here for three days, and before that she was sick. It doesn't have anything to do with her."

"Everything was fine until that girl came. That's when the animals started to disappear. And Lorna's cat was found in your yard. It doesn't make sense that it is anyone but her."

"Tamara couldn't have had anything to do with it. It's pure coincidence."

"You're blind. I'd think that after all of the kids you've fostered, you'd be able to see what was in front of your own face. I've never liked having to live near a foster home, but this is a whole different story. You've got to get rid of her. Can't you see that?"

"Tamara has not had any opportunity to interfere with your dog. I'm sorry, but it's someone else."

"She's back today, isn't she? I saw her earlier, wandering the streets. You'd better keep her indoors, or I'll call the police."

"Mr. Allen," Mrs. Henson's voice was reasonable, persuasive. "I saw Tamara when she found that cat. The poor girl was sick to her stomach, nearly fainting. I promise you, she didn't have anything to do with it getting... killed."

"She's a good actor, that's all. She's enjoying leading you along. She's like a fire-setter who goes back to watch the fire burn and help the firemen. She gets a sick enjoyment out of pretending to be distressed like everyone else."

"No, sir. You're wrong. I'm sorry you've lost your dog, but it does not have anything to do with Tamara. If you don't believe me, you are welcome to check our yard. But there's nothing there. Good-bye."

The door shut with a jarring clatter. Tamara looked down at the vegetables and cut them studiously, not saying anything or looking up as Mrs. Henson came back in and looked at her. Mrs. Henson went back to preparing supper, without further comment.

(iv)

Jesse came down later while the table was being set and dinner dishes assembled. Tamara watched him covertly while she got out the salad dressings and helped to arrange the table. Even though he'd never made any kind of move on her, she was still nervous around him. He seemed to sense it and kept his distance, but there was a watchfulness between the two of them.

"Who was at the door earlier?" Jesse inquired.

"Mr. Allen," Mrs. Henson said. She pressed her lips together into a thin line.

Jesse looked at his wife, brow furrowed.

"What was he here for?"

Mrs. Henson glanced toward Tamara. Jesse followed her gaze. They both saw that Tamara was listening to the conversation, and looked awkward.

"Not another one," Jesse said lowly.

Mrs. Henson nodded.

"His dog. Taken right out of his yard. It was chained." She pressed her lips together and shook her head. "I don't know what to do."

"Well, it's not up to us to do anything," Jesse said with a shrug. "It's a police matter."

"I suppose. I just worry," another covert glance toward Tamara, "about a confrontation."

Jesse nodded and didn't answer. Everybody drifted toward the table and sat down.

"Hey, Tamara, good to have you back," Nita said, smiling.

"Have a nice break?" Harry asked, eyes dancing with mischief.

Tamara had to laugh at him. She appreciated the comic relief, when everyone else was being so nice and careful.

"Yeah, always good to get away," she returned, and then stared down at her plate, her face getting hot.

No one chided them for being inappropriate, and conversation moved on while they dished up. Jesse looked over at Tamara.

"Enjoy your walk today?"

Tamara froze, and looked up from the salad bowl to his face. He was casual, not appearing to have a motive in asking her.

"Yeah," Tamara said. "Nice day."

"Was that your friend Sybil that you were with?"

Tamara darted a glance at Mrs. Henson, then back at Jesse. She coughed into her arm and passed the salad to her left. It wouldn't do to tell Jesse that she'd been with Sybil; if Tamara ended up inviting Sybil over like Mrs. Henson had suggested, Jesse would know immediately that it wasn't the same girl.

"Uh—no," Tamara fumbled. "Just a girl from school that I ran into. So we talked for a while."

"Oh, who was it?" Mrs. Henson asked. "You didn't tell me you ran into anyone."

"Just a girl. I—I don't remember her name. I've seen her... I guess she knows who I am... everyone knows who I am, after the locker search."

It sounded fake to her own ears. Her heart raced, and Tamara looked briefly at Jesse, sure he would detect the lie. He frowned, considering her answer.

"You looked pretty... close," he said.

"Why're you always getting on my case about my friends?" Tamara demanded, her voice rising. "I can be friends with who I want!"

"You said you weren't friends," he said calmly. "I'm just trying to figure out the truth, here."

"The truth is it's none of your business," Tamara snapped. "I don't need anyone telling me who I can have for friends."

"I didn't, Tamara. I just asked you who she was, and I think you're feeding me a line."

Tamara pushed herself back from the table and stormed off to her room. After she slammed the door, she could hear someone mounting the stairs after her. Tamara grabbed a pillow and threw it across the room, swearing. She swore repeatedly as the footsteps grew closer. The door opened, and Tamara's fists went up, ready. Jesse entered her room. Tamara shifted her feet, glancing around the room to establish the advantages and drawbacks of her situation. It was a small room, but she had trained in close quarters and he probably hadn't. That was to Tamara's advantage. The room was pretty bare, not a lot that could be used as a weapon. That was a disadvantage. Jesse was bigger and stronger than her, a weapon would help to even the odds.

"Whoa, chill," Jesse said, stopping short and holding his hands up in a 'halt' command when he took in Tamara's stance. "I'm not going to hurt you, Tamara. Stand down."

She didn't move. Of course he was going to say that. If he could get her to lower her guard, he would have the advantage of surprise. Right now, he didn't have it. Tamara was ready.

"Stay back, then," Tamara countered.

He put his hands down, at his sides. Tamara looked him over anxiously. Putting his hands down did not mean that he was less dangerous. He could have a concealed sheath that was more accessible with his hands down. Something in his pockets. Tucked in his waistband behind his back. Tamara bounced on her toes, ready.

"I just want to talk, Tamara."

"I don't want to talk. Just leave me alone."

"You think I'm attacking your choice of friends but I'm not. I'm just asking about what's going on. I get the feeling that you're lying to me, concealing something, and that's not helpful. We need to be open with each other if we're going to work things out. If there's a problem, let's sort it out."

Tamara shook her head. "There's no problem," she insisted.

"Then what are you hiding?"

"I want some privacy," Tamara insisted. "I haven't had any for three years. I'm not in prison anymore!"

"No. I'm glad you realize that. This isn't prison. This is family. People who want to help you. If you'll just let us."

"You don't have to know everything about me."

"Tamara..." Jesse laughed a little. "We know next to nothing about you. You keep everything wrapped up and hidden. You say you just want a little privacy, but you keep everything private. Every thought. Every feeling. The past. The present. You don't want to share anything. Risk anything."

Tamara shifted her stance.

"About all we know about you is your parole release papers," Jesse said. "And that doesn't give us a picture of who you really are."

Tamara swallowed. She cleared her throat and blurted it out.

"In my last foster family... they beat me, if I didn't work hard enough. And even if I did. And he... he got me pregnant."

She could see his shock at her words. Had Social Services

really not told them that? Did they think that those details were so unimportant? Just a footnote on her file? It had changed the person Tamara was. Had led her to do things she still couldn't talk about. It had shaped who she had become.

"That's not going to happen here," Jesse said quietly. "I won't lay a finger on you. I'll never touch you without your permission."

Permission. Tamara wondered if Mr. Baker had thought she gave him permission. She had been lonely, isolated, had lost everyone she loved. Without the Bakers, she would have been homeless. It wasn't hard to get someone's permission when they were so wounded and their body was all they had left. But never again. She was strong now. She knew how to fight, how to protect herself. She knew that she had the right to protect her own body and self, and she would. She wouldn't give up that fight again. She would do whatever she had to.

"Just keep away from me," she warned, vivid flashbacks of Mr. Baker making her anxious. "Leave me alone."

"I'm not moving," Jesse reassured her. "I won't get any closer."

Tamara watched him, her heart thumping. He didn't come toward her. Didn't raise his hands. Just stood there, waiting.

"I'm sorry you were hurt by your foster parents," Jesse said. "That makes it hard to trust."

"Duh."

"Thank you for sharing that with me."

Tamara watched, waiting for his next move.

"Why don't you tell me about your friends," Jesse suggested. "The girl you met today. And Sybil. We don't know them."

"You wouldn't like them."

Jesse smiled slightly. "Why not?"

"They're not like you. Not... normal."

"What's normal?" he laughed.

"They're... they're okay with me being different. They're different." She relaxed her stance just slightly. "I dunno."

"Rebellious?" Jesse suggested. "The girl I saw looked sort of like a biker or something."

Tamara nodded.

"How old is she?" Jesse frowned. "She looked a bit old to be in your school."

"That's just because she's big," Tamara dismissed, mentally kicking herself for saying that Glock went to school with her.

"I guess. You don't know her name?"

Tamara hesitated. If she gave Glock's real name, they might check it out and find out that she was a convict, not a schoolmate. And if she made something up, she might not remember it next time.

"No."

Jesse leaned against the doorframe, in a relaxed posture.

"My wife informs me that you may be getting together with Sybil tomorrow."

"Yeah. Maybe she'll come here."

"I'd like to meet her. You understand the rules? No sleep-overs. No going to someone else's house without checking first."

Tamara nodded.

"Missus already told me."

"The other kids have been through this before," Jesse said. "Don't feel like you're alone. We'll help you out. You can do it, just like the others have."

Tamara rolled her eyes.

"We're here for you, Tamara," Jesse reiterated. "Think about it. Thank you for being open with me."

He withdrew from the room, pulling the door shut as he left. Tamara waited until the noise of his footsteps took him downstairs. Then she relaxed her muscles with a long sigh. She swore again under her breath, and melted onto her bed.

(v)

The next day, Tamara had been texting with Sybil, but she waited until the doorbell rang to run down the stairs and let her in. Sybil gave her an impulsive hug.

"Hey, babe. I missed you!"

Tamara swallowed a lump in her throat, touched by the remark. She gave Sybil a squeeze and then let go.

"Come on," she invited, taking off up the stairs. Sybil followed.

Mrs. Henson came out of her room to greet them at the top of the stairs.

"Hi. I'm Mrs. Henson, Tamara's foster mom. Sybil?"

Sybil nodded.

"Yeah. Good to meet you."

"You guys are going to work on homework, not just gossip?"

Sybil laughed.

"Sure. Probably about half-and-half."

Mrs. Henson smiled at this.

"Okay. Let me know if you need anything, Tamara."

Tamara led Sybil into her room and shut the door. Sybil looked around the room, then sat down on the bed.

"So," she grabbed Tamara's hands. "Tell me. What was it like?"

"What, jail?" Tamara asked. Sybil nodded. "Boring. At least at juvie, we had classes, and TV in the common room, and all. The jail at the police station... just sitting, waiting."

"There wasn't anyone else to talk to?"

"There were women in the other cells. No juvies. No one I wanted to talk to."

"That sucks."

Tamara nodded.

"Glock's really ticked about me coming over here to visit, and she can't," Sybil said.

Tamara waved this aside.

"I saw her yesterday. We talked."

"Yeah, well. Just be warned. She's not happy."

Tamara nodded.

"Yeah, okay. We'll go see her later. For a few minutes. But the parents wanted me to make nice and invite you over. I gotta keep them happy first."

"You don't want to be sent back," Sybil agreed.

"I gotta figure out how to get rid of Glock."

"What? Why do you want to get rid of her? You guys have a good time together."

"*She* has a good time," Tamara countered. "I'm not supposed to be around anyone with a record. And I can't exactly argue that I didn't know she had a record if we get caught."

"Well, so don't get caught. Why would she have to leave? Nobody's figured it out yet. You're safe."

"It's not safe. I don't want to do anything that might get me sent back. Mr. Henson—Jesse—already saw her yesterday. What if he reports it to Collins? I gotta get her to leave."

Sybil shook her head.

"Good luck with that," she said. "She's pretty... attached to you. She waited, what, a year for you to get out?"

"Little more than that."

"That's a long time. You'd be better off leaving with her. Get both of you out of here. But then I'd be sad." She made a mournful face. "Maybe you could run away, but still stay in town."

Tamara shook her head.

"I'm not running away at all. I want to do the right thing. I want to make it work."

(v)

Sybil and Tamara arrived at Glock's place. Tamara didn't

have to knock, Glock must have been watching for them, because she was standing at her door in the hallway as they arrived. She was scowling. As Sybil had warned, she was not in a good mood.

"Hey," Tamara greeted.

Glock motioned them in.

"We can't stay long," Tamara said. "I just told Missus that we were going to the mall."

"I got a movie," Glock said curtly, motioning to the television. "Just press play."

Tamara obeyed. Sybil hung back, saying something quietly to Glock. Tamara watched the TV for a minute, wondering what kind of movie Glock would pick out. It appeared to be a pirated version of an action movie that had been released recently and was still showing in the theaters.

"Cool," she said, glad it wasn't something that was going to make her sick to watch. With Glock's predilections, you never knew.

"I got you a drink," Glock said, brandishing what looked like a champagne bottle toward Tamara.

Tamara frowned.

"I'm not drinking," she maintained.

"No, look," Glock insisted, bringing it over to Tamara and thrusting it in front of her face. "It's not alcohol."

Examining the label, Tamara discovered that it was sparkling grape juice, clearly labeled 'non-alcoholic'. She smiled at Glock, genuinely pleased.

"You did that for me? Thanks!"

"Had to toast your release with something, didn't we?" Glock said, giving her a rough hug around the shoulders.

"Can I open it?" Sybil offered. "I want to pop the cork."

Glock handed it to her, shaking her head in amusement.

Tamara watched Sybil take it back to the kitchenette to unwrap the foil and pop the cork. Sybil giggled. Glock sat down next to Tamara on the bed, watching the opening action of the movie.

"Did you hear about Chips?" she asked.

Chips was one of the girls who had been with them at juvie. Not a friend or someone you could get close to. She was independent, not in any of the gangs, but that didn't make her friends with Glock and Tamara, or any of the other girls who weren't in the gangs. Tamara shuddered, remembering a particularly brutal fight between Chips and Glock that Tamara had accidentally provoked.

"No," she said, looking at Glock's face. "What happened with Chips?"

"Big high-speed chase with the cops," Glock said with a laugh. "Ended up in a huge crash, smashing into a police barricade, rolling the car, gas tank exploding and everything."

Tamara gaped.

"Was she... did she die?"

"They got her out before it exploded. Lots of damage, crippled bad. Still life-threatening condition, last I heard."

"Whoa. You think she'll be okay?"

"Would you want to survive that? What's the point in living if you don't have control over your body anymore?"

Sybil put a glass into Tamara's hand, and she took the first few swallows without even tasting it, she was so horrified by Glock's story.

"How did you hear about it?" she asked.

"I got connections, kiddo. You may want to cut yourself off from everyone from juvie, but I keep my ear to the grapevine."

Tamara sipped at the drink.

"That's really awful."

"Yup," Glock agreed cheerfully. "Good old Chips."

They watched the television screen, thinking about Chips. Tamara started to relax, feeling warm and comfortable. She watched the car crashes on the TV, thinking about Chips' accident. It was a funny coincidence, Glock getting a smash-up movie when Chips had just been in a terrible accident. She started to giggle.

Glock glanced at her and smiled in approval, then looked at Sybil.

"Princess needs a refill," she pointed to Tamara's glass.

"Sure," Sybil agreed.

"What's so funny?" Glock asked Tamara.

"The show... and Chips... it's—it's funny, isn't it?" Tamara laughed.

"Yeah," Glock agreed, brushing Tamara's face with the back of her fingers. "It is, isn't it?" Glock took a deep draught of her own drink.

Tamara accepted a top-up from Sybil and took another sip. She looked at Sybil, frowning.

"That's not the same bottle."

Sybil laughed.

"Yes, it is!" she teased.

Tamara drank it down. She stretched, feeling relaxed and loose for the first time in weeks.

"What are we doing tonight?" she asked.

Glock raised an eyebrow.

"What do you want to do?"

"I dunno. Let's go out. Have some fun!"

"Sure," Glock agreed. "How about you, Syb?"

"I'm game," Sybil agreed.

ELEVEN

(i)

TAMARA STUMBLED, AND GLOCK held her under the elbow, keeping her on her feet and steadying her.

"Slow down, baby doll. You're going to end up flat on your face."

"We need a car," Tamara said.

Glock nodded.

"A car would be good," she agreed. "How about it, Sybil? You gonna get us a car?"

Sybil scratched her ear.

"Uh... I can't get a car..." she protested.

"Well, I can," Glock chuckled. "Here. Hang onto Miss Priss for a minute, while I rustle up a ride for us."

Sybil took Tamara by the arm.

"Just stay here a minute," she urged, trying to keep Tamara still. Tamara tried to go after Glock, but Sybil held tight. "Stay and talk to me. She'll be back."

"Where's she going?" Tamara asked.

"Getting you a car."

"Where?"

"Don't ask, I don't think we want to know the details."

It seemed to Tamara like it was a long time before Glock drove up beside them, giving the horn a tap in greeting.

"There she is," Sybil said. "Climb in."

"I want to drive."

"No," Sybil laughed. "Glock's driving. You'll just get in a wreck."

"I want to drive," Tamara insisted. Why shouldn't she be allowed?

Sybil opened the door for her, and Tamara shook her head. Sybil attempted to push her into the seat. Tamara resisted.

"What's wrong?" Glock demanded, leaning over to talk to Sybil through the open door.

"She won't get in," Sybil explained. "She wants to drive."

Glock laughed. She put the car into park, and climbed out.

"You wanna drive?" she offered. "Go ahead."

Tamara made her way around the car, holding onto it to steady herself. She slid into the driver's seat.

"You can't let her drive!" Sybil protested.

"Why not?" Glock challenged. She got into shot-gun, forcing Sybil to get in the back seat, or be left behind. Glock looked at Tamara. "You ever drive before?"

"How hard can it be?" Tamara asked.

Glock laughed again.

"Not hard at all." She looked out at Sybil. "You coming, or not?"

Grumbling, Sybil climbed into the back seat.

"She's going to kill us all."

Tamara couldn't reach the pedals. She stretched to reach them.

"You gotta move your seat forward," Glock advised.

Tamara groped for the release, but couldn't find it. Glock

leaned over to release it, and shoved the seat, sending Tamara rocketing forward.

"Whoa!"

"How's that?"

Tamara nodded, touching the pedals.

"Yeah, that's good."

She looked for the gear shift, and noticed that Glock had started the car with a screwdriver rather than keys. Tamara giggled at this. Who knew you could start a car with a screwdriver? Why didn't everyone do that? She shifted into drive and the car crept forward. After a few minutes of jerky starts and stops, she was getting the hang of it.

"Take this exit," Glock pointed.

Tamara cornered a little wildly, and made the off ramp. She found herself on the freeway, with cars whizzing by. She stepped on the gas to bring the car up to speed with that of traffic, and laughed with exhilaration.

"Wheee! This is great!"

"Go girl!" Glock encouraged, leaning forward, grinning madly.

"We're all gonna die!" Sybil squealed from the back seat.

Tamara and Glock thought this was hilarious, and Tamara pushed the gas pedal to the floor, edging past other cars as the engine roared. She found a clear lane, and watched the scenery and other cars whipping by the window.

"It's fun!" she laughed.

Tamara decided to see how many other cars she could pass. Glock egged her on. Then suddenly, Glock froze.

"Cops," she said, twisting around to look behind them. "Pull over to the side. Turn off your lights."

Tamara stomped on the brake and pulled the car over with a screech of tires. She looked for the button that would turn off the lights. Glock reached across her and twisted a knob. She shifted into park.

"Feet off the pedals," she instructed.

Tamara obeyed, and they turned to watch the approach of a couple of police cars. They rocketed past the darkened car without even slowing.

"Okay. We gotta get off this highway before they figure it out," Glock said. "Keep your lights off, and take this exit. Nice and slow."

Tamara followed Glock's instructions, and in a few minutes they were back to cruising the city streets.

"We need to stop for some more drinks," Tamara suggested.

"Sure," Glock agreed. "Let me find a club that will let you guys in."

"And pot," Tamara said. "A whole lotta weed."

It seemed unfair that she had been accused of having pot in her possession and using it, when she'd never even tried it. If she was going to be convicted of using it, she should at least have a taste of what it was like.

Glock grinned over her shoulder at Sybil.

"We got us a whole different girl here this weekend," she observed.

"Do you think we should get her back?" Sybil asked. "We don't want her to get into too much trouble."

"She's already missed curfew, and she's drunk as a skunk. You take her back now, and she's going straight back to juvie."

"Oh."

"There's no more parole anymore," Glock said, a hard-looking smile on her face. "She's gotta run, now."

Tamara drove slowly down the strip, carefully avoiding the partiers who kept crossing the street in front of the car, until Glock indicated the club that she wanted to go to.

"There. Moby Dick. I can get us all in there."

There were no spaces that Tamara could see in the parking lot, so she simply pulled close, double-parking beside a black Mercedes, and they all got out.

"Won't it get towed?" Sybil asked.

"We'll get another one," Glock said.

"You got another screwdriver?" Tamara giggled.

"I always have another screwdriver, baby. Come on."

(ii)

Tamara had been dancing with Glock and Sybil, but there was a period of missing time, and she didn't know how she had ended up in the dimly lit hall with a heavily jeweled man who seemed to be all hands. Tamara struggled to free herself from him, but he held her pinned against the wall and forced his mouth over hers. He smelled and tasted foul. Tamara squirmed and tried to kick, but he had her effectively immobilized, and she couldn't escape. She tried to turn her head away, but he gripped her jaw tightly, not letting her move. Tamara was having trouble breathing, between the pressure of his body on her chest, and the smothering kiss. She gagged, and he withdrew slightly for a moment, staring at her with glinting black eyes. Tamara coughed, and tried again to push him away.

"There you are!"

The man was startled by Glock's voice, and turned to look around at her.

"Get lost," he ordered in a hoarse, out-of-breath voice. "None of your business."

"She is my business," Glock countered, moving in quickly on them. "She's my girl, so unless you want to be hurtin', you'd better make nice and apologize."

"Apologize?" he repeated. "For what?"

"For even thinking of touching her," Glock growled.

The man's body went suddenly rigid. Tamara couldn't see what was happening in the space between Glock and the man. He released Tamara. She stayed leaning against the wall, not sure where else to go. The man held his hands up.

"I let her go," he pointed out. "So why don't you just take her and scram?"

"I told you to apologize," Glock insisted.

But he didn't apologize. His body, still touching Tamara's, though no longer pressing her against the wall, convulsed, and twisted around toward Glock. He made a strangled sound, a gurgle, and started to crumple to the floor. Glock grabbed Tamara's arm, and pulled her.

"Come on. Scram."

Tamara let herself be pulled along, out of the hallway, back to the dance floor, full of dizzying motion and lights and blaring sound with a heavy beat. Glock quickly found Sybil.

"Oh, you got her," Sybil observed, with a sloppy grin.

"Move. We're leaving," Glock instructed in a hard voice.

"Why?"

"Now."

Glock's grip on Tamara's arm was hurting. But she knew better than to try to pull away. She stroked Glock's fingers with her other hand.

"Hey Glock..." she coaxed.

"What do you think you're doing, wandering off like that?" Glock demanded angrily, gripping more tightly and giving her a shake. "You want to get hurt?"

Tamara saw stars and swayed on her feet. Glock swore and released Tamara's arm, winding her arm instead around Tamara's body and supporting her.

"Hold this," she told Sybil, thrusting something into her hand. "And come on. We gotta make tracks."

Sybil didn't argue any more, and the three of them made a beeline for the door. One of the bouncers held up his hand as Glock approached, studying Tamara.

"She okay?"

"Just went a bit over her limit," Glock said. "Needs some fresh air."

He nodded and let them leave. Glock hustled Tamara over to the parking lot. She looked around and picked a car in the far corner of the lot, under a burnt-out security light. She propped Tamara against the car.

"Just hold on there, okay?"

Tamara nodded her thick head. Glock glanced around quickly, and put her elbow through the driver's window. She unlocked the door.

"Screwdriver," she snapped at Sybil. Sybil and Tamara looked down at Sybil's hand, at the object that Glock had told Sybil to hang onto. It was a screwdriver. The blade and shank glistened with blood. Glock snatched the screwdriver away. Sybil stared down at the blood smeared on her hand, her face pale in the moonlight.

"Get her in the back. Hurry up," Glock barked.

Sybil wiped her hand on her pants and swallowed hard. She helped guide Tamara into the back seat. Tamara laid down and closed her eyes for a moment.

(iii)

Tamara shifted around uncomfortably and sat up. She was still on the back seat of the car. The vehicle wasn't moving, engine just idling. Glock and Sybil sat in the front seat, their voices low. Glock looked over her shoulder.

"Sleeping Beauty awakes," she observed.

Tamara rubbed her eyes.

"What're we doing?" she demanded.

Glock passed her a cigarette. Tamara look at the slightly squashed, hand-rolled tube. She took a cautious inhale and held the smoke in her lungs. Glock motioned for her to pass the roach on and she did. She coughed, releasing the smoke all at once. Tamara cleared her throat, trying to calm down the burning in her chest.

"Is that it?" she asked, a little disappointed that the pot didn't give her an instant high.

Glock grinned at her.

"Takes a few minutes. Be patient."

"Where are we?" Tamara looked out the back window and didn't see much but trees.

"Lookout point," Glock said, gesturing to the front windshield.

Tamara looked out over the city, thousands of pinpricks of light. Around the halo produced by all of the lights, she could see an ocean of brilliant stars glinting.

"Oooh," she breathed. "It's beautiful."

Glock and Sybil nodded. They all sat in silence for a few minutes.

"Gimme another hit," Tamara said.

Glock passed her the joint. Tamara breathed in the smoke.

"D'ya know what?"

Glock gazed at her.

"What, Princess?"

"We gotta get some food."

Glock laughed. She looked at Sybil.

"How about you? Hungry?"

"I'm dying," Sybil admitted. "What are we gonna get?"

"Whatever we feel like," Glock said, putting the car into reverse and backed away from the edge of the cliff.

(iv)

They pulled in in front of a convenience store and Glock looked around, her eyes sharp and wary.

"You two stay put," she ordered sternly, opening her door.

"I want to come in," Tamara protested.

"Just stay in the car. What do you want?"

"I dunno... chips, candy, hot dog..."

Glock licked her lips.

"I'll get them."

"Why can't I come in?"

"Because I said. You just stay here." Glock looked at Sybil. "Make sure she stays. Got it?"

Sybil nodded. Glock got out of the car. Tamara couldn't understand why Glock kept treating Tamara like she needed a babysitter, or why she thought Sybil should be in charge. She waited until Glock was in the store for a minute before reaching for the door handle.

"No," Sybil warned. "Stay."

She grabbed Tamara's hand and tangled Tamara's fingers with her own so that she couldn't grasp the handle.

"Look," Sybil said, indicating the store, where they could see Glock gathering together a mountain of snacks. "Watch. Don't you know what she's doing?"

Tamara let go of the door and watched. Glock carried their snacks to the check-out counter and put them down. The clerk rang everything up and bagged it, and opened the till while reaching for Glock's payment. In the blink of the eye Glock had her hand at the clerks' throat. Tamara couldn't tell whether she had another screwdriver or a knife or something else. With the other hand, Glock reached into the register drawer and pulled out a handful of cash. She released the clerk, grabbed the bags of snacks, and left the store at a leisurely pace. Mouth open, Tamara watched Glock return to the car. She tossed the bags to Sybil, got in, and pulled out. The clerk pulled out a phone and dialed, watching their departure.

"Why'd you do that?" Tamara cracked up. The whole thing seemed utterly ridiculous. *Glock?* Maybe she should be called 'Tool' or 'Screwdriver'. She hadn't shown a piece all night—in fact, Tamara had yet to see her with a gun—but she certainly had a myriad of uses for an innocent looking slot screwdriver. And the idea that Glock would leave the store with all of the food and more money than she came with was absolutely hilarious to Tamara. Who did that? Tamara dissolved into giggles.

"Just needed to replenish the funds," Glock said, grinning widely.

Sybil dug into the snack bags and began distributing the food.

(v)

Tamara awoke slowly, her head thick like she had a fever, her body feeling sticky and sore. She moved, and found herself intertwined with other limbs and bodies. She opened her eyes and tried to extricate herself from Glock and Sybil. They were all piled together on the bed, like sleeping puppies.

"Stay here," Glock muttered, reaching for Tamara as she pulled away from them.

Sybil shifted and started to awaken. She moaned. Tamara's head pounded, and her stomach roiled with nausea. Sybil broke loose from the pile and dashed for the bathroom. Tamara lay still, hand over her stomach, trying to keep it from reacting to the noise of Sybil being sick. She rubbed her eyes, squinting at the window.

"What time is it?"

"Shaddap and go back to sleep."

Tamara closed her eyes again obediently, but sleep had fled. The pain and the nausea were overwhelming, and her worried brain chattered away like a squirrel.

"What happened?" Tamara asked, propping herself on her elbows. "What day is it?"

"Nothin' happened."

Disjointed images forced their way into her consciousness. "No... wait a minute..."

Tamara sat up the rest of the way, but it was too much for her stomach. Sybil was already in the bathroom. Tamara barely made it to the sink in the kitchenette before erupting. She hung onto the counter, weak-kneed, her head spinning. Tamara reached for the tap to wash the vomit down.

"What the heck did I eat last night?" she moaned.

Glock's low chuckle came from the bed.

"Whatever you could get your hands on, Princess."

That's about what it felt like. Tamara heaved again. She was seeing spots and worried that she was going to pass out right there on the kitchen floor. She hung on tight to the counter. Sybil came out of the bathroom behind her.

"Yuck. I don't usually get this hung over," she groaned. And at Tamara: "Morning, sunshine. How are you doing?"

Tamara laughed between heaves. "Oh, just great, Syb."

Her knees buckled and she was barely able to hold onto the counter to keep her feet.

"You gonna be okay?" Sybil worried.

"Oh..."

Sybil walked over to her. She fished around in the cooler and held a piece of ice to Tamara's forehead, rubbed it on the back of her neck. Tamara steadied herself. The ice helped her dizziness. The faintness faded.

"Thanks."

Sybil started the water running again.

"You done now?"

"I dunno."

Sybil rubbed her back. After a few minutes, Tamara felt okay to leave the sink, and she and Sybil wobbled back over to the bed. Glock rolled over as they sat down on the edge of the bed.

"Come lie down," she invited. "Go back to sleep. Gonna take a while before you feel up to anything."

Tamara stretched out against Glock, closing her eyes.

"What happened?" she asked.

"Nothing happened. You had a bit to drink, that's all."

Tamara rubbed her temples. "I didn't have anything to drink," she pointed out.

"Sorry, baby, but yes, you did."

Tamara opened her eyes. "No, you gave me—"

"We gave you a little something to loosen you up. And it did, didn't it?" Glock said to Sybil.

Sybil reddened.

Tamara stared at them. "You got me drunk?"

"We got you a bit tipsy," Glock amended. "Then you got yourself drunk."

Bits and pieces of the evening were coming back to Tamara. "Did I... drive...?"

Glock grinned. "Sure, you did," she agreed. "Like a veteran drag racer."

The more Tamara remembered, the worse she felt. "Oh, no..."

Glock massaged her shoulders and neck. "Go back to sleep" she urged. "You'll feel better when you wake up."

Tamara covered her eyes with her arm and tried to find sleep again.

(vi)

When Tamara awoke the next time, Glock was watching television. Tamara was feeling better. Not one hundred percent, but not quite so sick and foggy as she had been. She got up and went to the bathroom. The space was cramped, hardly big enough to turn around in. Tamara wasn't sure how Glock would maneuver her big frame in there. There was a mirror, and Tamara looked at herself as she washed up.

She had a black eye, but had no recollection of where she had gotten it. She touched it with cautious fingers. It was puffy and tender. Tamara splashed water on her face and rinsed her mouth. She went back out to the main room.

"Bit better this time?" Glock asked, glancing at her.

Tamara nodded. Looking at Glock, she frowned, images of the previous night coming back. Cars, screwdrivers, the man who had assaulted her in the hallway.

"What?" Glock frowned at her.

"Nothing. Just trying to remember."

"Don't hurt yourself."

Tamara sat down on the edge of the bed. "I gotta go home," she said.

Glock guffawed. "Seriously? Think it through, Frenchie!"

Tamara frowned. "Why?"

Glock glared at her, shaking her head. "Did you make it home before curfew?" she demanded.

"No. But that's just one..."

"What are you going to tell Collins?" Glock asked.

"I don't know..."

"That the only violation?" Glock pressed.

"No... but that was because you gave me alcohol... it wasn't my choice..."

"You think you can convince him of that?"

Tamara looked at the brightly-lit window.

"What time is it? If I get back early enough..." She pulled out her phone to look at the time. It was already afternoon. Tamara stared at the little LCD screen in dismay. "I had an appointment with him today."

Glock nodded.

"And... I was supposed to see the new therapist today. I missed that too."

"And what's he gonna find out if he drug tests you after last night?" Glock asked.

Tamara tried to remember the details of the previous night. "Did I...? I don't remember..."

Glock chuckled. "Doesn't matter anyway," she said cheerfully. "He's already issued a warrant."

Tamara's stomach clenched. "What? How do you know that?"

"I have my sources."

"No..." Tamara groaned.

"What did you think? You already violated once and been given a warning. Then you disappear overnight again? You think he's going to wait any longer?"

"But that's not fair. It wasn't my fault."

"If you think you can convince him..."

Tamara buried her face in her hands. "No! No, I don't want to go back. I won't go back to juvie!"

"You don't have to," Glock told her, grasping one hand and pulling it away from her face. "You don't have to go back. You and me, we'll stick together. You don't have to go back to the Hensons, or Collins, or anywhere. Just stay with me. Together."

"Me too," Sybil said.

Glock glanced at her, but didn't say anything to her. She continued to focus on Tamara.

"Just like at juvie. You and me. I'll look after you. Just like juvie, except we'll be free. Do whatever we want to."

"Like last night?" Tamara said, thinking back in horror of how the man who had attacked her had crumpled to the floor. The blood glistening on the screwdriver blade. Her black eye and how sick she had been on waking.

"Yeah, just like last night," Glock agreed with a broad smile.

(vii)

Glock had gone out to restock supplies, leaving Tamara and Sybil at the apartment. They were both still feeling too queasy and tired to go anywhere.

"Your mom won't be worried?" Tamara asked, lying on her back and staring up at the stained ceiling.

"No, not yet. She might ground me, but she won't be worried. I've spent plenty of nights out before."

"She won't beat you?"

Sybil turned her head and looked at Tamara.

"No. She won't lay a hand on me."

"And your step-dad?"

"Him either. They'll just try to talk it out. Lecture."

"Will they call the cops?"

"What for? They don't..." Sybil dropped her voice. "It's not like they know anything that happened last night. Just that I stayed out."

"What *did* happen last night?"

"We don't have to talk about it. We didn't get caught. Nobody knows. And we weren't the ones who... robbed the store or anything."

Tamara tried to sort it out in her head. "It's not all Glock. I drove the car. And we both smoked pot, and... drank."

Sybil rolled over and propped herself on her elbows, so she was looking down into Tamara's face. "I wasn't trying to get you in trouble or anything," she said guiltily, biting her lip. "We just wanted... to help you relax... loosen you up and make you feel better. It wasn't to get you in trouble, to get your parole violated or something."

"Maybe not for you," Tamara said. "It was for Glock."

"You don't know that! She cares about you, she just wanted you to feel better! You've been so stressed out. It was just to celebrate and help you relax."

Tamara shook her head. "She wants me to stay with her. That's what it was about."

Sybil frowned. "She talks about when you and her were in juvie..."

"It wasn't like she says."

Sybil looked at her, waiting for more.

"You'd think we were on a picnic or something to hear her

talk," Tamara said. She heard the resentment in her voice and tried to soften it, but it was there, harsh and raw. "Maybe it was for her, but it was no picnic for me. You've seen what she's like when she gets in a mood. You imagine being stuck in a six-by-six cell with that for a couple years."

"But you weren't in a cell the whole time. You had classes and common areas and everything."

"And Glock twenty-four seven. Whether she was in a good mood or not. Locked up together every night. Every night!" Tamara's voice cracked.

Sybil picked at a scab on her arm, refusing to look at her and acknowledge her words.

"So you don't want to stay here with her?"

"How's your wrist?"

Sybil rotated her wrist slowly, testing it. "Still sore," she admitted.

"And what if she'd broken it? Or if she'd been alone with you, without a food fair full of witnesses and me to stop her? What do you think she would have done then?"

Sybil shuddered, and didn't answer.

TWELVE

(i)

GLOCK WAS GONE FOR a long time. Sybil kept checking the time and fussing about having to go home soon. Glock finally returned. Tamara figured she'd have a big load of grocery bags, for having been gone for so long, but she only had a couple. One with drinks, and one with snacks and a few canned foods.

Tamara got up to help put them away. She was bored and wanted to do something useful, even if it was only to unpack a couple of bags. Sybil stood up too, inching toward the door.

"I gotta get home," she said. "I'll pop in for a while... umm, tomorrow afternoon, I guess. You guys going to be doing anything?"

Tamara put drinks and fresh ice in the cooler.

"No particular plans," Glock said. She stood between them, her back to Sybil. "We'll do whatever we're in the mood for."

She handed Tamara a couple of bottles. Tamara reached to take them, and stopped. There was a red crust around Glock's nails. Like the cuticles had been bleeding. But Glock didn't pick or bite her cuticles like Tamara did. There was a black line of dirt under the nail as well, on all of her fingers. When Tamara didn't take the bottles, Glock put them down on the counter, and then looked at her nails to see what Tamara was staring at. She used her thumb to flake away some of the red crusts, and studied the dirt under her nails.

"Guess I should have worn gloves," she observed. "But I don't like the loss of sensation."

Tamara swallowed, feeling suddenly ill again.

"What did you do?" Her voice was suddenly hoarse.

Glock smiled. "I'll scrub up, if it bothers you. You put the rest away."

She retired to the bathroom.

Tamara looked at Sybil.

"I gotta go," Sybil repeated. "You be okay?"

Tamara looked at her, unable to find her voice. Sybil was through the door and gone in a flash. Tamara put the canned goods into the tiny cupboards and took a bag of potato chips over to the bed to eat while watching TV. Glock was out a few minutes later, and showed her hands to Tamara, pink and moist, the nails now scrubbed clean.

"There, that meet with Princess's approval?" she questioned.

Tamara nodded. Glock sat down next to her, digging into the chips.

"You want to go out again tonight?"

Tamara cleared her throat and tried to answer in a clear and confident tone, despite her shakiness.

"I'm still recovering from last night."

Glock chuckled at that. "It was a good night, wasn't it?" she reminisced. "Real nice. We'll just watch some tube, then? Hit the sack early like regular folks?"

"Yeah," Tamara agreed.

And she had to figure out how she was going to get out of the situation. She couldn't go on living with Glock indefinitely.

She couldn't go back to the Hensons. She wasn't sure how she would make it on her own. She didn't have any street smarts. She might have to stay with Glock just long enough to get a handle on how to take care of herself, and then make her break...

"I've been thinking about your problem," Glock commented, crunching down some chips and staring at the TV, not looking at Tamara.

Tamara was startled. "What problem?" she asked.

"You want to go back to parole, with that family."

Tamara's mouth twisted bitterly. "Yeah, but there's no way to do that. Not when Collins has already issued a warrant."

"Maybe there is."

Tamara frowned, looking at Glock. Glock did not look at her, but kept staring at the TV. "What do you mean?"

"Your other problem with this coach. What's-his-name."

"McClure," Tamara filled in. "But there's not really anything I can do about that. I already told Collins. He didn't believe it."

"Exactly," Glock agreed. "So the pervert's just going to be allowed to go on, messin' around with the girls on the team. And who knows who else? Maybe he's got little girls at home too, or access to nieces or whatever."

Tamara shifted uncomfortably. "I didn't really think about that," she said. "But I've already told. What else can I do?"

"What would you say if I told you there's a way to stop him and to get back onto Collins' good girls list at the same time?"

"No way. Not possible."

"But there is," Glock coaxed. She looked at Tamara, her eyes big and black. Dangerous eyes. "You don't want to let a perv like that get away with it, do you?"

"No..."

"So you go see him. After school, after practice. You tell him what you know and threaten to expose him. He has to quit, or you'll out him publicly."

Tamara was disappointed. "But I already told Collins. No one would believe it."

"McClure doesn't know that. And he doesn't know that you don't have proof, either. You say that you recorded him on your phone. Whatever. He doesn't know it's not true. He has to resign, or you'll air it. Online, or the ten o'clock news. To his wife, to the school, everybody he knows. Guys like that operate in the dark. They can't stand being exposed."

"Why do you care?" Tamara challenged. "I thought it wasn't any of our business. The girls could just take care of themselves."

"Yeah." Glock cleaned a nail that apparently wasn't clean to her satisfaction. "I said that. But I've been thinking about it. I don't think it's right, just letting him get away with it. If someone had turned in guys like that before they messed up our lives..." Her eyes were distant. "Your foster dad. Other guys that take advantage of little kids... things would be different for us, right?"

Tamara nodded. If it wasn't for Mr. Baker... her life would be a lot different now.

"So we gotta take care of him. You, I mean. Force his hand. Get him out of the school. We should, right?"

Tamara nodded. "Yeah, but—"

Glock shook her head. "But what? Now you don't want to?"

"How's that gonna help me get back on parole? After messing up, and having a warrant out, and all?"

Glock laughed. "You'll be a hero. Get his confession on tape. Then out him for real. You get it in the news, and they'll have to release you. You can't put someone who's just exposed a child molester in jail. A hero. They'll forget all of the technical violations. And that's all they know about. They don't know about me, or about you drinking or anything. Only about missed curfew and appointments. Who'd put a hero in prison over that?"

Tamara pondered on this. "Do you think so?" she said tentatively. "It sounds sort of... I dunno... too easy."

"We get McClure out of there. Save the team and whatever other little girls are in his life. Get you back on parole. Where's the downside? What are you hesitating about?"

Tamara thought about it. She was wary of Glock's new insight, when it was such a reversal to what Glock had said to her before. But there was genuine emotion in Glock's voice when she talked about the damage that a man like McClure could do. Who knew what men had taken advantage of Glock over the years that she should have been able to trust. Maybe it had gotten to her. Maybe as Glock thought about Coach McClure, she had started to feel sorry for Lotta, instead of looking down on her for being so weak.

"If anyone sees me at the school, I'll get arrested. And what if Coach doesn't believe me? What if he doesn't care, or he calls the police on me?"

"I'll go with you," Glock offered. "You'll be safe. He won't be able to do anything to you. I'll keep a lookout."

Tamara watched the TV, frowning. "I don't know... I told Collins, so he should investigate it, right? He'll find out..."

"That won't get you out of trouble like going public would."

"Can't I go public without talking to him?"

"What do you have? No one is going to believe you or do anything about it without proof. You need his confession. Get his voice on tape."

Tamara looked at Glock. The bigger girl gave her a smile, and put an arm around her shoulders. "You think on it," she said. "You'll see it's the only way."

(ii)

The next morning, Glock was out of sorts. Tamara saw the signs as soon as she woke up. Glock was pacing, muttering under her breath. Her hands clenched and unclenched. Tamara went to the bathroom without commenting, and when she came out, grabbed a drink from the cooler and handed it to Glock.

Glock looked at it for a moment before taking it. "Thanks, sweetie."

"What's wrong?" Tamara asked.

Glock paced heavily across the little room. She popped the tab on the beer and chugged it down. "Nothin' you need to worry about," Glock said.

"What, then?"

"You wanna come with me?"

Tamara shook her head. "Where?"

"We just go out, find a stray cat or dog..."

"No," Tamara said firmly.

"Come on. It's not like it's little kids, or something. It's not like they're people."

Tamara shook her head adamantly. "No! No, I can't."

Glock went nose-to-nose with Tamara. She grasped Tamara's chin tightly. "Think you're too good for me, don't you?" she demanded. "You think you're so much better than me? Maybe you'd rather it was you I took the knife to."

Tamara heard the chilling whisper of Glock pulling a knife from its sheath. She tried to back away, pull her chin gently out of Glock's grasp. But Glock held on, and with the other hand, pressed a blade to Tamara's throat. Tamara could feel the cold, sharp edge. She gulped and held very still.

"You want me to cut you?" Glock whispered.

"No."

Glock slid the knife slowly right to left. Tamara felt it bite into the skin. Glock kept it razor sharp. Tamara shuddered, her body quaking even though she strove mightily to remain still. Glock grinned.

"Yeah."

Tamara's heart pounded so hard that it hurt. She breathed heavily, unable to get enough air. She could feel blood start to trickle down from the knife. "Glock," she said in a voice much calmer than she felt.

"What?"

"I thought you were going out."

Glock started to laugh. She withdrew the knife, but continued to hang onto Tamara's chin. "You're not coming?"

"No," Tamara repeated firmly.

"I always forget you've got guts, when the chips are down."

Glock released Tamara's chin and swiped her thumb along the cut, drawing it away bloody. She sucked it off.

"I'll be gone a while, then. You think about what I said about that sicko coach, right?"

Tamara nodded. Glock left the apartment without another word. Tamara breathed out. Her stomach twisted with nausea. The cut on her throat was itchy and stung. Her whole body was shaking. She knew now she couldn't stay with Glock. Not even for the short time it would take her to learn how to get along on her own. If Glock's bloodlust had reached the point where she couldn't even go one day... Tamara wouldn't be safe for long.

Maybe Glock was right about one thing. Nobody would want to put a hero behind bars. Not for technical violations. The only chance for her to clear herself and get back on parole was to expose Coach McClure to the world.

(iii)

Tamara was ready when Glock got home. She looked at the time on her phone as Glock entered. Glock raised her brows.

"What? I didn't know I had a curfew," she growled.

"Well, if we're going to get to the school before McClure leaves for the day..."

Glock's face broke into a grin. "Yeah? You changed your mind? We're gonna do this?"

Tamara nodded. "If you really think it will work."

"Sure. Of course it will work."

"Well, let's go, then."

They left the apartment, Glock eagerly in the lead. Tamara was nervous about being out of the apartment in broad daylight, knowing that there was a warrant out for her arrest. If they saw anyone she knew... But Glock seemed totally oblivious to any possible danger. She watched coolly out the bus window, making the occasional comment to Tamara. Tamara kept looking at her phone, hoping to time their arrival at the school for after classes let out, but before McClure left for the day.

"Quit worrying," Glock said.

"What am I going to say to him?"

"That you know what he's doing. You have proof."

"And so he should quit, or I'll go public with it?"

Glock nodded.

"What if he wants to see the proof?"

"It's somewhere safe. You wouldn't bring it with you."

Tamara chewed on her nail. "What if he doesn't believe me?"

Glock shrugged. "It doesn't matter, Princess. Just keep him talking. He'll give himself away, if he talks long enough."

Tamara nodded, her stomach fluttering with anxiety. When Glock said it, it all sounded so simple.

"I'll be close by," Glock murmured, misinterpreting her anxiety. "He can't hurt you."

"Thanks," Tamara said.

They reached the school bus stop, and Glock and Tamara got off.

"What if the doors are locked?" Tamara asked. Didn't they lock the doors once school let out?

"Try before you start fussing," Glock advised.

Tamara bit her nail.

Glock caught her hand and pulled it away from her mouth. "Focus," she ordered. "Quit being so nervous. You're strong."

Tamara nodded. She moved purposefully toward the door. The handle gave under her hand, and swung open freely. She started down the hall. It was deserted. Her footsteps, quiet though they were, echoed off the walls. She felt like it had been a year since she'd been in the school last. It had been just over a week, but it felt like forever. She didn't belong there anymore. If she succeeded, and Collins and the court agreed to put her back on parole, would she feel like she belonged here again? Or did it mean that she would never have that feeling of belonging again?

Glock followed close behind her. Maybe that was one reason for Tamara's nervousness. Tamara looked at Glock over her shoulder. Glock nodded.

"Lead the way," she encouraged. "I don't know where his office is."

Tamara kept going. She passed empty classrooms and the gym. The showers. She felt like she was going to the dungeons. She stopped outside Coach McClure's door.

"This is it," she whispered to Glock. "You'll wait here?"

Glock folded her arms and stood as still as a statue.

Tamara breathed deeply, and stepped in through the doorway. McClure was sitting at his desk, piled high with binders and paperwork. Tamara wondered briefly why a gym teacher or coach would have so much paper to deal with. He didn't see her at first. Tamara walked further into the room. He saw or heard her movement and looked up.

"Tamara," he said, frowning. "What... what are you doing here?"

Tamara cleared her throat. "I know what you're doing," she said, in as strong a voice as she could muster.

"What are you talking about?" It wasn't his usual kind voice. Even when he harangued the team for stupid mistakes, his voice held a hint of humor, of understanding. But his voice now was cold, angry, brazen.

"I know about you and Lotta. And you and Holiday. I don't know how many others."

His eyes were like ice, with none of his usual warmth. "There is a warrant out for your arrest," he said.

Tamara shrugged. "So?"

"What are you doing here? I could call the police now, and you'd go straight back to juvie."

"And I'll show them the video."

She watched the sweat break out on McClure's forehead.

"What video?"

"The one I took on my phone, the day I saw you in the showers with Lotta."

He half rose from his chair. Then he froze, eyes focused on something behind Tamara. Tamara turned her head, but knew already what she would see. Glock stood behind her.

"Siddown, Coach," Glock said in a low, gravelly growl. "You just sit down and listen."

Tamara glanced at Glock again, not understanding why she was interfering.

"I know what you did," she repeated, like a broken record, stuck, not knowing what to say next.

"You don't know anything," McClure said flatly. "You're mistaken."

"I do. And I—I want you to resign, to quit, or I'll release the video. To the news," Tamara stumbled through her script.

"I don't know what you're talking about. I haven't done anything."

"Does your wife know you like to mess with little girls?" Glock demanded.

McClure grew paler, more grim. "Who are you? And what are you doing here?"

"Just admit what you did," Tamara persisted, trying to get him to confess. Glock had promised that he would confess. The whole scenario of making Tamara a hero hinged on McClure confessing. "You are molesting players. Just admit that, and I'll go."

"Are you crazy? Why would I do that?"

Glock surged forward. Tamara tried to grab her, hold her back. But Glock had always been too strong for her to control physically.

"Glock, no, we gotta do this right."

Glock turned, leering at her.

"*This* is what we're here, for, baby."

Tamara's heart sank. That was why nothing Glock had said had rung true. She wasn't here to protect Tamara. She wasn't interested in helping Tamara get back on Collins' nice list. It was revenge on the men who had damaged her. Lust for violence. For blood. Not a desire to help her friend and make things right again.

"No," Tamara protested weakly.

Glock shook her off.

(iv)

"Who are you?" McClure demanded, his voice shaking. "I'm calling the police."

He reached for the phone but he never got that far. As Glock traversed the small office, she grabbed a trophy from on top of a filing cabinet, and she brought it down on McClure's head as she reached him. He tried to protect himself, and it only hit his head with a glancing blow, not the full force with which Glock had intended.

"Stop!" Tamara pleaded, her voice hardly more than a squeak.

Her feet were frozen to the floor. She couldn't move a muscle to interfere, to try to help McClure. She knew Glock, knew how strong she was, especially in a rage. There was nothing that Tamara could do to stop her.

Yelling incomprehensibly, Glock swung the trophy again, landing a dull thud on the side of McClure's face. It had sharp corners, and both his head and his face were bleeding. In the frenzy that followed, McClure fought back against the attack, but was no match for Glock with the heavy trophy. Tamara couldn't believe how long he fought. She kept expecting him to go down, and he kept fighting back, kept trying to protect himself from the crushing blows and to pull the weapon out of Glock's hands. Tamara flinched at every blow as if she herself was being struck. At every gurgle of protest that McClure made. Glock continued to rage, hitting him over and over. Shouting curses.

"No, no, please..."

But Tamara wasn't in juvie anymore. There were no alarm bells. No guards. No batons and pepper spray. Just Tamara; too small, and too weak, and too afraid to stop Glock.

(v)

Finally McClure slid from his chair to the floor, and after a couple more smashing blows, Glock ceased, and was still. They just stood there, hearts pumping, breaths rasping in the stillness of the room. Tamara was frantic.

"Is he dead?" she shrieked.

"He deserves to be, doesn't he?" the older girl countered, grabbing Tamara by the arm and hauling her toward the door. "Come on, we gotta get out of here."

Tamara looked back at the form laying crumpled on the floor, bloody and broken.

"You've wrecked everything!" she cried. "I had one chance, and now you ruined everything!"

"Shut up, Frenchie. You never had any chance. You're just too stupid to know it."

Tamara tried to break Glock's grip.

"You set me up! You told me you were going to help me, and

you just set me up! Why? Because you wanted to kill him? Why do you care?"

"I told you to shut up," Glock repeated, squeezing Tamara's arm harder. "You want to get caught? Someone's going to hear your bellyaching."

Tamara shut up. Glock continued to haul her along until they got to the outside doors. She let go of Tamara and crashed through the door. Tamara followed close behind. Glock looked around. She put out her arm to stop Tamara.

"No running," she whispered. "Just walk calmly. People will notice you if you run. They're not going to notice two kids leaving the school who are just walking."

Tamara forced herself to walk sedately down the sidewalk beside Glock. Her heart was just about bursting out of her chest. Her head felt like it was going to explode. She should have known. She should have known that Glock had her own agenda. Why would she do something just to help Tamara get back on the right side of the law? When she wanted Tamara to stay with her, on the other side. She wanted Tamara to be on the run.

"What am I going to do now?" she asked bitterly. "You've ruined everything."

"I didn't ruin nothing. You're free, aren't you? Free to come and go as you like. You're not in prison. Not stuck with some foster family. Not stuck reporting every move you make to a parole officer. You're *really* free."

"You said you wanted to help me."

"Come on, Frenchie. I did help you. You were worried about that scum back there molesting Lotta or other girls? I took care of it. He's never gonna do that again. You don't have to worry."

"You killed him!"

"Maybe I did. Maybe I didn't. Won't know until we hear the news tomorrow. But either way, he's not going to be hurting anyone else again anytime soon."

"Why did you do that?" Tamara demanded, feeling a little hysteria take over. "Why did you have to do that?"

"Keep your voice down if you don't want to attract attention, Princess."

"Everyone is going to think that I did this!"

"Just a little bonus for me," Glock agreed. "There's no way you're going crawling back to Collins now, is there?"

"You've been sabotaging me the whole time. You just wanted me to run away. It was all one big set-up."

"Don't flatter yourself. Most of the time you screwed yourself up without any of my help."

"You got me drunk. You made me come down here to force McClure to confess. I suppose you were the one who planted weed in my locker too?"

"Nah. Like I said, you managed to screw things up on your own. The weed was nothin' to do with me."

"What am I going to do now?"

"Just chill. You can do whatever you want. Don't you see that? You're not trapped anymore. Now you're free!"

"Free to do what? Spend the rest of my life on the run?"

"So dramatic, my little princess," Glock squeezed her shoulders. "We can go wherever you want. We don't have to stay in town. You can change your name. Start a new life with a new identity. No one will know you were ever in juvie."

Tamara didn't point out that there was no way she was staying with Glock. Glock would just dig her deeper and deeper into trouble. Or else totally lose it one day and Tamara would be the next victim.

Could she really start fresh somewhere new? A new name, a new life? Tamara touched the teardrops tattooed on her face. Glock glanced at them.

"Well, yeah, those could be a giveaway," she acknowledged. "But you can get tattoos removed, or changed into something else. No problem."

(*vi*)

Tamara was oblivious to where they were. They'd been walking for a long time, but Tamara was still so overwhelmed and emotional that she took no note of their location. She wasn't crying. The hysteria had subsided. But she was cold and her brain foggy and she supposed she was in some kind of shock.

A car pulled up beside them. Glock and Tamara looked over at it as the window went down.

"Tamara?"

It was Deshawn. She looked out the window at Tamara and Glock, her face missing the usual brilliant smile.

"Tamara? You okay, honey?"

Glock scowled at Tamara. "Get rid of her," she said under her breath.

"I'm fine," Tamara said. "I'm... I'm sorry. Things just didn't work out."

"Mrs. Henson's really worried about you. Climb in. I'll take you home. We'll get it sorted out."

Tamara shook her head. "I—I can't, Deshawn. I can't go back, they'll send me back to juvie."

"They'll help you. Mister and Missus, they really care. They'll help you get straightened out again."

"There's nothing they can do when I'm in juvie," Tamara pointed out.

"You can get paroled again," Deshawn urged. "Just 'cause the first try didn't work, that doesn't mean you can't get out again. It's hard work. We all know how hard it is. But you can do it. We'll help you."

"Can you believe this bleeding heart?" Glock asked. "She wants you to go right back to juvie. She thinks you'll just walk back in, like a lamb to slaughter."

"Tamara, honey," Deshawn tried again. "Come on. Come home. You know it's the right thing to do."

Tamara wished that she could. Just go home to the family, and they would take care of things. Make everything right. But Deshawn didn't know the whole story. She only knew about missed curfew and appointments. Not about stolen cars, drugs, and maybe murder. The family couldn't take care of that. No one could take care of that. You couldn't just walk away from assault and murder.

"I can't," Tamara said. "Please. Just leave me alone."

Deshawn looked at her pleadingly, but when Tamara didn't give in, she drove on. Tamara saw Deshawn tap her ear as she pulled ahead of them.

"She's calling the cops," Tamara warned Glock.

Glock nodded, taking a quick survey of their surroundings. She pulled Tamara into an alley, out of sight of the road that Deshawn was on.

"Give me your jacket."

"What?"

Glock motioned impatiently. Tamara took off the denim jacket and handed it to her. Glock stripped off her black studded jacket and handed it to her.

"Put it on."

Tamara obeyed. The jacket just swam on her, way too big, and she opened her mouth to protest. Glock shook her head, anticipating Tamara's objection.

"Roll up the sleeves. But keep it on. Can you do something with your hair?"

"What?"

"Put it in a braid or a bun or something. They're going to be looking for a girl with long blond hair in a jean jacket. Come on."

"Oh," understanding trickled into Tamara's brain. "Oh, yeah. Okay."

She gathered her hair back and started to french braid it. It had been a long time since she had done that, but her fingers remembered the sequence. Glock nodded. She groped Tamara, and it took a confused moment for Tamara to recognize that she was trying to get something out of the pocket of the black jacket. She shifted her stance, and Glock pulled a red scarf or kerchief out. She wiped her hands, which were speckled with blood, then gathered up her own lanky black hair and tied the scarf around it in a doo-rag.

"Okay. We'll split up. Even dressed like this, we're too recognizable together. Me especially. You go that way..." Glock motioned at the playground behind a nearby building. "You know the way back to my pad?"

Tamara looked around, trying to get her bearings. Glock gestured impatiently.

"That's Main over there, right? You follow it to Delaware. Right? You got it?"

Tamara nodded.

"Yeah, okay."

Glock took off at a lope in the other direction. For a few heartbeats, Tamara just stood there. Now that she was separated from Glock, it was her chance. She could decide for herself what she was going to do. Follow Glock's directions and meet her back at the apartment? Make a run for it in another direction? Go back to the house or turn herself in?

A high siren was picked up by the wind. Tamara's heart raced even faster than it already had been. There was no time to think. She couldn't let them catch her. Glock had told her what to do, and Tamara couldn't sort out any other path to follow. She started walking across the playground.

(vi)

Tamara realized as she got to Glock's apartment that she didn't have keys to get in. If Glock hadn't made it back yet, she was going to be hanging around in the hallway or outside the building, conspicuous to the police or any witnesses or bad guys who wanted to make trouble for her. She had to be smarter. Think ahead. It felt like she had just been running from one bad situation to worse, without any time to think things through. To really get her head on straight. She was just reacting to everything, rather than acting on her own.

She tried the door handle, and it was unlocked. Tamara went into the apartment and shut the door behind her. Glock gave her a big grin.

"You look so cute in my coat," she laughed, reaching out to give Tamara a hug.

Tamara exploded. It was all just too much. Running from the cops. Seeing McClure bludgeoned in front of her. The pressure of following the rules and being in a family and not fitting in and Sybil's kid sisters and everything else was just too much, and she blew her lid. She punched Glock as hard as she could in the stomach as Glock approached with her arms held out. Glock gave a little 'oof,' and looked surprised.

"What was that for?"

Tamara hit her again, wanting to really hurt her. She wasn't strong enough or a good enough fighter, but she wanted to anyway.

"For screwing me over!" she shouted. "You messed up my whole life!"

Glock took the repeated blows with good grace, and enveloped Tamara in a bear-hug with a muffled laugh. Tamara was caged, she couldn't move, couldn't hit Glock anymore. She struggled to free herself. Glock lifted her up, walked the few steps to the bed, and dropped her onto it. As soon as she was free, Tamara looked for a way to continue the fight. She grabbed the nearest projectile, a pillow, and threw it at Glock's face. Glock caught it, and swung it back at her, whumping it across Tamara's face, nearly knocking her down.

"You want a pillow fight?" she teased. "All those sleepovers at juvie, and we never had one!"

Tamara jumped up, and launched herself from the bed at Glock's head, trying to get her arms around Glock's neck in a chokehold. Glock flipped her off, back onto the bed with a crash and squeak of springs. Someone pounded on the wall.

"Keep it down over there!"

"See?" Glock said. "You're disturbing the neighbors."

Tamara tried again, throwing herself at Glock, pounding with her fists, trying to hit something that would hurt her. Really hurt her. Again, Glock wound her arms around Tamara in a bear hug, and she fell onto the bed, her weight on top of Tamara this time, knocking the wind right out of her. Tamara gasped, trying to catch her breath again. There was a blinding pain in her side, and she could no longer fight Glock. She was still, and waited for Glock to release her. Glock's arms remained tight around her. Tamara squirmed.

"Leggo," she protested, between gasps.

"I don't think so," Glock countered.

Tamara thrashed, trying to break free, but it just sent further stabs of pain into her side and she was no closer to getting out. "Lemme go," Tamara ordered. "You hurt me."

Glock didn't move. Tears came to Tamara's eyes. They weren't tears of pain. She wasn't a baby. They were angry, furious tears. Furious at not being able to move. Not being able to protect herself. Not being able to do what she wanted to. The whole world was against her, and Tamara was too helpless to even move a muscle.

"Let go!"

Glock just continued to hold her tightly. After several minutes of weeping, a heaviness started to overtake Tamara. She couldn't keep her burning eyes open. She couldn't fight Glock's hold anymore. She was too tired. Too exhausted. The day had been so overwhelming. It didn't make any sense, but Tamara fell asleep.

(vii)

There were voices around her. Tamara didn't know who they were or where they were coming from. Everything seemed hazy and confused, like she had a fever. Tamara rubbed her sticky eyes, groaning.

"Hey, baby girl, have a nice nap?"

Tamara knew *that* voice. She opened her eyes, trying to see through the blur of sleep. Her eyes were itchy and gritty.

It was dark. The only light came from the big screen TV. Glock was beside her, smacking her lips, eating something with relish. Tamara had no appetite, no interest in what it was. She listlessly watched the television, waiting for her brain to warm up and start making sense.

Tamara shifted her weight to a new position, and gasped at the pain in her side. Stars danced in front of her eyes, and she felt herself slipping in and out of blackness, stuck somewhere in the gray light before unconsciousness.

"What's the matter?" Glock questioned, without looking at her.

"Dammit," Tamara breathed. "I think you busted a rib when you fell on me."

Glock turned and looked at her curiously.

"Yeah?" She reached out to examine Tamara's rib cage. "Let's see."

Tamara slapped her hand away.

"Don't think so," she growled. She knew what would happen if Glock got her hands on the broken bone. "Don't touch me."

"Aw, puppy's got her bark back," Glock cooed.

But she'd apparently been sated with the day's violence and didn't pursue it, turning her eyes back to the TV program. Tamara closed her eyes and continued to drift in and out.

"Hey," Glock nudged her, trying to rouse her. "Look. We're on."

Tamara opened her eyes, staring at the screen and trying to take it in. A news report. Somber looking anchorwoman. Outside shots of the school, with yellow tape across the doors. Tamara's most recent mugshots, from her arrest for drug possession. Older mugshots of Glock, eyes bloodshot, staring out somewhere past the camera.

"Coach McClure... bludgeoned... in ICU..." A few words made their way into her consciousness. "...Wanted for questioning... warrant for arrest... dangerous... may be armed..."

"Armed," Tamara echoed in dismay, "I'm not armed!"

Glock laughed.

"It's good," she declared. "Shows they respect us."

Tamara lay there, watching the screen. She was surprised to see Mrs. Henson's face.

"I think Tamara will do the right thing," she said. "I think that things got out of her control, but she knows what's right. She'll do the responsible thing."

Glock snorted. Mrs. Henson's face was replaced by Collins' serious one.

"It's always a disappointment when a parolee goes bad," he said soberly. "Rest assured that they are vetted and supervised very closely; this is a very rare occurrence. I think that there are some issues here that will need to be investigated."

"What's to investigate?" Tamara moaned. "All he needs to do is find me."

"Shh," Glock hushed her, gesturing at the screen.

"...true that there were allegations of inappropriate behavior by Coach McClure?" the anchorwoman was asking.

Tamara held her breath. So someone had leaked that detail. But Collins wouldn't be able to say anything about it.

"I can't comment on an active investigation," Collins said. "That's a police matter. Not something being handled through the Parole Division."

The anchorwoman went into her wrap-up, and the next story was announced. Tamara didn't move.

"At least we stopped McClure," she sighed.

Glock looked down and stroked Tamara's head. "That's right," she agreed.

THIRTEEN

(i)

THERE WAS A KNOCK at the door. Tamara tried to stir, but was still heavy with sleep and the fog from the day before. Glock was immediately on her feet. She reached behind the TV and when she pulled it out, a big black gun had magically appeared in her hand. Glock slid along the wall like a shadow. In order to look out the peephole, she would have to stand squarely in front of the door. Instead, she stood flattened against the wall.

"Who's there?" she demanded in a low, hoarse voice.

"It's Sybil," an impatient voice cut through the door.

"Are you alone?"

"Who would I be with?"

Glock stepped in front of the door and looked out the peephole. Her body relaxed and the gun hand dipped down. She slid the bolt and opened the door.

"You couldn't call or text before you came?" she demanded.

Sybil came in, shaking her head.

"I don't have your number, and Tamara's must be dead. Did

you let the battery run out?" she asked Tamara, looking down at her on the bed.

Tamara considered this. She worked the phone out of her pants pocket and flipped it open.

"Yeah, I guess I did," she admitted.

"I've been *freaking out* trying to get a hold of you! Did you know that you guys are all over the news?" Sybil's voice was shrill.

Glock shut and re-bolted the door. She slid the gun away into her waistband. Sybil caught a glimpse of it and her mouth dropped open.

"You take your life in your hands coming over here without warning me," Glock said. "You coulda been the cops. Or had the cops with you."

Sybil cleared her throat and shifted nervously. "Sorry. Like I said, I tried to reach you."

Glock took Tamara's phone from Sybil's hand, and looked at the connector pins.

"Won't work on my charger. Where's yours, Princess?"

"At the house."

Glock rolled her eyes.

"What's your number?" Sybil asked Glock.

Glock sighed and gave it to her. Sybil keyed it into her own phone.

"I might have a spare charger for Tamara. I'll have to search for it."

"Probably easier to just pick up a burner," Glock said.

Sybil sat down on the bed. She looked down at Tamara.

"So are you guys okay? You need anything?"

Glock glanced at Tamara, lying there listlessly.

"I think she's just tired. Things have been sort of... busy."

Sybil gave a single-syllable laugh of disbelief.

"Busy? Is that what you call it? Sheesh, I couldn't believe it when I saw the news. Both of you were on, not just Tamara. How did they know about *you*?"

"Her foster sister saw us together," Glock said. "I guess she got a pretty good look."

"Jesse too," Tamara said. "He saw us together the day I got out of jail."

"Who's Jesse?" Sybil asked.

"Foster dad."

Glock made an uncaring gesture. "People were bound to figure it out sooner or later. I'm a bit easier to spot, but I know how to lay low."

"Yeah?" Tamara's eyes half-closed as she started to drift again. "Does that include not drawing attention to yourself by eviscerating people's pets?"

There was only silence for a response.

"That's what I thought," Tamara grunted.

Glock sat down on the bed, and when Tamara resisted rolling toward the depression Glock made in the bed, she jarred her ribs again. She breathed in sharply through her teeth and tried to adjust to a position where they wouldn't hurt so much.

"You okay?" Sybil asked.

"She thinks she might've broken a rib," Glock said.

"Ouch. Should we take her to a doctor?"

"Nah. Can't do much for ribs. I can tape them up myself, if she'll let me get close to them."

Sybil reached over to Tamara and rubbed her shoulder soothingly.

"That sucks. What about painkillers? You want me to get something?"

Glock brightened at this suggestion.

"Nah. Why don't you stay here and keep her company, and I'll go rustle something up?"

Sybil shrugged.

"Sure, if you want."

Glock grabbed her jacket and pulled it on, taking a moment to unroll the sleeves that Tamara had adjusted when she wore it.

"I'll see you later."

The door closed behind her and she was gone. Sybil got up and threw the bolt again. She went over to the bed and stretched out beside Tamara, their faces close together.

"So how are you doing?" she asked. "You okay?"

Tamara opened her eyes briefly, and closed them again.

"I guess."

"Coach McClure... was that you, or Glock?"

"What d'you think?"

"Glock," Sybil agreed, nodding. "But you were there?"

"Yeah."

Sybil was quiet for a bit. Tamara opened her eyes. Sybil's eyes were wide with curiosity and excitement.

"Well?" she breathed. "What was it like?"

Tamara turned carefully to lie on her back.

"Awful. It was... he was fighting back, and she just kept... kept hitting him." Tamara shook her head. "The blood was splattering everywhere... the expression on Glock's face... and the yelling..."

Sybil gave a low whistle.

"Brutal. I can't imagine." But clearly, from her flashing eyes, she was doing just that.

"I never should have taken her there," Tamara said. "I never should have listened to her. I should have known..."

"What else are you going to do?" Sybil questioned. "She was your cellie, you have to be able to trust your cellie."

Tamara glared at Sybil, who giggled in embarrassment.

"The question is," Tamara said, "what to do now?"

"Lay low, like Glock said," Sybil said. "You're probably safe here, right? No one knows where she's living. They won't know to find you here."

"I can't live here," Tamara said flatly.

Sybil looked taken aback. "Why not?"

"I just can't. It's too dangerous."

Sybil still hadn't figured out just how dangerous Glock was. She was here to talk to them about a man being beaten so badly he was in ICU and might die, and Sybil still didn't seem to make the connection. She seemed to think that just because Glock liked Tamara, she wouldn't hurt her. But of course, the opposite was true. Glock was most likely to hurt the people closest to her.

(ii)

Glock returned to the apartment, banging on the door in irritation for Sybil to unlock the deadbolt. Sybil unlocked it and let Glock in.

"Shouldn't be locked out of my own place," Glock muttered.

"Sorry."

Glock dug into her pocket and pulled out an orange prescription bottle, tossing it to Sybil.

"Some oxy for Princess," she said. She put a couple of plastic baggies on the counter. "And something a little more fun for me. And you, if you want."

Sybil came over and fingered the baggies. "Yeah, if you don't mind sharing," she agreed.

"Just as easy to share a pipe as smoke it alone," Glock said.

Sybil dug in the cooler for a moment, then just filled a glass from the sink faucet, and took it over to Tamara. "Here, hon'," she handed the glass to Tamara and fished a tablet from the prescription bottle, which she also passed to Tamara. "You might wanna sit up a bit, or you're gonna spill."

Tamara attempted to prop herself up a bit, but the pain in her side flared, making it impossible. She washed the pill down the best she could, and wiped the dribble from her face and neck with the back of her hand.

"Oxy's good stuff," Sybil assured her. "You'll feel lots better."

Tamara nodded, holding her ribs, and breathing shallowly. She couldn't see what it was Glock was fiddling with over on the counter, but it wasn't long before Sybil abandoned Tamara and went over to join her. Tamara closed her eyes, waiting for the painkillers to take effect. She drifted off dreaming restless dreams.

(iii)

Tamara awoke with a start. Something was burning. She coughed and gagged at the foul, sickly smell. She sat up, trying to clear her lungs.

"What is that smell?" she demanded.

Glock passed a glassy pipe to Sybil, grinning.

"Smells like cat pee, doesn't it?" she laughed.

Wide-eyed, Tamara watched Sybil put the pipe to her mouth and suck on the stem, holding a lighter underneath the bowl.

"That, and burning plastic or something," Tamara coughed. It was sweet, but not pleasant. She rubbed her nose, looking around. "Can't we open the window?"

Sybil walked over to the bed and sat down, still smoking.

"Try it," she offered with a broad smile, holding the pipe up to Tamara's face. "It may stink, but it feels fantastic!"

Tamara pushed it away, then jerked back from the hot glass.

"Ow! No, I don't want any."

Sybil passed the pipe back to Glock.

"Looks like that oxy is helping," she observed.

Tamara was surprised. She realized that she was sitting up without pain. She took an experimental breath. There was a little discomfort, but nothing like what it had been before.

"Yeah, I guess it's helping," she agreed.

Sybil got up and cracked the window open. She waved her hands as if she could waft all of the rancid-smelling smoke out.

"Tell her how good it feels, Glock," Sybil prompted. "She should try."

Glock looked at Tamara and shook her head. "She doesn't want to feel good. Thinks she's better than anyone else."

"It's not that," Tamara protested.

She wondered why she was still arguing. *Did* she think that she was better? She could sit here and watch Glock and Sybil smoke crack, and think that she was better than them because she didn't? She had done everything else. Drank, smoked pot, participated in grand theft, assault, maybe murder. How could she still hold herself to a higher standard?

Glock sucked some more on the pipe. "That's okay," she told Sybil. "More for you and me."

(*iv*)

Glock and Sybil had partied late into the night, but both were now obviously on the rebound after their high. Sybil was passed out on the floor, and Glock lounged on the bed beside Tamara, looking more dour than ever, drifting alternately between unconsciousness and morose commentary, most of it random and not even directed at Tamara.

"Why are you still holding out?" Glock questioned suddenly, startling Tamara. "All the trouble, all the ugliness you've seen, why do you still think you're better? You don't do drugs. You don't even get drunk, unless we slip you something. You don't wanna be involved in any of my stuff. Why?"

Tamara looked at her for a moment, wondering if Glock was even in a state to comprehend her reply. But Glock continued to look at her steadily, waiting for an answer.

"Not because I think I am better," Tamara insisted. "I just want... to *be* better. I want to do the right thing. To be a good person."

"Why?" Glock demanded, a frown creasing her forehead. "What's the point of that?"

Tamara tried to pin it down. "I dunno... I was mostly raised by my Gramma, before the Bakers... I guess that's what she taught me. If you do good, you feel good. You help others, it comes back to you."

"That's bull," Glock complained. "That ain't true."

"Are *you* happy?"

Glock snorted. "I'm happy when I'm doing what I want."

"What about right now?"

"Right now, I feel like a piece of crud on the bottom of someone's shoe," Glock admitted. "But that's just the low from the crack."

"Is that how you want to feel?"

Glock closed her eyes briefly. "The high is worth it."

"What about feeling good without getting high?" Tamara suggested.

"Yeah? That what you were thinking about when you killed those kids? That you were being a good person, doing the right thing?"

Tamara's jaw dropped. "What?"

Glock chuckled, and opened her eyes in a squint to look at Tamara.

"You gonna preach to me about what's right? Don't forget I know your history."

Tamara was silent.

"It was a bad scene," she said after a few minutes. "I was all mixed up..."

"Don't tell me," Glock said. "I know what they did to you. Made you into."

Tamara watched the flashing pictures on the TV screen, which seemed to always be playing at Glock's apartment, twenty-four hours a day. She shifted uncomfortably.

"I know what I am," Glock said. "Why do you have such a hard time accepting what you are?"

"I'm... I'm still working on it," Tamara fumbled.

"Working on what?" Glock demanded.

"On... on what I want to be," Tamara said lamely.

"You think what you want to be has anything to do with it?" Glock derided. "Did you choose how you were born? Who you were raised by? You choose to go to that stinkin' foster home and be abused?"

"No."

"They're the ones who made you what you are. Just like my deadbeat junkie parents and broken system made me what I am. I don't fight it. I know what I am. Embrace it, quit fighting it. That's how to be happy."

"I still have choice," Tamara insisted.

"Yeah, be what you are and be happy, or fight who you are and be miserable. Either way, it's not going to change who you are, just how happy you are."

"And you think what I am is... what? A... criminal?"

Glock laughed and elbowed Tamara in the ribs. Luckily the opposite side from her injury.

"A *criminal*," she mocked. "You always denied what you are, Princess. A murderer. Infanticide, at that. And don't tell me it was a bad scene, I already know that. You started out a good, honest, innocent kid. And they twisted you up. And that's what they made you. You can't help that." Glock stared at the TV for a few minutes, then got up and got herself a beer, stepping carefully over Sybil. "Unfortunately, that granny of yours raised you with a conscience. So you got all this guilt. If you were like me, you wouldn't have to feel guilty."

Tamara frowned at Glock. "You think that's all there is to it? I was raised to be good, so I want to be good? But I can't be, because of the Bakers?"

"Yeah," agreed Glock. "You got it." She took a swig of her beer. "Just like I was made who I am by the system."

Tamara said nothing. Glock stared steadily at her.

"I'm a psychopathic sadist," she said. "I can't help that. That's not my choice. And when I see a perv like Coach Cutie, I can't control what happens. Sometimes I can resist an impulse for a while, but sooner or later, *you* know what's going to happen, don't you, Princess?"

Tamara nodded wordlessly.

"And when you see Sybil's little sisters, what do you see?" Glock's eyes were cunning. "What do you feel?"

Tamara chewed on her thumbnail. She tried not to think about Sybil's little sister. Because she knew thinking about Sybil's little sister would lead to thinking about Corinne and Julie, and she didn't want to think about Corinne and Julie.

"Don't block it," Glock said. "Feel it! Those sweet little girls..."

"I don't want to kill Sybil's sisters, if that's what you think," Tamara shot back. "I'm not a killer!"

"You are," Glock said. "Quit lying to yourself! You're a killer just like I am."

"You choose to kill," Tamara insisted. "I don't. I didn't."

"It's not a choice," Glock said. "It's... destined. You can fight it, but sooner or later, you're just going to blow. I know. I've been there."

"You chose. You made me take you to McClure. You wanted to hurt him. Kill him. That wasn't fate. That was a choice."

"If it wasn't him, it would have been someone else," Glock said with a shrug. "At least he deserved it."

"It was a choice," Tamara repeated.

Glock gulped down more beer, and folded her arms across her chest.

"And you didn't choose?" she said. "Frenchie, I don't get you. I chose to kill, but you didn't? You can choose to be a good girl now, but you didn't choose to kill those kids? That just happened? Are you schizo or what? How can you believe both at once?"

Tamara stared at Glock, frowning. She knew that Glock had chosen to hurt McClure. It wasn't fate. It wasn't just an impulse she couldn't control. It was premeditated. Not like what had happened with the Baker children. What had happened to the Baker children was different. But Tamara didn't know how to explain it to Glock.

"I was sick," she insisted. "They were beating on me, and treating me like a slave, and all of the pregnancy hormones messed with my brain. They made it all foggy and mixed up. I didn't know what I was doing. That's different."

Glock laughed and sat back down next to Tamara. "Oh, that's different," she agreed sarcastically. "Those kiddies just died because you were confused, right? What, you accidentally put rat poison on the cereal instead of sugar?"

Tamara shook her head. "No..."

"Little kids," Glock said knowingly, "like Sybil's little sisters. Think about it. Quit hiding from it. Sybil's sweet little sisters..."

"No. They were younger. Not that big." Their faces flashed repeatedly before Tamara's eyes. "Two years old, and a baby."

"Oh, just tiny ones, huh? Hardly worth worrying so much about."

"I just... I couldn't take care of them. It was too hard. All of the crying, the demands. Taking care of everything, while the Bakers partied. That's the only reason they got me, to be their slave. It was too much," Tamara insisted.

"So you were confused," Glock repeated. "And you accidentally throttled the babies while they slept?"

"No!"

"Why do you always play coy about what happened? Is it because you don't want to admit it to yourself? I've known you three years, protected you, taught you to take care of yourself, and you still won't tell me?"

Tamara closed her eyes, shaking her head.

"Say it out loud," Glock insisted. "I know you confessed to the court and the parole board. So tell *me*."

"I didn't... I didn't talk to them about the details."

"Tell me."

Tamara rubbed her eyes, trying to banish the images. Corrine in the water. Julie limp and flaccid in her arms, face blue when Tamara put her in the crib. "If I talk about it, will it go away?" Maybe she could stop the flashbacks, the nightmares.

Glock narrowed her eyes.

"Maybe it will," she said. "Maybe you gotta stop holding it in. Expose it to the light of day."

Tamara gulped and tried to form the words. "The older one... Corrine... she drowned in the bathtub. And the baby, Julie... they said it was shaken baby syndrome."

"*You* did it," Glock said, her voice harsh and grating. "*You* drowned her. Say it. Admit it. Not 'she drowned.' *You* drowned her."

"I... I drowned her." Tamara's voice broke. Tears started to run down her cheeks. Real tears.

"And the baby?" Glock pressed.

"I... I shook her to make her stop crying. Shook her and shook her."

Glock nodded. "Yeah. *You* did it. And if they hadn't treated you like that, hadn't abused you and messed with you and made you take care of the little kids all by yourself, you wouldn't have done it, would you?"

"No." Tamara's whole body was shaking, the tears coursing down her cheeks.

"They made you into a killer. It was their fault. Not your choice."

"But..." Tamara looked up at Glock's face. "Maybe I coulda

got out some other way. I could have run away. Or asked the social worker to move me. Or," she sniffled loudly, "told a teacher at school, about what they were doing."

"Then they just put you in a new home where it's twice as bad," Glock said, shaking her head. "They don't like kids who complain about their foster parents, make it look like the system is broken. They'd put you in a home where you were whipped black and blue and pimped out every day. That's what they do to complainers."

Tamara wiped tears from her eyes.

"I could have done something else," she said, more steadily. "I could have... made a better choice."

"They made you," Glock maintained. "He got you pregnant. You couldn't control that. You couldn't control the mood swings and confusion from the pregnancy and abuse any more than you could control throwing up."

"I could still... I didn't have to kill them," Tamara's voice broke again. "I didn't have to do that. Those poor babies. Corinne fought back so hard." She sobbed, unable to go on for a minute. Seeing Corinne in front of her, feeling her soft, baby smooth skin in her hands. "She was only two, and I could hardly hold her down. And Julie just kept getting sicker and sicker. Throwing up. Her face got blue."

Glock whipped the beer can furiously at Tamara's head, and Tamara barely avoided it. "It wasn't a choice!" Glock bellowed. "You just shut—your—face!"

Tamara covered her eyes with her arm and curled up into a ball, continuing to weep, her whole body shuddering. The door slammed, and Glock was gone.

(v)

When Tamara woke up, it was quiet. She turned over and the

pain ripped through her side again, taking away her breath. She breathed as shallowly as possible, head spinning, and glanced around to see what was going on. Sybil straightened up, having just shut off the TV. It must have been the silence that woke Tamara up, after listening to the drone of the TV for days on end.

Sybil's face was drawn, looking old and tired. She smiled weakly at Tamara. "Sorry, I wake you up?"

Tamara attempted a shrug.

"You look about due for another oxy," Sybil said.

"Yeah. Please."

She rested her head back as Sybil went to the kitchenette and got a glass of water for Tamara to wash down the pill. When she came back, she scanned Tamara's face.

"You look as bad as I feel."

Tamara's head was thick. Her eyes were itchy and swollen from crying. Her dreams had been haunted all night by images of the children. Sometimes Corinne and Julie, sometimes Sybil's sisters, and sometimes children she didn't even recognize. Guilt weighed heavily upon her. She hadn't felt so bad in the three years since it had happened.

"Yeah," she whispered.

She took the oxy pill from Sybil and drank it down.

"Where's Glock? Did she... hurt you?"

Tamara shook her head. "We had a... a discussion."

Sybil snorted. "I'll bet that was interesting. Is she coming back?"

"It's her place. I assume so. Meantime, I gotta figure out what to do..."

"Well, you probably don't want to jump right into anything. Let things quiet down a little before you show your face anywhere. If you're not going to stay with Glock... I don't know what you're going to do. You'll have to be careful."

"Even if I wanted to stay with her," Tamara said, frowning at

Sybil, "sooner or later she'll kill me. And... I don't think that's what I want."

Sybil reached over and pushed a lock of Tamara's hair behind her ear. "She wouldn't kill you."

"She would."

Sybil paused for a moment, their eyes meeting. Then Sybil looked at her phone.

"I gotta get going. You need anything?"

Tamara breathed out. "You'd better leave me the pills."

Sybil looked reluctant to part with the bottle of oxy. Tamara couldn't figure out what Sybil would want them for. Tamara was the one with broken ribs. Sybil handed it over with a sigh.

"We need to think of a place we can meet later," Tamara said lowly. "Not your house. Not anywhere Glock knows about."

"You're serious. You're going to walk out on her?"

Tamara nodded.

"Sheesh," Sybil said. "I dunno. I can't think right now. My head's messed up. And you don't have a phone that works; I can't call or text you later."

Tamara shook her head.

"Can you get a phone? Or money to buy one?" Sybil suggested.

"I don't have any money. Do you?"

"Are you kidding? I can't even get my hands on my mom's credit card. Where's Glock's money? Does she leave any here?"

Tamara looked around the apartment. It was so small, and sparse. There were really no hiding places.

"Check behind the TV," she suggested.

Sybil went over to the big screen and squeezed her face against the wall to look. She poked about with careful fingers, then withdrew, shaking her head.

"Um, no. No cash back there."

Tamara looked at Sybil's pinched white face and decided not to ask for further details. She shook her head.

"I don't know where else she would put it. A coffee can or the toilet tank? She's probably just got it all with her."

Sybil performed a brief search of the tiny apartment, and shrugged widely.

"Sorry. She must not have stashed any. You know my number, if you can get a phone. I'll try to get my head straight and think of somewhere safe to meet. But... you'll have to make sure that you're not followed."

"Or you," Tamara pointed out. "The cops will know by now that you're my friend. They might follow you, looking for me."

Sybil considered that for a moment.

"They already talked to me at school. I think I convinced them I didn't know about Glock, or where you might go or anything."

"Well... I guess you weren't followed here yesterday, or we wouldn't still be around."

Sybil nodded. "I'll be careful though," she promised. "I dunno where to meet you. I want to pick somewhere there's lots of people; you know, hide in a crowd... but that means more people around that might recognize you."

Tamara nodded. "I'm not very experienced at this. Never really even watched spy movies..."

"I'll figure out a place. You figure out the phone. And then... what are you going to do next?"

"I'll tell you when we meet. I'm still figuring it out."

Sybil touched Tamara's face, where the tears were tattooed, now puffy from real tears. The tears that should have come years ago. Sybil's touch was feather-light.

"And you're okay? Is it just the ribs?"

Tamara shook her head. "No. It's... hard to explain."

"I know you won't like this, but maybe... have a drink. It might help." She lifted her hands in a shrug. "Just sayin'. Your choice. I'll see you later. We'll talk."

(*vi*)

Tamara hung out in the convenience store for a long time, looking at the cell phones and watching the clerk. There was a security camera, but Tamara thought after watching it for a while that it was broken. It was old, and the light on it was out, and the angle it was pointed at wouldn't actually take in the cashier's counter.

"Miss? Miss?"

Tamara realized that the cashier was trying to get her attention. She walked toward the check out counter. "Yeah?"

"You need something? You can't just hang out here. You waiting for someone, or what?"

The knife in Tamara's pocket was slippery with her sweat as she shifted her grip on it. She'd seen Glock do this. Simple. Just threaten him with a knife. They were all trained to just cooperate with an armed assailant. He would do what she wanted. Give her the money in the cash drawer. Activate one of the prepaid phones. A coffee to go, if she asked. She didn't actually have to hurt anyone, just threaten. And it was for the good. So that Tamara could start a new life and escape from Glock. She wanted to be a good person, so one small criminal act could be excused. No one had to get hurt.

"What do you want?" the clerk demanded. "Is there something wrong?"

He eyed her suspiciously. Tamara turned around and walked out. She didn't look back.

After that, Tamara just walked for a while, trying to sort things out. She dry-swallowed another oxy as her ribs started to pulse with pain. She got on the bus and had barely enough change to cover the fare. She sat down and looked over the other bus patrons. A few were talking on phones. Or playing games or reading books on them. A few just sitting, staring out the window. Tamara frowned, thinking back to Mrs. Henson's response when Tamara had asked for a phone. Everyone carried a phone. She could borrow one if it was an emergency. Well, why not?

She shifted closer to a mom with a squirmy toddler and a squawking baby in a stroller.

"Excuse me?"

The woman looked up, and looked her over uneasily.

"Yes?"

"I, um, my phone died, and I gotta find out where my mom wants to meet me. Do you have a phone I could borrow, just for a couple minutes?"

The woman's expression softened. "Yes, I guess. For a minute."

She dug into her backpack, then pulled out a phone and handed it to Tamara. Tamara pushed the button to wake it up. A smart phone, much fancier than the old flip she'd been using.

"This is different than mine. Where do I go to text?"

The woman gave her a puzzled look. But she looked at the phone and swiped and tapped until Tamara was in the messaging app. The woman tapped the compose button.

"There. Just put in your mom's phone number there, then tap there, and type your message. And send."

"Thanks."

Tamara tapped in Sybil's number carefully, and then her message.

Where do u want to meet?

She waited, looking at the time and wondering what class Sybil was in. Some teachers were more laid back about phones than others. Sometimes you had to be really careful about texting during class without letting the teacher see.

Know the youth club across from the mall?

Tamara thought about it, trying to visualize. Then she nodded to herself. It was a good choice. A sort of outreach program for at-risk kids. No cops or social workers, just teen mentors, who hopefully would not recognize her or want to get her in trouble. She texted back.

Yes. C U there after school.

She hesitated a moment.

Don't text back. Not my #.

Tamara handed the phone back to the woman with the children.

"Thanks."

FOURTEEN

(i)

TAMARA GOT TO THE youth club before Sybil did. She'd never been there before and didn't know the leaders, so she just hovered around the fringes, watching the boys playing basketball, trying to look like she fit in and knew everyone there, when she actually knew no one. A few teens glanced at her and whispered to each other, but mostly they ignored her. No one seemed like they recognized her or knew that there was a warrant out for her arrest. No phones were whipped out upon sighting her, though there were plenty of kids already talking or texting.

Tamara paced across the sidewalk by the basketball pavement, looking toward the school, impatient for Sybil to arrive. Eventually, she saw the familiar figure approaching.

"Hey."

Sybil nodded, smiling. "Hey, girl. Are you okay?"

Tamara nodded. "Yeah. Okay."

"So..." Sybil looked around carefully. "No Glock?"

"No."

Sybil seemed slightly disappointed. "Are you going back there, then? Where else can you go?"

Tamara shook her head. She took a deep breath, and related what she had been thinking about after leaving the convenience store.

"I... I guess I realized... I can't exactly get along on my own, without breaking more laws... I mean... even to get my own phone... I got no money, no way to work or get any money... without lying, using someone's social insurance number, all that... I can't..."

"What are you saying?" Sybil asked.

"I... I always thought it wasn't fair, me getting sent to juvie. I thought... it wasn't my fault." Tamara started to think about the children again, and tears came to her eyes. "But that was wrong. It *was* my fault, my choice..."

Sybil's eyes were wide, uncertain.

"You're not going to..."

Tamara nodded.

"You're not going back to juvie!" Sybil insisted in disbelief.

"What else am I going to do? I killed those babies, Sybil. It was my choice. I gotta pay for it."

"But you already served your time."

"No... I served part of my term, and made parole. But I broke my parole."

"It wasn't your fault," Sybil protested. "Glock got you drunk, and she's the one who hurt the coach."

Tamara noticed with dark humor that Sybil didn't include herself as one of the parties complicit in getting Tamara drunk. Sybil had poured the drinks. It had been her doing as much as Glock's. But Tamara had made enough mistakes of her own.

"I broke my parole," Tamara said. "I wasn't supposed to have anything to do with Glock. I should have reported it the first time she showed up. Maybe they could have proven she was the one who tortured and killed the pets... or something else. I don't know. Everything else that happened... I guess I'm sorta responsible for the stuff Glock did too, since I never reported her."

Sybil was shaking her head, distressed. "No, Tamara. Come on. You're a good person. You don't deserve to have to go back to juvie."

Tamara sighed. Sybil's phone vibrated, and she pulled it out and looked at it. Tamara saw her lips tighten, and her eyes darted up to Tamara's face.

"What?" Tamara asked.

Sybil handed the phone to Tamara. Tamara looked down at it. A text message from the number she knew must be Glock's.

Where is Frenchie?

"Tell her you don't know," Tamara said. She had hoped that Glock would stay away from her apartment longer, not notice that Tamara was gone until Tamara could get things straightened out. But before Tamara could hand the phone back to Sybil, it buzzed again, and she looked down at it.

I'm at your house. The little girls are home.

Tamara's heart sank. She slowly handed the phone back to Sybil. Sybil looked down at the text message. The color drained from her face.

"Tell her we'll come there," Tamara sighed.

Sybil tapped a message back. Tamara leaned in to see Glock's response. Sybil held the phone out flat between them so that they could both see it. In thirty seconds, there was another buzz and the new message appeared on the screen.

No hurry. I can amuse myself here.

Sybil clutched at Tamara, her eyes wide with alarm.

"Come on. We gotta go."

(ii)

They walked quickly without conversation. What was there to say? Neither one wanted to talk about Glock, or the danger to the girls. And talking about anything else under the circumstances would seem inappropriate, almost blasphemous. Both of them were a little bit out of breath, and Tamara was reminded of Coach McClure telling her that she needed to give up smoking if she wanted to get in proper shape. She couldn't even walk quickly without puffing. Each heavy breath brought a stab of pain in her ribs, like the worst stitch she'd ever had in her side. There was no leisurely smoke out in front of the house today. Sybil hurried up the sidewalk and turned the handle, but there was no need. The door swung free, not properly latched. Tamara looked down at the doorframe as she followed Sybil into the house. It was splintered, the strike plate ripped out of the wood.

Tamara had sort of expected things to be in chaos when they got to the house. Shouting and banging and crying. But it was very quiet. Tamara blinked, her eyes adjusting from the bright afternoon sun to the dimness of the living room. The blinds and curtains were pulled. The two older girls were at the far side of the room, as far from Glock as possible. They were holding each other, their faces streaked with tears. Glock looked thoroughly comfortable in an easy chair, with the youngest girl on her lap. Tamara's nostrils flared with the strong smell of urine that hung in the air. She wiped her nose with the back of her jacketed arm. Glock watched her, stroking the hair of the little girl that she was holding, patting her like a cat. The girl's eyes were wide, her face damp and blotchy, a river of snot running from her nose all the way down her chin.

Tamara tried to control her breathing. Tried to avoid going back, seeing Corinne's face again and hearing Julie's open-mouthed wails. She hated it when they cried. It got under her skin and drove her crazy. If the Bakers were home and heard either of the girls crying for long, Tamara was sure to be punished for it. So even if they weren't home, Tamara was still conditioned to shut them up as quickly as possible, panicking that they were going to be heard.

"Thought maybe you ran away," Glock commented, her voice casual and unconcerned.

"No. No, I just needed to get out." Tamara swallowed, trying not to sound out of breath. "Get some fresh air."

Glock nodded. She grasped the little girl's long hair, pulling it, forcing the girl to tip her head way back to try to reduce the pressure. Her ivory throat was exposed; long, smooth, and unmarked. Glock ran her nails down the pale skin, light enough not to leave a scratch. The girl sobbed or gagged, making her small body convulse once. Tamara heard the sharp intake of breath beside her, and looked at Sybil. Her face was just as pale as her sister's, stark under her dark make-up. Sybil's eyes were wide, showing the whites all the way around the iris. Her chest was heaving.

Tamara forced herself to move. She covered the space between her and Glock in a couple of strides. Without worrying about the inadvisability of such an action, she reached over and plucked the little girl up off of Glock's lap. Glock hung on for a moment to her hair, but when Tamara kept pulling, Glock released it, letting the tot go. Tamara hugged the girl to herself. Her pants were soaked, but Tamara paid no heed. The girl's tiny arms encircled Tamara's neck and held on tightly. Her fine hair brushed silkily across Tamara's cheek. Tamara could feel her start to sob.

Tamara felt like she was swirling down into a dark vortex. The flashbacks were so strong now that she could barely focus on the physical world around her. The guilt was overwhelming. Two children like this; even younger and more vulnerable, completely innocent, and Tamara had snuffed the life out of them. As cold and unfeeling as anything Glock ever did, Tamara had simply found them inconvenient, and taken the easy way out.

She rubbed the little girl's back soothingly. "It's okay, Boo," she whispered in the girl's ear. "You're safe now."

She handed the child to Sybil, who enfolded her eagerly in her arms.

Sybil motioned to the other children. "Come on now," she snapped out. "Come to your bedroom, guys."

The other children approached hesitantly, keeping as far from Glock as they could. Sybil gathered them around her and took them down the hall to the bedroom, shutting the door behind her.

Tamara looked down at Glock, her heart pounding. Glock stood up. She grasped Tamara's hands, and intertwined her fingers with Tamara's on both hands. They stood face-to-face, palm-to-palm, uncomfortably close together.

"It's time to stop this dance," Glock hissed. "Let's get something straight here. You're mine. That's not over because we're out of juvie. You're still mine, and you do what I tell you."

Tamara said nothing.

"Don't run away from me," Glock warned.

"Do I look like I'm running?"

Glock stared at her, eyes narrowed.

"Come on."

She let go of Tamara's hands, and headed for the door. Tamara followed after her, letting out her breath. Whatever happened to Tamara now, at least she wouldn't be responsible for Sybil's sisters getting hurt. They would be safe. Hopefully, Sybil would have the sense to call the police. Put them on Tamara's and Glock's trail. Send them to Glock's apartment. Sybil knew that Tamara was resigned to going back to juvie anyway. Sybil had to protect her little sisters. She had to do what was right for them. Or what was to stop Glock from coming back again the next time? And next time, maybe she wouldn't just play games. Tamara knew Glock wouldn't hesitate to hurt the little girls.

Glock didn't look back to see if Tamara was coming. She just strode off. Tamara quickened her pace to keep up. She got up beside Glock, but kept lagging behind and having to run a few strides to catch up again. Tamara's side was burning, and she had to stop, hands on knees, breathing heavily. She couldn't seem to get enough oxygen, and the stabbing pain in her side wasn't receding because she had stopped. Tamara coughed painfully, hurting all the way from her hip to her heart. Her face twisted in a grimace of pain, and she tried to control her breathing, hoping the pain would subside.

At first Glock paid no attention, striding on, expecting Tamara to catch up again. Tamara was seeing bright flashes of light, crowding out her vision, making it difficult to see the physical world. Still bent over, she stared down at her feet, trying to see the details. Trying to force herself to stay conscious and aware.

There was a light hand on her back. Glock's big, powerful fingers.

"Breathe, Frenchie. Take it easy."

"Hurts," Tamara gasped. She swallowed, and tried to slow her breathing down again.

"What hurts? Your ribs again? Why won't you let me take care of them?"

Tamara nodded.

"Where's your pills?" Glock asked. "Don't tell me Sybil ran off with them."

"No..."

Tamara tried to find her pockets, but couldn't sort through the folds of her coat with her shaking fingers. Glock felt for them, and delved into Tamara's pocket to pull them out. Tamara could hear her shaking them out.

"Here. I'm hoping you don't need a drink to swallow them."

Tamara held out her hand, but Glock pressed it directly to her lips. Tamara sucked it in and swallowed. Glock rubbed her back lightly in circles.

"Just breathe, Princess. It'll take a few minutes to work."

Tamara nodded wordlessly. She just stood there, bent over, focused on nothing but breathing. Eventually, the pain started to recede. Tamara coughed. She still didn't feel like she was getting enough air, but at least breathing wasn't so painful.

"Can you walk, or am I gonna have to carry you?" Glock questioned. "You know, that might attract some attention."

"Walk slow," Tamara requested.

"Sure, Princess."

Tamara cleared her throat and straightened up. With Glock walking slowly by her side this time, they progressed down the street.

After a few minutes, Glock huffed impatiently. "This is gonna take forever."

"We can catch the bus," Tamara suggested, rolling her shoulder, trying to relax the muscles in her side.

"Too many people who might know you," Glock disagreed. "I'm thinking we'd better get a car."

"No," Tamara protested. "I'll try to go faster."

"No point in making yourself sick. Driving will be a lot easier."

"I don't want—"

"I'm not askin' your opinion," Glock snapped.

Tamara stopped arguing.

"Here," Glock directed her toward a bus stop bench. "Wait here. Rest. Just don't get on any buses, okay? Wait for me."

Tamara eased herself down onto the bench, and sighed. "Okay."

Glock nodded. "I won't be long."

(iii)

Tamara was dozing a bit when Glock pulled up in the car, and wasn't sure how long she had been waiting. She decided the oxy must be making her dopey. Glock tapped the horn to wake her up, and Tamara squinted at her for a moment before remembering where she was and what she was doing. She got up creakily from the bench, rubbing her back and stretching the kinks of out her neck. Glock opened the passenger door and Tamara got in.

"You like the wheels?" Glock inquired with a grin.

Tamara rubbed her eyes. She hadn't noticed anything special about the car; but then, she wasn't a car person. She couldn't tell the difference between a ten-thousand-dollar compact and a hundred-thousand-dollar sports car. She forced a smile.

"Yeah, pretty sweet," she approved, hoping that was the right response.

Glock seemed satisfied with this, and shifted into gear, racing the powerful engine for a moment, and then pulling out.

"Takes longer to get a car during the day," she apologized. "In this area, anyway. Too many people around."

"It's okay," Tamara said. "I had a nice nap."

Glock chuckled. "Good. You had anything to eat today?"

Tamara thought about it, then shook her head.

"What do you want? Burgers?" Glock asked.

"Sure. Whatever you want. I'm not really that hungry."

"You're never that hungry. But I'm starving. Nothin' good to eat at Sybil's. I swear, that family must live on Kool-aid and mac and cheese. Me, I need my red meat."

Tamara nodded. "Sure. Burgers are fine."

She paid little attention as Glock selected a fast food drive-through, and ordered a pile of food. Tamara dug through the bag to find a small burger, and nibbled at it while Glock snarfed down burgers, fries, a pie, and a shake. Tamara got about half-way through her burger and couldn't finish. She held it out to Glock. Glock took it, shaking her head.

They pulled over, and Tamara frowned, looking around. "Where are we?"

Glock didn't answer, her big bites making short work of the

remaining half-burger. She chewed, and motioned for Tamara to get out. They were in a back alley, but Tamara didn't recognize the buildings. It wasn't the alley behind Glock's apartment. She followed Glock around the car and to a door that had a chain with a padlock running through it. Glock pulled out a key and unlocked the padlock. She led the way into the dark building. It was dusty, some kind of warehouse. There were crates, broken furniture, some kind of abandoned equipment. Glock took Tamara into a room with a boarded-up window. There was some sunlight that made it into the room through the cracks between the boards. Glock motioned to a dusty swivel chair.

"Siddown."

"Why—"

"Just do it."

Tamara obeyed. She looked around the room, trying to figure out what it was and why they were there. Glock put a shopping bag down on top of a crate beside Tamara. She pulled out a roll of tensor bandages.

"Off with the shirt."

Tamara moved slowly, removing first her jacket, and then her t-shirt. When she had the t-shirt half off, Glock gave it a tug, pulling it the rest of the way and dropping it on the floor. She started wrapping the bandage around Tamara's torso.

"This is going to be tight," she said. "Best I do it while the oxy is still working."

Tamara nodded stiffly. She looked around, trying to stay distracted. It wasn't the first time that Glock had been in the building. There were pathways through the dust where she had walked. Some of the bits of crates and furniture had been reposi-tioned. Tamara's eyes roved over what looked like a makeshift counter or desk. There were dark stains on it and Tamara wondered in a disjointed way if Glock had been painting here or something.

Glock snugged up the bandage and bent down to fasten it in place. "Okay. That's got you fixed up. Here."

Glock handed Tamara her shirt, and waited while she put it back on. Glock held out Tamara's jacket and helped her thread her arms through the sleeves. There was a ratchet sound and pressure on Tamara's wrist, and as she swung her head around to see what Glock had done, Glock attached the other end of a pair of handcuffs to a pipe that ran from the floor to the ceiling.

Tamara stared.

Several seconds passed, and Tamara's brain couldn't quite process what was happening. Glock grinned at her. Tamara pulled on the chain as if testing to see if it was real. Of course it was. She knew it was. But she couldn't quite comprehend it.

"Comfy?" Glock demanded.

"What are you doing?"

"Making sure you stick around this time."

"I wasn't going anywhere—"

"Nope," Glock agreed.

"Glock..."

"Don't whine, Princess."

"You don't need to lock me up."

"You think you want to go back to juvie? How about you live in my prison instead?"

"I didn't... I never told you I wanted to go back to juvie!"

Glock smiled, her eyes narrowing like a satisfied cat, purring over a captured mouse.

"Glock..."

Glock pinched her cheek roughly. "You've had your drugs, something to eat, and got your ribs bound up. You should be fine for a while."

With that, Glock walked out.

(iv)

Tamara supposed she should be happy that she had a comfortable seat, if she was going to be held prisoner for any length of time. That was thoughtful of Glock.

She was aware that her brain wasn't quite operating the way that it was supposed to. She should be upset. She should be trying to escape. Yelling for help. But instead she just sat there. She'd been in handcuffs before. There was no point in pulling on them. Her hand wasn't going to come out or the chain miraculously break. And Glock certainly was not going to suss out a location where anyone was going to be able to hear Tamara yell. If Glock was waiting somewhere close, outside the room, Tamara wasn't going to give Glock the satisfaction of hearing Tamara panic or break down.

By now, Tamara had sorted out that the dark stains on Glock's work bench were not paint. This was where Glock disappeared to in order to carry out her recreational activities. That meant that it was close to the Hensons' house. Tamara wasn't sure how that helped her, but somehow it made her feel a little better, knowing the Hensons were close by.

She was still feeling dopey from the oxy and closed her eyes.

(v)

Tamara had been dozing, slipping in and out of consciousness, having nightmares of Glock drowning Sybil's sisters. She woke with a start, and lifting her head, found she had a crick in her neck. Sleeping sitting up was not terribly comfortable. Each time she awoke, the ache in her side was a little more insistent, reminding her that Glock had not left her with any additional painkillers. She explored her side with careful fingers, feeling the uncomfortably tight bandage and trying to pull it a bit looser. The fasteners were on the other side, below the armpit of the arm that was handcuffed to the pole. Tamara found herself breathing heavily, even though she wasn't running or walking fast anymore. She managed to fish her cigarettes out of her pocket, and wormed a couple of fingers down into her jeans to retrieve her lighter.

The cigarette helped to relax her heaving chest, and reduced the headache pounding at the back of her head. She breathed in the smoke, trying to ignore the pain in her side. Glock would be back sooner or later. She knew Tamara was dependent upon her. Tamara was in too much pain to go back to sleep again. She shifted her position. It occurred to her that she could stand or lie down on the floor if she wanted to. The handcuffs gave her some range of motion, and the wheeled swivel chair could be pushed out of the way if she wasn't using it.

She got up and walked in circles around the pole. It felt good to stretch her legs after sitting for so long, but her side wouldn't allow her to keep it up for long. Her breathing became too labored, and Tamara slipped back into her chair to wait.

The temperature in the warehouse was falling. Tamara started shivering, deep down in her stomach. She did her best to wrap her arms around herself to try to keep warm. It didn't seem to help.

Tamara heard a clanking and raised her head. She tried to sort out the sounds. Was it the noise of the chain being unlocked? Footsteps, panting, growling? Tamara wondered if she was starting to hallucinate.

"Did'ja miss me?" Glock asked, moving into the room.

Tamara swung her head around. It *was* Glock. At least, she seemed too substantial to be a hallucination. She had a full shopping bag. Not the thin plastic kind, but a heavy canvas reusable one. And for some reason, a dog.

It was a small dog, shaggy, square faced, with bright, curious eyes. It was on a leash and heeled for a moment or two, then wandered off to sniff at something new. Glock yanked on the leash, jerking it back.

"Come on, mutt," she ordered.

The dog resisted getting too close to Glock, and when she pulled it closer, growled deep in its chest. Glock just laughed.

"Stupid little thing," she observed.

Not too stupid to fear her. Glock set down her heavy shopping bag and took a moment to look at Tamara. "What's wrong with you?"

Tamara's teeth chattered. "Cold. And need more p-p-p-pills."

Glock frowned, glancing around the room as if she thought that Tamara was trying to fool or distract her. "Cold?" she repeated.

Tamara bobbed her head. Glock touched Tamara's cheek with the back of two fingers. She withdrew again.

"You're like ice." Glock removed her jacket and pulled it around Tamara. "I'll bring blankets or something. I don't know if it's cold in here," again she frowned, looking around, "or if it's because you're in shock or something. From your ribs. We'll get some more oxy in you. That'll fix you up."

Glock dug out the prescription bottle and shook it, looking at the remaining pills kicking around the bottom.

"I'll have to get some more. Here, swallow."

Glock put two pills in Tamara's mouth. Tamara obeyed. Glock dragged the little dog over and tied it to the same pole as Tamara was chained to. The dog yipped and growled, and when there was no reaction to its threats, sat back on its haunches and gazed at Glock and Tamara.

"I brought you a friend," Glock said, nodding at the dog.

Tamara looked at it, then away again. "Great," she murmured.

"Thought you'd be happy for the company," Glock said.

Tamara made no comment. Glock picked her shopping bag back up and rifled through it. She placed one of the warehouse crates beside Tamara, and set a takeout box on it.

"Not hungry," Tamara said.

"It'll help to warm you up. Get something hot on your inside. Perk you up a bit. You were never a big eater and oxy takes your appetite away. So you're going to have to force yourself to eat, even if you're not hungry."

Tamara looked at the box, her stomach writhing. It smelled like Chinese or Thai or something. A heavy, spicy, sweet aroma. She hoped that once the oxy took effect, her stomach would settle so that she could eat something as Glock suggested. Otherwise, she might not be able to keep it down.

The dog nosed at her leg, and Tamara kicked it away. Glock grinned. She delved back into her bag and laid some tools down on her workbench. Tamara didn't look at them. She decided there was nothing else in the bag that concerned her, and let her chin fall to her chest, closing her eyes. Glock continued to unpack and organize her supplies in silence.

"Bathroom break?" Glock suggested.

"Not yet."

"That oxy not working yet?" Glock felt Tamara's face again, studying her.

Tamara shook her head. "Little bit."

"A few more minutes, then, you should be fine."

"Mmm."

Glock trailed her fingers lightly through Tamara's hair. She curled the ends around her fingers, stroking the lock with her thumb. Tamara breathed, waiting for the oxy to take the rest of the pain away. The dog snuffled around their feet. Sweat broke out on Tamara's face. Tamara wiped it with her free hand, and pushed Glock away from her.

"Okay? Better?" Glock verified.

Tamara stretched and touched her side. "Yeah."

Glock unlocked the handcuffs and took Tamara to a back office with an ancient bathroom attached. Tamara had figured the most she would get was a bucket, so she was grateful for the modern plumbing, however old and rusty. She came out of the bathroom and Glock gave her a rough hug around the shoulders.

"What else you need?" she asked, as she escorted Tamara back to her restraints.

"Nothing."

She was used to waiting. She was used to being locked up. Glock would visit and keep her company, bring her food and oxy. Glock locked Tamara's handcuffs again. She pulled a radio out of her bag with a flourish and set it down next to Tamara.

"Something to occupy you while I'm gone," she said.

"Are you leaving?"

"Yeah. If I gotta get you blankets, I'd better duck out. Back in an hour or two."

Tamara nodded. "Okay."

"You eat something," Glock pointed at the takeout box. "I mean it."

"I'll eat."

"More than a bite, I'm saying."

Tamara nodded.

"Okay," Glock said. "Catch you in a while."

(vi)

Glock had not turned the radio on before leaving. Tamara stretched as far as she could, and just managed to grasp it. She couldn't get a good grip, and dropped it on the concrete floor, which made it closer and easier to reach, but she was worried that it would be broken and not work. Tamara turned it on and got nothing but static. But she'd played with her Gramma's old radio plenty of times; so she didn't panic immediately. She turned the tuner knob slowly, listening for a clear station. She found some jazzy saxophone music and sighed in relief. But sax wasn't going to keep her from getting bored. She ran through the full tuning band, and then reversed back through it again, eventually picking a more modern station and putting the radio down.

She picked up the takeout box that Glock had left for her and found General Tso chicken, chow mein, and white rice. She took a few bites. General Tso had been one of her favorites when she had lived with her Gramma. Not something that they had been able to have very often. So in spite of her lack of appetite, she did enjoy it for a few bites. Chow mein was of less interest, and two mouthfuls of rice were about all she could manage.

The dog kept pacing around her feet, whining, nosing at her and begging for food. Tamara tried to ignore it. She did not want to get attached to this dog. It was cruel of Glock to bring it to her, encourage her to be friends with it, and then to torture and kill it as Tamara sat a few feet away. Tamara had no intention of making any kind of connection with the dog. It was like a pig on a farm. Don't get sympathetic with an animal that was just going to be slaughtered. Tamara shoved it away from her several times, but it kept begging for food. Finally she put the rest of the food in the take-out container on the floor, and it left her alone to gobble the Chinese food down. She hoped the table scraps weren't anything that would make it sick.

Glock was right about the hot food helping to warm her up. She still had Glock's coat wrapped around her, but it was the heat from the inside that really made a difference. It felt like her body was finally functioning again. Glock had given her two oxy pills this time instead of one, and Tamara's side was almost entirely pain-free. She turned up the radio and reclined back as far as the chair would let her.

(vii)

Tamara wasn't sure how long it had been before Glock returned. She heard the clanking of the chain being removed from the back door again, and Glock came in a couple of minutes later.

"Hey, Princess. How're you feeling?"

"Okay."

"Good." Glock looked around and saw the takeout container on the floor. "How much did you eat, and how much did the dog?"

"I ate."

Glock was carrying a garbage bag. She set it down and started to pull blankets out of it. Tamara shed Glock's jacket and took one of the blankets from her, and started to wrap it around her. She gagged, and examined the blanket with disgust. It stank horribly, and when Tamara took a look at it, she could see unidentified stains and crusty spills across it. Tamara pulled it back away from her body.

"What's wrong?" Glock asked, grinning.

"It's... it's..." Tamara wiped her nose, pushing the blanket onto the floor and swearing. "What'd you do, roll some homeless person?"

"Take it or leave it, that's what I got."

Tamara pawed through the blankets that she could reach, looking for something reasonably clean. Everything was tattered, worn, and stained. And it all stank of sweat and urine and vomit. Tamara pushed it all away.

Glock pulled her own jacket back on again. "Princess," she mocked.

"Uggh. How could you even touch something like that?"

Glock chuckled. She listened to the radio for a minute, and Tamara saw her eyes wander over to her work bench and linger there for a short time. Then Glock looked back at her again.

"You miss juvie?" she asked.

Tamara stared at Glock's shirt collar, not wanting to look at her face. She frowned.

"I don't *miss* it..." she said slowly, feeling her way, "but it's not easy being out. When I was in the jail after they found the pot..." Tamara sighed. "I didn't have to think. I didn't have to make any more decisions. I didn't have to do anything. It was... such a relief."

Glock nodded. "Yeah," she agreed. "Everything is scheduled... predictable. You don't have to get stressed out over things..."

Tamara ran her finger down the seam of her pants. She tried to remember when she had last changed clothes.

"You been getting pretty stressed lately...?" she suggested to Glock.

In juvie, Glock hadn't been so wound up. Her blood lust, easily pacified with a fight or two, had only surfaced occasionally. Now, Glock couldn't seem to go a day. She had that hungry look in her eyes constantly. Glock was being reckless with the number of animals that she was taking from a limited geographic area, showing no concern she might get caught. Tamara wondered if she had been ramping up for a year, or if it was sudden, triggered by Tamara getting out, or something else that had happened recently.

"What've I got to be stressed about?" Glock laughed. "I do whatever I want."

"Then why do you want to go back to juvie?"

Glock snorted and shook her head. "I never said I wanted to go back to juvie. *You're* the one who wants to go back to juvie."

"Not the same without you there," Tamara said impulsively.

Glock looked at her, eyes widening slightly. "Yeah?" she said. She moved closer to Tamara. "You never said what it was like for you, after I left," Glock said. "You get a new cellie right away? Have to defend your rep? You never said nothing."

Tamara considered.

"Didn't get a new cellie right away," she said. "Weird, sleeping without someone else in the room. No one keepin' me awake snoring."

"Snoring. You were the one always keeping me awake, tossing and turning. Or talking half the night. I never had a chance to snore. You have to fight it out? You were a reasonable brawler, by the time I left."

"Mmm... no, not much. Few confrontations, not too many got physical."

Glock went over to Tamara. "It was simple in juvie." She touched the chain of the handcuffs holding Tamara. "It was good, wasn't it?"

"You want to get sent back?" Tamara challenged. "Is that why you're being so reckless?"

"Reckless? Me?"

Tamara nodded. "Yeah, you."

Glock made a brushing-off motion, shaking her head. "Nah. I don't want to go back. I just wish..."

"It's not the same anymore," Tamara agreed.

"No. It's not." Glock looked around abruptly. "I gotta get out of here. You got everything you need for the night."

Tamara looked at 'everything'... the blankets on the floor. "Did you get more pills?"

"Oh," Glock patted her pockets. "Yeah, sure." She found the bottle and shook it. "There you go." She put it down within Tamara's reach. In another pocket, she found a flashlight, and set it down.

Tamara wet her lips. "Got any water?" she asked.

"No. You can swallow them dry."

"Yeah, but I'm thirsty," Tamara protested.

Glock grunted. "I'll bring you some tomorrow."

With that, Glock departed. Tamara stood and stretched, circled the pole a couple of times, and then sat down again. She turned the radio up. Since Glock had taken her coat back, Tamara had started to shiver again. She looked at the blankets with distaste. She didn't want to have to use them. But she couldn't be choosy. There was no other way for her to stay warm.

She picked out the blanket that looked the least filthy, and wrapped it around herself.

Eventually, it got very dark, and Tamara could see nothing without the flashlight. It was better that Tamara couldn't see the stains on the blankets. After some time had passed, she couldn't smell the stench anymore either. Tamara wrapped herself up as much as she could, and lay down on the floor. It wasn't comfortable, but she was exhausted after the long day, and after downing two more pain pills, she found that she could sleep.

(viii)

When she awoke in the morning, Tamara found the dog cuddled up to her. At first she didn't move, comforted and happy for the companionship. And the dog was warm and didn't smell as awful as the blankets. But after a couple of minutes, she forced herself to move.

"Get out of here, dog!" She shoved it roughly away and sat up. "Go on, just stay away from me!"

Her ribs were on fire, and Tamara got down a couple more oxy as quickly as she could. She was parched and hoped that Glock would be there soon with some water. At least in juvie, they had brought three meals a day, and each one included a drink, even if it was just orange Tang. Tamara wasn't sure if she was going to be able to dry-swallow any more pills. Her throat was getting so dry she didn't think they would move down. Just stay there stuck in her throat. Licking her lips didn't bring any relief. They were still chapped and dry, rough as sandpaper.

Once the drugs started to take effect, Tamara walked around the pole a few times, and sat down in her chair. She felt unaccountably exposed and vulnerable sitting there. The only person in the room. It was like a throne, the only chair there. Conspicuous. But it was warmer and more comfortable than sitting on the floor. Her back and her tailbone had been stiff and sore from lying on the floor while she slept. At least oxy took care of that soreness too. Tamara wondered if she was getting too dependent on the pills. She supposed they were probably narcotic, and you weren't supposed to take narcotics for too long. But how long was too long for broken bones? Broken bones didn't heal in a day, or even in a week. She'd already moved from taking one at a time to taking two at a time. Even two weren't taking away the heaviness and pain that had been growing in her chest. Could a fifteen-year-old die of a heart attack? Tamara got out a cigarette and lit it. It made her cough a bit, but the oxy kept the pain under control. It was probably good that she was coughing, loosening the mucus up. The tightness did not go away.

Glock eventually showed up. She tossed a takeout container that smelled like bacon on the crate next to Tamara. "How'd you sleep, Princess?"

Tamara coughed. "Not good."

"Too bad," Glock said, without any emotion in her voice. "Have something to eat."

"Did you bring water?"

"Better. I brought coffee."

Glock supplied her with a tall insulated cup from a local coffee shop. Tamara picked it up and breathed in the steam. It was still too hot to drink, but she was so thirsty...

"I figured it would warm you up better than cold water."

Tamara blew on the surface of the coffee, hoping to cool it down more quickly. "That dog made a mess. You should take it out for a walk. And clean it up."

Glock scowled.

"Why don't you just get rid of it?" Tamara suggested, then choked on her own words. "I mean—take it back where it came from, just let it loose so they think it escaped on its own, or something."

Glock just stared at her.

"It was nice of you to think of me," Tamara fumbled. "I just... don't want a dog."

Glock shook her head in disgust.

Trying to take the focus off of her words, Tamara retrieved the takeout container that Glock had brought her, and opened it with shaky fingers. Eggs, bacon, a rather soggy English muffin. She looked back at the crate, and retrieved her fork from the previous night's dinner. Apparently Glock hadn't thought about needing cutlery for her breakfast. She shoveled a forkful of eggs.

"Mmm, this is good," Tamara moaned. "Do you remember the eggs at juvie? Those reconstituted egg whites or whatever they were?"

Glock's mouth turned up slightly.

"Those were awful," she agreed. "I almost couldn't finish them." She grinned. "Almost."

Tamara shook her head. "You finished everything. Yours and mine."

"Well, it takes a few more calories to keep a body my size going. I never could understand why they gave everyone the same amount. Giving me the same amount as you or that little slip of a Chinese girl." Glock shook her head.

Tamara crunched through the crispy bacon. The dog was underfoot again, whining and begging. Tamara shoved him away with her foot.

"Can you do something with it, please?" she demanded. "It's driving me crazy. You bring any dog food?"

Glock looked surprised at the question, raising her brows. "No."

Tamara rolled her eyes, and kicked the dog away again. "Just get it out of my way, okay?"

Glock came over and grabbed the dog's leash, pulling it away from Tamara with a hefty yank. The dog yipped, and darted toward Glock, snapping at her legs. Glock lifted the dog off of its feet, letting it dangle in the air.

"You think you can order me around?" she demanded of Tamara.

"No—no, it's just making me crazy. I didn't mean to snap."

Glock continued to let the dog hang.

"It's going to choke," Tamara protested.

"Yeah," Glock agreed.

"Please, stop! I'm sorry. I am. Being locked up has got me irritable. You know what that's like."

Glock's eyes were dancing, enjoying Tamara's reaction. Tamara forced herself to look away. To relax her face and show more interest in her cooling coffee than in what was happening to the dog.

"Oh, that tastes good. I feel like I haven't had coffee in a week. But it's only been... what..." She pondered. "Huh. Maybe it has been a week. Well, it's good, anyway."

She picked up the soggy biscuit and nibbled at it. She heard the dog's nails skittering on the floor again, and Glock readjusting the leash. Tamara fiddled with the radio tuner, looking for something with a heavier beat.

"What do you want to listen to?" she asked.

"Whatever you want, Princess. I'm not going to be staying long."

Tamara risked looking at her now. "Why would you bring me here if you're not even going to spend any time with me? I thought the whole point was that you wanted me to yourself."

Glock shrugged. "More to make sure that you can't run off on me. I'll spend more time with you later. Right now, I have other things to take care of."

"Could you bring a book or something? I'm bored out of my mind."

"Yeah, maybe."

Glock picked up her own coffee and took a few big gulps. "I'll never get that Sybil," she said, shaking her head. "That's one messed-up chick."

Tamara was surprised. "What do you mean?"

She had thought that Sybil was pretty stable. She had a nice family, helped take care of the kids. Sure, she liked to give the impression that she was a bad girl, but so did a lot of people. That was nothing. So she wore some dark make-up and had a few piercings. She still seemed pretty normal to Tamara.

"You know she came by my place today, looking for you?"

Tamara thought about it. "Well, she probably wondered where I was."

Glock shook her head. "If she had any sense, she wouldn't be coming anywhere near me. There's got to be something wrong with her."

Tamara shrugged. It did surprise her that Sybil would go to Glock's apartment the day after Glock had held Sybil's family hostage. But Sybil had refused to consider Glock a real danger before she threatened the little girls. Maybe now that the imminent danger to them was gone, Sybil had returned to her willful ignorance.

"I guess," Tamara conceded.

"She oughtta be lookin' after her little family, not messing around with me."

"Yeah..."

Sybil's infatuation with Tamara and Glock, even knowing all that she did, was a *bit* extreme.

"You, on the other hand," Glock cocked her head, looking at Tamara. "You are messed up if you think you can do anything other than stay with me."

Tamara nodded, keeping her breathing even. "Where else would I go?" she agreed.

Glock looked at her with narrowed eyes. "Yeah, where else?" she asked.

Glock took a look around the room for anything that was out of place, and Tamara recognized that she was preparing to leave.

"A book," she reminded Glock. "Okay?"

"Sure, Princess."

Glock picked up her coffee cup, and walked out without another word. Tamara sat still thinking about the conversation. The dog coughed a couple of times. Tamara glanced at it, worried that Glock had injured its throat.

"Sorry," she apologized to the dog. "Didn't mean to get you in trouble."

FIFTEEN

(i)

WHEN GLOCK ARRIVED THE next day, Tamara was still on the floor, in the strange blurred space between asleep and awake. The dog was curled up against her once again, even on the shortened leash. Tamara had awakened enough to take her pills, and then had fallen back asleep again. She had fed the dog the remainders of her breakfast after Glock had gone, but then Glock had not shown up again with lunch or supper. Ravenous, Tamara sucked down the cold, bitter remains of her coffee, and prayed that Glock hadn't forgotten about her or gotten caught by the police.

Glock's arrival the next day woke Tamara up. She was confused and disoriented. She sat up, rubbing her eyes, trying to remember where she was. When she remembered where, she struggled to remember how long she had been there; something to help ground her in time as well as space.

"We got company," Glock announced. "Get up and make yourself decent."

Tamara struggled to get to her feet. After a few unsteady

moments she slid into the chair to rest, wheezing. "Company?" she repeated hoarsely.

"Come on in," Glock called.

Sybil peeked around the corner, then hurried in to greet Tamara, her eyes wide as she looked around at the warehouse. "Hey, Tamara! How's it going, girl?"

Tamara ran her fingers through her hair, realizing that she probably looked a wreck after several sleeps without a brush or comb.

"Hey," she greeted weakly.

Sybil's eyes went over Tamara. She glanced at Glock, and then back.

"Lookin' a little worse for wear, there," Glock commented in a tone of unconcern.

Glock dropped a takeout box on Tamara's crate, sending the prescription bottle spinning. Sybil retrieved it, and shook it to see how many tablets were left.

"Leave'em be," Glock warned.

Sybil rolled her eyes and set the bottle back down. "I wasn't taking them." She looked at Tamara. "You had any lately?"

Tamara nodded. She coughed and cleared her throat. "Yeah. Not long ago."

Her lungs felt heavy, like she was drowning. She tried to take a deep breath in, but was limited by the tight bandages around her ribs.

"Glock, is there a sink or something where I can help Tamara get herself cleaned up?"

Glock snorted. "And you wouldn't just run off with her again? I'll take her."

"Let me come too. I don't want to be in here alone." Sybil took a glance around the room and shuddered. Glock moved toward Tamara and unlocked the handcuff bracelet from the pipe. Looking from Tamara to Sybil, she caught Sybil's wrist, and in a lightning-fast movement, slapped the empty bracelet over Sybil's wrist.

Sybil swore loudly and jerked away hard, causing Tamara considerable pain and making her stumble hurriedly to her feet. Sybil swore repeatedly, pulling on the chain as if it would magically break or come undone.

Tamara pulled back. "Cut it out! Settle down!"

"She handcuffed me! You're not going to hold me here too," Sybil shouted at Glock. "No way, no how! Don't even think of it!"

Glock was smiling, thin lips turned up in a smile of satisfaction. "I thought you wanted to go to the bathroom with Frenchie. Now you can go with her and I don't have to worry about you wandering off. What's the problem?"

"Unlock it now!"

"I'll unlock it when you're done," Glock smirked.

Sybil jerked the handcuffs again, and Tamara grasped the chain to protect her own wrist and yanked Sybil up close to her so that they were staring at each other eye-to-eye.

"I said cut—it—out," Tamara said fiercely.

Sybil's eyes were wild, but she relaxed her arm and stopped pulling on the cuffs. "Sorry."

Tamara nodded. She started toward the back bathroom. Glock joined them, chuckling. Tamara did her best to ignore Sybil, pretending that she was on her own. She used the toilet, then stood at the sink to wash up. Sybil looked her over.

"You're filthy," she commented. "I don't know how you could get so dirty in a few days."

Tamara got her hands wet and applied them to her cheeks. "You try sleeping on the dirty floor with a dog and some hobo's blankets and see how you look after a day or two."

Tamara was glad that the mirror was too dusty and stained to see herself clearly. Sybil tried to help with a few smudges that Tamara had missed, and to straighten out her hair. Sybil had her purse with her and dug out a comb and some make-up and went to work. Tamara watched Sybil's face, still feeling disoriented, removed from herself.

"Who cares how I look?" Tamara questioned. "You think Glock cares?"

Sybil looked confused. "I don't know…" she admitted. "I just figured… you'd feel better if you looked better."

"I don't."

"Okay, well…" Sybil trailed off. She started to pack her makeup back away. "Will you be okay?"

Tamara just shook her head and didn't answer. Sybil looked at her for a moment, then they exited the bathroom together.

Glock looked them over. "Very pretty," she observed ironically.

"Glock," Sybil said. "She's sick. Don't you think you could let her go?"

"Sick? She looks fine to me."

Glock led them back to the holding room. Sybil held out her cuffed hand toward Glock insistently. Snickering, Glock took her time unlocking the cuff. She closed it over the pipe again, and Tamara sat down, holding her side and breathing shallowly.

"See?" Sybil pointed out. "She already had oxy, she should be fine. But she can't breathe, and all she did was walk to the bathroom."

"Eat your dinner," Glock said to Tamara, pointing to the takeout box.

Tamara opened it. French fries. No ketchup or gravy. No burger. No matter, she was starving. She started chewing her way through the fries. "You get a drink? I need a drink."

Glock gave her a soft drink cup. Tamara slurped down the top half, until her stomach started to hurt and she lost her breath. She went back to eating the fries.

"You said you were taking good care of her," Sybil said. "You're not taking good care of her."

"I'm not a nursemaid. She's got everything she needs. Look. I even got her a book."

Glock tossed a worn paperback at Tamara. Tamara fumbled, dropping it on the floor, and picked it up again. She looked at the front cover. A gory horror novel. Well, what did she think Glock would choose? Even with the mind-numbing boredom of her imprisonment, Tamara wasn't sure if she could force herself to read it. Tamara wrinkled her nose and continued to eat the fries.

"Look how pale she is. Listen to her breathing." Sybil watched Tamara scarfing down the fries. "When's the last time she ate?"

"She never eats much," Glock dismissed.

"That doesn't mean you don't have to feed her as often. Didn't you get three meals a day in juvie? She's still going to get hungry, even if she doesn't eat very much at a time." Sybil shook her head at Tamara. "And I think she's going to finish it this time."

"I'm right here," Tamara growled. "Don't talk like I'm an animal or a baby or something and can't understand you."

"It's a good thing I made you bring me today," Sybil groused. "Tamara, tell Glock that you're sick."

Tamara turned her head sideways as she ate to look at Glock. "You know I'm sick," she said.

"You got a sore side and some side effects from the oxy," Glock said. "It's not like you're dying or something. You're not throwing up or collapsing or anything."

Tamara looked toward the boarded up window. There was still light between the cracks. She took a drink. "What time is it?"

"Four o'clock or something."

"You haven't been here since breakfast yesterday? I've been sleeping practically that whole time."

"Because you're bored," Glock agreed. "What else are you gonna do? That's why I brought you the book."

Tamara shook her head and ate the last few fries. She used

her fingers to wipe up the rest of the grease and salt, licking off her fingers. She drank down the rest of her pop.

"Maybe I should stay with you tonight," Sybil suggested, looking doubtfully at the pile of stinking blankets. "Just to make sure you're okay."

"You're not staying with her," Glock contradicted, shaking her head. "No way."

"Why? Are you?"

"I don't trust you."

Sybil raised her eyebrows. "You trusted me enough to bring me here."

"So you could see she was okay and would stop nagging me. You said that was all you wanted, and you'd leave me alone, once you saw her." Glock caught Tamara's eye and rephrased. "Once Sybil saw you. And now she's seen you're all right, so tell her she has to go."

"I'm okay, Syb," Tamara said firmly. "Really. Don't cause any trouble."

She stared at Sybil fiercely, trying to communicate with her gaze. If Glock thought that Sybil was going to call the police or something, she wasn't going to make it out the back door alive. And if Glock thought there was a danger that Sybil had already told someone, had started the police on Glock's trail, then Glock would have to either move Tamara or dispose of her. And moving her would be too dangerous.

Sybil bit her lip, meeting Tamara's gaze, and nodded slowly. "Okay," she agreed. "Tamara's okay. I agree. I'm not going to cause any trouble. But can I come back again? Tomorrow?"

Glock scratched her ear, considering Sybil with her brows drawn down. "I don't know. We'll see."

"Okay," Sybil agreed lightly. She swallowed and looked at Tamara. "There anything else you need, babe? Now that you've got a book?"

Tamara shook the beverage container. There was still ice in

it. She took off the lid and put a couple of cubes in her mouth. "Water. And more food."

Glock rolled her eyes.

Sybil was looking at the dog. "He's not looking too good. Is he all right?"

Glock grinned. "Frenchie feeds him from her leftovers," she said. "He'll be fine."

They all looked at Tamara's empty takeout container. Tamara felt sick. She hadn't even thought to save anything for the dog this time. She'd been too hungry herself. She looked at the dog, something that she avoided doing as much as she could. He wasn't getting in the way anymore. And not just because he was on a shorter leash. He lay on the floor listlessly, just following her movements with his eyes. Tamara looked away again.

"Okay," Sybil said. She gave Tamara a nudge in the shoulder. "You take care of yourself, okay? Keep taking the oxy. Those ribs will heal up in no time, and you'll be up and around again."

Tamara nodded. "Yeah," she agreed. "I'm gonna take another one soon."

"Not too many," Sybil warned. "You said you took some right before we got here. If you take too many, they're going to give you problems."

"I'll be careful."

"Well, okay..."

Sybil looked at Glock, who jerked her head to indicate the back entrance. "Let's split."

"Will you be back tonight?" Tamara asked.

"Tonight? No. Tomorrow sometime."

"Those eggs were really good..." Tamara hinted.

"Subtle, Princess," Glock chuckled.

Glock and Sybil walked off together. Tamara ran her fingers around the inside of the takeout container, hoping she'd missed some of the salt. But it was clean. There was nothing left to do but go to sleep or read the book.

(ii)

Reading did help, even if Tamara didn't like the subject matter. She could certainly see what had attracted Glock to the book. Though she wondered if Glock had actually read it. Tamara couldn't remember Glock ever reading a book in juvie. More likely she had just seen the book and liked the cover or the description, or had heard something about it from someone else. It was awful, and Tamara hated reading it, but it at least helped her to stay awake and alert. For a few hours. Then it was done, and she stared at it, wondering if she should read it over a second time. Her thoughts were getting fuzzy, so she decided she needed more sleep, and lay back down again.

(iii)

It had, perhaps, not been subtle to suggest that Glock bring her more breakfast, but it worked anyway. Glock was there sometime after the room started to get light, and did have another takeout container of eggs and bacon for her. Tamara was not as ravenous as she had been for supper the night before, but she was still getting pretty hungry. This time, though, she ate more slowly, flicking little bits at the dog between bites, not wanting the guilt of having starved him again. He snapped up the food that she flicked toward him, but he did not sit up and beg or whine at her. He continued to just lie on the floor watching her with his sad eyes.

"At least for breakfast, it's just you and me," Glock grunted, watching Tamara eat. "Without Sybil getting underfoot."

"She doesn't mean to annoy you."

"I dunno. Sometimes I think she does. Testing to see how far she can go."

"She shouldn't do that," Tamara said, shaking her head.

"No. She shouldn't," Glock agreed, the corners of her mouth twitching. She sipped at her coffee. "You know who I miss from juvie?" she asked.

Tamara considered. Glock had never really had any friends in juvie. She didn't hang out with anyone, joke around with anyone, talk. She was a loner. She often went days without talking to or acknowledging anyone but Tamara.

"Who?" she asked curiously.

"Chips," Glock said. "And the others that I used to rumble with. There was always someone who could give me a good fight."

Tamara nodded. It figured. "Too bad about Chips."

"What about Chips?" Glock raised her eyebrows.

"About her accident," Tamara reminded her. "That crash that she was in. How is she doing now, do you know?"

"Chips is fine," Glock said, with a rumbling laugh. "Nothing wrong with her."

"What?"

"There was no crash," Glock said, her eyes dancing. "Man, are you ever gullible, Frenchie."

Tamara frowned at her and sat up straighter. "What? Why would you tell me that if it wasn't true?"

Glock grinned at her. "To distract you from Sybil pouring the drinks. So we could get some alcohol inside you."

"What?" Tamara's voice climbed upward.

"Sure. Once I showed you the sparkling juice, Sybil had to pull the switch. Couldn't do that with you watching. So... I had to find a way to distract you."

"You guys are unbelievable."

Glock grinned proudly. "And you walked right into it," she said. "I gotta say... you're a lot more fun drunk."

Tamara chewed a strip of bacon, flicking a small piece over to the dog. "Then why don't you just make friends with someone who likes to drink?"

"That wouldn't be the same. Someone like Sybil? Or someone who only cares where their next drink is coming from? I don't want a lush. Just someone who can let her hair down now and then."

Glock ran a lock of Tamara's limp hair between two fingers. Tamara pulled back from her.

(iv)

Time stretched on interminably. Tamara couldn't keep track of the hours or days anymore. Glock brought Sybil back again, and Tamara glanced at the doorway that Glock had disappeared through, hoping that she'd be gone for a few minutes.

"You gotta help me get out of here," she whispered.

Sybil nodded. "Yeah... but I don't know what to do. She doesn't exactly trust me. Asking for her keys might be a bit of a giveaway."

"You'll have to think of something. What about getting her drunk, or drugging her, or something? Then you could get the keys."

Sybil shook her head. "She can drink me under the table any day. I could just call the police. That would make the most sense, right? Just tell them where you are, and they could break in and get you. What about that?"

"Then the cops will be looking for Glock, and Glock will be looking for you."

Sybil didn't look too keen on that.

"She knows where to find you... and your family."

"I know where she lives. They'll be able to arrest her."

"You sure enough to count on it? She won't catch wind and escape the cops, and go after the little girls?"

Sybil stared at Tamara, thinking it over. She knew enough about Glock to realize she was expert at avoiding the police and had connections on the inside.

"No," she admitted.

They both froze as there was a noise from the back. Glock returning?

"You gotta figure out how to get her keys," Tamara whispered hurriedly. "And get me out. We'll make it look like I just escaped. Then she'll come after me, and not you. And maybe…"

Glock walked back into the room. Sybil gave Tamara a quick nod.

"What's going on?" Glock questioned. "You two look like you're making some pretty serious plans."

Sybil laughed. "Just asking what kind of muffins she likes. In case she gets tired of eggs."

"Muffins." Glock raised her eyebrows at Tamara. "Blueberry, isn't it?"

"Blueberry's good. Pretty much anything except bran."

"I had these ones the other day," Sybil said. "They got them at the food fair in the mall. Cranberry and orange. Those are seriously good muffins."

"Yeah?" Glock asked. "Maybe we'll get some of those. You like cranberry, Princess?"

"Sure."

"Huh. I never had cranberry and orange."

"I could get some," Sybil suggested. "Bring them over tomorrow morning."

"Morning?" Glock repeated. "You said you couldn't get anymore truants."

"No school tomorrow. I could bring breaky."

"Maybe."

Tamara could see Sybil weighing her words, trying to decide whether she could ask for a key. She shook her head infinitesimally. Sybil pressed her lips shut, and didn't say anything further.

(v)

Tamara awoke groggily to someone shaking her. She shifted her position, pushing the hands back and then rubbing her eyes. She looked around blearily, disoriented. The room was barely lit, the sun low in the sky, either just going down or just coming up. It was Sybil who had woken her up. Tamara looked around, but didn't see Glock. She had to be in the bathroom or one of the other rooms. Tamara rubbed her side tenderly, and coughed, her chest feeling sore and congested. The cough set her ribs aflame, bringing tears to Tamara's eyes.

"Oooh."

Sybil was quick with the pills, passing a couple of tablets to Tamara to take. Tamara blinked and looked at Sybil narrowly. There was an extra movement she had caught out the corner of her eye, in which Tamara thought that Sybil might have popped one of the pills herself. Tamara lay still, squeezing and twisting the blanket in her hands, waiting for the pain to ebb.

"Can you get up?" Sybil asked. "We should move quick."

"Why?" Tamara croaked.

"Because I don't know how long it will be before she realizes."

Tamara blinked several times, trying to focus. "Realizes what? Where's Glock?"

"She's still at her apartment. So we should move."

"How did you get the keys?"

Tamara watched while Sybil unlocked the handcuff around her wrist. Sybil looked around anxiously. She helped Tamara to her feet and held her steady for a moment. Tamara glanced around.

"Untie the dog too."

Sybil looked irritated. She nudged the dog with her toe. "Is it even alive?"

Tamara's heart sank. She knelt down and lifted the dog's head. Its eyes were dim, but it was still alive. She could see its nose quivering. Tamara's fingers shook as she unclipped the leash from the dog's collar. She gathered it up in her arms. She could feel the dog's heart beating very fast under her fingers. Lifting it made her gasp in pain.

"Let me," Sybil protested. "You shouldn't be trying to carry it with those broken ribs."

Tamara let Sybil take it from her arms. "Where's Glock?" she asked, looking around.

"She's not here. We need to get out so she can't find us. Come on."

Tamara let Sybil lead her out of the building. The chain hung loose outside.

"Leave it loose so she thinks I just escaped on my own."

"Can I just put the dog down here?" Sybil asked. "Someone will find it."

"No, they won't," Tamara objected. "It'll just die here. Bring it."

Sybil shook her head, leading the way. She coughed. "Man, it stinks," she complained.

"It can't help that. I probably do too."

Sybil looked at her and didn't comment. They stopped beside a car.

"Yours?" Tamara asked.

"My mom's. Here, get in."

Tamara opened the door and got into the front passenger seat. Sybil dumped the dog unceremoniously into her lap. She went around to the driver's door.

"I'm gonna be in crap if I take the car home smelling like dog," she groused as she got in.

After pulling out, Sybil reached into the back seat and brought out a cardboard box from the muffin shop.

"Here, I got you some," she said, offering it to Tamara.

Tamara juggled it open. Warm orange and cranberry muffins. Tamara inhaled the scent. She moaned, closing her eyes. "Oh, that's good."

"You haven't even tried one yet."

"I can still tell."

Tamara took one of the big muffins out of the box and broke a piece off the top. She held it in front of the dog's snout, and he licked it up out of her hand. Sybil looked appalled.

"It's not for the dog!"

"He's starving."

"It's for you!"

Tamara broke off another piece and put it in her mouth. "It's good," she approved, savoring it, chewing slowly.

Sybil shook her head and put the car in gear. "That's disgusting."

Tamara broke off a piece and held it out to Sybil, and Sybil took it, laughing.

"You're awful," she complained. She popped it into her mouth. "...But it is good!"

They drove for a few minutes in silence. Tamara alternately fed the dog and herself. Sybil looked sideways at her.

"So, what do you want to do?" she asked.

Tamara sighed. She stretched her neck and rubbed it. Too many nights sleeping on the floor. She ached all over. Every joint felt swollen.

"I dunno," she said. She knew what she had to do. But she wasn't looking forward to it.

"Why don't I take you back to Glock's?" Sybil suggested. "Then she'll know that she can trust you, 'cause you went back there, and she'll let you just stay at the apartment, instead of..."

She jerked her head indicating the way that they had come, "back there."

Tamara shook her head adamantly. "No way."

"Come on, Tamara. I don't know what you're planning, but it's not going to turn out good. You gotta know that."

Tamara shook her head stubbornly. "I'm not going back to Glock! I can't believe you would suggest it, after she broke my ribs. After she locked me up like that! Come on!"

Sybil frowned, watching the road ahead of her. "So where am I going? Where do you want me to drop you off?"

"Can I borrow your phone?"

"You're not going to call Glock?"

Tamara shook her head.

"Who, then?"

"Collins, I guess," Tamara sighed.

"Block the caller ID, then," Sybil said. "If he figures I'm involved, that I knew where you were, I'm gonna be in big trouble."

"How do I do that?"

Sybil pulled her phone out, and while driving, thumbed through the settings, then handed it to Tamara.

"There. But that doesn't mean I'm happy about it. Even if you're not going to go back to Glock, I still think you should just go out on your own. You don't have to go back to Collins, back to juvie. That's just... not fair."

Tamara shook her head. "And being locked up by Glock is?"

"I didn't say that. I just said... live on your own. Lots of kids do."

"You don't," Tamara pointed out.

"Yeah... well, I got things pretty good at home. I don't figure I have any reason to leave. But if I did... I'd be out in a minute. I could get along on my own. So can you."

Tamara dialed the phone. She ignored Sybil shaking her head in disapproval. The phone rang a few times before it was answered, but Tamara had learned that cell phones didn't actually connect as fast as landlines, even if it made a sound like it was ringing, and tried to be patient. She didn't know what she would say if she got Collins' voicemail. For that matter, she wasn't sure what she was going to say if he answered. If he didn't, she would probably hang up rather than leaving a message.

"Hello. Collins here."

"Mr. Collins... it's Tamara."

"Tamara?" his voice was surprised. "Well, I didn't expect to hear from you again. Where are you?"

"Umm... I guess I'm in trouble."

"Some," he allowed. "But we can get it straightened out."

Tamara's hopes rose. "Really?" she said. "I might not have to go back to juvie?"

"I can't really say right now. Why don't you and I meet?"

"Yeah..." Tamara trailed off. "I killed those kids," she said impulsively. She'd been stewing in the guilt for days. She had to get it off of her chest, she couldn't wait until she saw Collins in person. When she allowed herself to think about it, the guilt over what she had done was overwhelming, and she had to tell him, get it out in the open. "I did it. I remember."

Collins didn't say anything for a moment. Then he spoke, his voice cool and unemotional. "What kids, Tamara?"

"The Baker kids," Tamara said. "Corinne and Julie. Before. Before I went to juvie."

"I know you did. You confessed to it and were convicted, remember?"

"But... I didn't really confess. I just said what they told me to say. The lawyer wrote it all out. I just read it. It's not... it's not the same as really confessing."

"But now you are confessing you did it. So it's not like you were wrongly convicted."

"No," Tamara said with frustration, not understanding why the conversation was going sideways. "I did it. And I..." Tamara's voice cracked. She tried to keep it under control. "I feel really bad."

"Have you been drinking, Tamara?" he questioned.

"No!"

"Okay... so this is something else you and I can discuss when we meet, all right? Let's set it up."

"Okay," Tamara agreed. "But... just you. No cops, right? I'll turn myself in to you."

"Sure. That's the best way. Shows responsibility, a desire to do the right thing without being forced. Then you and I can take the next step together."

Tamara breathed shallowly, finding herself out of breath again. The dog on her lap whined, and Tamara scratched his ears.

"Where should we meet?" she asked.

"Well, since you're turning yourself over to me, why don't you pick the place? Where would be comfortable for you?"

Tamara glanced at Sybil, who could probably hear both sides of the conversation, but Sybil offered no solutions. Tamara thought about it. Not at the Hensons' house, she didn't want to face the disappointment of the family. Not at the school, where the coach had been beaten. She didn't know many other places that would be private. Sybil's house, Glock's apartment, the warehouse... none of them were acceptable.

"How about... there's a sportsplex where we played volleyball..."

"Okay. Which one?"

"Um, Three Peaks or something like that."

Collins made a ticking sound with his tongue. "Yeah, I know where it is," he agreed. "Are you heading over there now? Or do we need to set a time?"

Tamara looked questioningly at Sybil. Sybil looked at the car stereo for the time. "Give us a bit of extra time. An hour, maybe."

Tamara relayed the information to Collins.

"Who are you with, Tamara?"

"I just asked a friend to drive me."

"Glock Spielman?" Collins questioned, his voice hard.

"No. She doesn't know I'm meeting you."

"I'll meet with you, but you'd better be alone."

"Yeah. It's okay. I wouldn't bring her."

"You said you wanted to do the right thing. So I'm trusting you."

"Nobody else," Tamara said. "Just me. And you."

"Okay. I'll see you soon."

Tamara pressed 'end' and breathed out, trying to relax. She tried to slow her breathing down, to catch her breath again, but felt dizzy.

"There. I did it," she said. "I really did it."

"Yeah," Sybil agreed darkly. "I don't know why you had to go and do that."

"Sorry," Tamara said, truly wishing that Sybil wasn't so upset about it.

Sybil motioned for her phone, and Tamara handed it back. She watched Sybil launching the messaging app, and typing while she drove, eyes darting back and forth between the road and the little LCD screen.

"Who are you texting?" Tamara asked.

"Gotta let my mom know I'm going to be a little later getting back."

"Oh, okay."

Sybil held onto her phone for a few minutes, getting a reply back and sending another message. Her grip on the phone seemed awkward. Tamara noticed that her little finger and ring finger were swollen, the skin stretched tight like sausages.

"What happened to your hand?"

Sybil slid the phone back into her pocket, and looked at her hand. "I was mad," she said. "Hit the wall. It... er... was a little harder than I thought."

Tamara shook her head. "You should get it looked at."

"Yeah, I'll go to the clinic or something. Get me one of those muffins, I'm hungry."

Tamara managed to reach the box in the back seat and got out a muffin for Sybil. Sybil ate it messily, strewing crumbs across every surface.

"What are we going to do with that dog?" she asked. "Can we ditch it now?"

Tamara looked out the window. They had gotten out of the industrial area with the warehouse. It wasn't a residential area, but little commercial places. Strip malls, houses that had been converted to offices, picturesque little places.

"There should be somewhere along here," she said. "Somewhere people will notice it... take it to a vet or feed it or something."

She fed the dog another piece of muffin.

"That's probably not even good for it," Sybil pointed out. "Dogs aren't supposed to have table scraps and stuff. It can make them sick."

"Well, it needs food."

"How about there?"

Tamara looked in the direction Sybil pointed. There was a little pet food store. Reading the signs in the window, Tamara discerned that it was a yuppie, exclusive sort of place, where they baked doggie biscuits and other treats by hand. People like that wouldn't let a dog starve to death on their doorstep, even if it was dirty and bedraggled.

Tamara nodded. "Yeah, that looks good. Pull up close, but not right in front. We don't want them to notice us right away."

Sybil nodded her agreement, and stopped a couple of shops down from the pet food store. Tamara opened her door.

"Can you carry it? With your ribs? Do you need help?" She wrinkled her nose, obviously hoping the answer was no.

"I can carry it that far," Tamara assured her. The oxy had

taken full effect now, and although she didn't feel well, she figured she could carry the dog that far. She was puffing pretty heavily by the time she got to the customer door of the pet food store. Taking a look around to make sure that no one was watching too closely, Tamara bent down to put down the dog. It whined slightly, a high-pitched squeak of protest. Tamara put it on the concrete, and fed it the rest of the muffin.

"You just stay here, and you'll be okay," she promised. "They'll feed you and look after you. Maybe..." she looked at the collar, but it had no tags on it. "Maybe they'll be able to figure out who your owner is, and take you back home."

Its tail thumped weakly a couple of times. Tamara got back up, swiping at tears that came to her eyes. How ridiculous. She was doing the right thing, returning the dog. She had tried so hard not to get attached to it. Not to get pulled in by the liquid brown eyes and sad face. It was a dog, and not even her dog. She should be happy that she had been able to save it from Glock. Not sad.

She swiped at her eyes again before getting back into Sybil's car. She tried to look nonchalant, like she didn't care anything about the dog and was just glad that it was off of her hands now. She rubbed her hands on her pants and wiped her nose with the back of her sleeve.

SIXTEEN

(i)

THEY HAD TO STOP for gas, and Sybil drove a round-about route to get to the sportsplex, both of them keeping a sharp eye out for police cars, marked or unmarked. Sybil circled the block a couple of times, eyes on the time, before she finally pulled into the nearly-deserted parking lot.

"What if it's locked?" she asked.

"Then we'll meet outside," Tamara said with a shrug.

She looked around. There were a few cars parked. She didn't know which was Collins', or if he was there yet. Tamara got out slowly, feeling slightly sick to her stomach. She rubbed her side, trying to breathe normally but feeling more lightheaded all the time. She bent down, looking back into the car at Sybil.

"Bye," she said. "Thanks for your help."

"Don't do this, Tamara. You can still change your mind."

"No. I have to do it. You take care, okay?"

"You want me to leave?" Sybil was reluctant to go.

"I told him I'd be by myself."

"Shouldn't I just stick around, to make sure he's here? That nothing goes wrong?"

Tamara shook her head. "No. Bye."

Sybil shifted into reverse and pulled out of the parking space. She waved a hand toward Tamara, not looking at her again, and sped out of the parking lot.

Tamara sighed. She was on her own now. This was all her. No one making her. No one forcing her or writing it out for her. Just Tamara, choosing to do the right thing, even if it meant going back to juvie again. Because she had a choice. She could do the right thing even if it hurt her.

She hadn't thought about the tall flight of steps to get into the sportsplex. When she'd played volleyball there, it had been nothing to her. A quick race up the stairs, then down into the change rooms, back up to play... Now with her ribs bothering her so much, Tamara felt like a gray old lady, barely able to toddle without a walker. She went up the steps one at a time, stopping on each stair with both feet, instead of lifting one foot above the other with each step. She stopped on the first landing, gripping the railing tightly, sweat streaming down her forehead and trickling down her back. The way that her heart raced and her chest burned, she was sure she was going to end up having a heart attack by the time she got to the top step. She forced herself to go on. Every three or four steps, she stopped and rested. No one came up behind her. Collins must already be in the building, awaiting her arrival.

On the very top step, her vision faded for a moment, and she was blind, ears ringing, heart pounding, gasping for breath. Tamara tried to discipline her breathing. She was all right. Just a broken rib or two. No need to act like a wimp about it.

She pushed the door open and looked around. It seemed dark and cool inside the sportsplex after being in the bright sun. She had expected Collins to be standing right there, waiting. But there was no sign of him.

"Mr. Collins?" Tamara called, barely above a whisper. "Mr. Collins, are you here?"

There was no sound. Then Tamara thought she could hear footsteps and movements, and a whispered exchange.

"Mr. Collins? Is that you?"

"Over here," his voice echoed in the big entrance hall.

Tamara cocked her head and tried to pinpoint the origin of the sound. "Where?"

"To your right. Toward the locker room."

Tamara walked slowly, her brain screaming at her that something was wrong. Why wasn't he out here, waiting for her? Who else was there that he was whispering to? He was supposed to be *alone*.

Tamara rounded the corner and looked down the stairs toward the locker room. And there was Collins. Glock stood behind him, her knife held at his throat.

"What...?" Tamara croaked.

Glock's eyes glittered in the shadows of the stairway.

"What are you doing here?" Tamara asked, bewildered.

How had Glock even known where she was? Tamara had just set up the meeting. She didn't even know herself where it was going to be until an hour ago. She had picked the place. So how had Glock known where it would be? Tamara should have been able to figure it out, but her brain wouldn't supply the answer. Denied the answer. Glock's smile was mocking.

"Sybil texted me the details about your planned get-together," Glock said. "And I was so disappointed not to be invited along."

"Don't wreck this for me!"

"Wreck it? Oh, you've done that already, Princess. You think I'm going to let you leave me?"

"Glock, please," Tamara begged. "You didn't need to come here. I have to do this. I have to... make it right."

"Make what right?" Glock demanded. "You don't have to

follow Collins' rules. He's just set you up. That's what they always do. First they warp your mind. In foster care and in juvie. Make you follow their rules, eat and sleep when they say, condition you to do what they want you do. And they make you think that you're going to get out someday. And when they let you out, you'll be free. And you can start over, and have a life again. But all the time, they're just setting you up."

"Nobody set *you* up," Collins disagreed, looking faintly angry about the knife being held at his throat. "You were released. You're out here living your life the way you want to. No one put you back in jail."

Glock laughed. "That's because I'm too smart for you. I know the system. I know the way it works. You gotta get outside it as soon as you can. If you're like Frenchie, and you try to follow the rules, it won't work! Because vermin like you are just slinking around in the shadows, waiting for her to make a mistake. You make it impossible not to. Nobody is supposed to be able to follow all the rules. You just want to funnel them all back into the system. And when you do, you pat yourself on the back, and say: 'oh well, they didn't follow the rules.' That's right, isn't it? It's not a system that's supposed to succeed. She's supposed to fail. You know she's going to, sooner or later. And you just sit there. Watching. Waiting."

"And what's your suggestion?" Collins said dryly. "Break the rules? Live outside the law? Get put back in prison for something big instead of something small?"

Glock pulled up on Collins' chin, her knuckles whitening as she gripped the knife harder.

"Give me one reason I shouldn't slit your throat right now," she snarled.

"Glock," Tamara protested. "It's not his fault... it's mine. It's me you're mad at. I'm sorry. I should have listened."

"I see right through you," Glock sneered. "You can't snow me with fake apologies. Don't try."

Tamara took a couple steps closer. If apology didn't work, she could try diversion.

"Why don't you and Sybil get together?" she suggested. "Obviously Syb' told you everything. She likes you, wants to spend time with you. And there's no danger of her going back to juvie. Why don't you set up with her instead? You don't want me. I'm the traitor. The enemy." Tamara stepped closer. "Sybil's the one who told you the truth. Set this whole trap up. Made sure you knew where I would be. She's smart."

"Sybil?" Glock repeated. "Yeah, she'd like that. She's a wannabe, Princess. She'll never be anything else. She just wants to play at being a JD. And then go home to the family and eat KD. She'll never be the real thing. You might have been soft when you got to juvie, but you weren't a wannabe. You killed those babies. *You* were the real deal."

Tamara was close to them now. Very close. She could smell Collins' sweat, rank with fear. Glock shifted her grip, pressing the knife blade against his bared throat. It scraped loudly on his stubble. Tamara reached out and touched Glock's wrist. Gently; not physically restraining her. Glock stared into her eyes, her pupils wide and black. Tamara breathed painfully, starting to wheeze. She slid her fingers lightly up Glock's forearm, past her elbow, stopping at the tattoo on Glock's bicep. The princess crown over the French flag.

"Let him go," Tamara breathed. "It's not his fault. If it wasn't him, it would be another PO. He's just a cog in the machine. He's not the one who decides."

Glock's grip on Collins tightened. "Get down," she ordered harshly. "Knees. On the floor."

Collins looked at first like he would resist, but Glock pressed the knife harder to his throat, and Tamara had to catch herself not to cry out.

"Knees," Glock repeated.

Collins sank to his knees, his eyes steadily on Tamara's face.

"Lace your hands behind your head."

He obeyed. Tamara swallowed, and breathed open-mouthed. Was Glock going to let him go, or was this the point at which she twisted the knife?

"Put your forehead on the wall."

Collins started to shuffle toward the wall on his knees, and Glock jerked back on the knife.

"No," she ordered. "Just lean forward, put your forehead on the wall."

He was still too far back from the wall. Tamara was sure that when he tried, Collins would end up facedown on the floor, with a broken nose. But he leaned forward, and ended up precariously balanced, leaning with his forehead on the wall, knees on the floor, and fingers laced behind his head. He couldn't easily get out of that position and was not a threat as long as he stayed there.

In slow motion, Glock turned to Tamara and put the tip of the knife to Tamara's throat.

(ii)

Time passed. Tamara wasn't sure how long she stood like that, frozen, waiting. Her brain was still stuttering to keep up with what was going on, trying to find a way out, an escape route. Her brain didn't know that it was already too late. Glock wasn't going to be talked out of this. She'd take Tamara back to the warehouse. Or somewhere else this time. And she wouldn't let Sybil around to criticize her care or make sure that Tamara was all right.

Or maybe she'd just slide the knife across Tamara's throat and end it there.

Tamara closed her eyes briefly, and there was an interruption in time. Like when you were watching TV when you were too tired or sick, and your brain kept trying to sleep in the fractions of seconds between spoken conversations, and you could have a whole dream in the pauses. Glock continued to stare at her. Was she waiting for Tamara to speak? To move? To fight? Why didn't she do something?

"You left me," Glock said finally. "You would leave me to go back to juvie. It's better to be locked up there than to be free? With me?"

Tamara shook her head. "I don't want to go back to juvie... I just want... there's a certain person I want to be. And..." Tamara shook her head, tears starting in the corners of her eyes.

"You can't," Glock finished. "It doesn't matter how much you want to be the little girl you were before you went to that foster home, you're *not*. They made you into a killer. And keeping all of your parole terms isn't going to do that. Serving more juvie time isn't going to undo that. You are what they made you. Neither of us can go back to what we were. Our lives have already been decided."

Tamara shifted, and the point of the knife dug into her throat.

"And don't try those sad puppy dog eyes on me," Glock growled. "You know what I do to puppies."

Tamara could suddenly feel the heat of Glock's anger pouring off her. Like when you open an oven, and the wave of steam and heat rolls out. Glock was not just hurt. Not just betrayed. Deep inside, she was converting those feelings into anger. Into hate and fury. At Tamara.

Tamara would be lucky to escape with a mere slitting of the throat. Glock intended to inflict far more pain than that.

(iii)

Tamara coughed. The blade bit into her throat, but she didn't care. What was one more scar on her throat? She knew that look in Glock's dark eyes. And she knew that there was no way to talk Glock out of it. The more she begged and pleaded, the more Glock enjoyed it. She wanted to squeeze the maximum of pain and fear out of the encounter. She wanted suffering. Tamara's suffering. Tamara was the one who had betrayed Glock. They had been cellies in juvie. Glock had protected her. Taught her. Mentored her. Yes, Glock had hurt her too, but had known just how far she could push it before Tamara broke, or a guard interfered. This time, there was no limit. She wanted to push Tamara past the breaking point. Past anything she had suffered in the past.

Tamara coughed again and cleared her throat. Sweat was dripping down her face. "Whatever," she said regretfully. "I guess that means you don't want to come."

Glock's eyebrows shot up. "What?"

"In juvie... it was best when we were together," Tamara reminisced. She stared off into the distance. "Things just weren't the same when you left."

Glock's eyes narrowed. She searched Tamara's face, suspicious. "What?"

"You don't want to go back. I didn't want to either," Tamara forced a chuckle. "But it's not like they don't know about McClure, right? I know I'm goin' back there. I thought at first... well, I thought from what you said before, maybe you wanted to go back with me. Be a team again. Like we were."

Glock studied her. "Are you crazy, French?"

"That's why I told Sybil to let you know where I was going," Tamara explained, as if it all made perfect sense. "I thought that you'd want to come. We could both go in, together. Isn't that why you came? Isn't that why you threatened Collins? So you could go back to juvie with me?"

Glock shook her head. "You didn't tell Sybil to let me know," she countered. "Sybil and me cooked that up together. So that I would know just how far you'd go to betray me."

Tamara forced a laugh. "Poor Sybil. So many stories to keep

straight. She told you where I was meeting Collins so that you could come back with me. Come back to juvie with me."

"No," Glock growled. "You think I'm stupid? Just what are you...?"

"She did tell me," Sybil's voice came from above them, and everyone turned their heads to look for her at the same time. Up the stairs, leaning over the railing, watching and listening to them from a safe distance. "She told me to let you know."

"This is crazy," Glock protested. Scowling, she pressed the knife into Tamara's throat. "I didn't come here to get taken back to juvie!"

"Well, what did you *think* was going to happen?" Tamara questioned. "That you could just take my PO hostage and *not* go to jail? Seriously? Why would you come here and threaten everyone, unless you wanted to get arrested?"

Glock lowered her knife. Her eyes searched Tamara's. "You never were a good liar, Frenchie."

"Oh?" Tamara stared steadily back, her heart pounding. She really hadn't expected it to work, but Glock was backing off. She was confused. Not ready to turn herself in, maybe, but confused enough that she didn't know what to do.

"You want me to go back with you?" Glock asked. Her voice was strange. Not the usual threatening growl. Something more vulnerable. Almost hopeful.

Tamara curled her fingers around Glock's knife hand. "Of course."

They stood like statues. Tamara's brain was flashing those microsleeps more strongly now. She felt like the whole thing had slowed down to an old movie, frame by frame. Each interval longer as the film drew to a close. She stumbled in place, finding it difficult to keep her feet. Glock's knife clattered to the floor, and she caught Tamara, grabbing her with both hands and steadying her.

"Hey. Careful."

"You're gonna have to help me," Tamara said. "I'm not feeling so good."

Glock held onto her, looking uncertain.

"I'm gonna pass out," Tamara explained.

Glock put her arms around Tamara and held her close. "Are you gonna help, here?" she asked irritably.

Tamara was confused at first, then realized that Glock was talking to Collins. Collins too seemed surprised. It took him a minute for him to make it to his feet. His fingers pressed gently over the pulse point in Tamara's throat for a moment, then he looked at one of her eyes, prying the eyelids wide apart when Tamara flinched away.

"What did she take?" he questioned.

"Nothing," Glock snapped. "She won't take anything."

"Oxy," Sybil called down from above. "She's been taking Oxycodone for a few days."

Collins felt Tamara's face and forehead with the back of his fingers. "She's burning up. How long has she been sick?"

Glock hung onto Tamara tightly. "What should I do?" she asked. "Put her in your car? Are you going to call an ambulance?"

"Let me make some calls," Collins said. "Can you just take care of her for a few minutes, until they come? Maybe she should lie down."

Glock lowered Tamara to the floor. She smoothed Tamara's limp hair back from her face. Collins was talking in a low voice on his phone. Tamara reached for Glock's arm.

"Hold my hand."

They intertwined their fingers. Tamara could see Collins watching her. His face was calm and relaxed, and she thought that he understood what she was doing, trying to keep Glock's hands busy, keep her focused on Tamara and not what was going to happen next.

The police arrived first. Collins handed Glock's knife to one of them, but kept them a short distance away until the ambulance arrived. When the paramedics had Glock move back in order to examine Tamara, Collins spoke to her.

"I need you to come over here, Glock," he said. "You go with these officers, and then you can see Tamara after she's released from the hospital."

Glock walked toward the police officers with no resistance. "Am I under arrest?"

"I can't very well send you to juvie if you're not under arrest," Collins pointed out.

Glock allowed the police officers to cuff her.

SEVENTEEN

T AMARA LOOKED UP FROM her lunch plate and saw Collins standing in the doorway of her hospital room, waiting for her to notice him.

"Hey," she said, dropping her eyes back down to her plate.

Collins came into the room. He pulled the visitor chair over and sat down beside her, stretching out his long legs.

"How are you feeling?" he asked.

Tamara coughed and cleared her throat. "Could use a smoke," she said.

"Considering the fact that you've got pneumonia, I don't think that would be a particularly good idea."

"Yeah. That's what the doctor said."

He nodded. "You're looking a lot better, though."

Tamara looked up at the IV bags hanging on the pole beside her, draining into the needle in her arm. Fluids, painkillers, antibiotics. All designed to help her feel better.

"Yeah, a lot better."

"You should have gone to hospital when you first broke your ribs."

"Wasn't that easy."

"No. But you might have been able to avoid your lungs filling up with fluid." He was silent for a few minutes, and Tamara didn't know what to say. "So... I've been trying to sort this whole mess out," Collins said.

"Uh-huh."

"Your friends are not making it that easy."

Tamara poked at the food on her tray. "They're not my friends... Glock's not my friend."

"Explain that to me."

Tamara picked at the skin around her thumbnail. "I didn't want her to come see me. I told her to go away. I told her I couldn't, because I was on parole. And she... they got me drunk, and Glock broke my ribs, and she chained me up and wouldn't let me go..."

"You're right, that doesn't sound like a friend," he said with a grimace.

Tamara nodded. "She was my cellie in juvie. She... missed me. But I didn't want her around."

"Why didn't you call me?"

"I know... I thought if I called you, you'd send me back to juvie. I didn't... I was wrong."

"If you'd called me, and said that she was around and wouldn't leave you alone, I could have done something about it. We could have had a restraining order issued. Arrested her if she broke it by continuing to contact you. But you didn't give me that opportunity, did you?"

Tamara shook her head.

"And because you didn't report the contact, you ended up with all of this bad stuff happening to you. And to McClure..."

Tamara pressed her lips together, and wiped the corner of her eyes. "Glock said that I should get McClure to confess. Get a recording of it, and expose him, so that he couldn't hurt any other girls. And then I'd be a hero, so I wouldn't have to go back to juvie."

"And why did you take her with you?"

"So that... she could protect me. From the coach."

"How were you supposed to record this confession?"

Tamara sighed. "On my phone. The phone Syb' gave me."

Collins held up a phone. "This one?"

Tamara looked at it. "Yeah..."

"Did you record it?"

"Well, he didn't confess..."

"Did you record it?" Collins repeated.

Tamara frowned. "Yeah, I tried..."

He handed the phone to Tamara. "Show me."

She opened it up and saw that it had been fully charged. She scrolled through the menus and found the recording app. There was one large file, the recording that she had made the day that she confronted McClure. Tamara looked at Collins, and selected it.

The audio wasn't great. She had left the phone in her pocket and could hear the fabric rubbing against it. The voices were muffled, but the louder voices were intelligible. When Tamara heard Glock's voice for the first time on the recording, her heart started to race. In a few minutes the argument had escalated, and Glock attacked McClure. Tamara closed her eyes, listening to herself begging Glock to stop, hearing the crashes and cries. She saw it all over again in her mind. Tamara had been so upset by the attack that she had never thought to turn the recording off. She heard herself yelling at Glock, their escape from the school, and the whole argument that followed the attack. Eventually, Tamara turned off the playback. It had apparently continued recording until the phone battery died. She looked at Collins. He wasn't surprised. He'd obviously already listened to it.

"So... you know," Tamara said. "You know it wasn't me, that I tried to stop it."

He nodded. "Since McClure's attack... the police investigation that I initiated after talking to you at the jail has confirmed a number of cases where McClure may, allegedly, have been involved with students or past students."

Tamara breathed out in a long sigh. She still didn't have much wind, and it hurt her ribs to breathe so deeply.

"You're still in trouble," Collins reminded her. "You still violated just about every one of your terms."

"I know."

"And Sybil..."

"She's not in trouble, is she?" Tamara asked in concern. "Sybil's not really *bad*..."

"I haven't quite figured out what was going on between her and Glock. But it looks like there was some... coercion."

"Glock threatened to hurt her little sisters."

"Sisters that you were not supposed to be around," Collins pointed out.

Tamara fiddled with her cup. "I know. And if I hadn't gone there, Glock wouldn't have known where she lived. Glock didn't hurt them, did she?"

"No. But it looks like she broke a couple of Sybil's fingers in securing her cooperation."

"Oh," Tamara remembered Sybil's swollen fingers. "She said she punched a wall." Tamara felt a little silly for having believed it.

Collins nodded. "I don't think she'll get any time," he said. "Maybe some community service and probation or something."

"Good. Syb's not really that bad... just... I dunno... confused. If it hadn't been for Glock..."

They were silent for a few minutes.

"Next time you're up before the Parole Board, I'll be happy to speak for you," Collins offered.

Tamara was thrown.

"What? That's... really nice of you."

"You saved my life," he pointed out. "You're the one that got both of us out of there alive. I didn't think either one of us had a chance with Glock. And... I think that you can turn things around. I think that without Glock showing up, you would have been able to manage your parole. You were on the right track. Your big mistake was not reporting to me as soon as you suspected that Glock was around. And certainly as soon as she made contact."

"Yeah."

"I want you to try again, when you're next up before the Parole Board. Don't give up on it."

Tamara nodded, her face warming. "Okay. I'll try," she agreed. "And... what's happening to Glock now?"

"She will not be sent to the same facility."

"So we won't be cell mates again?"

He frowned. "You didn't *really* want that, did you?"

"No!" Tamara was horrified at the thought.

"I didn't think so. Once you're released from here, you'll be headed back to juvie. Keep your nose clean. It will work out."

Tamara nodded. It wasn't the fresh start that she had expected a few weeks ago. But she'd learned a lot in that time. And next time... next time it would be different.

Did you enjoy this book? Reviews and recommendations are vital to making a book successful.

Please leave a review at your favorite book store or review site and share it with your friends.

Don't miss the following bonus material:
Sign up for mailing list to get a free ebook
Read a sneak preview chapter
Other books by P.D. Workman
Learn more about the author

Sign up for my mailing list at pdworkman.com and get Gluten-Free Murder for free!

PREVIEW OF TWO
TEARDROPS

ONE

TAMARA HAD SOMEHOW EXPECTED things to be different when she was readmitted to the juvenile detention center. She had changed during her short period of release, and she had subconsciously expected that juvie and the people there would have changed as well.

But old Eli was at the wheel of the bus that picked Tamara up from the city jail after she had recovered sufficiently to be released from hospital. He looked Tamara over as she was escorted onto the bus and chained in place. He shook his head and made a clicking sound with his tongue.

"Tamara French," he observed. "Right back where you came from."

Tamara gave him what she hoped was a hard stare to discourage him from further comment. She had a rep to reestablish. She couldn't come off as sorry or embarrassed by her return to juvie.

"Saw your mug on TV," Eli went on. "You and Glock. What are you doing hanging around with Glock Spielman? You know she's bad news."

Tamara gave a wordless shrug and turned her face away from

him to stare out the bus window. A couple of girls were loaded onto the bus. Newbies she didn't know. Young and green, looking terrified behind their masks of indifference. Then a girl Tamara recognized. A tall, Hispanic girl, crooked nose, face acne-pocked. Vernon. She'd been the boss of the TMJ gang in juvie when Tamara had first arrived, released around the same time as Glock.

Vernon's eyes flicked over Tamara. "Yo, French. Saw you on the news," she greeted, raising a shackled hand at waist-height to high-five her.

Vernon was showing her respect, acknowledging Tamara as an equal. Tamara was just able to lift her hand far enough to slap Vernon's white-scarred palm in response. The guard escorting Vernon in gave her a jerk, pulling her away from Tamara.

"No personal contact on the bus," he growled. Then Vernon was past Tamara and she couldn't see the older girl's response. She listened to the guard anchoring Vernon in place and then he headed for the door.

"That's it for today," he told Eli.

The guard who had been seated at the back of the bus when Tamara got on, a man Tamara didn't recognize, walked up the aisle, checking that each girl was securely anchored by jerking on their wrist-chains. He sat at the front of the bus, in a seat that faced them, watching for any sign of trouble. Eli closed the door with a hiss and secured it. Then they were on their way home.

The same general observations were made on the other end as the guards who processed intake recognized Tamara and greeted her by name, mentioning that they had seen her on TV or heard of her pending return.

"Didn't think I'd be seeing you again," Bonner commented.

Tamara shrugged and started to strip, gazing up at the ceiling.

"Remove all your jewelry and put it in the tray."

"Came from city jail," Tamara pointed out. "They already got it all."

"Everything?" Bonner demanded, scrutinizing Tamara's less-visible piercing sites with brows drawn down and her head slightly cocked.

"Everything," Tamara confirmed. She awaited further instructions, knowing there was no point in trying to move on until Bonner was convinced she wasn't trying to smuggle in any contraband. Bonner walked her through the strip search, making Tamara display every fold and crevice where she might have something hidden, then finally nodded.

"Okay. You're clean. Anything else I should know about?"

"No, ma'am."

"Showers."

Tamara walked over to the door that led to a single semi-private shower. She moved quickly. Water that never heated up properly; harsh, coarse soap; and yellow, chemical-laden anti-lice shampoo that burned for hours if she got it in her eyes. All familiar. All reasons not to linger under the spray any longer than was necessary. Hot showers were something she would miss. She shut off the water and grabbed a thin towel, rubbing her body briskly to banish the chill. Bonner, still supervising the process, handed her the orange jumper and her whites.

"Suit up."

"Thank you, ma'am."

Tamara pulled the skivvies and jumpsuit on over damp skin, her movements automatic and requiring no thought. She waited for Bonner to buzz her through the next door. When Bonner didn't push the button immediately, Tamara looked back at her. Bonner shook her head.

"I figured that was the last we'd see of you," Bonner repeated. "You were one we weren't going to see back through here again."

Tamara chewed on her lip, trying to sort through the rush of emotions Bonner's comment brought. Anger, guilt, shame, denial. Her stomach knotted, and the feelings were all jumbled together, rocketing around her brain and refusing to be corralled.

"Guess we were both wrong," she said finally. "It... wasn't like I thought it would be."

Bonner hit the door release. Tamara turned back around, opened the door, and walked through it.

She was the first one to be processed, so it was just her and the staff in the orientation room. She moved automatically to one of the benches, then paused, looking to Rice, the highest-ranking official in the room. Rice looked back at her for a moment.

"Have a seat," he eventually said, giving a nod.

Tamara sat down.

"We heard you were on your way back," Rice commented.

"Here I am," Tamara said, not sure what else to say.

"Yes. Here you are."

Tamara sat in silence. She recognized all of the guards and staff. Her memory of her initial admission three years before was foggy. She had been so exhausted and sick and overwrought, she could remember little between the strip search and being shown to her bunk. But she knew the procedure by heart. The previous year, she had been a senior mentor, sitting up at the front where Karim and Lawson were now, shepherding the greenies through the admittance process. Showing a friendly face to the scared little newbies, helping to de-escalate the anxiety and hostility that went with being in a strange place for the first time, surrounded by intimidating adults.

One of the greenies from the bus came through the door and looked around the orientation room, eyes wide, looking like a deer caught in the headlights. Eyes flashing to Tamara, she saw where she was supposed to be and slid into the seat next to her.

"Waterson?" Rice addressed her.

Her head snapped up. "Yeah?"

"You will stand until you are given instructions and told to be seated."

Her throat betrayed a hard swallow. Waterson looked at Tamara again, unsure what to do. Then she rose slowly to her feet again. The room was silent. Everyone waited while she stood there uncomfortably, face red.

"If you are not sure what to do, you should ask," Rice said finally. "We are here to help you. If there is ever any question about what you are or are not allowed to do, you should ask. You will never be censured for asking permission or asking for clarification. Understood?"

Waterson nodded. "Yeah. Okay." She swallowed again and licked her lips.

"We use 'yes, sir' and 'yes, ma'am' here."

"Oh... yes, sir."

Rice gave a warm smile of approval. "Have a seat."

Waterson collapsed back into the space beside Tamara breathing fast. Hyperventilating was not uncommon with scared admittees.

"It's okay," Tamara whispered to her. "Try to relax."

The other girl's eyes widened. Relaxing was the farthest thing from her mind.

When the door opened next, it was the other greenie, and the process was repeated. Her name was Perez. Not the first Perez in the facility, she would probably end up being addressed by her first name. She was eventually seated in the other bench, and glanced over at Tamara and Waterson, looking isolated and alone.

Tamara felt a chill each time the door opened and air rushed over her wet hair and the wet spot that her hair had made on the back of her coveralls between her shoulders.

Vernon entered. Like Tamara, she was familiar with the rules and procedures at juvie. She didn't even make her way over to the bench, but stood there as the door closed behind her, head tipped up to look at the ceiling, waiting.

"Vernon," Rice acknowledged. "You may be seated next to Perez."

Vernon didn't answer, but took the two steps over to the bench and sat beside newbie Perez.

"So, two newbies and two... experienced," Rice observed, looking them over. "Nice symmetry. Waterson and Perez, this is your orientation. French and Vernon, a refresher. Stay awake." He gave Tamara in particular a stern look. Considering the fact that Tamara couldn't remember her initial orientation, it was logical to assume that she may, in fact, have slept through it, and Rice remembered the fact. Rice proceeded to introduce the staff members who were present and what they were there for. Tamara's mind wandered. He ran through policies, rules, and schedules. Most of the administrators had a set speech they followed. After attending a year's worth of orientations, Tamara had pretty much memorized Rice's.

Tamara looked up at Karim and Lawson, the mentors. Their expressions were blank. They had mentally checked out, waiting for Rice to get through his patter. When he reached the part where he introduced the two of them, they blinked and sat up straighter. Tamara knew Rice was drawing to a close. She rubbed her eyes and shifted in her seat, preparing to get up.

"You will each be assigned an intake officer." Rice's eyes flicked over the four admittees. Tamara knew he assigned the intakes on the fly, matching the new girls to their counselors based on his first impressions of them. He was remarkably good at assessing attitudes and personalities to pair each girl with the right professional.

"French, would you see Dr. Sutherland?"

Tamara stood up and faced the facility psychologist. The other girls were assigned to other staff members. The two senior mentors approached their assigned greenies to help them through the process. Tamara worked her way across the room to Dr. Sutherland.

She looked down at his shoes, her face hot, too embarrassed to meet his eyes.

"Uh, hi, Dr. S."

"Tamara. Nice to see you again." Dr. Sutherland paused, reconsidering. "Well, it would have been nicer not to see you again, under the circumstances, but here we are." He scratched at his silver goatee.

Tamara chewed on her thumbnail. "Uh-huh."

"Let's take a conference room, shall we?" He put his hand over hers, pushing her hand gently away from her mouth.

Tamara followed him out of the orientation room and then beside him down the hallway to a meeting room. Tamara twisted a lock of hair around her finger, fidgeting, while Sutherland sat down and opened his folder.

"Your name is Tamara French?" He looked up from the folder to her, eyes smiling.

"Yes."

"You are currently... fifteen?"

"Yes."

"You've been remanded for breach of your parole conditions?"

"Yes."

"Remind me your original charges."

Tamara swallowed. Sutherland knew very well what Tamara's original charges were. It was just one of their psychological tricks for getting an intake to be forthcoming and cooperative. Ask questions that would get several yeses in a row. Then ask factual questions requiring short answers. Once the intake got into the habit of answering, move into open-ended questions, and the momentum would carry them on to keep answering openly and honestly. As a senior mentor, she'd been taught how it worked.

"Two murder convictions," she told him, trying to keep her voice calm and even.

"And you've served how much of your sentence?"

"Three years." She anticipated his next question. "Of five-to-ten."

"Your parole officer was..."

"Chad Collins."

Sutherland jotted down answers on his intake forms.

"How are you feeling, Tamara?" He looked up at her, eyebrows raised.

"Better."

He waited for more details, letting the silence draw her out.

"Ribs are still sore. But they're healing. My lungs are clear. Doctor said not to do any running for a while."

"That shouldn't be a problem."

"No, sir."

He didn't say anything for a minute, studying her. Tamara tried to keep her hands down away from her face and just to focus on her breathing. It would be a good time to practice one of the relaxation exercises Dr. Frank had given her.

"How do you feel about being back here?"

Tamara blew out her breath slowly. She hadn't had a cigarette in two weeks, so she was past the physical withdrawal from nicotine, but she still desperately wanted one to calm her and to keep her hands still.

"It sucks."

Sutherland chuckled.

"And it's... a relief. I feel... like I belong here. I didn't on the outside."

He nodded his understanding. "Three years of institutionalization has had an effect on all areas of your life."

"It was so hard. When Glock showed up... it was like... it was so much easier just to do what she said."

"Even though you knew it was in breach of your parole."

"Yeah. Making my own decisions was... really hard."

"So now you're back with us... at least until your case comes before the parole board again. What do you think that's going to be like?"

"I dunno. Back to normal."

His eyes searched her face. "Have you had any thoughts of suicide?"

"Oh." The suggestion surprised Tamara. "No... no, not at all."

"Good. No thoughts of self-harm? Or finding yourself taking risks you normally wouldn't?"

"No... not since I was in hospital."

"How do you feel about being put in the general population here? Is there any reason you feel unsafe or in need of special supervision?"

Tamara thought back to when she was first remanded. Had anyone asked her those questions then? When she had felt so scared and vulnerable? That early-morning admission was mostly a blank. They must have interviewed her, but she could remember nothing about it.

"Tamara?" Sutherland probed, eyes sharp, looking concerned.

"No. No, I'm fine. General population is fine. Everybody knows me. No problem. Really."

"You have something else you want to talk about? You seem... distracted."

"No. It's just... this is weird. Sort of like *deja vu*. Except backwards. I've done this all before, right? But it doesn't feel like it. I should be able to remember... but I can't."

Sutherland wrote a note on Tamara's file.

"*Jamais vu*," he said.

"What?"

"*Jamais vu* is when something that should be familiar seems new and foreign. But I don't know if that applies here... It's been three years since you were admitted. It's not like something that happened daily. It was a long time ago for you."

"I guess. Do you remember? Who did my intake then?"

Sutherland considered. "I'd have to look back at your file," he said. "You were in pretty bad shape when you came to us. It wouldn't have been a routine intake."

Tamara nodded. "It's all foggy. Like bad dream."

"You weren't... yourself. Physically and emotionally, you were very *sick*..."

"But you put me in the general population then."

Sutherland shook his head. "No. Not for several weeks."

"Really?"

He nodded.

Tamara gave her head a little shake. "I don't remember."

"Let's try to stay focused on today."

"Oh. Yeah, okay."

"Maybe that's something we could talk about in regular sessions."

Tamara nodded. Before her release, they had been working on transitioning to life on the outside. That had obviously not worked out so well.

"You're feeling strong?" Sutherland asked. "Ready and willing to resume your normal activities here?"

Tamara frowned, considering. Not the words that she would have chosen. Was she prepared to be dropped back into the maximum-security block? Prepared to defend herself and reestablish her rep if she needed to? Mentally prepared for constant vigilance? While she craved the strict routine she'd been conditioned to and not having to make her own decisions again, she would also have to face the familiar violence and high-pressure politics.

"I... I guess I gotta be."

On completion of her intake interview with Dr. Sutherland, Tamara was passed off to Zobel, one of the guards, a familiar stocky figure Tamara had grown used to seeing over the previous three years. Sutherland nodded at him and didn't give him any instructions on Tamara's 'housing' situation. Which meant they had already figured on her being placed in the general population and no changes needed to be made to her anticipated assignment.

"Didn't think we'd see you back here again so soon," Zobel remarked, taking Tamara by the arm to escort her to her new cell.

"Wasn't exactly my plan." Tamara sighed.

"Hear you put Glock Spielman back behind bars."

Tamara turned this over in her mind. She supposed that technically it was true; but it wasn't like she had informed on Glock. All she had done was try to talk Glock out of killing her and Chad Collins. The fact that she was successful, and Glock had ended up being arrested didn't make Tamara a snitch. Glock had done it to herself.

"Wasn't my doing," she said. "I was just there."

"I told you a long time ago that girl was trouble. You should have just stayed away from her from the start."

"Yeah."

She didn't remind him that Glock had been her cellmate. Sort of hard not to associate with your own cellie. Or that Glock had been her protector, keeping Tamara from being beaten up by the gangs. He was right. They had gotten too close. And Tamara should have stayed away from Glock while on parole. She should have reported contact with her right from the start and saved herself several weeks of misery.

They walked past Tamara's previous cell. It was going to take a while to adjust to a new cell. She'd be walking back into her old one and wondering what the hell the other girls were doing there. They passed a couple of inmates walking down the hall. Nothing was said, but Tamara felt their eyes on her.

"Relax," Zobel told her, feeling her tense. "Nobody starting any fights today."

"Who am I bunking with?" Tamara's anxiety ratcheted up another notch as she considered all of the unknowns.

"New girl. Blacksnake."

"Who's she with?"

Zobel gave her a sideways look. Tamara wasn't sure if he was going to try to tell her that he didn't know which gang the girl was affiliated with, or to take the party line that there were no gangs inside the facility. He apparently decided against this approach and gave her the straight goods.

"Sharks."

Tamara bit her lip. "And Vernon's back." The leadership of TMJ had been unstable since Vernon's release. A good thing for those who didn't want to be forced into a gang, but something that caused the guards no end of grief as they tried to stay on top of the changing political climate and keep all-out war from breaking out. "Who's heading TMJ? Still Rosie?"

"For now."

They both knew it probably wouldn't last. She was lucky to have retained power for as long as she had. With Vernon back on the inside, that wasn't likely to continue.

Tamara thought about the two new inmates. Perez and Waterson. While neither one was an obvious asset, they both looked tough and streetwise. If TMJ could recruit two more bodies and Vernon regained her position at their head, it might be enough to throw the balance of power. TMJ could take control of the block.

Zobel stopped abruptly and Tamara jerked to a halt. She looked at him, wondering what she had done. He indicated the cell.

"This is it."

"Oh. Right. Thanks."

She slipped into the cell. Blacksnake had only been there a

few weeks at most and hadn't collected any personal items in that time. So there was little in the cell other than her bedding and hygiene items. The bottom bunk was made, and a stack of new bedding was neatly folded on the thin, worn mattress of the top bunk. Tamara's hygiene kit was tucked into the pillowcase. They used to pass them out to inmates in large, zip-seal plastic bags, until someone had discovered they were large enough and had just enough stretch to pull over someone's head. It took only one suffocation for every plastic bag in the place to instantly disappear.

Tamara stretched her sheet over the mattress and tucked it neatly. The rules didn't say she had to do it immediately, but it would earn her points with the staff and she wouldn't have to do it at lights-out, when she was too tired.

There was no reason to stay in her cell any longer except to delay the inevitable, so Tamara went back into the corridor. Gomez was taking Vernon to her new cell. Unlike Tamara, Vernon had been handcuffed; she stood waiting for Gomez to unlock her.

"Don't cause any trouble," Gomez warned as he removed the cuffs.

Vernon sent an amused look in Tamara's direction. "What trouble?" she asked with mock innocence.

"Just behave yourself. Don't know what they're doing, putting you straight into general."

"I was good for my intake," Vernon sneered.

Gomez shook his head and walked away. With no desire to be left in the corridor with Vernon, Tamara headed toward the common room.

"Frenchie!" Vernon hadn't entered her cell. She fell in quickly beside Tamara. Her smile was more like a sneer. Tamara remembered what Glock had said about her in the early days of Tamara's incarceration. *Vernon's a sly one, always sneaking around; she'd just as soon stab you in the back as smile at you.*

Tamara had no intention of getting stabbed in the back. Vernon already knew that Tamara was the enemy, intent on staying out of the gangs. She wasn't going to waste any time courting Tamara. "Where's the Glock? I thought they got you both together."

"Didn't come here. Sent her upstate, I think. Didn't want us mixing."

"Not after putting that teacher in ICU," Vernon agreed with a snort. "Though why they care about scum bashing scum, I don't know."

"Who can figure it out?" Tamara agreed. While she was trying to appear casual, she was watching Vernon like a hawk, evaluating every movement and expression. Vernon had just been searched by Bonner, who was very conscientious and knew her business. She had been handcuffed and she hadn't had time to make or acquire a weapon. She hadn't had a chance to talk to her gang yet, so she didn't know where she stood or what she was going to have to do to take over control of TMJ again. She wouldn't want to waste any energy on Tamara. Vernon was unarmed and had more important things to do than fight Tamara.

Unless she were looking for an easy warm-up to loosen up her muscles. Then Tamara was the perfect target.

"You get either of those newbs for a cell mate?" Vernon asked.

"No. Some other girl who's been here a few weeks."

Vernon grunted. "Me neither. Listen..." She grabbed Tamara's shoulder before they entered the common room, stopping her. Tamara froze. She stood there staring at Vernon, not pulling out of her grip or fighting back. Either reaction was likely to provoke violence. Vernon pulled Tamara a little closer, lifting her chin slightly in a gesture of defiance and dropping her voice to a hoarse whisper. "You have contact with either one of them, give them a little nudge my way. Make sure they know TMJ rules the block. And anyone who's *smart*," she gave Tamara a hard stare, "knows to sign on with us."

Tamara swallowed. She didn't say she would; she didn't say she wouldn't. She didn't acknowledge TMJ's rule over the block or which gang she would recommend if someone were so stupid as to ask her opinion. She stared into middle distance, past Vernon. Not at Vernon's face. And not at her own feet. Showing respect, but not agreeing nor arguing. She didn't flinch under Vernon's close scrutiny and eventually Vernon pushed her away.

Tamara breathed a long, slow sigh of relief, which made her ribs ache.

She entered the common room. It was just exactly the same as it had been when she had left. It hadn't been long. It seemed like an eternity. Like a lifetime. But it had only been a few weeks. The room was exactly the same. The faces were exactly the same, with very few exceptions. The temperature and the smell and the sound of the circulation fans were all exactly the same. It was as if she'd never left.

No one jumped up to meet her. Tamara didn't have any close friends in the block. A few people that she could talk to if she ended up standing next to them in the canteen or bathroom sinks, but no one that she could confide in or who told her all of their secrets. Tamara suddenly missed Sybil. As annoying as Syb's fascination with Tamara's criminal past had been, it had been nice to have a friend again. Like going back to her childhood.

And then there was Glock. She didn't miss Glock's closeness.

Everyone looked past Tamara to Vernon. Tamara was a nobody. She didn't get in the way. She wasn't in the gangs. She wasn't worth looking at or talking to. But Vernon was going to be making some waves.

There was a spurt of curses from the corner of the room. Tamara's eyes darted over to the source. Rosie jumped up from her seat and was pushing her lieutenants out of the way as she bee-lined toward Vernon. Tamara was caught right between the two girls.

Of course, the guards had been expecting just that kind of trouble, and immediately moved in, larger numbers than usual in the common room. They split between Rosie and her girls and Vernon, as if everything had been arranged ahead of time, assignments made to A team and B team, with A team surrounding Rosie and B team surrounding Vernon. It was as neat and polished as if they had been practicing on the parade grounds all week.

Rosie was spitting and cursing and didn't go quietly. She was easily overcome by the guards, but still struggled against them to show her strength and determination to fight Vernon at the earliest opportunity. She cat-called and smack-talked while they hauled her out of the room and to isolation. Her lieutenants and a couple of other TMJs too eager to take up the fight were escorted out as well. The isolation unit was going to be busy. Some of them would probably end up locked down in their own cells instead.

Vernon, meanwhile, had not reacted to Rosie with her own threats and gestures. The guards were left surrounding a single girl who was just standing there, watching the whole operation with amusement. They looked at each other for guidance. The plan had obviously been to take both girls to isolation. If the administration was smart, they had already made applications to have one or the other of the girls transferred to a different facility. But with Vernon standing there calmly, there was nothing the guards could do without violating her rights. They had no reason to lay hands on her or write her up.

"Nice job," Vernon said coolly. "Now if you'd back off, I'd like to go watch some TV."

More confused looks, and then the guards gave her some space, going back to their previous positions or leaving the common room. Vernon looked at Tamara and raised an eyebrow.

"Doesn't look like there's going to be any more excitement today."

Tamara unclenched her fists and tried to relax all of her muscles. There was a shot of pain through her broken ribs that she hadn't been aware of until the danger was past.

"Yeah. Right," she agreed in a voice that sounded too weak and vulnerable.

"I appreciate the sentiment, and all," Vernon said, chuckling.

"Oh—I wasn't—" Tamara fumbled her words.

Of course Vernon knew Tamara hadn't been prepared to fight to protect Vernon. Only herself. Vernon knew that; she was just teasing Tamara. Poking fun at her reflex reaction.

Vernon ignored Tamara's babble and walked toward the TV. Directly to the space that Rosie had previously occupied. The remaining TMJ members looked at Vernon and at each other anxiously. Vernon had moved in and usurped Rosie's place just like she had planned. TMJ was going to be forced to take action against Vernon or to accept her without relying on the results of a show-down fight between the two potential leaders. All of the powerful TMJs had been removed from the equation and only the rank and file remained. Or those who had been reluctant to ally themselves with Rosie's cause.

Vernon really was brilliant, Tamara realized. She was going to be able to position herself without ever lifting a finger.

Vernon leaned back in her chair nodded at Alicia Brett, one of her old sidekicks. "'Sup, Brett?"

Everyone was watching and listening, waiting to see what happened.

Brett nodded. "Vernon."

"Fill me in. What's been happening around here lately?"

Brett reluctantly drew up one of the other vacated chairs so that she and Vernon could talk in lower voices and not be overheard by the guards and other girls. Brett looked at the other TMJ members, but there was no one there who ranked high enough to tell her what to do or who was confident enough to advise her. Brett leaned in toward Vernon.

The conversation was too quiet for Tamara to hear. She didn't try to get closer to listen in, but kept an eye on the little knot of girls as she found a seat of her own and pretended to be watching the TV. Most of the others were also watching to see the outcome of the convo. The TMJ girls started to relax, and it was obvious from their body language that they had made the decision, conscious or not, that Vernon was the new leader of the TMJ.

Without one punch being thrown, Vernon had placed herself as the *de facto* leader of the TMJ. Tamara wasn't sure what was going to happen when Rosie got out of iso, but she wouldn't be resuming leadership of TMJ as she expected.

It seemed like so long since Tamara had eaten breakfast, and so much had happened since then, that she was surprised when the meal bell rang that it was only lunch and not supper. She had lost track of the days, but decided it must be the weekend, since most of the girls had been in the common areas and not in classes.

Her brain was so imprinted with the mealtime routine after three meals a day for three years that her hands and feet moved of their own accord, with no conscious direction on her part.

The canteen was the same. The food was the same. The faces around the room were mostly the same. Tamara got in line, picked up her tray and dishes, and moved along the serving counter, oblivious to what they were putting on her plate. Instead, her mind was on the rest of the room, radar active for any potential problems. The canteen was one place that problems happened. The guards couldn't keep track of every fork, every bowl of hot soup, and every potential for contamination or poisoning. There were no knives, but it was less restricted than isolation, where there was no cutlery and food was served cold in lightweight paper bowls.

"Thought you weren't coming back here."

Tamara swiveled to look at the girl behind her. Tabitha Smith. Tabby. When she had arrived at juvie, she'd had fine, bleach-blond hair which, together with her delicate, almost translucent skin, made her look as fragile as a china doll.

She wasn't.

"Yeah. Things didn't go according to plan," Tamara agreed.

"What happened?"

"Assault. Breach of parole. Associating with a felon."

Tabby snorted. "So much for being a good girl."

"Yeah."

"It's always the quiet ones," Tabby said. "People think you're such a sweet little thing, cuddly little kitten. Until you show your fangs."

Tabby liked cat metaphors and Tamara had heard this one before. She didn't bother to answer, hoping the conversation would terminate.

"You're looking piqued there. You been sick?"

Tamara turned around to face Tabby fully. If Tabby or any of the others thought Tamara was weak, she would be an instant target. She shoved Tabby, making her topple backward into the girls behind her in line before she could regain her balance. A plate went sliding across her tray and crashed to the floor. The hum of conversation in the room was instantly silenced. Tamara waited, ready to throw her tray down and fight Tabby if necessary. She certainly didn't want to with her injured ribs, but she had to show them she was strong before there could be any question of it.

"Chill!" Tabby protested. "What's your problem?"

Millican was there, stepping between them, giving both girls an angry scowl. "Break it up. You both know how to behave in the canteen. What's going on here?"

"I don't know what her problem is," Tabby growled. "I didn't do anything, she just shoved me, out of nowhere!"

"Uh-huh. Go to the back of the line and get a new plate. Put some space between you."

Tabby protested against having to wait longer for her lunch, but obeyed and went back to the end of the counter to pick up a new plate. Millican stared at Tamara. "What's up with you, French? Forget how to behave while you were gone?"

Tamara didn't answer. She just stood there stone-faced. Millican stooped to pick up the dropped plate and its contents. When he grabbed the edge, they both saw what had been camouflaged by the food Tabby had been dishing up. The plastic plate, supposed to be unbreakable, had shattered. The piece that he picked up was a long, sharp dagger of plastic. Millican's knuckles whitened. His eyes widened in alarm. He met Tamara's eyes and his other hand shot to his panic button. Tamara winced at the loud shrill of the siren.

Guards shot across the room to Millican's assistance. More were summoned by a remote alarm, every spare security staffer pouring into the canteen.

"Get your hands up," Millican ordered.

Tamara stared back at him. Her hands were occupied, both holding her lunch tray. She didn't move. Other guards cleared nearby inmates away, creating a perimeter.

"Put your tray on the counter." Millican spoke through clenched teeth. "Put it down gently. Do *not* drop it."

Maybe they had a whole shipment of defective dishes. Maybe every plate in the room could be broken to produce multiple weapons. If Tamara felt threatened, she could arm herself. She wouldn't win against his taser and service weapon and all the rest of the security staff surrounding them, of course.

But that hadn't stopped juvies from trying in the past and injuring themselves or the security staff before they could be subdued.

Smaller shards than the one Millican held could be tucked in a pocket, underarm, or braid to be used later. They wouldn't be turned up by x-rays or metal detectors. If the staff didn't identify every splinter of plastic that had come from Tabby's plate, the whole block would be on general lockdown.

Tamara didn't move immediately. She let Millican sweat it. Reminded him and everyone else in the room that she wasn't any shrinking violet to be bullied or ignored. Asserted her position.

"French!" Millican barked.

Tamara startled at his shout and let the dinnerware slide to the edge of her tray. She balanced it there, right at the edge, looking Millican in the eye. Then she moved slowly to lay it flat on the counter and raised her hands to shoulder height.

One of the guards behind her grabbed her hands and pressed them together to handcuff her. There was a collective sigh of relief. Millican turned around to spot Tabby.

"Her too. Tabitha Smith." He pointed a finger at her and made sure that Tabby was handcuffed as well.

"What happened?" Weiler, one of the administrators, hurried into the canteen, her sharp eyes darting around the room.

Millican showed Weiler the knifelike shard of plate. "It broke. We have to be sure she didn't get a piece of it." He indicated Tabby with a hooked thumb.

They both crouched down by the broken plate. Millican pushed the spilled food out of the way and fitted his shard of plastic into its place in the plate. They adjusted the now-visible triangles, looking for any gaps that would indicate a missing piece that could be used as a weapon. Weiler shook her head.

"I don't think so. It's all here."

Millican nodded his agreement. "I couldn't stop to check. If she or someone else had already grabbed a piece..."

Weiler nodded. "You did what you had to. Let's get this cleared away, then we can resume lunch." She looked at Tamara. "What about French? Already in trouble?"

Tamara gave a shrug, looking away from her.

"She and Tabby were scrapping. That's how the plate got broken."

Weiler shook her head at Tamara. "You're only back a few hours, and you're causing trouble? You were always one of the good girls."

"Yes, ma'am," Tamara agreed.

If Weiler knew she was a model inmate, then why was she assuming Tamara had done anything wrong?

"You can't be causing me grief! Leave that to the gangs. Fly straight and behave yourself."

"Yes, ma'am."

Weiler stared at her for a long moment.

"I'd say you miss your lunch today over this little scene, if I didn't know how little you eat." She glanced aside at the tray Tamara had put down.

Tamara didn't care if they sent her straight to her bunk for the rest of the day. The food looked so thoroughly unappetizing, she didn't know how she would get any of it down anyway.

Weiler sighed. "She can eat after this is cleaned up. Nobody has to miss lunch."

A couple of guards scooped the wreckage of Tabby's lunch into a dustpan and took it out of the room rather than throwing it in the garbage in the canteen. The guards allowed everyone to return to the counter to finished dishing up and to the tables to eat. Millican unlocked Tamara's handcuffs. She centered her dishes on her tray before picking it back up. She could still feel his gaze on her as she walked along the remainder of the counter and sat down to eat.

TWO

THE DAY PASSED SLOWLY. The worst part of incarceration was the mind-numbing boredom. There were activities offered in juvie that were optional. Training, crafts, working with teachers to upgrade skills outside of their usual school classes. But after a few crafts, they were all the same. Tamara felt like an adult stuck with a coloring book. She just wasn't interested in what they had to offer anymore. She'd tried it all.

So she sat in the common room. She sat and watched the TV, but mostly she watched the other inmates. The political upheaval was worrying, but she was on the outside. She couldn't do anything but watch.

Eventually, it was back to the canteen for supper, and this time there was no trouble and everyone showed Tamara the proper respect. She noted that the "unbreakable" plastic dishes were gone, replaced by a combination of tin and paper plates retrieved from storage or the isolation unit. It made her feel less than human, like they no longer warranted decent plates like civilized humans. Another thing taken away from them. She hoped it wouldn't be long before they had tested the plastic plates and either returned or replaced them.

Tamara dished up on automatic pilot. Found a seat and ate on automatic pilot. Finally, the evening bell rang and she returned to her cell for quiet time. She could have gone back to the common room to watch more TV, but her mind was burned out. It had been a long day and she didn't want to be with everyone else.

Tamara changed into her nightwear and climbed up into her bunk. She probably wouldn't be able to sleep for several more hours, but she couldn't face anything more difficult than lying in her bed after the long and trying day.

She hadn't been there long when her cellmate arrived. Tamara turned to look at her.

"Oh. Hey."

The other girl looked back at her. Tamara had been hoping that the new girl would be younger, green, and smaller than she was. But the girl who looked back at her was probably sixteen. She had the prison-hardened look Tamara was familiar with. The new girl was no newbie.

Tamara took in her bigger size, black hair, dark skin, and native features in a quick glance before looking away. She didn't want to be accused of staring or showing too much interest.

"Hey," the girl grunted. "Who are you?"

"French. Tamara French."

"French," she repeated. "I've heard of you. You were bounced from parole."

"Yeah."

"I'm Blacksnake." The girl gave a humorless smile, showing off a couple of missing teeth. "You've been warned."

Tamara took a deep breath and let out the air very slowly. Tamara had dealt with tough cellies before. She turned her head for another quick assessment of Blacksnake.

Blacksnake started to strip off her day uniform. Tamara

pretended to close her eyes, but continued to watch Blacksnake. She had round white scars on her shoulders and back. Cigarette burns. She had tattoos: a variety of prison tats, professional-looking ink, and what looked like tribal art. While overweight, she wasn't flabby, lots of bulky muscles under the layer of fat.

Blacksnake started to dress in her pink night wear. "I know you're watching me."

Tamara opened her eyes the rest of the way, turning to face the ceiling.

"You're not in a gang?" Blacksnake asked.

"No. I stay out of all that."

"I'm in Sharks. You should join up."

"No offense," Tamara said. "Just not interested."

"We'll see."

Tamara darted a glance in her direction, but it didn't look like Blacksnake planned to convince her immediately. She was still dressing, her movements slow, eyes watchful. Tamara rubbed her own eyes, aching and puffy with lack of sleep.

"You see what happened with Vernon and Rosie?" she asked.

"I heard."

"Not good for the Sharks."

"Sure it is," Blacksnake glowered at her. "TMJ leadership in upheaval, that's good news for the Sharks. Gives us a chance to get the upper hand."

Tamara bit her lip. She wasn't going to argue with Black-snake, but Tamara knew she was wrong. She had been there before when Vernon was running TMJ. Vernon knew what she was doing. She would run TMJ like a well-oiled machine. That wasn't good for the Sharks; it was very bad.

———

Tamara stared past Dr. Sutherland, waiting for him to begin. Usually, he started with a lecture. A lot of nonsense about self-examination, therapy or exercises she should be doing to prepare herself for her new life when she left juvie, and whatever other navel-gazing he had been doing since she had talked to him last. But he didn't start, and she slid her gaze over to him, checking to see what was wrong.

"You were asking before about what happened when you were first admitted," Sutherland said. "So I thought maybe we should start there today. How does that sound to you?"

Tamara was surprised. "Yeah, that would be good."

He slid out a file folder she hadn't seen before. Not the usual tattered one filled with his notes of every week, but a slimmer one with her name on the faded edge. It had obviously been sitting on the shelf untouched for most of her stay there. He tipped it up before opening it, so that she couldn't see the contents, and considered what he was looking at for a few minutes before offering anything further. He worked a couple of photos out of the pockets they were stored in and pushed them across the desk to her.

Tamara looked at the mugshots of a young girl, the breath going out of her. She barely recognized herself.

"Look at how young I was! Can you believe that's me? What a baby face. Twelve years old." She swore softly and shook her head. She studied the face. Blank of emotion during the taking of the photo, but her face was visibly streaked with tears. There were dark circles under her eyes and she looked like she hadn't slept in three days. She probably hadn't.

"Do you remember any of this?" Sutherland asked. "Being questioned, arrested, and booked?"

"Bits and pieces. Like it was a nightmare. Not specifics, though. Just that they took me to the police station... I was there for a long time, talking to different cops... tired, anxious... thought I was going to get out of there. That they were just going to let me go, or send me to a new foster home. I never figured they were going to arrest me."

"Even though you knew what you had done."

"I just thought... they wouldn't figure it out. They would think that Corrine just drowned by accident, like I said. And Julie... I don't know what I thought about Julie. Just that she had the croup or the flu and she'd get better. Not... that she'd die." Tamara felt tears start in her eyes and wiped them impatiently away. Who was she crying for? Julie? Or for the little girl she herself had been? When tears came unbidden, instead of her squeezing them out on cue, she always felt like her body was betraying her. She needed to stay in control. She tried to freeze out her emotions and keep a mask over her features.

Dr. Sutherland waited a few moments before continuing. He pulled another photo from the folder and slid it across to her. Tamara saw herself on her intake into juvie. She remembered it only vaguely. How during her strip search they'd made her wait there in the search room, cold and vulnerable, while the matron conducting the search left to retrieve a camera and second witness.

Tamara was naked in the picture, black bars across her private parts and eyes. She never understood why they put bars over people's eyes. Like they too were indecent.

But the arresting thing about the photo was the bruises. Whip marks striped Tamara's legs black and blue. There were places where the lashes had torn the skin and dried blood edged the bruises.

Tamara felt nauseated. They had abused her. The memories had blurred; she hadn't remembered individual incidents. Looking at the picture, the details of that last one came back to her in a rush of sensations. The burning lashes that made her cry out in pain, even though she tried not to give Mrs. Baker the satisfaction. The curses and invectives. Lying there on the floor afterward, exhausted, her body pulsing with pain at each heartbeat.

Getting back up and dressing for school.

Her plan had already been in place at that point. She had known she risked a beating if the theft of Mrs. Baker's money was noticed, but she was determined to get out and she would need money. She would get put into an emergency placement and she would run. Then she would be free. With the money, she would have a chance of survival. The beating was an acknowledged risk, one she had decided was worth taking.

"Do you remember that?" Dr. Sutherland asked, his pale blue eyes intent.

"Yeah." Tamara stared at the skinny, undeveloped figure. She had been a *child*. She had wondered time and again how they could treat another human being the way they had, but she had never realized so clearly that *she had been a child*. How could they do that to a little girl?

Tamara had thought herself partially responsible for the beatings. She wasn't able to take care of the children or complete her housework or other duties to their satisfaction. She needed to try harder and they wouldn't hurt her.

But she *hadn't* been responsible for what they had done to her. She had only been a child.

She swore and looked up at Dr. Sutherland.

"Were they ever charged? Did they ever have to pay for what they did to me?"

"Some people would say they paid by the loss of their two children."

"I hope so!" Tamara growled, her emotions getting the better of her again. "I hope they cried every day over the loss of their babies! But I doubt they did. They didn't care about them or they wouldn't have made me take care of them all the time. They would have taken care of them themselves."

"You don't think they loved their children?"

"No. They didn't care about them." Tamara thought about it. They had cared for the babies more than for her. There had been tender times: Mr. Baker reading to them before they went to sleep, Mrs. Baker playing peekaboo with Julie before leaving them in Tamara's care as she headed off to work, singing the silly songs that made Corrine laugh. They liked to take them off to McDonalds for a meal or buy them frilly new clothes.

Tamara had been on the outside. Seeing the children doted on while she was treated like a slave. Being punished for letting one of them cry. Corrine had figured out she could get her way by crying. Either from Tamara, afraid of the consequences of letting Corrine cry, or from her mother when Tamara was removed from the picture. So she would fake-cry just to get her own way. It was infuriating.

"I don't know. Maybe they did care, in a way. But not like real parents are supposed to."

Sutherland nodded. "As far as their being charged... if I recall correctly, they were, and worked out a plea deal."

Tamara was happy to hear that. At least they had been punished. They hadn't just walked away with everyone thinking they were innocent victims.

"What else do you remember about when you first came here?" Sutherland asked.

"I don't know... I remember them taking pictures of me. Being embarrassed. But I was so tired and foggy... all the stuff that had happened... I don't remember policies and procedures or any of that stuff. Being interviewed. Just... finally getting to lay down and go to sleep."

He nodded. He didn't add any information or demand more, he just watched her. Therapists were like that. Always watching and evaluating, writing little notes in their unreadable hand-writing.

"The next day," Tamara said slowly, "or sometime after that... I had to go to the infirmary."

"Yes," he agreed. "You were in pretty rough shape."

"Not just *this*," Tamara said, pushing the photo back across the table to him, looking at the whip marks one last time. "That's when I found out I was pregnant."

"You didn't know before then?" His eyebrows lifted.

Tamara rolled her eyes and shook her head. "He told me I couldn't get pregnant, so I never even thought of it... I was twelve; I was naive. And I never knew... how bad it would make me feel. I knew about morning sickness, but not how tired and foggy it would make me. Or all the crazy feelings and thoughts..."

Sutherland drummed his fingertips on the desk, considering this. He was frowning. "Tell me about that."

"About what?"

"The crazy thoughts and feelings."

"I don't know... I was emotional all the time. All over the place. I wasn't sleeping. I was always either mad at Mister and Missus or crying my eyes out. Losing stuff, dropping things, wild psychedelic dreams..."

"So you were getting *some* sleep."

"Sometimes... a few hours here and there. Not every night. And not all of the dreams... uh... happened while I was sleeping," Tamara explained awkwardly.

"You were hallucinating?"

"I don't know. It's all mixed up, I don't remember it very well. I think... yeah, sometimes."

"When you put together your... escape plan... were you hallucinating or lucid?"

Tamara shifted restlessly and tried to figure out what to do with her hands. She scratched at the already-worn varnish on the arm of her chair.

"I don't know. Does it matter?"

"Not to anyone but you and me. Does it matter to you?"

Tamara stared off into space, working it through in her head. She scratched another track in the varnish on the arm of the chair. "I always blamed the Bakers... for what happened."

"They were responsible for what they did to you."

"But I blamed them for what I did. For... what happened to the children."

Dr. Sutherland looked at her, not saying anything. Tamara remembered how Glock had dogged her, insisting that Tamara admit what she did instead of talking about it as if it were just something that had happened. She sensed that Sutherland too was waiting to see if she would use first-person language.

"I blamed them for... for making me kill Corrine and Julie."

He nodded. "I see."

"I know I confessed and everything, but I never... I never really admitted to myself... that it was my choice. Not... not the Bakers' fault."

"So you said all the right things, but you never actually took responsibility in your own mind."

"Yeah. So now... does it make a difference that I was hallucinating? Does that mean... it wasn't really my choice? It really was just something that happened because he got me pregnant?" Tamara rubbed the center of her forehead. "Everyone doesn't feel like that, when they're pregnant?"

"No. Most women do not hallucinate when they are pregnant. Pregnancy can trigger some forms of psychosis. It was... an extenuating circumstance. I'd be interested in exploring this further in future sessions. Before we meet again, I'd like you to consider... explore what it was you were thinking and feeling when you made those plans and choices."

"It was so long ago..."

"It was three years ago. I understand that a lot has happened since then, and that you were confused at the time, but I'd like you to think about it. And we'll talk about it again next time."

"Okay." Tamara looked down at the floor.

"I'm sure you would like to have a better understanding of what happened three years ago as well. You want to be able to recognize if you start having disordered thoughts in the future. If you truly want to be able to live a new life, you need to understand what it was that happened."

"Yes. I do."

He gave her a smile of approval and opened his desk drawer. Tamara couldn't resist a little grin, knowing what was coming. Sutherland pulled a bag of candy out of his desk and held it out to her.

She knew that it was a psychological trick. A way of conditioning inmates to have positive thoughts and feelings about their counseling sessions. But knowing that didn't stop it from working. He was the candy man. The purveyor of sweets, something they didn't often have access to on the inside. She couldn't help but look forward to the end of a successful session, when she would get that one little bite of sugar. Inmates who were uncooperative and had to be taken out of their sessions early by the security staff didn't get a treat.

Halloween was approaching, so instead of the usual wrapped gummies, nougats, or hard candies, the bag held treat-sized chocolate bars. Tamara helped herself to one of her favorites. Her mouth was watering and she could hardly wait to get the bar unwrapped.

"I'll see you next week," Dr. Sutherland said, putting the bag back away in his desk drawer.

"Okay." Tamara took a small nibble of the chocolate bar. All of those good brain chemicals went rushing to her pleasure centers, conditioning her brain to anticipate her therapy sessions as something positive. But she didn't care that he was training her like one of Pavlov's dogs. At least Pavlov's dogs got fed.

———

The free time bell rang. Blacksnake was sitting across the table from Tamara and met her eyes.

"You going out to the yard?"

Tamara shifted uneasily. "Not today. I was gonna go to the library."

"Library?" Blacksnake snorted.

Tamara knew what Glock's reaction would have been to Tamara going to the library instead of yard time. She had drilled it into Tamara for two years. Only weaklings and victims went to the library. If she wanted to fit in and not to be bullied, she needed to go to the yard, put in an appearance. Make sure that people saw her there, strong and unafraid.

Tamara was leery of Blacksnake. The bigger girl had already made it clear that she wanted to recruit Tamara to the Sharks. Sharing a cell could be difficult if the inmates didn't share political factions. Blacksnake showing Tamara particular attention about getting out to the yard was a red flag. Tamara intended to stay far away from her and to fly under the radar as much as possible until Blacksnake got used to her.

"I got some work to do," Tamara explained, getting up from the table and starting to move away. "Legal stuff to do with my next parole hearing."

"You just got bounced from parole," Blacksnake said, her eyes narrowing. "You aren't going to be up again for a year."

"I gotta work on it," Tamara said, shrugging.

Mercifully, Blacksnake made no attempt to stop or pursue her, so Tamara headed for the library.

It was quiet. Few people chose to use the library during yard time. They had weekly access during their classes anyway and few of them had any reason to be there more than once a week. Tamara scanned the meager shelves of books.

"Tamara French," Ms. Ruth greeted warmly. "It's good to see you. What can we find for you today?"

Tamara shrugged. "I've already read most of these... Can I use the computer?"

Ms. Ruth looked around, as if she needed to check to see if

there was a lineup for the computer. "Yes, of course." She tapped her wrist. "Twenty minutes."

They operated on the basis that if an inmate only had twenty minutes in a session, she would get on, go straight to whatever she needed to do, and not get in any trouble. There was, of course, a child-safe filter set up on the internet, but a knowledgeable person could get around that with enough tinkering. The twenty-minute session rule was far more restricting.

Tamara sat down and tried to decide what to do. She hadn't actually planned the visit ahead of time. She didn't have anyone to write letters to. She wasn't actually researching legal strategy.

Thinking about her session with Dr. Sutherland, she opened the search page and typed in Denny and Christina Baker's names. She wasn't sure what she was expecting to find. The computer ground away and slowly refreshed the screen with news articles about Tamara's trial, with some of the new stuff that happened while on parole at the top. Tamara scrolled down, looking for information about the Bakers' trial. There was nothing.

Dr. Sutherland had said that they struck a plea deal, so Tamara tried a few revised searches with the words plea and bargain added to the search terms. The list shortened, the bigger, splashier headlines disappearing and pictures of Tamara being replaced with some thumbnails of the two Bakers. Tamara opened an article and skimmed the details.

Her mouth dropped open and the world spun around her. She actually had to hold on to the desk to keep herself from falling right out of her chair.

"No."

Ms. Ruth looked over at her. "What?"

"Oh, sorry. No. Nothing."

"Do you need help with something?" Ms. Ruth's eyes moved over Tamara's face. "Are you okay, Tamara?"

"No. Yes. Everything is fine."

Ms. Ruth walked over toward her. Tamara's fingers moved lightning-fast to close the browser tab. Ms. Ruth looked at the blank screen, a frown line appearing between her plucked eyebrows.

"Do you need something? What are you working on today?"

Tamara held her hands up defensively, and shook her head. "I... I changed my mind. I don't want to do this today. I want..." She had no idea what to say. She just shook her head again, getting up from her chair and shoving it clumsily back under the desk with a bang. She fled from the library, aware that Ms. Ruth was watching her retreat until she turned the corner.

There weren't a lot of options. She could go back to her cell. She could go to the yard. There might be some alternative activities being offered, but she hadn't paid any attention to what sessions were advertised on the calendar. She didn't want to go back to her cell. A fire was burning in her belly and she didn't know what it was. Anger? Fear? She hadn't yet had a chance to process her emotions and all she was aware of was the building pressure. She needed to get outside to let it burn off. Maybe she could shoot some hoops. With her ribs, that probably wasn't an option even if any of the girls did want a pick-up game and there was a ball that wasn't flat.

She tried not to run down the hall. That would just attract attention from the guards or staff. She didn't want any extra attention. She just wanted to get outside into the fresh air.

Tamara stopped when she got out the door and took a deep lungful of air. She forced herself to stop and take a careful look around. Just darting out into the yard in a tizzy, with no thought as to who was there and what undercurrents might be running through the other inmates was not a good idea. She needed to be smart.

Everything seemed quiet. The guards were relaxed. Tamara didn't pick up on any body language from the other inmates indicating trouble was brewing. She separated out the

Sharks and TMJ, two groups studiously not looking at each other. Rosie was not in evidence, so Vernon was the nucleus of the TMJ. Blacksnake was on the fringes of the Sharks. Still the new girl. Unproven. She was a member of the gang, but didn't rank.

Blacksnake turned her head, catching Tamara's entrance in her peripheral vision. She raised an eyebrow.

"French. I thought you were going to the *library*."

Tamara glared. The anger in her stomach was building to the point where she felt like she could melt Blacksnake with her laser beam gaze. "Get outta my business," she growled.

The bigger girl actually took a step back. She raised her hands slightly in an automatic gesture to calm Tamara or defend herself.

"No offense."

Tamara stared at her for a few more seconds before finally releasing Blacksnake from her gaze. She saw Blacksnake's shoulders dip as she breathed out. Blacksnake gave a little nod.

Gomez circulated through the yard, eyes sharp. He met Tamara's gaze. "All good?"

Tamara nodded. "Fine."

He lingered for a moment before moving on again, watching for any trouble.

Tamara made a motion toward Blacksnake. "Got a smoke?"

Blacksnake's eyes widened. Her hand moved to her uniform pocket, then she hesitated. Tamara wasn't in the Sharks. They were cellies, but they weren't friends or even acquaintances. Tamara was just a small white girl, not affiliated with anyone.

Tamara raised her brows. She was worked up and in desperate need of the nicotine. Nothing else was going to help her relax.

If Blacksnake had cigarettes and refused Tamara, she might as well declare war. And being new, she couldn't be sure that she would have the Sharks behind her. She didn't know enough about Tamara to judge her rep and what political cachet she held.

There was a tense moment while Blacksnake held her hand over her pocket, their eyes on one another.

Blacksnake dug into her pocket and produced a slightly mashed cigarette, which she handed over to Tamara. Tamara nodded her thanks and moved over to Gomez, who lit it for her. She could see that he wanted to ask again if she was okay, if something was going on. But he kept his mouth shut. Tamara took a few steps away from him, again facing Blacksnake, keeping an eye on her.

Tamara brought the cigarette up to her mouth and closed her eyes while she breathed in the smoke. Her first nicotine hit since... when? Since she had been with Glock. In the warehouse, suffering with pneumonia. Not her finest hour. She held the smoke in her lungs and then released it slowly. The knot in her stomach eased slightly.

She opened her eyes again. Probably not the brightest idea to have her eyes closed while facing off against a potential adversary. They watched each other warily.

"You been here how long?" Blacksnake asked finally, when Tamara was about halfway through her cigarette.

"Three years."

"So... you know how things work."

Tamara nodded. "Yeah. This is my crib. I know how it works."

Blacksnake mirrored her nod. Her attitude was far different from what it had been when she and Tamara had talked in their cell or at breakfast. Tamara knew that it was her own attitude that had made the difference. She knew better than to act shy and self-effacing with a new cellie. Caution and respect had their place, but there was nothing like a little rage to back everyone off.

"You don't think it's good, Vernon being sent back, fighting for the presidency of TMJ?"

Blacksnake looked toward Vernon. Tamara did not, dragging on her cigarette and staring into middle space.

"She's not fighting for the presidency," Tamara said. "She's got it. They probably won't put Rosie back in general. Not unless they want her to get shanked. They'll transfer her out."

"Yeah...?" Blacksnake considered. "And you think that's bad."

"Not for TMJ."

"But for the Sharks?"

Tamara blew out her smoke. "Yep."

Blacksnake looked toward Lewis, the current leader of the Sharks. Blacksnake's voice was low as she spoke to Tamara, but she was still looking too much at Lewis. That was going to get her in trouble.

"*They* don't seem to think it's a problem."

"It's just my opinion. I'm not anybody."

Blacksnake contemplated this. "But you are," she said. "You've been here three years and stayed independent. You know how it's going to work out."

"It's an opinion. I could be wrong, just like anyone else. And I've been away. A lot could have happened in that time."

"This Vernon, what's she like?"

Tamara couldn't help a quick glance toward Vernon, but she looked away again immediately, not long enough for anyone to accuse her of staring and not making eye contact.

"Vernon's back in the presidency within hours of being readmitted. What do *you* think?"

Tamara remembered Glock's words. *She'd just as soon stab you in the back as smile at you.* Vernon was as dangerous as they came. And the fact that she knew Tamara and they had avoided hostilities for two years did not mean that Tamara was home free. If Vernon decided Tamara was poking her nose where it wasn't wanted or that Tamara posed some kind of threat, Tamara would have to be transferred or she'd be leaving in a bag.

"Blacksnake."

Their heads both snapped up. Lewis had noticed their conversation and didn't like it. Blacksnake's eyes and body language had been broadcasting the subject of the conversation as clearly as if she held a billboard.

"What are you talking to French for?" Lewis demanded. "She ain't a Shark and she don't know nothing. You go it?"

Blacksnake cleared her throat and nodded. "Yeah. No problem. Just... she *is* my cellie."

Lewis looked at Tamara, considering this new information. She obviously hadn't clued in to the fact that Tamara had been bunked with Blacksnake.

"Not for long, she's not."

It was a threat.

The anger that had been gradually loosening came back full-force. Tamara didn't just let it flare up; she intentionally prodded it and threw gasoline on top. She took three wide strides toward Lewis, knowing the other Sharks would never let her get within striking distance. And the guards were well-trained to deal with fights emerging in the yard.

"You got a problem with me?" Tamara demanded, pushing against the hands that restrained her. She let the words out in a snarl that left her throat raw. "Three years; have I ever interfered in Sharks business?"

Lewis shifted into a defensive stance. She didn't tell the Sharks to let Tamara go.

"You never caused me no trouble," Lewis admitted.

Tamara still fought back against the hands that restrained her. "*You've* only been here a year. I *ever* caused any trouble for any of the Sharks?"

Lewis was forced to look at her lieutenants for help, put in a position where she didn't know the answer to Tamara's question. There were quick head-shakes from the Sharks who had been around for longer. Few inmates had been there as long as Tamara. She had a rep as an old-timer.

The guards were pushing their way through the girls to reach Tamara and the inmates holding her back.

"Stand down, French! What's going on here?"

"Let go! No contact in the yard."

Tamara was released by the Sharks and everyone watched to see if she were going to go after Lewis. The guards were at the ready, their batons already out or hands on their tasers. If it escalated to actual violence, they would have the yard shut down in thirty seconds.

"No trouble," Lewis said, eyes down, not liking having to make peace. But she didn't have much choice. Her gang was already in danger from the coup in TMJ, she couldn't afford to chance any injuries to herself or other Sharks in a fight with Tamara. They couldn't be distracted from the real danger. And she had to know her girls wouldn't be impressed if she made an enemy of an inmate who previously had remained neutral.

"You planning on taking me out?" Tamara challenged, determined to have it settled. "You don't like me being cellies with Blacksnake and you're gonna take me out?"

The guards exchanged looks. They would now be on the lookout for anyone who might be wanting to do just that.

"No," Lewis protested. "No, I... I didn't say that. I won't do nothing."

"Yeah?" Tamara took a calculated half-step forward. Enough to crowd Lewis and make her feel uncomfortable. Enough for one of the guards to put a warning hand on her arm. But not enough to make them cuff and remove her. "I'm not gonna get any trouble from you and your girls?"

Lewis shook her head grimly.

Tamara finally nodded and backed away slightly. A sigh and a murmur went through the yard.

"Why don't you head back to your cell?" Gomez suggested.

Tamara dropped the butt of her cigarette on the pavement and ground it out.

She left the yard and headed back to her room.

———

Two Teardrops, Book #2 of the *Tamara's Teardrops series* by P.D. Workman can be purchased at pdworkman.com

ABOUT THE AUTHOR

Award-winning and *USA Today* bestselling author P.D. (Pamela) Workman writes riveting mystery/suspense and young adult books dealing with mental illness, addiction, abuse, and other real-life issues. For as long as she can remember, the blank page has held an incredible allure and from a very young age she was trying to write her own books.

Workman wrote her first complete novel at the age of twelve and continued to write as a hobby for many years. She started publishing in 2013. She has won several literary awards from Library Services for Youth in Custody for her young adult fiction. She currently has over 60 published titles and can be found at pdworkman.com.

Born and raised in Alberta, Workman has been married for over 25 years and has one son.

———

Please visit P.D. Workman at pdworkman.com to see what else she is working on, to join her mailing list, and to link to her social networks.

———

If you enjoyed this book, please take the time to recommend it to other purchasers with a review or star rating and share it with your friends!

facebook.com/pdworkmanauthor

twitter.com/pdworkmanauthor

instagram.com/pdworkmanauthor

amazon.com/author/pdworkman

bookbub.com/authors/p-d-workman

goodreads.com/pdworkman

linkedin.com/in/pdworkman

pinterest.com/pdworkmanauthor

youtube.com/pdworkman